CONTENTS

Dear Reader,

Let me introduce you to the characters in *Risky Business*...no, not Tom Cruise and Rebecca De Mornay. (Can you believe it's been over twenty-five years since the movie was in the theaters? Think of all the parodies of the dance in boxers to Bob Seger's "Old Time Rock & Roll"!)

I'm talking about the characters of my two-in-one novels, *A Dangerous Precedent* and *Double Exposure.* Kirsten McQueen and Dane Ferguson are two passionate people on opposite ends of a discrimination lawsuit. They just might be the most unlikely people on earth to be attracted to each other, but when they square off in the courtroom—look out! The sparks fly.

As for Melanie Walker and Gavin Doel—boy, do they have a past, and now it's come thundering to the present and the secret she's kept from him. She'd promised she would wait for him, but fate had driven them apart. Now he's a world-class skier with a cast on his injured leg and a bad attitude, and she knows it's only a matter of time before the past will catch up to both of them.

I had lots of fun writing these stories of ill-fated love. I hope you have a lot of fun reading *Risky Business* and that you're still dancing! For more information on the book and what other projects I'm working on, check out my Web site, www.lisajackson.com. Who knows, you might enter a contest and win a copy of *Risky Business!*

Keep reading,

Lisa

Praise for *New York Times* bestselling author

"When it comes to providing gritty and sexy stories, Ms. Jackson certainly knows how to deliver."
—*Romantic Times BOOKreviews* on *Unspoken*

"Provocative prose, an irresistible plot and finely crafted characters make up Jackson's latest contemporary sizzler."
—*Publishers Weekly* on *Wishes*

"Lisa Jackson takes my breath away."
—*New York Times* bestselling author Linda Lael Miller

COLD BLOODED

"*Cold Blooded* grabs you by the throat from page one and does not let you off the edge of your seat for a moment after that."
—*Romance at Its Best*

"Taking up where last year's phenomenal *Hot Blooded* left off, *Cold Blooded* is a tight, romantic, edge-of-your-seat thriller."
—*Romantic Times BOOKreviews*

"*Cold Blooded* is an exciting serial-killer thriller… an entertaining tale."
—*BookBrowser*

"Crisp dialogue, a multilayered plot and a carefully measured pace build suspense in this chilling read that earns the WordWeaving Award for Excellence."
—*WordWeaving.com*

THE NIGHT BEFORE

"*The Night Before* is a page-turner that will have you racing toward the finish."

—*Reader to Reader*

"A typical thriller is a meander through a dust bowl compared to *The Night Before*'s tumult down a rocky mountainside."

—*Affaire de Coeur*

"Lisa Jackson sets her own standards [in] women's fiction today, weaving her magic and providing us with literary works of art."

—*The Road to Romance*

"An exciting romantic psychological suspense filled with plenty of twists."

—*Allreaders.com*

WHISPERS

"Author Lisa Jackson delivers a tour-de-force performance with this dynamic and complicated tale of love, greed and murder. This is Ms. Jackson at her very best."

—*Romantic Times BOOKreviews*

"What a story! This is a perfectly put-together, complex story with more than one relationship and mystery going on...a perfect meld of past and present. I loved it!"

—*Rendezvous*

"Author Lisa Jackson has delivered another must-read romantic suspense novel."

—*Gothic Journal*

LISA
JACKSON
RISKY
BUSINESS

HQN™

Recycling programs
for this product may
not exist in your area.

ISBN-13: 978-0-373-77373-2
ISBN-10: 0-373-77373-0

RISKY BUSINESS

This edition published by arrangement with Harlequin Books S.A.

www.HQNBooks.com

Printed in U.S.A.

A DANGEROUS PRECEDENT

CHAPTER ONE

Dane Ferguson hated theatrics. He was a quiet man and usually direct. Though sometimes forced by his profession to become overtly dramatic, he was never comfortable in the role and preferred the straightforward approach—the right combination of questioning and evidence to coax a witness into saying what Dane wanted the jury to hear. By nature Dane wasn't melodramatic; he expected the same of others.

Tonight he was disappointed. He had been in the room for nearly fifteen minutes, and Harmon Smith had yet to get to the point. Just how much of this theatrical demonstration was for his benefit, he wondered as he swirled his untouched drink and eyed the opulent surroundings of the president of Stateside Broadcasting Company.

Dane suspected that he had been summoned to Smith's townhouse on the Upper East Side because of the briefs he had received from that attorney in Portland, Oregon. He had scanned the documents without much interest and passed them along to a junior associate in the firm. Now he wished he had paid more attention to the neatly typed pages.

Undoubtedly the McQueen decision was more important than Dane had originally assumed. Why else would Harmon have insisted upon this evening meeting with several of the prominent vice-presidents of SBC? Television people, Dane thought distastefully, they all love an audience.

"I think we're about ready," Harmon finally announced,

motioning toward the far wall with his free hand. In the other he balanced his drink and a cigarette. A servant placed a cartridge in the video recorder.

The television seemed out of place to Dane. The twentieth-century machine was tucked between leather-bound editions in a cherrywood cabinet, and the rest of the room had been tastefully decorated in period pieces. Leather wingback chairs, antique brass reading lamps and highly polished mahogany tables were arranged perfectly around a rare Oriental carpet of deep emerald green. There was little doubt in Dane's mind that the decorator who had created the stately effect would have preferred to exclude the television. But that was impossible. Harmon Smith lived and breathed for the tube and the six-figure income that television provided him.

Dane's deep-set hazel eyes fastened on the screen, as had all the other pairs of eyes in the room. Harmon Smith wiped an accumulation of sweat from his receding hairline before taking a long swallow of his Scotch and water. The muted voices in the room quieted as an image on the screen flickered and held.

"There she is," Smith whispered through tightly clenched teeth. He pointed a condemning finger at the woman who dominated the screen.

The object of Smith's contempt was an attractive woman who wore her smile and expensively tailored suit with ease. She descended the concrete steps with unfaltering dignity and managed to hold her poise despite the wind blowing against her face and the throng of reporters that had engulfed her.

"That's Kirsten McQueen?" Dane asked dubiously as he studied the graceful woman. His dark brows rose speculatively and a smile tugged at the corners of his mouth.

"The bitch herself," Harmon Smith answered vehemently after taking a long drag on his cigarette.

"Now, wait a minute—" Dane began to interrupt, but Smith silenced him by shaking his balding head.

"Shh… I want you to hear this."

"Ms. McQueen?" A pleasant-featured woman reporter with long dark hair and almond-shaped eyes accosted the graceful cause of the commotion. "We know about the decision against KPSC. Would you care to comment on the fact that the judgment in your favor is a small victory for women's rights?"

Kirsten's even smile never wavered. Her clear green eyes looked steadily into the camera. "I doubt that the decision has anything to do with women's rights, Connie. I think mine was an individual case that was brought to an equitable conclusion." It was obvious to Dane that the slender woman with the soft brown hair and the intriguing green eyes was at ease in front of a camera. There was a quiet dignity about her that was captured on the film.

The reporter persisted. "Then you don't see the decision as a vote of confidence for feminism?"

"This was a lawsuit concerning age, not sex," Kirsten emphasized, holding her hair in place with her free hand. Raindrops had begun to shower on the crowd.

"But feminist groups throughout the state are supporting you and what you're fighting."

"And I appreciate it," Kirsten replied with the flash of even white teeth and the hint of an evasive smile.

"The women's movement could use a new heroine," the plucky newswoman suggested.

Kirsten laughed lightly. "I hardly think I qualify," she responded. Her eyes had warmed by the compliment she apparently considered absurd.

The reporter was placated. "All right. What about the rumors that the station might appeal the decision?"

Kirsten sobered. "It's their right."

"Do you think another jury would rule in your favor, considering the outcome of this trial?"

Kirsten hesitated. "That remains to be seen," she volunteered carefully. "At this point it's only conjecture and I never like to borrow trouble." The clear green eyes had clouded.

The thin blond man with the thick moustache who had been walking next to Kirsten took charge. "That's enough questions," he insisted authoritatively. His protective position of holding lightly onto Kirsten's bent elbow suggested that he was either Kirsten's husband or attorney. Dane suspected the latter—the neatly pressed three-piece suit gave the man away.

"Who is he?" Dane demanded with a frown.

"The prosecuting attorney," Frank Boswick, Smith's assistant replied.

"Is he any good?"

"Rumored to be the best Portland has to offer," Boswick allowed.

Dane's concern was evidenced in the knit of his brow and the narrowing of his eyes. "So why isn't he on our side?"

Smith waved off Dane's question with the back of his hand. "Are you kidding? Lloyd Grady has a reputation of working with the underdog. He's originally from Seattle, and apparently thought he could get some national attention through Kirsten McQueen."

The television screen darkened. Dane considered everything he had learned about Kirsten McQueen as he shifted his gaze from the television to Harmon Smith. The balding man's skin had flushed from the combination of alcohol and anger. He stubbed out his cigarette with a vengeance.

"I want to nail Kirsten McQueen," Harmon Smith spat out. His watery blue eyes lifted to meet Dane's inquisitive stare. "And I want you to do it."

"I'll consider it."

Harmon Smith's lips compressed into a thin white line. "I'm calling all of my markers, Dane. You owe me a favor—a big one—this is it."

The amused smile that had tugged at the corners of Dane's mouth slowly disappeared and his square jaw hardened. "I said I'd consider it," he acquiesced before sitting in one of the stiff chairs. "I think you had better explain everything about this case to me—from the beginning."

"Didn't you get the information from our Portland attorney?" Smith asked. Dane's gaze sought Frank Boswick. The young assistant seemed to have a more objective approach to the case.

"The attorney in Portland is Fletcher Ross," Frank stated.

Dane took a thoughtful swallow of his brandy. "I saw the notes, but I'd like to hear your side of the story." His dark hazel eyes had returned to Harmon Smith. Why was this so important to him?

Smith paced nervously to the window and fumbled in his pocket for his cigarettes and lighter. He looked into the dark Manhattan night before responding. "Basically, the story is this: Kirsten McQueen is a local gal. Grew up around Portland somewhere."

"Milwaukee," Frank clarified.

"Right. Anyway, KPSC hired her right out of college." Harmon Smith blew a thick cloud of smoke at the window as he reconstructed the events that had thrown him and his corporation into the middle of this mess. "She had all the right qualifications—"

"Which were?" Dane inquired.

Smith shook his head as if it didn't matter. "You know, a degree in journalism, some work in another station, brains, interest in the news. Anyway, she worked her way up through the ranks. It was good publicity for the station to make her a full reporter because of her local connections. People eat that kind of thing up. Everybody likes to hear that a local girl made good."

Dane nodded pensively, his studious eyes never leaving

Smith's worried face. Why did Kirsten McQueen get under Harmon Smith's skin? She was just a small-town reporter; he was the head of a national broadcasting corporation.

"So," Harmon Smith continued, warming to his subject, "as time went by she started throwing her weight around, making ridiculous demands, becoming a real pain in the neck. Finally she was let go."

"And she sued KPSC?" Dane surmised.

"Right."

Dane thought it odd. The woman on the screen had appeared dignified, not likely to throw her weight around. In his profession he often had to size someone up by first impression. It helped that he had an intuitive understanding of most people's motives. In Dane's estimation, Harmon Smith must have gotten some bad information on Kirsten McQueen, or else he hadn't as yet completely leveled with Dane.

"But she didn't sue for sex-discrimination?" Dane thought aloud, conjuring mental image of the conservatively dressed woman with the slightly seductive smile.

"Hell, no! She wouldn't have a leg to stand on and she's smart enough to realize it. Even her replacement was a woman!" Harmon Smith declared.

"A younger woman," Dane guessed.

"Yeah, right," Smith grumbled. "I really don't know how old Carolyn is."

"Twenty-two," Frank supplied with an unappreciative glance at his superior. "Carolyn Scott is twenty-two."

"Whatever," Smith acknowledged with a wrinkled frown. "It really doesn't matter."

"And this new woman… this Carolyn Scott… she's qualified?" Dane asked.

"Yeah, sure."

"All the right qualifications," Frank agreed.

Dane tugged on his lower lip. "I really don't understand

something here," he admitted. "Kirsten McQueen doesn't look all that old to me."

"She's not!" Smith stated angrily. "My point exactly. That's why this whole goddamn mess is so hard to swallow!"

"How old is she?" Dane inquired evenly.

"Somewhere around thirty."

"Thirty-five," Frank corrected him. "You may as well level with Dane, Harmon," the young assistant advised. "He's on *our* side."

"Wait a minute," Dane interjected. "How can a thirty-five-year-old woman win an age-discrimination suit?"

"Beats me," Smith allowed. "Only in Oregon. Those people out there aren't in tune with the rest of the nation. They're always on some new crusade! It's either a bottle or a bill, or a clean-water act, or easier laws on possession of marijuana—whatever. I even think an Oregon woman prosecuted her husband for rape, for God's sake!"

"That's right," Frank agreed. "The competition made a television movie out of it."

"Figures," Smith snorted angrily. "Now it looks like it's KPSC's turn."

Dane set his drink on the table and stood to face Harmon Smith squarely. "So you think public sentiment won the case for Kirsten McQueen?"

"It sure as hell didn't hurt it!" Smith waved angrily in the air and shrugged his shoulders as if Dane's questions were irrelevant.

"How many women does KPSC employ?" Dane's gaze shifted to Frank Boswick.

"Eleven," the young assistant replied.

"And how many are over thirty-five?"

"Two."

Dane's dark brows arched. "And neither of them is in front of the camera—right?"

Frank Boswick smiled and shook his head. "One woman who's forty does special interest stories once a week," he stated, shooting his boss a glance that dared the older man to dispute the facts. "However, she wasn't promoted until after Kirsten McQueen filed suit."

"Great," Dane muttered, starting to see the evidence stacking against KPSC. His eyes narrowed with the challenge and he concentrated on a premise for defense. "So why are you involved, Harmon? Isn't this a problem with the station in Portland?"

"It should be," Frank agreed.

Smith let out a disgusted sigh. "The reason Stateside Broadcasting is involved is because we own a percentage of our affiliated stations. Granted, that percentage is small, but we're still involved."

"And that includes KPSC," Dane surmised.

"Right." Harmon Smith thought Dane was finally becoming interested in the case. "And Kirsten McQueen's decision is dynamite. Not only will it affect our other affiliates throughout the country, it could have ramifications for the entire industry."

"A dangerous precedent?" Dane asked.

"Exactly." Smith refilled his drink from a well-stocked bar. "That clip you saw is three months old. We've appealed the decision and the State Court of Appeals in Oregon has ordered a new trial; the date is set for early October, I think. I want you to represent KPSC. You can work with the Oregon attorney for the station."

Dane eyed Smith warily. "How involved will I be?"

"You'll call the shots."

"That will be difficult from New York."

Smith's eyes turned cold. "Then you'll have to go to Oregon."

Dane was reluctant. "I don't know if I can spare the time. I've got several cases scheduled for trial this summer here, in New York."

Smith pursed his lips. "Can't some associate handle them?"

"One of the partners… maybe, but you can't expect me to spend all my time working on this one case across the country in Oregon."

"I don't give a damn how much time you spend out there. I just want to win and end all of this. And I expect you to keep it quiet. We don't need any more publicity." Harmon Smith's icy blue eyes narrowed with suppressed rage. "Don't worry about your fee. I don't care how much this case costs, I just want to be certain that we overturn that McQueen decision once and for all."

"That might be difficult."

"That's why I want you!"

KIRSTEN RAN HER fingers over the rim of the plastic insert of her coffee cup. She twirled it in her hands while she waited for Lloyd. What was taking him so long? The building was unseasonably warm and Kirsten was nervous. She never felt completely at ease talking with lawyers, even her own. And the thought of facing Fletcher Ross again turned her stomach.

Maybe she was foolish to continue her battle against the television station; maybe she should give up. They seemed to have inexhaustible sources of money to try the case. She didn't. She stared unseeing at the watercolors adorning the walls. The seascapes she had once found fascinating didn't interest her today. Nor did the clean blond modern furniture or anything else to do with Grady and Sullivan, Attorneys-at-Law. She was wrung-out—tired of lawsuits and even wearier of smug attorneys in stiff business suits. The less she had to do with them, the better.

Lloyd entered the room and Kirsten knew at that instant that something was wrong. His smile was tighter than normal, his brown eyes worried.

"Sorry I kept you waiting," he said as he slipped into the chair next to hers.

She returned his disturbed grin. "It's all right. What's up?"

He shifted in the chair and crossed his arms over his chest. "There's been a couple of changes in the strategy of the defense."

She arched her brows inquisitively. "Such as?"

"They've got another lawyer."

She wasn't surprised. Fletcher Ross hadn't been well prepared or convincing, even to her. "So they're replacing Ross…."

"Not exactly." He looked her steadily in the eyes.

"What do you mean?"

Lloyd let out a disgusted breath of air. "They've hired someone to help Ross with the defense." His dark eyes were serious and his smile had all but disappeared.

Kirsten ignored the sense of dread his words had inspired and stiffened her spine. "Someone whom you consider a worthy opponent," she guessed.

"At the very least," Lloyd reluctantly agreed.

"You act as if the guy is F. Lee Bailey." Lloyd leaned back in his chair. "Or maybe God," Kirsten continued, trying to lighten the mood.

"Not quite," Lloyd admitted with only a hint of a smile.

"But a close second?"

"You might say that. The guy's name is Ferguson, Dane Ferguson."

Kirsten shrugged her slim shoulders. "I don't think I've ever heard of him."

"I'll bet you have—think."

Kirsten tossed the vaguely familiar name over in her mind. She couldn't identify it with any particular incident. She shook her head pensively.

"He comes from New York."

"That explains it," Kirsten joked. "KPSC never let me

cover any of the national stories… you know, too much thinking involved for a woman."

"Look, Kirsten, this is serious," Lloyd stated.

"Of course it is."

"Ferguson's got a reputation in the East."

Kirsten's smile fell from her face. "A big gun?"

Lloyd nodded. "Yeah, I guess you could call him that. He's not as flamboyant as Bailey, but he's sharp, very sharp." Lloyd thought for a moment. "He usually handles corporate cases—mergers, takeover bids, that sort of thing."

"Then why does he want to bother with me? What's a hotshot New Yorker doing out here?" The absurdity of the situation did not amuse Lloyd Grady. Not at all.

"From what I understand, he's been hired by SBC to turn this case around."

"Why? What does Stateside Broadcasting Company care about this?" Kirsten asked, feeling suddenly very small.

"I looked into it. They own a part of KPSC."

Kirsten was incredulous. Her green eyes widened in amazement. "And so they want to spend a lot of money on this case. It doesn't make any sense, Lloyd. They'll probably pay this Ferguson character more than the two hundred thousand the jury awarded me."

"I don't think this was a purely economic decision," Lloyd stated, pinching his lower lip.

"It's not the money?" Kirsten was dubious.

Lloyd shook his head. "I don't think so. It's the principle of the thing that bothers Stateside. They want to make an example of you to all their affiliates."

"Dear God." Kirsten sighed. "Can't they leave me alone?"

"That's precisely what they're asking themselves about you," Lloyd surmised. "The way they see it, you're the one rocking the boat."

Kirsten raised her hand to her forehead and gently rubbed her temples. The headache that had been threatening all morning had begun to pound behind her eyes. "So what are you suggesting, Lloyd," she whispered, "that we throw in the towel?"

"Not yet." Lloyd drummed his fingers on the table. "Let's wait them out and see what Ferguson's strategy is. He's flying in tomorrow to take your deposition."

"Tomorrow!" Her eyes met Lloyd's. "Good Lord!"

"Don't worry."

"Don't worry?" she echoed, astonished. "You just told me that Dane Ferguson is one of the most prestigious lawyers in New York City and now you ask me not to worry?"

"I just wanted you to know what to expect."

"But I already gave my deposition."

"Apparently Ferguson wants to do the questioning."

"Great," Kirsten murmured sarcastically.

"You can handle it," Lloyd predicted with more confidence than he felt. "It doesn't matter who defends the case. I still think it's solidly in your favor."

"Then why the scare tactics?"

"I want you to be ready for Ferguson. He's slick. Don't let him con you into saying anything you don't mean."

"You act as if that might be easier said than done."

"Just remember that you're in the right," Lloyd advised.

"Let's just hope you can convince the jury of that."

Lloyd smiled resignedly. "We did once before."

"And look where it got us."

"Come on, Kirsten, we're not defeated yet. Don't be so pessimistic. Where's your spirit? Think of the challenge of it all!"

A spark of life lighted her eyes. "I suppose you're right," she conceded with a wan smile. "It's just that I'm getting tired of all this legal nonsense. I don't know if it will ever end."

"The wheels of justice turn slowly," Lloyd kidded her. "Think of it as fun," he suggested, but his face remained grim.

"Fun?" Kirsten repeated. "If you think this is going to be fun, I'd hate to see what you do for a good time."

He cocked his head. "What if I offered to show you?" he asked suddenly.

"I'd say forget it. We have too much work to do," she countered with a convincing toss of her head. Long ago she had learned how to deal with forward men, and she knew that Lloyd had harbored more than a casual interest in her for the past several weeks. He was a reasonable man. After a few pointed rebuffs he would get the message.

"All right, but the least you can do is have dinner with me."

"With what you charge per hour," she teased, "no way."

"Be serious."

Her eyes turned suddenly cold. "I am, Lloyd. And I'm not in the market for a man. You should know that as well as anyone."

All too well he remembered the details of her divorce. "It was only a suggestion."

Kirsten nodded. "I know—why don't we wait until the case is tried? Maybe we can have a victory celebration." She hoped to spare his feelings while inwardly acknowledging that the chances for dinner with him were slim. She just wasn't interested in Lloyd Grady, or any man for that matter. What she needed was a job. She hoped the position she had applied for in San Francisco would work out.

"Okay," Lloyd agreed. "You're on. Now, about Ferguson. Can you be here tomorrow afternoon?"

"To meet with him?"

"To be grilled by him," Lloyd corrected her.

Kirsten's features tightened. "I wouldn't miss it for the world."

CHAPTER TWO

Dane decided that Fletcher Ross was a second-rate attorney at best. As he watched the husky lawyer he came to the conclusion that Fletcher Ross was hiding something. Dane studied all of Ross's exaggerated movements while listening to the Portland lawyer's remarks concerning the McQueen decision.

Ross puffed importantly on a cigar and paced near the window as he described in detail all of the shortcomings of the original trial. The wily man had more excuses than New York had taxicabs—everything from surprise witnesses to the baffling change of trial dates, and that didn't begin to include the fact that the jury was preponderantly unbalanced, composed of two women to every man. In Ross's inflated estimation, he didn't have a prayer going into the courtroom, and he was trying desperately to convince Dane of the same.

He failed. Dane Ferguson had too many years of courtroom experience and he knew just how frail Fletcher Ross's excuses were. After hearing for the third time about how Ms. McQueen had conned the jury, Dane looked pointedly at his watch. It was a gesture that Ross didn't miss. He cut short his long-winded explanation.

"I suppose we should head over to Grady's office," the hefty lawyer suggested. "My car is in the lot."

"Let's walk," Dane replied with authority. "I could use some fresh air."

"It's nearly ten blocks—" Ross began to argue, but thought better of it when he noticed the surprise in Ferguson's eyes. Obviously the New Yorker was used to having his commands obeyed. The last thing Ross could afford was to offend Dane Ferguson or anyone remotely associated with KPSC. He should have won that McQueen case, and the look in Dane Ferguson's dark eyes accused him of that fact. Ross managed a well-practiced smile. "Sure, why not walk? It's a great day." He gathered his correspondence and notes before pushing them carelessly into his briefcase.

Dane rose from his chair and handed Ross's copies of the depositions taken earlier back to the Portland attorney.

"I hope they were helpful," Ross offered, accepting the documents and snapping his case shut.

Dane nodded absently. "Some of them… but I have a few more questions for Ms. McQueen and I want to *see* her reaction to them."

"Good luck," Fletcher Ross muttered as he opened the door to his office and held it for his New York colleague.

"Will I need it?" Dane inquired.

Ross cocked his head. "It wouldn't hurt," he conceded, stepping into the bright sunlight. Secretly he hoped that Dane Ferguson would put the screws to Kirsten McQueen—she deserved it. Losing that case had placed an irrevocable black mark on Ross's career.

Dane had to squint against the brilliance of the sunshine reflected by the minute particles of glass in the concrete sidewalk. At the intersections, where part of the concrete had been replaced by brick, the reflection wasn't so hard on his eyes. "I thought it always rained out here," he remarked, remembering the image of Kirsten McQueen talking to reporters against a darkened sky.

"It usually does," Ross responded breathlessly. He had to

walk briskly to keep up with Dane's longer strides. "I guess we're having an early summer."

The offices of Grady and Sullivan were situated on the twentieth floor of a red brick tower located one block away from the Willamette River. This was the heart of the city, the business district of Portland, and the rent was considerably higher than that of the office Fletcher Ross occupied near Old Town. It made him uncomfortable and served to remind him of all his shortcomings.

During the elevator ride Dane was silent, immersed in private thoughts of how he was going to question Kirsten McQueen. From what he had read of her, and his own impression from the film clip, he knew that his job wasn't going to be easy. He smiled at the thought. He always had enjoyed a challenge, and Ms. McQueen was certain to be that and more.

AT PRECISELY TWO-THIRTY the secretary called Lloyd on the intercom. "Mr. Ross and Mr. Ferguson are here," she announced without any trace of inflection.

"Good. I'll bring Ms. McQueen and meet them in the boardroom." Lloyd turned his attention away from the intercom to focus on Kirsten. "We're on," he stated, rising from the desk. "Just remember to remain calm and answer any of Ferguson's questions directly. If you don't understand a question, ask him to rephrase it. If you get into trouble, let me know—I'll try to get you out of it. Remember: We're not on trial."

"Not today," she replied, straightening her jacket and walking with Lloyd to the door.

"Any other questions?" he asked. When she shook her head he touched her lightly on the shoulder. "This will be easier than you expect," Lloyd promised.

"It has to be," she replied wryly, "because I expect it to the worst couple of hours of my life."

"You're kidding...." It sounded like a question.

"A little."

"You'll do great," the attorney said, holding the door for her before leading her to the reception area. A young girl with doe eyes and straight blond hair turned from her typewriter as they approached.

"Mr. Ross and Mr. Ferguson are in the boardroom. I already gave them coffee."

"Good."

Lloyd pushed open the door to the boardroom. Sitting on the far side of the long oak table were Kirsten's opponents. They looked up as she walked into the room. Ross slid a disdainful glance down her body, but the other man, the one who had to be Ferguson, held her gaze boldly as he straightened from his chair to acknowledge her presence. Kirsten swallowed back the sudden dryness in her throat and managed to hold Dane Ferguson's uncompromising stare. His eyes were hazel and suspicious, his chin strong and jutted, his physique lean, but broad-shouldered. He looked as if he knew exactly what she was thinking.

Fletcher Ross was making introductions. Kirsten nodded politely on cue, managed to accept Dane Ferguson's brief handshake, and then gratefully sank into a chair opposite him. In a corner of the room, wedged between the bookcase and her machine, sat the court reporter. She was in position and ready to record every word of the conversation for future use in the courtroom.

Kirsten had been through this procedure before the original trial. At that time she had felt violated, strong and ready for a challenge. There was no doubt that she could meet the opposition head-on. But today she felt uncharacteristically weak. Like a caged animal trapped behind imprisoning bars. She attempted to hide her frailty behind a cool facade of poise, the same poise she assumed when she was in front of the camera.

Lloyd cast her a reassuring glance as the questions began. It was Dane who spoke.

"All right, Ms. McQueen, I'm going to ask you a few simple questions." He ignored the skeptical rise of one of her finely arched brows. "I want you to answer them honestly and if you don't understand a question, I expect you to tell me so." He paused and his hazel eyes drove into hers. She sensed a danger in their vivid depths. This man's one intent was to discredit her. He would attempt to trap her—entice her into saying anything that might destroy her credibility. He wanted to prove that she was nothing more than a greedy liar bearing a grudge against KPSC. He was still waiting for her response.

Slowly she nodded her head.

"You'll have to speak," he reminded her pointedly. "The stenographer can't record head movements."

Her green eyes were a study in indifference. "I realize that, Mr. Ferguson."

"Good. Then if you're ready, we'll get to it. Your name is Kirsten McQueen?"

"Yes." Her expression told him how ridiculous the preliminary questions were. He ignored the disdain in her eyes.

"How old are you?"

"Thirty-five."

"And how long did you work for KPSC?" He eyed her steadily. Though his voice remained toneless, she could feel the intensity of his words.

"Nine years and eight months."

His eyes darted to his notes. "I thought you were hired directly out of college."

"I was."

Dane Ferguson smiled familiarly and Kirsten was instantly wary. He folded his arms over the tabletop and studied every small detail of her face, realizing uncomfortably that hers was a disturbingly understated beauty that could melt the hearts of a jury. "That doesn't add up, Ms. McQueen."

Kirsten froze. There was something in the cajoling smile and coaxing eyes flecked with gold that made her muscles tense. "Pardon me?"

"Just how long did it take you to finish college?"

She felt an old anger beginning to surface, but she managed to hold it at bay. "Less than four years."

He looked genuinely puzzled. "How then do you account for the time discrepancy?"

She surveyed him coolly. Lloyd nodded, encouraging her to let go of a few personal facts. "I worked between high school and college at KRCT radio."

"To put yourself through school?"

"Yes." She bit out the answer as if he were getting too close to her. She was beginning to feel uncomfortable; the questions were getting much too personal, reminding her of a time she would rather forget.

Dane hesitated a moment. He was beginning to rattle Kirsten McQueen. Though she tried to hide it, he could see the quiet anger resting just beneath the surface of her intriguing green eyes. She began to play with her coffee cup, and then as if she suddenly realized her actions were a display of weakness, she folded her hands in her lap. He closed in.

"Did you help put your husband through college?"

For a moment her voice failed her. "Yes," she finally whispered.

"You were divorced… when was it? Two years ago?"

"Four. It was four years ago this month." She had to clear her throat.

"Why did you divorce him?" The question hung stagnantly on the air. Anger colored her cheeks and her delicate jaw tightened.

"I don't see that this has anything to do with—"

"Why did you divorce him?" Dane repeated a little more loudly. Lloyd motioned with his hands for Kirsten to calm down.

"It…it didn't work out," she replied lamely.

"Why?"

Kirsten bristled. Her eyes narrowed. "My husband was having an affair, Mr. Ferguson. He couldn't seem to make a choice between me and… this other woman."

"So you divorced him?" Was there disdain in his cold dark eyes?

There were so many other factors involved in the divorce. How could she begin to explain to this stranger the hurt and the hours of torment she had endured because of Kent? Even if she could tell him about it, he would only use it against her in the courtroom. "Essentially, yes," she replied.

Dane had hit a sensitive nerve. It was apparent in the flush on Kirsten's skin and the deadly gleam in her eyes. She was daring him to proceed with this line of questioning, but he had no choice. Empathy didn't enter into the case. The truth did.

"The woman with whom your husband was having this affair—was she younger than you?"

Every muscle in Kirsten's body was beginning to ache with the tension taking hold of her. She felt an accumulation of sweat between her shoulder blades. "Yes," she admitted, her chin rising just a fraction of an inch.

"Much younger?"

"Twelve years."

"I see," he commented dryly. It was obvious from the emotionless expression on his face that he didn't see—not at all.

He quickly scanned his notes and pretended interest in them. "And the woman who replaced you at KPSC is also younger than you, isn't she?"

"Yes." Kirsten drew in a long breath. She understood Dane's line of thinking. Though it was ridiculous, it bothered her.

"By how many years?"

"I'm not sure—about thirteen, I think." An angry tide of scarlet crept up her neck. "Look, Mr. Ferguson, if you're insinuating—" Lloyd raised his palm, reminding her of the danger of straying from short, succinct responses to Dane Ferguson's questions.

Dane was interested. "What do you think I was insinuating?"

"Nothing," she replied in a vengeful whisper. "Let's get on with it."

"All right, Ms. McQueen. Now, tell me. Why do you think you were discriminated against—what was the reason—age? You're hardly what I would consider ready to be put out to pasture."

He was leading her, putting on a little of the country-boy charm through his light eastern accent. Kirsten didn't buy his ploy for a minute.

"What, exactly, is your question?"

He smiled. It was a genuine smile that slowly spread over his rugged features, and it let her know that he appreciated her perception. *My God,* she thought to herself, *he thinks I'm a challenge!* She had to remind herself that his smile was deadly. "Tell me why you think you were discriminated against."

"Isn't that all written out in the court documents?"

"I want to hear your side," he countered. "Humor me."

From the corner of her eye she saw Lloyd nod. She looked Dane Ferguson squarely in the eyes, mustering all the conviction she felt on the day she was let go. "They fired me because they thought I was too old to be in front of the camera."

"At thirty-five?" He was dubious.

"Yes!"

"Does the station have a written policy about such matters?"

"I don't think so."

"Then why do you think you were too old?"

An amused smile tugged at the corners of Kirsten's full lips. "I didn't think I was too old, the station did."

Dane settled back in his chair. "I find that hard to believe." It wasn't a question and she didn't respond, refusing to be baited. "If KPSC doesn't have a written policy, how did you come to the conclusion that you were discriminated against? Many people are let go and replaced by younger, less expensive employees."

"No woman at KPSC is in front of the camera after she turns thirty-five," Kirsten stated, immediately regretting her words when she noticed the widening of his boyish grin. Damn it, she'd let him goad her into saying something she shouldn't have.

"So this is sex—not age—discrimination."

Lloyd interrupted. "This is an age-discrimination suit," he reaffirmed.

Dane was attempting to lure Kirsten into dangerous territory and she had to fight the urge to tell him where to get off. "Very few older men are allowed under the lights," she added, amending her earlier statement.

The New Yorker again surveyed his notes. "But KPSC does employ one woman near forty for on-camera work—and there's a gentlemen. Ted Sharp, who's been with the station for nearly ten years as the weatherman. He's forty-seven." Dane's eyes drove deeply into hers. "Certainly you can see my problem in understanding your case," he stated calmly, imploring her without words to enlighten him. He rested his square chin in his hand and waited patiently for her response.

Kirsten swallowed back the hot, infuriated words she felt forming on her tongue. She wanted to tell him how she loathed what he was doing to her, how her past was none of his business, but she didn't. She felt her fingernails digging into her thighs, carefully hiding her tension beneath the edge of the table. Forcing a smile to her lips, she faced her attacker and remained quiet, letting the waiting game continue. She braced herself against another onslaught of questions, evidence to be used in the unending assault against her character. It took all of her concentration to hide her true feelings.

"Did you have any other problems at KPSC?" Dane asked, suddenly lifting his eyes from his notes.

Kirsten shifted uneasily in her chair. Just how much did Dane Ferguson know? How much more could he guess? His eyes were unreadable, his jutted chin unforgiving. She guessed him to be a loner, a solitary man living in the city. "What do you mean?"

"For the most part, Ms McQueen, your employee records are impeccable." Was he kidding? Kirsten suspected that Aaron Becker had crucified her once she was gone. "But there is some mention about your dissatisfaction with your job."

"Some mention?" Kirsten repeated, incredulous. "You mean a memo from the station manager, Aaron Becker? Was that dated before or after I was let go?" she inquired with just the trace of sarcasm. Lloyd stiffened and shot her a warning glance.

Dane's eyebrows rose fractionally as he watched Kirsten brush back a strand of her light brown hair.

"Were you dissatisfied?"

"Not really—"

"What does that mean?" he prodded, knowing he was on the verge of discovering her weakness. Lloyd Grady shook his head slightly. It was intended for Kirsten, but Dane saw it.

"I mean that I was as satisfied as the next person."

Dane was onto something. He could see it in the nervous glances passing between lawyer and client. The personnel records for the station lay in front of them. And he sensed that within the thick folder was the key to the puzzle. Why couldn't he see it? Just what the devil was Kirsten McQueen trying to hide? The woman and the mystery piqued his interest. Something was definitely bothering Ms. McQueen, and Dane doubted that it had much to do with age discrimination.

"Your employee records indicate that you continually demanded more challenging work. You asked to cover more diversified stories." His gold-flecked eyes rose questioningly. He searched her face for a clue.

"That's true," she admitted hastily, her palms beginning to sweat.

"Then you weren't satisfied with your work?" That same damned question.

"Not completely, no."

"Your job lacked challenge?" Dane was obviously surprised. "But you were a newscaster. That in itself is quite an accomplishment, and, I would think, a challenge." Kirsten remained silent. "Ms. McQueen," Dane said, leaning forward and pushing his angular face closer to hers, "didn't you enjoy your job at KPSC?"

"Yes."

"I want you to level with me. Something isn't right here." He pointed to the employee records with one long finger. "Something between you and KPSC. Now, I can't do my job until I understand what it is that's bothering you—and you can't expect a jury to come to an equitable decision if you withhold evidence."

"Is that what you're trying to achieve, an equitable decision?" she asked dubiously.

"Of course."

Fletcher Ross looked as if he were finally going to make a comment, but he decided against it and nervously turned his attention to the window of the large room. He pretended interest in the view of Mt. Hood while he fidgeted with the hem of his sleeve. Anxious beads of perspiration began to dot his wrinkled brow.

Lloyd intervened on Kirsten's behalf. "I don't think this is the time or the place to accuse my client of withholding evidence. If you don't have any more questions"—his gaze included both attorneys on the opposite side of he polished table—"then let's end this thing and all go home."

The New York lawyer was frustrated. He anxiously rubbed the knuckle of his forefinger with his thumb. "I'll agree to that, Lloyd, if you can assure me that Ms. McQueen will agree to another deposition should I need any further information." His response was directed to Lloyd, but his eyes never left Kirsten's face.

Lloyd's brow puckered. "I don't think that will be necessary. You've asked enough questions today, and you have all the testimony from the first trial—"

"It's all right, Lloyd," Kirsten interjected, glad for any excuse to be done with the interview. She rose from the table to her full height and managed to rain her most disarming smile on Dane Ferguson. "Anytime Mr. Ferguson wants to ask me more questions, I'll be glad to answer them."

Dane was suspicious of Kirsten's motives, but he hid his skepticism by standing and taking her outstretched palm, shaking it briefly. He had to hand it to her; she had guts—and class. An enticing mystery was Kirsten McQueen—daring one moment, vulnerable the next. Dane had trouble understanding her, and that bothered him—a lot.

"Thank you for your time," Dane stated as he released her hand.

"My pleasure." The words sounded sincere, but there was a coldness in her gaze that detracted from her polite sophistication. "If you'll excuse me," she requested with a stiff smile. When no one objected, she picked up her purse, turned on her high heel and left the boardroom.

Thank God, Kirsten thought to herself. *Thank God it's over. I hope I don't have to face Ferguson again until the trial!*

CHAPTER THREE

Dane was left with an uneasy feeling in the pit of his stomach and the sour taste of deception in his throat. Something wasn't right about this McQueen case, and he didn't know exactly what it was. That fact alone irked him.

As he paced impatiently in his hotel room, he slid a glance at his copy of all the depositions taken earlier in the week. The papers were where he had left them, scattered over a small table near the bed. Not only had he deposed Kirsten McQueen, but also several of the employees of KPSC who had known and worked with her. And the statements didn't seem to go with Fletcher Ross's evaluation of the case. That wasn't surprising, what was disturbing was the fact that Dane felt something—some piece of evidence—was missing from the neatly typed documents and he couldn't for the life of him figure out what it was.

He felt the weight of an angry frustration settling on his shoulders. He'd been up half the night reviewing the depositions and still hadn't been able to find the answer to his problem. He swore silently to himself as he walked between the bed and window of his hotel room. Alternately he studied the expensive weave of the carpet and the view of the Ross Island Bridge stretching over the silvery waters of the Willamette River.

The airline ticket for a flight back to New York weighed heavily in his pocket. He had business back in Manhattan, a pressing matter that couldn't be put off indefinitely, and yet Dane knew that he wasn't finished in Oregon. The McQueen case stuck in his craw, and he was forced to admit to himself that it wasn't just the issue that held his interest; it was the intriguing plaintiff as well. Kirsten McQueen had managed to get under his skin. The thought galled him, and he spread his fingers before raking them through his unruly dark hair. If she had managed to permeate his thick wall of indifference, there was no doubt that she would be hell on a jury. This case was going to be a lot rougher than he had hoped.

He checked his watch. It was noon in Manhattan. Dane scowled as he picked up the phone. He'd wasted too much time in Portland as it was. Within a minute he was connected with his office near Wall Street.

His secretary wasn't pleased. He could hear her disapproval in the clipped tone of her response when he explained that he might not be back in New York as early as he had planned. "What about the Taylor hearing on Tuesday?" Madeline asked.

"I'll be back for it," Dane replied thoughtfully. He couldn't afford to anger Clarise Taylor, and the hearing couldn't be delayed.

"Mrs. Taylor expects to see you Monday afternoon—"

"See if she can make it Tuesday morning—better yet, tell her I'll call her the minute I land at LaGuardia."

"She won't be pleased."

"Is she ever?" Dane asked, and the frosty tone of his secretary instantly melted.

"I suppose not. I was just trying to avoid another scene."

"Impossible," Dane muttered. "Don't worry. If things go as I hope, I'll be back in town early tomorrow morning and I'll see Clarise as scheduled."

"God help you if you don't," Madeline said.

When Dane hung up the phone he wondered if he had

made the right decision. What could he expect to accomplish in a few extra hours? The meeting with Fletcher Ross had reinforced Dane's assumption that the Portland attorney wasn't worth the time of day. The help Ross had offered Dane had been minimal, and there seemed to be a shadowy distrust in Ross's eyes. Whenever Fletcher Ross couldn't answer a question directly, a deep-seated resentment surfaced on his round features. At first Dane had dismissed Ross's actions as inconsequential. After all, the man had a right to feel indignant. The fact that Dane had been asked to oversee the defense of KPSC was in effect a slap in the Portland attorney's face. But now Dane suspected there was more than professional indignation in Fletcher Ross's silent wariness. It was as if the husky lawyer were covering his tracks. Why? Had Fletcher Ross blown the first trial so badly that he thought his career was on the line?

Dane knew he had to talk to Kirsten again, but he loathed the idea of another deposition. Confronting her within the crowded confines of an attorney's sterile office stuffed with opposing lawyers, disinterested secretaries and grim-faced court reporters wasn't what he desired. He felt compelled o see her alone to study the depths of her wide eyes with no one else to disturb him. He cursed himself for his own impetuosity. Though it wasn't illegal to seek her out without counsel, it was unethical and Dane was used to doing everything strictly by the book. If he'd learned anything, it was that he would never again be coerced into talking behind closed doors.

"Don't be a fool," he uttered out loud, chastising himself as the memory of that one fatal error surfaced in his tired mind. His lips thinned as he considered the unfortunate Stone Motor Company decision and what it had cost him personally. Everything of value in his life had been savagely ripped from him—cruel punishment for the pain he had inadvertently caused others. His reasons for living had been destroyed, and he had vowed to himself that he would never make the same unconscionable mistake again. And yet, here he was, pacing in an overpriced hotel room in Portland and contemplating the unthinkable.

His square jaw hardened and his eyes narrowed speculatively when he telephoned the law offices of Grady and Sullivan. There was only one answer to his dilemma: He had to see Kirsten McQueen and her attorney. And he had to shake her story.

It was a full five minutes before Dane managed to get through to Lloyd Grady. He could hear the restraint in the other man's voice.

"I'd like to depose Kirsten McQueen again," Dane announced after exchanging preliminary civilities with Kirsten's attorney.

"I'm sure we could arrange it."

"Is it possible this afternoon?" Dane inquired, knowing his request to be somewhat out of the ordinary.

"I'm afraid that's impossible. My afternoon is full."

"Perhaps your partner could sit in?"

"Out of the question," Lloyd replied smugly. This case was his baby and he wasn't about to let anyone, not even Sullivan, handle any aspect of it. Already there had been some national coverage of the McQueen decision, and if he played his cards right, Lloyd Grady could make a big name for himself.

Dane wasn't put off easily. When push came to shove, he usually got his way. "Is there another time this weekend that might work out?"

"I don't think so."

With each of Lloyd Grady's quick objections Dane's persistence grew. "I'd like to meet with Ms. McQueen before Monday because I have to be back in New York for a hearing on Tuesday."

"Then I guess you're out of luck," Lloyd responded, feeling suddenly very relieved. "Unless you want Fletcher Ross to handle the deposition."

Over my dead body, Dane thought to himself and smiled at Lloyd's obvious ploy. Too bad he was the opposition. "I don't think so."

"Well, then, you'll have to wait until you're back in town," Lloyd observed, wiping an accumulation of sweat from his nose. Dane Ferguson, or at least the man's weighty reputation, unnerved him.

"Or perhaps I can speak with Ms. McQueen myself?"

The request stunned Lloyd, but he quickly found his tongue. "I don't think so," he said hastily. "Let's keep this strictly aboveboard." There was a pause in the conversation, and Lloyd wondered if Ferguson had heard him. "I've advised Kirsten not to speak with you or any of your associates without my presence."

"And she's agreed to that?"

There was the slightest hesitation. "In essence, yes."

"Then find another time for a deposition before next Monday."

"I'm afraid that's impossible."

"This is only Thursday," Dane reminded the stubborn Portlander.

"But Ms. McQueen is out of town."

Dane smiled to himself at the small piece of information. "Can't you get a hold of her? She might consider my request."

"The point is, I'm not about to ask her," Lloyd stated with renewed authority. "You had your chance, Ferguson, and I was happy to comply with your schedule. But I'm not about to inconvenience my client again, not now. If you want another deposition at a time suitable to both parties, I'll agree to it." The Portland attorney's voice was firm.

"Perhaps you should talk to Ms. McQueen," Dane suggested.

"I will—when she returns. Now, if there's nothing else..."

Dane ended the conversation politely, but his temper seethed. He knew his request was out of the ordinary, and if the situation were reversed, he might act in the same manner as Lloyd Grady. Somehow he expected a little more courtesy from the plaintiff's counsel. Closing his eyes, he rubbed the strain out of his neck muscles. Why did he have the uncomfortable feeling that everyone in this Oregon town was trying to hide something from him? Even his associate, Fletcher Ross, couldn't be trusted. As for Lloyd Grady, the respect Dane originally felt for the man was beginning to dwindle. It was as if he were afraid of something. Dane had noticed the dark glances he had shot to his client during the deposition. And Kirsten McQueen—there was a wariness in the depths of her eyes that worried Dane.

The most expedient decision would be for Dane to return to New York and forget Kirsten McQueen until he could depose her again. Perhaps Harmon Smith, or that assistant of his, Frank Boswick, could clear up some of the enigma. But they couldn't help relieve him of the attraction for Kirsten.

Her image teased his mind. Even now, when he tried to concentrate on the peak of Mt. Hood rising above the wispy clouds, he envisioned the slant of Kirsten's mouth when she smiled, the gentle slope of her shoulders and the provocative green tint of her eyes. "You're a fool," he muttered to himself. His broad shoulders sagged as he realized his motives for staying on the West Coast. The lawsuit was an easy excuse. He wanted to be with Kirsten McQueen alone—as a man to a woman. Something in her mysterious verdant gaze dared him to touch her.

"This can't happen," he warned himself, throwing his clothes into his garment bag. *I have to remain objective.* Dane's vexation was apparent in the furrow of his dark brows and the pain in his eyes. It had been a long time—maybe too many years—since he had wanted, really wanted a woman. In the last six years no woman had come close to reaching him the way Julie had, and if the secret truth were known, he preferred it that way. He didn't want another woman. Ever. It hadn't been a problem. Until now. Instinctively he knew that Kirsten McQueen could be the one woman who could change his life.

"It's too late for you," he scolded himself as he scooped up the keys to the rental car and zipped his garment bag. Rather than let the faded images of Julie enter his mind, he hoisted the bag over his shoulder, snapped the loose papers into his briefcase and strode out of the small hotel room.

He still had a few hours before his plane was scheduled to depart, but the thought of staying any longer than necessary in the room made him restless. He decided to have breakfast at the airport and hope to find a copy of the *New York Times* at a newsstand.

Once inside the rental car, he carefully maneuvered through the narrow streets of Portland's west side before crossing the Marquan Bridge and following the Banfield Freeway toward the airport.

It was time to return to New York and end all this folly about Kirsten McQueen. She was an enchanting woman, but he couldn't allow himself the luxury of seeing her. Not now. For the time being Kirsten remained the opposition, nothing more. And when the lawsuit would finally be resolved, Kirsten would hate him for defeating her. That was the way it had to be; there were no choices. He gripped the black steering wheel until his knuckles whitened. Damn Harmon Smith for dragging him into this mess!

PORTLAND INTERNATIONAL AIRPORT was a madhouse. The pilots for Westways Airlines had made good their threat to strike, leaving the fleet of jets grounded in eight western states. The sprawling terminal building, set on the banks of the muddy Columbia River was crawling with desperate travelers hoping to find alternate routes to reach their planned destinations. To complicate matters, there was the ominous possibility that the pilots for Flight USA Airlines would soon join suit. Their contract had expired yesterday and negotiations were rumored to be breaking down.

Kirsten edged her way toward the Westways desk. She had to pick her way between angry travelers, abandoned luggage and tired children. A red-faced woman turned on her heel, shouted an oath at the weary blond girl behind the counter and jostled Kirsten, who was approaching the tired reservation clerk.

"Is there anyone I could speak with concerning the strike?" Kirsten asked the blond.

The girl turned her weary eyes in Kirsten's direction. She frowned slightly before replying. "You're Kirsten McQueen, aren't you?" A smile pulled at the corners of her mouth. "You won that big case against the television station, didn't you?"

"Not yet, I'm afraid," Kirsten responded.

"Hey—give me a break," an angry male voice interjected. "I need to get to San Francisco!" The balding man behind Kirsten shoved his way forward.

"What can I do for you, Ms. McQueen?" the reservation clerk asked, ignoring the protests of the angry man.

"I'd like to speak with Larry Whitehall. I'm doing a story on the strike."

"He's not here," the blonde said with a shake of her neatly cut hair. "He's supposed to be in Seattle, trying to renegotiate with the union."

Kirsten had guessed as much, but refused to be deflated. She needed a story, and this was by far the most newsworthy on the West Coast. "Then who's taking responsibility in Portland?"

Before the desk clerk could answer, the man behind Kirsten exploded. "Look, lady," he shouted, pointing an accusatory finger in Kirsten's face, "I don't give a damn about a story on the strike. I have to be in San Francisco by three o'clock, and I imagine the rest of the people in this line have better things to do than wait while you conduct an interview, for God's sake!"

"That's right," a female voice concurred.

The desk clerk shot a killing glance at the loud customer before returning her perturbed gaze to Kirsten. "I doubt if he has time to talk, but you might try to speak to Bob Ryan. He's probably at the United desk. United's agreed to try to move our customers."

"Thanks a lot," Kirsten said as she turned and nearly collided with the angry traveler.

"About time," the man muttered as he hoisted his elbows onto the counter. "Now, how the hell am I going to get to San Francisco in time for my nephew's wedding rehearsal?" he asked the blonde.

Kirsten didn't linger to hear the reply. Instead, she hurried toward the crowd centering itself around the red and blue sign indicating the desk of United Airlines, Portland's largest carrier. Kirsten's eyes scanned the sea of faces near the desk, looking for the ruddy complexion of Bob Ryan. Her gaze collided with the arrogant hazel eyes of Dane Ferguson. She felt her throat constrict. He was walking away from the desk and striding toward her. His eyes never left her face. The gleam of determination in the darkness of his glare promised an impending attack. His jaw had hardened and there was a tension in his walk.

"Ms. McQueen," he said in a tightly controlled voice once he was near her. "I thought you were out of town."

"Pardon me?" She met his gaze unwaveringly, but the smile she attempted was thin.

"I called your attorney earlier this morning and he said that you weren't in Portland." He stopped only inches from her, seemingly oblivious to the confusion in the terminal.

A smile hovered on Kirsten's lips as she regained her composure. Seeing Dane here had been a shock, but she managed to recover. "I had planned to be away, but something came up."

"And you didn't bother to inform your attorney?" Dane was skeptical. A storm of doubt was brewing in his eyes.

"Lloyd's my lawyer, not my keeper." She drew her eyes away from the power of his gaze and looked past him, toward the United counter, where she spied Bob Ryan. "If you'll excuse me…"

A strong arm reached out and powerful fingers clamped over her forearm. "I'd like to talk to you."

She let her eyes drop to the fingers surrounding her arm before she met his gaze boldly. "Then I suggest you set up an appointment with Lloyd Grady."

"I tried that." His voice was cold; his jaw tilted arrogantly.

She was clearly skeptical. "And Lloyd wouldn't comply?"

"He said that he didn't want to bother you, that you were unavailable."

She inclined her head and her honey-brown hair fell away from her face. "Because that's what he thought," she explained. "I told you that I would talk to you again, and I will. I'm a woman of my word."

"Are you? Then why don't we talk now, in the coffee shop." His fingers relaxed slowly.

"I can't. I still work for a living, you know. But I'll be more than willing to talk to you when Lloyd agrees." She felt herself warming to him, and she couldn't allow that. As she took a step backward he reluctantly released her arm. Her eyes took in everything about him—his thick, slightly windblown hair, the crisp business suit, the power of his shoulders and his incredible, omniscient eyes. They were deepset and slightly brooding and Kirsten realized that there was little Dane Ferguson didn't see. A feeling of cold misgiving took hold of her, and she couldn't shake it.

"I suggested that we meet tomorrow or later this weekend," he suggested.

"And Lloyd said no?"

"Right."

"Well, look, Mr. Ferguson, I have a very important story to cover right now, and I think you would agree that I really can't discuss anything about the case unless my attorney is present." Out of the corner of her eye Kristen noticed that Bob Ryan was walking briskly toward the glass doors of the modern terminal. A noisy throng of travelers and reporters followed in his wake. He looked as if he hadn't slept in days. Kirsten watched him leave the building. Within a few minutes he would be out of her sight and the story she was writing would have to be postponed.

"I'm sorry, Mr. Ferguson," Kirsten called over her shoulder as she hurried toward the doors of the terminal, but her words sounded false. She was relieved to be away from the power of the New Yorker's scrutiny, glad to put some distance between her body and his. As she half-ran after Bob Ryan, Kirsten told herself that it was just the thought of the lawsuit that bothered her. The hammering in her heart was the result of a number of things—the upcoming trial, the chaos in the airport terminal and her desperation for a good story. It had nothing to do with the fact that Dane Ferguson was a very intriguing man.

THREE WEEKS LATER Kirsten was once again in the law offices of Grady and Sullivan. True to his word, Dane Ferguson had asked for another deposition. He obviously hadn't been satisfied with Kirsten's answers to his earlier questions. Though she knew what to expect, Kirsten was still uneasy. This whole affair had dragged on too long and the thought of Ferguson's relentless questions worried her. She had only to remember the promise in his eyes when she had seen him in the airport. Too many nights she had considered those enigmatic eyes staring at her from across a courtroom. He would be deadly on a jury. The thought made her stomach twist with dread.

"What more could he possibly want to know?" she asked her attorney. Lloyd's wan smile was meant to be comforting.

"You tell me. You know as much as I do. Didn't he say anything at the airport?"

"I wouldn't let him."

"That's good. Besides, we'll find out when he gets here," the young attorney promised. Lloyd wished he could find a way to put Kirsten at ease, but he found it impossible to erase the deep lines of concern lining her flawless forehead.

"Can't we just say no thanks?"

"I don't think so." Lloyd's grin was nervous but genuine. He cared for Kirsten McQueen, and his dark eyes hardened at the thought of what Ferguson might try to do to her. "Look, Kirsten, we can't back down. Not now. We can't show the least little hint of weakness. You have to appear righteously indignant because you know that the truth is on your side."

"I don't want to perform, Lloyd. I just want to get it over with."

"I know," he consoled her with a worried frown.

When the secretary announced Dane Ferguson's arrival, Kirsten felt a stab of cold doubt enter her heart. There was something about the tall man from New York that took hold of her and wouldn't let go. Fletcher Ross had been easy to deal with because Kirsten disdained him. With Dane it was different. She respected the man and the honesty in his hazel eyes. It was difficult not to trust his lazy, easygoing smile or the gentle way he stroked his chin in confident reflection as he watched her. The trust he inspired was precarious. She had felt it the first time they met and again, fleetingly, at the airport.

He was waiting for her. He stood on the far side of the narrow room, leaning casually against the windowsill. His broad shoulders nearly filled the window frame. When she entered the room he straightened and adjusted his shirt cuff. There was warmth and humor in his knowing gaze as he appraised her, and Kirsten had the unlikely sensation that he was glad to see her. The trace of a smile curved his lips in the awkward moment when introductions were reaffirmed.

When seated across the heavy table from him, Kirsten attempted to relax. Though a professional smile crossed her lips, her spine remained rigid, poised for the verbal attack that was sure to come. Kirsten regarded Dane Ferguson as the enemy. Cool green eyes held his gaze firmly as if she were daring him to proceed with the inquisition.

"Good afternoon," Dane said. Fletcher Ross cocked his head in Kirsten's direction, puffed on his cigar and watched the proceedings through narrowed eyes.

Kirsten returned the New Yorker's greeting and noticed that the court reporter was already in position to record everything that was said in the uncomfortable room. The smile on Kirsten's lips didn't falter. She reminded herself that she had to remain in complete control of the situation. Nothing Dane Ferguson or Fletcher Ross could say would rattle her.

"I'm going to pick up where we left off the other afternoon," Dane announced. He opened his briefcase and slapped some neatly typed pages onto the modern oak table. Kirsten remained silent, patiently waiting for the first of his questions. "I want you to tell me about your workday at KPSC," Dane suggested, resting his elbows on the table and propping his chin in his hands.

"What do you want to know?" Her poise never wavered.

"How did you get along with the station manager… what was his name?" Dane quickly perused his notes, but Kirsten suspected he hadn't forgotten the name. This was all a part of the show—to lure her into saying something she would regret.

"Aaron Becker," Kirsten supplied with a tight smile.

"Right. How did you and Becker get along?"

"Very well, I think," she replied cautiously. "At least, professionally speaking."

A dark glance from Lloyd warned Kirsten that she was straying into forbidden territory.

"And personally?" Dane demanded, his voice controlled but a darkness gathering in his piercing gaze.

"We didn't socialize."

"Why not?"

The question wasn't necessary. "I don't see that the fact that I didn't socialize with Aaron Becker has anything to do with the case," she answered calmly.

Dane noticed the slight puckering of her delicately arched brows. He was getting somewhere. Quietly tapping the end of his pencil on the paper, he grinned slowly and in a manner meant to ingratiate himself to her. "I was just trying to establish the relationship that existed between you and your boss."

"It was professional—nothing more." She withheld the urge to tell him it was none of his damned business and managed to mask the resentment in her eyes.

He seemed puzzled. Thoughtfully he glanced at Lloyd Grady before returning his gaze to Kirsten's face. "But the other day, the last time we talked, you said,"—his dark eyes left her strained face to scour his notes—"…here it is: I asked you about dissatisfaction with your job and a memo to that effect and you responded with 'Some mention? You mean a memo from the station manager, Aaron Becker? Was that dated before or after I was let go?'" Dane paused before raising his eyes to hers. He contemplated the anger he saw in her eyes. "That question indicates that you and Mr. Becker had a misunderstanding."

"Not a misunderstanding really," she explained. "I wanted more involved assignments—"

"Such as?"

"Oh, I don't know." Kirsten tried to think. She wanted more examples than that of Ginevra, the most explosive issue, which had ignited her dismissal. "There were several big stories around at the time, and Aaron refused to let me cover them."

"Because of your age?" Obviously Dane doubted it. "Or was it because you were a woman?" He paused for dramatic effect. "Or was it something else entirely?"

"Kirsten has no way of knowing what went through Aaron Becker's mind," Lloyd cut in.

"Don't you?" Dane impaled Kirsten with his demanding gaze. Gold flecks sparked angrily in his eyes before his voice softened. "I just want to hear your side of the story, that's all." In the flash of an instant his entire demeanor had changed from that of inquisitor to one of an old, interested friend. Kirsten witnessed the ease with which he changed his expression, and her stomach knotted. He was good, damned good, and it was frightening. Very easily this man with the taunting hazel eyes and congenial smile could lure her into saying something she really didn't mean.

"Just before I was let go," Kirsten began evenly, her gaze never wavering, "there were several big stories. One was a political scandal involving a state senator, another was about a suspected drug ring south of Oregon City, and another involved a proposed site for a nuclear reactor near the coast. Aaron didn't want me to cover any of those stories."

Dane rubbed his chin pensively. Fletcher Ross pulled at the tight knot in his tie. Nothing seemed to be adding up to

Dane. He felt the strain in the air. "Becker didn't want you involved because you were too old?" She didn't respond. "Forgive me, Ms. McQueen, but I'm having a little trouble understanding all of this." There it was again—the well-practiced country-boy charm, a direct contradiction to his expensively tailored suit and determined jaw. Kirsten wasn't fooled.

"Then perhaps you should ask Aaron Becker about it," she suggested.

"I intend to," Dane promised, leaning back in the oak chair and regarding her silently.

Fletcher Ross squirmed. The conversation was uncomfortable and the warm boardroom made him sweat. He could feel the dampness running down his back. Looking at his watch, he frowned before leaning over to Dane. "I think we've gotten all we need today," the portly man said, running nervous fingers through his hair. "I've got an appointment back at the office in half an hour."

"I have a few more questions," Dane responded, his determined tone warning Ross not to interfere. The authority in his intense gaze brooked no argument. Quickly his eyes returned to search Kirsten's intriguing face. "Why don't you think Aaron Becker let you work on any of those stories?"

"I don't know," she said. Her clear green eyes were shadowed. Dane knew he was getting near the truth.

"Was there another reporter better suited for the job? Say, one with more experience?"

"Not in my opinion."

"Isn't that a little lofty?"

"You asked; I told you the truth."

Dane looked to Ross for an explanation, but the Portland attorney averted his gaze. Fletcher Ross scowled and lifted his hefty shoulders, indicating that he thought Dane's line of questioning was of no importance.

"Were younger reporters given the choicest stories?" Dane

asked, trying to understand exactly how the elegant woman seated sedately across the table from him felt.

"In one instance, yes. Another was given to a man who had been at the station about the same length of time as I had and the third... well, Aaron Becker didn't seem to place too much importance on Ginevra."

"Ginevra?" The name was vaguely familiar to Dane. Once again he turned to his associate, but Fletcher Ross shook his head, as if he couldn't fathom Kirsten McQueen or her interest in the town with the strangely familiar name.

Kirsten understood the exchange of confused glances, and the indifference on Ross's round face made her blood begin to boil. All of the anger she had fought so desperately to suppress had threatened to erupt. Ross's attitude was the same as Aaron Becker's had been when Kirsten had first gone to her boss with ideas on the Ginevra story. For a reason she couldn't name, it was suddenly very important that Dane Ferguson understand. "Ginevra is the proposed site for another nuclear power plant. It would be Oregon's second, but no one at KPSC seemed to have much interest in it."

"Except for you," Dane guessed, returning his interested eyes back to Kirsten's incredibly beautiful face. She caught herself and didn't answer immediately. "Is this story significant?" Dane prodded, aware that Fletcher Ross was shifting in his chair and twirling an unlit cigar in his fingers.

"In this part of the country—yes. At least I think so."

"Why is that?"

Kirsten was about to expound on the subject, but understood the look of caution on Lloyd's even features. The perfectly groomed blond attorney spoke for his client. "This has nothing to do with the matter at hand. Ginevra is still in the planning stages and the only significance it bears on this case is that it was a small bone of contention between Kirsten and Aaron Becker."

Dane pushed up his sleeves, propped his elbows on the table and pressed his lips against his folded hands. His eyes reached out to hers in the thickening silence. "Ms. McQueen," he said softly. "Just why do you think you weren't allowed to cover the Ginevra story?"

"I wish I knew," she answered honestly, feeling the need to let this man understand her frustration.

"Then you think it might be more than just age discrimination?" His hazel eyes dared her to tell the truth. She felt herself wanting to reveal her deepest secrets before she shifted her gaze and forced her fingers to coil in resolution.

"I don't know what to think, Mr. Ferguson," she replied. "And—and I don't see that rehashing a dead issue such as Ginevra will help either of us with this case."

He raised a quizzical eyebrow. "You might be right, Ms. McQueen." Snapping his briefs into his case, he graced her with a smile. "I think that should do it," he stated, "unless, of course, I discover something else I need to discuss with you."

"Of course," she replied, settling back in her chair and breathing deeply for the first time all afternoon.

His dark, gold-flecked eyes swept the room to include everyone. "Thank you," he stated, rising to leave. A satisfied smile cracked across his rugged features and Kirsten had the impression that she hadn't seen the last of him.

Dear God, she thought to herself, *Dane Ferguson thinks of me as a challenge*. Involuntarily she squared her shoulders and her cool, emerald-colored eyes appraised him. *Well, if it's a fight he wants,* she promised herself as she watched his retreating figure, *it's a fight he'll get!*

CHAPTER FOUR

It certainly doesn't get any easier, Kirsten groaned to herself as she massaged her aching calf muscles. She was winded from the run and collapsed on the bottom step of the staircase, ignoring the gritty layer of sand on the rough boards. After completing four miles along the surf's edge, she realized that the early-morning exercise had taken its toll on her. Her leg muscles ached rebelliously as she pulled herself upright and began to mount the weathered stairs that led from the beach to the cabin. Her lungs burned from her accelerated rate of breathing and the cold sea air. Between her own sweat and the thick fog, her hair had been reduced to a wet mass of dark ringlets framing a flushed face.

"Wonderful," she grumbled as she pushed the damp hair out of her eyes. "So much for keeping fit." The usual exhilaration she had come to expect from the run was missing, and she hadn't been able to dispel the ugly mood that had been her constant companion since yesterday afternoon. She paused to catch her breath and leaned over the bleached railing in order that she could survey the wet beach as if it were an uncompromising opponent. "Tomorrow I'll run five!" she promised herself, and slapped the railing with newly felt conviction. Her green eyes rose to pierce the fog, searching for the horizon. Try as she would, she was unable to discern the difference between the cold sea and the sky. The threatening gray waters of the Pacific seemed to bleed into the equally opaque sky. "Gonna be a storm, unless I miss my guess," she murmured, absently repeating the words she had heard from her grandfather time after time.

The wind coming from the north was raw as it blew against the strained contours of Kirsten's face. She hurried up the few remaining steps and walked briskly down the overgrown path leading to the house. With one hand placed against the weathered siding to support her, she pulled off her Nikes and placed them on a corner of the porch, convinced that she would need them for the next day's run. Why did she have such a lack of energy and enthusiasm for jogging? Kirsten had always enjoyed an early morning run on the wet sand. The smell of the salty sea had been invigorating.

Blame it on a lousy night's sleep, she decided, or better yet, on Dane Ferguson for robbing her of her slumber. She leaned against the doorjamb before entering the cottage. Why was it that she couldn't get him out of her mind? What was it about him that set him apart from the rest of the men she had met recently? She had considered the fact that she felt an eerie fascination for him because it was his task to defeat her—to prove her nothing more than a money-grubbing employee with an incredible chip on her shoulder. But there was something more to the intrigue she felt for him, something she couldn't define.

Though she had tried, she hadn't been able to put yesterday's inquisition or Dane Ferguson out of her mind. Shaking her head disgustedly while running her fingers through her tangled curls she entered the cabin and let the screen door bang closed behind her.

What was she attempting to prove by going after KPSC? Her righteous indignation and need for revenge had faded and she faced another time-consuming and costly trial. The thought of Dane Ferguson with his knowing eyes and sophisticated self-assurance only made it worse. No doubt the man would torture her on the witness stand, twist her words until the meaning was lost in a jumble of legal maneuvers and double-talk. Was it worth it? What had happened to her fire and determination? Weren't there any simple answers anymore?

She stepped into the shower and tried not to think about Dane Ferguson and the threat he posed. The rusty pipes groaned as she turned on the spray and felt the sharp sting of cold water against her overheated skin. Her cramped muscles began to relax.

Just when the water had warmed to a comfortable temperature, and she had finished washing her hair, she heard her phone ring. "I'm not interested," she said aloud, but the phone continued to shrill insistently. Her dark mood hadn't improved.

"Wouldn't you know," Kirsten muttered as she turned off the water and stepped hastily into her robe. She managed to make it to the telephone before the ringing had subsided.

"Kirsten, is that you?" Lloyd's worried voice called to her through the wires.

She closed her eyes. That was the trouble with Lloyd; he was so damned overprotective. As a lawyer it was a quality in his favor. As a man it was a fault to his detriment. Where did he get off calling her and then asking if it was she? "Yes, Lloyd," she said wearily. "It's I." She tried to mask the disappointment in her voice. It wasn't Lloyd's fault that she hadn't slept well or that she was doing a pretty good impersonation of Oscar the Grouch.

"Good." He sounded relieved.

"What's up?" she asked, toying with the phone cord and hoping that she wasn't dripping on the parquet floors. She attempted to ignore the fact that she was shivering and concentrated on the telephone conversation.

"It's Ferguson," Lloyd explained. "He's been looking for you."

Kirsten's heart stopped for a second. "Wait a minute—it's barely nine o'clock and I saw him yesterday. What do you mean, he's been looking for me?"

"Just that. He called this morning about eight. He asked me where he could find you." There was a note of anxiety in Lloyd's voice.

"I thought he would be back in New York by now."

"So did I."

"You didn't tell him where I was, did you?" Kirsten asked. Her anger had given way to dread. The last thing she needed was another confrontation with Dane Ferguson. He could read her too easily. His intense stare seemed to penetrate the darkest corners of her mind.

"Of course not," Lloyd replied. "I also reminded him that I was your attorney and that you wouldn't talk to him unless I was present."

Kirsten leaned her shoulder against the wall, as if she suddenly felt the need for support. "Did that discourage him?"

There was a heavy pause. "I don't know, Kirsten," Lloyd admitted. "Believe me, I can't imagine why he would come looking for you, but he might. The guy's damned unpredictable."

"But not stupid, Lloyd. He knows that I won't say anything without your advice, so he would be wasting his time even if he did find me. From the looks of him, I doubt that he makes a practice of doing that." She almost talked herself into believing it, until she remembered Dane's penetrating stare. Those dark hazel eyes had silently made promises to her from across the table yesterday afternoon. She hadn't understood the meaning of those promises until now.

"I wouldn't think so," Lloyd replied, but he didn't sound convinced. "And you're right. Ferguson's not stupid—a far cry from it. All you have to do is look at his record to realize that."

"What record? You started to tell me about it once before, but you never finished. Just what is it that Ferguson's done?"

"I can't believe you don't remember. Think back. Remember the Stone Motor Company decision about six years ago?"

"Vaguely—something about a defective transmission?"

"Brakes. There was some controversy over a new type of disc brake that Stone had manufactured and put on its elite line—the Zircon. There was a class-action suit against Stone."

"And Stone Motors won."

"Right," Lloyd agreed.

"I take it that Dane Ferguson defended Stone," Kirsten guessed.

"You got it."

"Great," she mumbled, wondering if she was making an incredible mistake taking on KPSC. Her thoughts flew back to the coverage of the Stone Motor incident. It was a national story—given to another reporter—but there was something out of the ordinary about the decision, an ironic twist or something. She couldn't remember. At the time she had been wrapped up in her own problems, the worst of which was that her marriage was falling apart. "Why didn't you tell me all of this before I met with Ferguson?"

"I thought you didn't need to worry any more than necessary."

"Hmph." Once again Lloyd had protected her. "Lloyd?"

"Uh-huh?"

"Wasn't there something else about that Stone decision, something…ironic?" She felt a twinge of dead at the question.

"I don't know if I would classify it as irony. Bad luck would be a better explanation," Lloyd allowed.

"For what?"

"Ferguson owned one of Stone's Zircons. It was his car,

but one day, supposedly without his knowledge, his wife used the Zircon to take their kid to a doctor. They lived in Upstate New York, somewhere near Buffalo, I think. Anyway, the road was icy—"

"And his wife and son were killed when the car slid off the road and rolled down an embankment," Kirsten finished, remembering the details of the horrible accident. How could she have forgotten it? Now that she had met Dane, it all seemed so personal. A wave of nausea threatened to overtake her.

Lloyd's voice was grim. "That's right. To my knowledge it was never proven that the brakes failed. Too many other factors were involved to prove that the car was defective. However, the accident renewed the speculation and controversy that the Zircon was unsafe. Because of decreased sales, Stone was forced to quit manufacturing the Zircon the next year. The company nearly went bankrupt."

Kirsten was sickened by the story. She didn't want to feel any empathy for Dane Ferguson. She didn't want to feel anything for him at all. It was better that she remain detached and objective about him. That way she would remember that he was the adversary. She couldn't think of him as a man, a human being with problems of his own. The woman in her cried for him, conflicting with her instincts as a reporter which reminded her that he was dangerous. Any feelings for him personally were contradictory to her best interest.

Though she didn't want to know more about Dane, she was compelled to listen as Lloyd continued. "For a while no one heard from Dane Ferguson. He quit practicing law, and what happened to him in the next eighteen months is a mystery to me. Then he suddenly resurfaced in Manhattan with enough money to start a practice in the heart of the city. Within the last couple of years he's reestablished himself as one of the top lawyers in the nation."

"And he's decided to defend KPSC," Kirsten stated with a trace of disbelief. "Incredible."

"Or unlucky."

"What about both?" she suggested humorlessly. She told herself she didn't need this aggravation. If she were smart, she'd get out now, drop the case and look for a job in L.A. But the thought of Aaron Becker and the rest of the smug bigwigs at KPSC gave her an angry new determination. Let them call in the big guns from back east. She had the truth on her side!

"Look, Kirsten, I just wanted to warn you about Ferguson. If he does manage to find you, you don't say anything!"

Kirsten drew in a deep breath. "How could he find me? You're the only one who knows where I am."

"But I'm not the only person who knows that you inherited a beach cabin somewhere around Cape Lookout," he reminded her. "Since you gave up your apartment, it wouldn't be too hard to guess where you're living."

"Lloyd, do you really think—I mean really think that he would track me down at the coast?"

"I wish I knew," Lloyd conceded. "It would help me immensely if I knew what that guy was thinking." There was a pause. "Hey, look, Kirsten, I've gotta run. Talk to ya later."

"Right," she agreed as she hung up the phone. She walked back into the bathroom and changed into her jeans and a sweater, letting her damp curls dry naturally.

She had only given up her apartment a few weeks ago, when she had decided to move, if only temporarily, into the small cabin her grandparents had owned. She had hoped that getting away from Portland would give her a fresh perspective and that it would take her mind off the trial. It hadn't. If anything, it had made the situation worse. Now she was that much closer to Ginevra, the site planned for Oregon's second nuclear power plant and what she considered the genuine reason she had been let go by KPSC. Her outspoken voice against the Ginevra plant had influenced Aaron Becker. And when she had asked to do a story on the proposed site, he had flat-out refused, insisting that her opinions were biased. She had sworn to be objective about the story, posing both sides to the controversy, but Aaron Becker had been adamant, demanding that she continue covering local social events such as the Rose Festival and the opening of the recently restored Grand Theatre on Broadway. Within two weeks she was fired with only a few weeks' severance pay to sustain her.

Fortunately, she had saved some money while working at the station and there was the small inheritance her grandparents had left her. She supplemented her income by writing freelance articles for magazines. It wasn't a lot of money, but she could live well enough on it because the small cabin overlooking the sea was unmortgaged. Now that she no longer had the rent on the apartment, finances weren't a major worry, although no one would believe her.

Her argument with KPSC wasn't over money, and the two hundred thousand dollars she had been awarded originally wasn't her primary concern. She wanted to see justice prevail, and she had no other means to fight KPSC than through a court of law. That she could be let go because she was a little older than the station would have preferred, and because she wanted to do more in-depth stories about controversial issues, certainly shouldn't be cause for dismissal. It would have been different if she had been a real pain in the neck, but she had always been a conscientious employee and had done anything that her superiors had asked—until Ginevra. There was something about that proposed site that really bothered Aaron Becker. She could read it in his stony gaze the first time she had broached the subject: Ginevra was off-limits.

Why? To date, she hadn't had a satisfactory answer. She wondered if she ever would.

She threw on a light jacket and stepped into her shoes before going outside. Though the fog had lifted, a light drizzle continued to fall from the overcast sky. She ignored the signs of a storm and hurried down the slippery steps to the beach. In one hand she carried a short shovel and a bucket, the other was used against the wet railing for balance.

The tide was out and the sand near the water's edge was saturated with seawater. Though it was late in the day for digging for clams, Kirsten scoured the wet beach for the deep round holes that indicated a razor clam was buried beneath the surface. Spying the first hole, she dropped to one knee and began to dig in quick, short strokes. She was mindless of tide, which would occasionally creep up on her, or the rain that had begun to fall. Her concentration was solely on the capture of the burrowing clam. When the sand became too wet and soft for the shovel, she tossed it aside and thrust her arm into the oozing hole until she felt the flat shell of the escaping mollusk with her fingertips. Her arm was wet and sandy to above her elbow, her sweater dirty and her jeans soaked by the icy salt water, but Kirsten didn't care. For the first time in weeks she wasn't brooding about the impending lawsuit.

DANE'S EYES SQUINTED in frustration as he stared at the crooked coast highway. He was traveling southward on the slippery asphalt two-lane road and the sudden rain shower impeded his speed. To the west, stretched out endlessly, was the gray Pacific Ocean. Frothy whitecaps rose on the choppy water, and the ominous color of sea and sky reaffirmed Dane's doubts.

He knew it was a mistake to track down Kirsten McQueen. There was no way he could justify his impetuous journey to the Oregon coast, but the short telephone conversation with Lloyd Grady earlier in the morning had nearly forced Dane to seek her. There was something overtly protective in Lloyd's voice, and without words the Oregon attorney had intoned that Kirsten McQueen was off-limits to another man. Dane had taken Lloyd's self-serving warning as a dare. He was certain he was making a grave error; he could feel it in his bones, but he was drawn to her, compelled to find her. Lloyd Grady's protective attitude toward Kirsten only served to reinforce Dane's determination.

He took a curve too sharply and the rental car slid into the oncoming lane. Regaining control of the car, Dane swore and forced himself to ease up on the throttle. He was behaving like a madman.

His hope that yesterday's deposition would end his desire for her had been frivolous conjecture. If it were possible, the confrontation yesterday had strengthened his need to be with her alone. He shifted the gears of the car as the road began to climb and he scowled at the threatening gray clouds in the distance. Each time he had been with Kirsten, even fleetingly at the airport, he felt his attraction for her increasing.

"Damn that woman for getting under my skin," he muttered with a deepening frown. "This is lunacy."

Trying to ignore the fact that the risk he was taking might possibly cost him the case, Dane searched the dense foliage of twisted pines for the side street that would lead him to Kirsten's beach cabin. Never in his life had he been so foolhardy, but never had he been so damned possessed by a woman. Not even Julie. The passion he had shared with his deceased wife paled in comparison to the ache he felt for Kirsten McQueen. Maybe that's what happens when passion lies dormant for six years, he thought to himself. When it finally arises, the lusting ache becomes so heated that the memory of another woman fades.

He turned onto a private lane leading to a cabin on the cliff overlooking the sea. Or maybe the fact that Kirsten McQueen represented the opposition enticed Dane to her. That she was unavailable added to her allure. Whatever the reason, he was

They reached the stairs. After setting her bucket on the lowest step, Kirsten crossed her arms over her chest and leaned against the railing. The wind blew her hair away from her face, allowing Dane a glimpse of her ears and throat. "Mr. Ferguson," she asked cautiously, "what are you doing here?"

He looked tired but sincere. "I came to see you."

"That much I guessed," she replied, cocking her head and eyeing him suspiciously. He noticed the curve of her neck and the way her full lips pursed when she was puzzled. "I want to know why. I assume it's to ask me some more questions."

"Possibly…"

"The answer is no," she stated firmly. "Mr. Grady has advised me not to speak with you—under any circumstances."

"I'm sure he did," Dane allowed, placing his shoe on the lowest step of the staircase and leaning on his bent knee. His eyes narrowed as he looked toward the sea. It was if he were seeing it for the first time. He noticed the white foam of the waves contrasting against the bluish-gray depths, the graceful flight of California gulls as they scoured the beach and the gnarled flat pine trees that clung to the edge of the cliff.

"Then why did you come here?" Kirsten inquired, her rage and indignation slowly giving way to curiosity.

Abruptly his dark gaze swept back to her. His smile was forced and conveyed a sense of self-derision. The wrinkles near his eyes had deepened. "I had a couple of reasons," he explained. "The first is that I don't completely buy the story you told me yesterday"—Kirsten started to interrupt, but he held his hand near his face in a gesture meant to cut off her angry retort—"and second is that I find you incredibly… fascinating, for lack of a better word."

Kirsten wasn't easily persuaded. "Because I'm your latest challenge—the opposition, so to speak," she threw out, daring him to deny her assessment of the situation. There was something about him that touched her and made her aware of him as a man. That alone irritated her. Kirsten didn't want to think of the dark-eyed stranger with the mysterious smile as a man. It was too disturbing. It would be wiser to think of him only as the enemy.

He shook his head and his thick coffee-colored hair ruffled in the wind. It gave him a boyish look that lessened the severity of his angular features and softened the intensity of his dark eyes. "The fact that you're the opposition has nothing to do with it."

"And a cat really does have nine lives," she responded caustically. "Give me a break." She rubbed her temple and tried to remain calm. "Look, Mr. Ferguson—"

"Dane."

"Mr. Ferguson, don't try and con me. It won't work."

"Oh, that's right," he agreed, mimicking her cynicism. "For a moment I forgot that you're a hotshot ace reporter who knows all the angles."

Her dark eyebrows rose slightly, and a smile dared to soften the pout on her lips. "Touché, Mr. Ferguson," she whispered.

"Call me Dane."

Once again he was rewarded with the elegant lift of her brow. She didn't respond to his request, preferring to hear him out.

His ever-changing eyes held hers in a cold embrace. "I just thought that it might be nice to meet you in less… confining surroundings."

"Forgive me if I'm skeptical," Kirsten announced with a slightly wicked gleam in her eye. "I tend to get this way when I'm around someone who's being paid to discredit me." She turned on her heel and began to mount the stairs.

Dane picked up the shovel she had left wedged in the sand before following her upward. He attempted not to notice how the tight wet fabric of her jeans hugged her buttocks, and grimaced to himself. How could a woman who was wet from head to foot, covered to the forearms in sand and still bleeding from an angry wound have the nerve to tell him where to get off? She appeared so damned lofty and self-righteous. Damn, but she was so hard to figure out.

Kirsten managed to hold her tongue as she climbed the staircase. She wondered what she was going to do about the man a few steps below. He was obviously not easily discouraged, and she had to admit that she enjoyed his company—in a perverse sort of way. At least he wasn't dull!

At the top of the stairs she faced him, determined to make a final stand. When he stepped onto the path that led to the small cottage, she knew it was now or never. She was angry with him for seeking her and angry with herself for secretly being pleased that he would take the time and trouble to find her. His dark eyes were so mysteriously inviting, and if she were inclined to be romantic, she could imagine erotic promises in their vivid hazel depths.

His skin was dark, as if he had spent some time in the sun, and it was stretched tightly over the uncompromising contours of his face. He was a handsome man, she decided, but not in the classical sense. His features were too large and bold.

"I wish you would forget that I was the defending attorney," he stated.

"I'll bet."

He leaned on the handle of the shovel and his eyes drove deeply into hers. "Just think of me as any other man."

"A little hard to do."

He pulled an exaggerated frown. "I suppose it is a lot to ask, but it would certainly help."

"Help what—or whom?" He was beginning to work on her; she could sense it.

"Look, Kirsten," Dane began, and she bristled at the

familiar use of her name. "I didn't come here to spar verbally."

"So you said." Her disbelief was evidenced in the dubious slant of her mouth.

"I really do find you extremely attractive."

There was a sincerity in his eyes that she wanted desperately to believe. She hated to admit it even to herself, but it was hard to ignore the fact that he was a very interesting man.

"And you expect me to believe that you came here just to get to know me better. This is a social call?" Her words were uncharacteristically caustic. What was the matter with her? Didn't she have the decency to be civil to this man?

A crooked smile exposed his straight white teeth. "Not entirely, no."

"I didn't think so." She managed to hide her disappointment under a veil of self-assurance.

"There are several things I have to discuss with you about the case."

"And you know that I can't. Not without Lloyd," she reaffirmed.

"This is strictly off the record." His voice was toneless.

"You've got to be kidding!" she exclaimed, but his eyes remained serious. "You can't expect me to believe that what you and I discuss will be kept confidential."

He folded his arms over his chest patiently. "As a reporter you sometimes heard things that were off the record." Kirsten nodded, her eyes still wide with disbelief. "And I expect that you never betrayed any of those confidences, did you?"

"Of course not! But this is a little different! We're talking about a lawsuit that I initiated against KPSC, and you're defending the station." She shook her head as if she hadn't heard him correctly. "You really can't expect me to trust your motives."

"I suppose you're right," he acquiesced, his features hardening. Once again his gaze traveled to the foreboding sea. The tidal waters were slowly encroaching on the sand. With each new wave the dark water came closer to the cliff.

A gust of wind blew across the ocean. Kirsten was chilled to the bone, and as the raw air rushed against her wet clothes her teeth began to chatter.

"You'd better go inside," Dane advised her, conscious of how uncomfortable she was. He cocked his head to one side and studied her with increasing interest. "You'll catch your dead out here," he observed.

That's the least of my worries, she thought to herself. You, Mr. Ferguson, are much more dangerous than anything I could possibly contract from the weather. "That's an old wives' tale," she retorted. "People catch cold from viruses, not bad weather."

Dane's patience was pushed beyond his limit. He placed his hands squarely on his hips and glowered at her. "What is it with you, Kirsten? Are you mad at the world because you lost your job? Do you argue with every person you meet—or is it just me?" His mouth pulled into a grim line of disgust and his jaw hardened. He felt the unfamiliar urge to grab her shoulders and shake her.

"Everyone I meet isn't trying to mutilate my character," she threw back at him.

"You asked for that, lady. You initiated the suit against KPSC, not the other way around. You're getting only what you bargained for."

Her green eyes flashed. "And that doesn't include the harassment of the attorney for the defense knocking on my door! I'd hate to see how you would react if Lloyd Grady started questioning Aaron Becker without your knowledge."

"This is a little different."

"How?" she demanded.

A crooked smile touched his lips and his eyes gleamed

with amusement. "Because I doubt that Lloyd Grady would find Aaron nearly as captivating as I find you."

She had to repress the urge to laugh at the image he brought to mind, but a twinkle of amusement sparked in her eyes. She was warming to the charms of the tall man from New York and her defenses were weakening.

Realizing that her behavior until this point had bordered on insolence, Kirsten felt a small stab of contrition. A drop of rain slid down her cheek, and she wiped it away with the back of her hand while she considered just what she was going to do about Mr. Dane Ferguson, attorney for the defense. He was persistent without being pushy, and there was something alluring about his ability to read her. It was as if he understood her innermost thoughts. His perception was precarious.

She wondered if it would hurt to talk to him as long as she steered the conversation away from the subject of the trial. Kirsten was a reporter, a good reporter, and she knew how to ask as well as avoid answering questions. Perhaps in talking with Dane she could extract information from him that might help her with her case against KPSC. It was possible that she could lure him into saying something she shouldn't. Just about anything could happen if she only dared take the chance.

Her most disarming smile formed on her lips and the suggestion of a dimple graced her cheek. "I didn't mean to be rude," she explained. "It's just that I'm a little wary of lawyers for the defense."

Dane made a sound of disgust. "And you should be," he said reluctantly.

"Then you understand why I'm cautious," she said, her green eyes warming.

"Certainly." Dane acted as if her worries were justified. He seemed to understand her position, and the woman deep within Kirsten wanted desperately to believe that he did. It was important that he realize how she felt.

"I'm sorry," she said, turning her back to him.

"So am I." His sincere words touched the deepest part of her, and she hesitated. Rotating to face him again, she had to struggle to hide the honest regret in her eyes.

"Under different circumstances…" she began, her voice fading into the wind.

He inclined his head and eyed her speculatively. He saw the hesitation lingering on her face and he damned himself because he couldn't let go. He had the advantage and he pressed it. A cold blast of air from the sea caught in her hair and made her shiver. "You'd better go inside—warm up," he suggested, knowing just what to say to disarm her. He pushed his hand into the back pocket of his jeans and his eyes held hers in a gaze that promised her the moon.

He seemed so genuinely concerned. The raw force of the wind had colored his face. It was a kind face and a strong face. She felt as if she could trust her very life to this stranger with the enigmatic smile and slight accent. Her resistance ebbed with the soft look of worry in his eyes. She paused only slightly, and then smiled wistfully.

"If you promise not to turn the conversation to the lawsuit, I'll make you a cup of coffee."

"I don't want to trouble you."

You already have, she thought, *more than you can possibly guess*. "No trouble at all," she said, wondering about the risk she was about to take. "If you're lucky, I'll make lunch."

His eyes moved slowly away from her face to rest on the grimy bucket of clams. "I take it I'm looking at lunch."

She laughed at his exaggerated dismay and he thought her laughter was the most inspiring sound he had ever heard. "Don't they appeal to you?" she asked, her smile broadening as he stared at the clams.

"You appeal to me," he responded, sobering as he took her injured hand in his own. Rotating the slightly swollen fingers, he surveyed the wound. "As to the clams, I don't think I've ever eaten anything so… vicious."

An evil twinkle danced in her eyes. "Don't worry." She cocked her head in the direction of the bucket. "They'll get theirs. Just you wait and see what I intend to do to them."

"My pleasure," he mocked, echoing the haughty words of dismissal she had cast him at the first deposition in Grady's office. He pressed her fingers to his lips and tasted her wound. Kirsten's breath caught in her throat at the intimacy of the gesture. She had to sink her teeth into her lower lip when the tip of his tongue probed the sensitive skin. The warmth of his wet tongue on her chilled fingers might have been the single most erotic gesture she had ever experienced, and she couldn't help but wonder where it would lead. Her heart nearly skipped a beat before beginning to pound as wildly as the angry surf against the wet sand. Her eyes never left the darkened intensity of his. It was as if her gaze were controlled by the power of his knowing hazel eyes.

Slowly she withdrew her hand, attempting to ignore the shivering sensations he had inspired. Her voice was barely a whisper when she picked up the bucket and turned toward the cottage. "Please come inside," she invited him, wondering how much she was willing to offer this man, this adversary.

Dane smiled. Kirsten felt that it was the most honest smile she had ever seen. He took the bucket from her fingers. "Let me do this," he suggested, as if he had known her all of his life. The gesture was a simple deference to her womanhood, and yet she didn't feel threatened by it. Had any other man attempted to take the bucket from her, she would probably have been offended. Her ex-husband had proven to her how important it was for a woman to be able to stand on her own, without the need of a man for anything. But with this man—

this stranger from New York—her feelings were vastly different, and if she stopped to analyze them, she would become even more uneasy than she already was.

CHAPTER FIVE

The size and condition of Kirsten's cabin were somewhat of a disappointment to Dane. When he had first discovered that Kirsten McQueen had retired to a private piece of property overlooking the Pacific Ocean, he had been expectant. For the first time since being introduced to the case, he had a glimmer of insight into the motives of the woman. Or so he had thought.

Dane had been certain that he would find her existing in an extravagant tri-level cedar house complete with hot tub, wet bar and sauna. He had been secretly pleased, hoping that the house would be an opulent symbol of her expensive tastes and lavish lifestyle. For his own peace of mind, Dane needed to know that there was a reason to believe that the intelligent woman he had met only a few weeks before would sacrifice any and all principles for the promise of a bundle of cash.

If he were honest with himself, he would have to admit that the case disturbed him—a lot. There was something about Harmon Smith's attitude that didn't ring true. It was almost as if the president of Stateside Broadcasting had a vendetta against Kirsten McQueen, and it didn't help that Fletcher Ross was a slimy excuse for an attorney. Dane hated the thought of trying to bail Ross out of the sticky mess his incompetency had created. So it would have been of considerable consolation for Dane if he could believe that Kirsten McQueen was the type of woman who would stoop to doing anything to continue living beyond her means.

Unfortunately, his theory had backfired right in his face. Yesterday afternoon he had surreptitiously noted that Kirsten was wearing understated but expensive clothes. The same had been true during the first deposition and at the airport. Her wardrobe indicated that she was accustomed to the finer things in life. But today she was dressed no better than any other beachcomber. Gone were the Dior suit and the Cartier bracelet. In their stead were well-worn jeans and a simple sweater.

Dane had expected to find an imported sports car in the drive. Once again he had been wrong. The small vehicle sitting near the garage was several years old, domestic and economical. The house proved no different. It was small, barely a cabin, and in need of several obvious repairs. It wasn't at all like he expansive estate he had hoped to find. The only thing of value was the land. With its sweeping view of the Pacific Ocean, the piece of property had to be worth a small fortune.

The entire McQueen case was becoming frustrating, damned frustrating, and the fact that he was becoming attracted to Kirsten didn't help matters. *You're going to slit your own throat,* he cautioned himself silently.

Kirsten eyed Dane with more than a hint of suspicion. She knew that he had been examining the grounds in an effort to understand her, and it made her uncomfortable. His practiced eye roved mercilessly over the weathered siding on the cabin, and she experienced the uncanny sensation that she was about to invite an unwanted intruder into her home.

"Are you going to stand out there all day?" she called from the porch after removing her shoes and opening the door. "Or would you rather come inside and dry off?"

Her questions brought his attention back to her. "What about these?" he asked, holding up the bucket of clams.

"You can bring them in; there aren't many."

"It makes a difference?" He seemed genuinely puzzled.

She was forced to laugh again. She hadn't laughed for a long time, and it felt wonderful. Dane appeared interested in the conversation, but she doubted that he gave two cents about clams or how they were cleaned. "If I've got quite a few, and the weather allows it, I clean them outside in a tray on the back porch. If not, I do them inside."

His suggestive smile was as enigmatic as it was contagious. "Then let me do the honors," he proposed before stepping off the front porch and walking briskly toward the back of the house. "You can work on the coffee—and make sure it's hot!" he called over his shoulder.

"Wait a minute… are you sure you know what you're doing?" Her voice trailed off as she realized that he couldn't possibly hear her over the whistle of the wind. The thought crossed her mind that she should help him with his task, but she decided against it, deriving a vengeful satisfaction at the thought of him tackling the unfamiliar work. "It'll be good for him," she thought aloud with a smile. "Character-building."

After cleaning and bandaging her fingers, Kirsten put a pot of coffee on the stove and started washing vegetables for a fresh spinach salad. From her vantage point near the sink, she had an unobstructed view of Dane through the window. She had to give him a little credit for the way he concentrated on his work. He looked up only once and that was to wink broadly in her direction. Why did that friendly gesture make her heart miss a beat?

He's an interesting man, Kirsten decided. He's full of surprises and contradictions. If it weren't for the fact that he was defending KPSC, she could envision herself getting involved with him.

By the time the coffee perked, Dane deposited the freshly cleaned mollusks on the kitchen counter. There was a twinkle in his eye and his grin was devilish. The clams were perfect;

it was a professional piece of work. "Not too bad for a city slicker," he drawled with a western affectation and slow-spreading grin.

Kirsten glanced at the clams before impaling Dane with her curious green eyes. "Looks like you've had practice."

"A little. My uncle owned a fish market in—"

Kirsten held up her hand to cut short his explanation. "Don't tell me," she joked. "It looks as if I've been conned after all. And I swore to myself that I wouldn't be fooled by you. All that sophisticated loathing of live sea food—it was just an act."

Dane leaned against the counter and accepted a steaming cup of coffee. "But a good act," he protested. His eyes danced with merriment as he took a sip from his mug and observed her over the rim. He could get used to spending time with this woman, he determined, and wondered why in the hell he had thought of that.

"Right. A good one," Kirsten agreed, shrugging her shoulders indifferently before turning her attention back to the scallions she had been slicing.

"You can't blame me for trying," he persisted. "I've got to find some way to keep you interested."

The rhythmic strokes of the knife faltered. "Is that what you're doing?"

"Isn't it?" he tossed back at her, his eyes narrowing just a fraction.

She reached for a dishtowel and, thoughtful, wiped her hands before turning to face him. Still holding the towel, she cocked her head and stared at him pensively, as if hoping for just a glimpse of his inner thoughts. "I wish I knew," Kirsten admitted with a sigh. "You've given me a lot of reasons for being here, but none of them entirely explain what it is you're looking for." She let out a long breath of air while she wondered if it would be wise to confront him with the truth—

all of it. "Look, Dane, I know you're not going to want to hear this, but it seems to me that despite all the excuses you've come up with, the bottom line is this: You're here looking for something… some motivation for my lawsuit against KPSC, a reason to argue against the age discrimination."

Dane frowned into his cup and deep lines etched his forehead. He hadn't counted on Kirsten's depth of perception. "All right," he acquiesced, "that much is true, at least partially." His dark brows blunted in concentration. "I'll be honest with you. I'm having a helluva lot of trouble believing the age-discrimination thing. It just doesn't wash with me. I think it's an excuse for a lawsuit, the only tangible reason you and Grady could come up with for taking KPSC to court."

"So you've determined that I'm just a woman with a grudge against her former employer and that I'm hell-bent to get some money out of KPSC and some national media attention for myself any way I can. You think I'm doing all this for money and publicity, don't you?" she charged, her eyes darkening and the skin drawing tight over her cheekbones.

"Aren't you?"

"Of course not!" she replied angrily. "Oh, what's the use…"

"What do you mean?" He had set his mug on the counter and was staring at her, listening to her every word, watching her slightest facial movement.

Kirsten's lips tightened over her teeth, but she refused to be drawn into the argument. It was too precarious and couldn't possibly help her. Perhaps she had divulged too much of herself to Dane already—and Lloyd had advised her not to say anything. "This isn't getting us anywhere," she whispered, attacking the hard-boiled eggs with a vengeance.

"That's where you're wrong."

"Aren't I always? Wrong, that is."

There was a sadness in his eyes, but he persisted, bringing

his point home. "You really can't blame me, you know. You're only thirty-five, and on top of that you're beautiful...incredibly beautiful."

Her assault on the eggs slowed, and she paused slightly, obviously affected by his words. She considered a response, but thought better of it, preferring to concentrate on the salad. It was safer, and she didn't have to look beyond his words to the meaning in his eyes.

"Kirsten look at me." Dane was standing behind her, touching her lightly on the shoulders. The warmth of his fingertips seemed to flow into her as his hands gently coaxed her to face the questions in his eyes.

"Why can't you believe me?" she asked weakly. "What's so hard to understand? Carolyn Scott is only twenty-two."

"And from what I understand, she's just as qualified as you are."

"You can't believe that! Don't my years of experience count for anything?"

Dane studied the soft contours of her face and the determined gleam in her eye. "And so you think that you were discriminated against because of your age?" The worry in his gaze stated more clearly than words how deep his doubts were.

"You're forgetting that one jury already believed me," she countered, attempting to step backward and put some distance between her body and his. Strong fingers restrained her, held her fast.

"Are you sure they believed you, or do you think that just maybe they didn't believe Fletcher Ross?" he demanded.

"It's the same thing."

"You don't believe that any more than I do," he charged, a challenging light appearing in his eyes.

Her chin rose defiantly. "It doesn't matter. The point is: I won!"

He openly mocked her. "You, dear lady, may have won the

first skirmish, but that's only the beginning. The battle hasn't really begun."

She glared at him angrily, unable to hide the indignation in the misty green depths of her eyes. "What you're saying is that I haven't got a prayer because you're defending KPSC! Is that why you came here? To try to talk me into dropping the suit?"

A muscle in the back of his jaw tightened and his eyes darkened to a dangerous hue. "I just want you to be prepared."

"That's a lie, Dane. The last thing you want is for me to be prepared to face you. You're hoping to wrap up this case quickly and add another notch to your briefcase before flying back to New York!" She struggled to free herself from his grasp, but he refused to loosen his possessive grip on her arms.

"Just listen, Kirsten," he advised, giving her a shake.

"Why?" She jerked herself free of his imprisoning grip. "Just give me one good reason why I should listen to you!"

"Because I care about you."

"You don't even know me!"

"Oh, but I do… much better than you realize," he countered, leaning lazily against the wall and rubbing his chin.

There was a self-assurance about him that reinforced the meaning of his words. The proud manner in which he carried himself, the confident tilt of his head as he watched her and the bold, sharp features of his face served to remind her of who he was and what he represented: the opposition.

She took the offensive. "Reading my testimony… or analyzing my deposition doesn't give you any insight into me as a person."

"And you're attempting to ignore one very basic fact," he accused her. The slow movements of his thumb against his chin had halted and his eyes drilled into hers. Kirsten felt all of the muscles in her body tense as if they expected an assault. His gaze promised that once he began pursuing her, he would never stop.

"What fact is that?" she managed to say though her throat had become desert-dry.

His smile was self-demeaning. "The fact that I'm attracted to you."

"I don't see that attraction has anything—"

"You're trying to hide from the fact that I like you, Kirsten. And I'd like to know even more about you."

"To use in a court of law!" she whispered, trying to disregard the subtle traces of passion lingering in his eyes.

She closed her eyes for a second and tried to concentrate. The light and airy kitchen was becoming too intimate, the conversation too personal. She had to fight the power of his compelling gaze. All too easily she could believe anything he might say.

She felt the tips of his fingers caress the contour of her jaw. Her eyes opened and she was staring into the most sensual hazel eyes she had ever seen. The promises in their depths couldn't be denied; the questions they silently asked demanded answers.

"Why can't you believe that as a man I'm attracted to you?" he asked roughly.

She swallowed with difficulty, but held his gaze. The feel of his fingertips was seductive and dangerous. She reached upward and grabbed his wrists, hoping to slow the erotic assault on her senses. "Because I don't want to think of you as a man," she admitted.

"It's easier to consider me the adversary."

"Because that's what you are…can't you understand that?"

He drew in a ragged breath before pulling her close to him and wrapping his arms around her shoulders. He buried his face in the golden brown strands of her hair, drinking in deeply of the clean fresh scent. She smelled so damned feminine and she looked so innocently wise. "Sometimes things aren't as simple as we'd like them to be," he replied. "Sometimes feelings get in the way of the simple facts."

"That's just it, can't you see?" she cried, forcing her head backward so that her eyes could search his. "I don't want to have any feelings for you. I can't afford to trust you! The fact that you're here with me now is crazy—suicidal as far as the courtroom goes!"

The strong arms around her tightened. She could feel the hard muscles pressing against her, the warmth of his body enveloping her, the passion lurking in his gaze inviting her. "Don't confuse what happens between us with what will occur in court."

"That's impossible..."

Hazel eyes impaled her and held her fast. "Haven't you learned by now that nothing's impossible?" He searched her face, studying the feminine contours and wondering how futile his efforts were. There was no reasoning behind his interest in her, no logic. He had always considered himself a logical man, a man who pondered all the solutions to a puzzle before ascertaining the truth. But the puzzle of Kirsten McQueen was as much an enigma as it had ever been, and his attraction for her was entirely without thought or plan. He had known from the first time he had gazed into her mysterious eyes that warm afternoon in Lloyd Grady's office that the battle lines were drawn. This was a no-win situation.

Despite the arguments forming in his mind, he wanted her. More desperately than he had ever desired a woman did he crave Kirsten McQueen. Yes, she was beautiful, but it was more than her beauty that captivated him. It was the combination of beauty, wit, dignity and fire that held him fascinated. The feelings taking hold of him, driving him mad with frustration, were sparked by the allure in Kirsten's bright eyes and the trembling of her lower lip. The urges buried deep within him were primal and possessive. He wanted to claim this woman for his own.

Kirsten witnessed the play of emotions on Dane's face and realized that his thoughts had taken the same traitorous path as hers. She also knew that he was about to kiss her and that at this moment it was the one thing she desired most in the world. She wanted to be touched by this man. She needed to feel the power of his body crushed passionately to hers.

His head lowered and the warmth of his lips met the cool invitation of hers. She didn't resist, nor did she encourage him. His fingers twined in the honey-brown strands of her hair and he murmured her name. Her heart began to drum irregularly and she felt the rush of blood in her veins when his slips slid deliciously over hers. Warm urges, impassioned vibrations she hadn't felt in years, spiraled through her body and made her tremble at his touch. Involuntarily she leaned closer to him, enjoying the feel of his hard body aching for hers.

He sensed her reaction and he pulled her hair gently with his hands, forcing her head backward in order that he could press his wet lips against the exposed column of her neck. A shiver of anticipation scurried up her spine when his tongue found the delicate bones encircling the hollow of her throat.

"Don't," she pleaded, letting her eyes close with the delicious sensations he encouraged from her. It was a feeble objection, the final protest from a woman lost….

His lips found hers again and this time the kiss they pressed against her was demanding. The gentle consideration for a woman Dane didn't know had disappeared as the fever within him had ignited. His hands pushed against the muscles of her back, forcing her breasts against the flat wall of his chest. His lips crushed to hers and her mouth parted to the insistent pressure of his tongue.

It had been so long since a man had caressed her as if he really cared. She gasped when the tip of Dane's tongue traced the serrated edges of her teeth and then probed farther, as if by physical exploration of her body he could understand her mind.

His hands stole up her back to finally rest at her shoulders. He pulled his head from hers and gazed deeply into her eyes, silently asking her questions she couldn't begin to understand. How much of herself could she give to this man?

"I want you," he said simply, and the honesty of his statement made Kirsten more aware of the danger therein.

"I know." She attempted to smile but was unable. The darkness in his eyes and the gentle pressure of his fingers promised sensuality and desire, surrender and satiation—if only she would take a chance.

"I want you more than I've ever wanted a woman," he whispered reluctantly, as if the admission itself were a betrayal. His warm breath moved her hair and his lips brushed seductively against her forehead.

"I don't know if that's enough for me."

His body became rigid. "What more could you possibly need?" he asked.

Kirsten's words were hesitant, as if she were unsure herself. How much of herself did she dare reveal to him and why did she feel the overwhelming yearning to make him understand her? Yesterday she wanted to hide from him; today she wanted to share her deepest secret with him. And yet she couldn't; she had to be cautious. Self-preservation had to come before physical desire. "I'm not asking for promises you can't possibly keep," she conceded. "And I don't expect to hear empty words of love."

His dark brows rose quizzically and his fingers rubbed the tired muscles near the base of her neck. "But there is something you want," he prodded. "Tell me—what is it?"

She tried to ignore the warmth of his hands on her skin, but she felt as if her entire body began and ended where his fingers touched her. "Dane, I have to know that you trust me…at least just a little. I have to think that this attraction isn't just because you consider me a challenge, an opponent that has to become a conquest."

"What are you trying to say, Kirsten?" he demanded.

"I need to think that what is happening between us isn't confused with what might happen in the courtroom."

The seductive movements of his fingers against her skin stopped. "I don't know what to think about you," he said.

"I don't understand."

"I think you're the one who has trouble with trust. If there's a problem between us, it's in your mind. You're the one who can't let go and forget, not for one moment, that I represent KPSC." His voice was even, and though the words accused her, they didn't judge. It was a simple statement of the situation.

"How can I, Dane? Think about it. Think about who you are and what you represent." She tried to pull away from him, but he refused to let her go. "It's not as if you're an accountant or even *my* lawyer, for God's sake. You're the opposition!" The conviction of her feelings was evident in the confusion in her eyes.

"Would it be any easier if I were on your side?"

"I—I don't know." Dangerous sparks made his eyes appear greener than ever.

Her small fist opened and closed against his back. He could feel the tension and frustration coiling within her body. "You have nothing to lose, Dane. I have everything!"

His jaw tightened and he took a step backward, releasing her. She felt as if she might collapse on the floor, but she willed her body to remain rigid. His voice was cold and emotionless. "Do you want me to leave?" His eyes bored into her, waiting for her response. She knew that it was in her power to force him out of her life. She had but to tell him to go and he would never bother her again…until they met in court.

She shook her head regretfully, knowing she was

making an unthinkable mistake. "Don't go," she whispered, inwardly longing for the protection and strength of his arms around her. "I—I don't want you to go." She paused and attempted to pull her scattered thoughts together as she raised her eyes to meet his unyielding stare. "The truth is that I think it would be best for you to leave, but if I'm honest with you, I'd have to admit that I want you to stay here."

"How long?" he demanded.

"What?"

His strong jaw hardened and the muscles in his neck stood out. "I asked you how long you want me to stay. A few minutes? For lunch? The rest of the afternoon? The night?"

She leaned on the back of one of the kitchen chairs. Her fingers dug into the hard wood. "I don't understand—why are you angry?"

"I don't like being toyed with," he stated flatly.

"That makes two of us," she tossed back.

The anger he had vainly tried to control snapped. The rugged features of his face became threatening, the hazel eyes bold. His lips thinned into a grim line of frustration. "I'm having one helluva time reading you. One minute you're vicious, the next seductive. I don't know whether I'm coming or going."

She lifted her head above his angry insinuations. "Don't give me that! I don't believe for one moment that you don't know exactly what you're going to do, and I'm appalled that you would expect me to. This entire charade"—she made a sweeping gesture with her arm, as if to include everything which had happened between them—"was just and act, and probably well-rehearsed." Her eyes had hardened to opaque emeralds. "I'll bet that you know exactly what your next move will be."

"With you? That would be impossible!"

"Aren't you the guy who just told me nothing's impossible?" Her lips curved into a vengeful smile and she hoisted her chin a little higher into the air. "And aren't you the man being paid an outrageous legal fee to prove that I'm nothing better than a money-mad disgruntled employee who would like nothing better than to see KPSC, and, for that matter, Stateside Broadcasting Corporation, go down in a ghastly conflagration of national publicity and ridicule!"

Dane watched her angry display and found his rage giving way to awe. She understood the defense's position much more clearly than he would have guessed. "Since you understand me so well," he encouraged her, managing to hide his sarcasm and attempting to seem less interested than he actually was, "why don't you tell me why Stateside Broadcasting Corporation is involved?"

"Beats me," she admitted.

"But surely you can hazard a guess?" he went on.

"I don't know why. They're your clients—the men responsible for sending you here in the first place." She turned her attention back to the salad and then went to work breading the clams.

"So why do you think Harmon Smith is so interested in you?" Dane continued.

She slid a glance in his direction. The conversation was ticklish; she would have to be careful. But at least it had turned way from the personal confrontation between a man and a woman. "So you want my opinion strictly off the record?" she asked.

"Right."

"I wish I knew," she conceded, casting another sidelong glance in his direction He was watching her, studying her with those intense hazel eyes. She had to be cautious in her answer, hoping to tell from his reaction if her suspicions were founded. "If I had to come up with a reason, I'd say that Stateside must be afraid of me. Why else would they send in their big gun from back east?" His eyebrows had quirked when she referred to him, but other than that one show of emotion, Dane's face had remained unreadable.

"And why would a national broadcasting corporation be afraid of one woman?"

"Because of what I represent, I suppose." She placed the pan on the stove and hesitated for a moment. "They must think that they have to make an example of me."

"So they hired me?"

She shrugged her shoulders. "I guess."

Dane asked his next question very carefully, for he thought he might finally understand just a little of the puzzle. "What about Fletcher Ross?"

"What about him?" Just the thought of the heavyset man with his thick jowls and habitual cigar made Kirsten's stomach sour. Her eyes were innocent when she raised them to meet Dane's inquisitive stare.

"I'm not one to upstage one of my associates..."

She smiled thinly. "Tell me another one."

"What I mean is, why would KPSC hire Ross in the first place? He doesn't come off very polished."

"You don't have to mince words with me. What you're trying to say is that he's a long shot from first rate. You know it and I know it."

"So why doesn't KPSC know it?"

Kirsten frowned as she prodded the clams and placed them on a platter. "They do, I suppose."

"But they would still hire the man?" Dane was clearly dubious but very interested.

"Sure, he's got a long-term contract. Besides, I think he's got money in the station or something."

"An investor?"

Kirsten thought for a moment before placing the dishes on the small antique table. "I don't know really. Anyway, don't quote me. Remember, we're off still off the record." As if realizing how risky the conversation had become, Kirsten managed to change the subject. If Dane noticed her reluctance to discuss the station, he hid it well. "We'd better sit down," she suggested. "If we don't eat this soon, we'll have to call it dinner."

Most of the meal was eaten in silence. Kirsten should have been ravenous but found it difficult to enjoy the efforts of her labor. Having Dane in her home made her uncomfortable. His watchful eyes noticed everything, and she couldn't help but feel that he would use anything he could find to his advantage. It had been an incredibly stupid mistake to allow him into her home and the fact that she was attracted to him only made it that much worse. He was smooth—too smooth.

"You haven't lived here long," he said, pushing his plate aside.

"A few weeks."

"Did you buy the place?"

She shook her head. "I inherited it from my grandfather. He lived here until he passed away last winter."

"Is this where you came to spend your summer vacations?"

Kirsten smiled wistfully, remembering the hours spent with her grandfather on the beach. "Some of them—when both Grandpa and Grandma were alive."

"What about the rest of your family?" Dane asked, leaning back in his chair. His eyes were warm and familiar. The lingering traces of suspicion had disappeared.

"I have one sister; she lives in Idaho near my parents," Kirsten replied with a thin smile.

"So what brought you to Oregon?"

He seemed to ask the question innocently, but Kirsten reminded herself that he already knew the answer. "I've always lived here."

"But not your parents?"

"They moved to Boise later…after I had graduated from

college." Her voice faded as she remembered those stormy years when she was married to Kent. Talking about that period of her life always made her uneasy, and though Dane was obviously just making small talk, she felt nervous, as if she were once again on the witness stand.

She picked up the dishes and took them to the sink, hoping that the conversation had ended. She didn't need to be reminded how alone she had felt when her parents had moved to Boise. Her marriage was slowly beginning to fall apart, and she had no one in whom to confide. The one thing in which she had taken consolation had been her job, and even that had eventually gone sour.

"You must have been the favorite grandchild," Dane observed as he rose from the table and helped put the dirty dishes on the counter.

"I don't think my grandparents played favorites."

"But you inherited the cabin."

"Actually my sister and I both did. She didn't want it, so I bought her out." Once again she felt as if she were revealing too much to this man. It was so easy to be honest with him—no wonder he had earned his reputation for winning in court. It was hard to discern between the lawyer and the genuinely interested and charming man. "The dishes can wait," Kirsten announced, walking toward the living room.

"Why didn't she want it?" Dane asked, knowing that he was disturbing her but determined to find out as much about Kirsten McQueen as he could.

Kirsten bristled, and her temper got the better of her. "Is it really any of your damned business?" she returned. "Why is it that you lawyers can never give up? Ever since you got here it's been one question after another!" She jerked her jacket off the hook near the door and turned her icy eyes on him. "You're all alike!" With her final insult she pulled the door open and started outside.

"Are you comparing me to Fletcher Ross?" Dane asked with an amused smile. *Damn the man, he knew how much he outclassed the likes of Ross.*

"You can take it any way you like!" She hurried down the steps of the porch and headed toward the garage. He was beside her in an instant and hadn't bothered with a jacket. Wind and rain from a blackened sky poured down on him.

"What're you doing?"

"Getting firewood before it really gets dark. I want to be prepared just in case we…I lose power!"

"Let me help you."

"I don't need your help," she shouted at him. The noise of the wind and the crashing surf made it difficult to hear. She pushed the garage door open with her shoulder. It was dark inside and smelled of dust and dried fir. She threw several chunks of fir and oak into a basket standing near the door.

"Being an independent woman doesn't include having your pride stand in the way of common sense," Dane advised as he took the heavy basket from her arms and turned toward the house.

She followed behind him with an armful of dry driftwood. "And you can take your male philosophy on life back to New York with you."

Once inside the cabin, he placed the basket near the brick fireplace and dropped several pieces of fir onto the smoldering flames. As the fire caught it cast a warm light into the otherwise dark room. When the flames were to his satisfaction he rose and dusted the palms of his hands on his jeans. Raindrops slid from his wet hair down the severe angle of his cheek. His eyes had turned as stormy as the sea. "I didn't come here to judge you."

"No, you're saving that for later, when you can really do a job on me in the courtroom," she accused him. The light fire caught in her angry green eyes and gave her soft hair highlights as warm as the golden flames.

His lips tightened into a tired frown. "If you let yourself, you can become a very lonely woman."

"If I do, it's my choice," she asserted.

"I don't understand why you're so angry with me," he stated, "but unless I miss my guess, I'm just an easy target. You're angry with men in general, aren't you?"

She held back the hot retort threatening to erupt. "It's not so much anger, Dane, it's freedom. I don't need a man telling me what to do. Nor do I need a man poking his nose into my personal life."

"Why don't you be honest with yourself, Kirsten," Dane replied, taking a step nearer to her. Steadfastly, she held her ground, refusing to be intimidated. "You're afraid of me… afraid of what I represent…"

"I'm not afraid of anyone at KPSC," she reaffirmed, the fire in her eyes emphasizing her assertion.

"I'm not talking about KPSC! Why can't you forget about the damned suit for a few minutes?"

"Because I'm talking to the defending attorney!"

"And the minute you forget that fact you think you've lost!" he charged, his penetrating eyes dark.

"Something like that, yes."

"Oh, lady," he whispered, coming close to her. There was a pain shadowed in the depths of his eyes. "If only it were that simple." He folded her gently into his arms, and she didn't resist, somehow finding an unknown comfort in the feel of his body stretched against hers. His head descended and his lips sought hers. She trembled in anticipation and accepted the touch of his mouth on hers. The soft pressure of his tongue gently parted her lips and she gave herself willingly to the bittersweet yearnings of her body.

Their tongues met, retracted and met again to mate in an intimate dance known only to lovers. She savored the taste of him, drowned in the smell of fresh raindrops against his skin, and relished the warmth of his body powerfully holding hers.

He kissed her eyes and let his wet lips touch each cheek. His hands pressed against the small of her back, rubbing her in anxious circles of desire.

"Let me touch you," he whispered, and the raw tone of her voice let her know of his frustrated longing. When she didn't respond, he brought his lips to hers and his fingers found the hem of her sweater. Slowly they crept up her back, tracing the soft muscles and inspiring a warmth within her she tried valiantly to deny.

"I don't think..."

"That's right, Kirsten, don't think... for once don't think, just feel—let yourself go."

His fingers caressed the slope of her spine as they inched upward. His lips were warm and persistent, his hands gentle and coaxing. They inched up her rib cage until they felt the weight of her breast. She gasped when his hand pushed upward on the firm flesh and a soft sound escaped her as he lifted the sweater over her head.

Involuntarily she crossed her arms over her breasts. As if to protect herself. He took hold of her wrists and forced her hands back to her sides. His eyes were gentle but determined. "Don't hide from me... you can't." Once again he held her fiercely to him and kissed the inviting swell of her breast. Her heart raced furiously, pounding in her head, warming her blood. Her breathing had become shallow, as if each breath were stolen from her lungs. A thousand reasons to pull out of his insistent embrace entered her mind, but fled when just as many excuses to stay bound to him argued in his favor. She wanted him to touch her, though she knew it was a mistake. She needed to feel his hands caressing her.

He took each manacled wrist and brought it to his lips, trying to physically ensure her that he wanted only what was best for them. With gentle prodding he kissed her again, and when he let go of her hands she didn't resist but wound her arms around his neck. She shivered as if from the cold, but the heat rising within her was the cause.

She felt the muscles in his arms flex as they wrapped around her and the soft hair of his forearms brushed invitingly against her naked back. Slowly he shifted his weight until he forced her onto the floor. The cool parquet sent a chill down her spine, but the warmth of the man leaning over her, pressing hot lips against hers, made her cognizant of nothing but him and the power of his passion.

"This is crazy," she sighed, watching as the firelight flickered in his eyes.

"This is right… you don't have to think of anything else." His lips lowered and lightly kissed the hollow of her throat before toying with the clasp of her bra. She could feel her breasts strain against the flimsy fabric when his tongue would touch her skin. Her nipples had hardened to stiff dark peaks rising against the sheer white lace. She quivered when his tongue rimmed her nipple, wetting the flimsy fabric and leaving a cool impression on her skin. The fires within her burned more ravenously, and a thin film of sweat began to collect on the small of her back.

"Oh, Dane," she murmured, her voice breaking with frustrated longing. "How can this be happening?"

"It's happening because you want it to," he whispered, his words ringing with the truth she felt in her heart.

"But I can't…I just can't," she cried, her small fist pounding relentlessly on his back, as if by striking him she could deny the feelings bursting within her.

"You have to let go."

"Oh, God, if only I could," she whispered, clinging to him and holding back the tears of frustration begging to be shed.

As if he finally understood that he was pushing too hard,

Dane gently released her, keeping his hands on her shoulders. Forcing her to look into his eyes. The strain on his face showed how he was willing back the tides of passion rising within him. He fought to ignore the powerful ache of desire that refused to subside. His voice was hoarse, his skin stretched taut over his cheekbones. "Don't get me wrong, Kirsten, I want you more than I ever thought possible. But I would never rush you into anything you might not be able to handle."

"What I want and what we can have are two different things," she replied, her green eyes pleading with him to understand her. "I can't deny that physically I desire you…but I want more than physical satisfaction."

He pushed back a wayward lock of his dark hair and stared at the ceiling, as if by studying the exposed beams he could come to terms with his traitorous feelings. "All right. That's for you to decide. I'm not about to get involved with a woman who can't accept a relationship for what it is."

"That's the problem, isn't it?" she asked. "You call it a relationship and I call it sex. In my book, a relationship is much more involved than one afternoon in front of the fire."

"Is that all it means to you?"

"No." She shook her head. Streaks of amber shone in her hair. "There's more to it than that," she admitted. "Under different circumstances… maybe things could have worked out. But I have a lot of trouble dealing with the fact that you are, for all practical purposes, hired to be here by KPSC."

"Not here, not with you, not now."

She closed her eyes. "If only I could believe that."

He eyed her speculatively. His voice was low. "I think I'd better go," he said softly. "Until you can understand that I'm a man as well as an adversary."

"Maybe when this is all over—"

"Be serious, Kirsten. When it's all over, one of us will be

the winner, the other will have lost. Do you honestly think that either one of us will be able to overcome that?" he asked, handing her the discarded sweater. She took it and held it protectively over her breasts.

"Then I guess we're at an impasse?"

He didn't notice the desperation in her voice. Nor did he see her vain attempt at poise. She felt as if he had come into her life and shattered it into a thousand pieces, but she managed a thin smile.

"Kirsten," he said, "I'd like to say the things you want to hear. Hell, I'd even be glad to make promises that I can't possibly keep. But I won't. I think too much of you to lie to you, and I expect the same in return." He touched her lightly on the chin, but she pulled her head away, afraid that his familiar touch would break the dam of tears burning behind her eyes.

"All I've ever wanted from you was the truth," she replied.

"Okay, so now you've got it. I hope you can live with it." He rose and reached for his jacket. "Goodbye, Kirsten."

He didn't wait for her response. In a quick movement he turned on his heel, opened the door and was gone, leaving the room more empty than it had ever been. Kirsten's throat swelled, but she refused to let go of her tears. She'd been through worse times than this, and she would weather this storm.

She ignored the sound of the car engine catching and told herself it was for the best when the noise had faded in the distance. The next time she would see Dane Ferguson she would be prepared. She wouldn't be so foolish as to let him see the soft side of her again. As far as that man was concerned, she had learned her lesson, and somehow she would be able to face him in the courtroom—that much she vowed.

CHAPTER SIX

The stormy afternoon slipped slowly into evening. Kirsten managed to finish a few tasks around the house. She paid the bills, cleaned the kitchen and tried to concentrate on rewriting a story about the decline of timber sales in Oregon, but found that the facts and figures in the recent slump didn't interest her. Her traitorous thoughts continued to return to the magnetic power of Dane's hazel eyes and how easily she had been captured by his seductive spell.

With a futile sigh she put the plastic cover on her typewriter and stripped out of her clothes. After a quick hot shower Kirsten slipped into her warm velour robe and poured herself a glass of Chablis. She stretched out on a small, slightly faded Oriental rug that covered the hardwood floor near the fireplace. Her back was supported by the couch and she stared restlessly into the amber flames of the dying fire.

"You're a fool," Kirsten whispered to herself as she sipped the cool wine and noticed the blood-red reflection of the coals in the crystal goblet. "You should have listened to Lloyd Grady and sent Dane Ferguson packing. What's the use of hiring an attorney if you're not going to listen to his advice? Anything you said to Ferguson will be used against you, sure as shootin'."

She sighed deeply, set down the glass of wine and let her eyes wander through the cabin. It was her home and she loved it, but tonight it seemed incredibly empty. It was as if Dane's presence of a few hours had altered the warmth of the interior. Everything looked the same, but the once cozy rooms felt lifeless.

"Honest to God, Kirsten," she muttered. "You're acting maudlin and morose, just because of one man." She chided herself repeatedly for being the kind of woman she abhorred before reaching angrily for the newspaper, grabbing her reading glasses from the coffee table and slipping them onto her nose. Expertly her eyes roved over the newsprint as she studied the local news, hoping to find an article of interest.

On the first page of the business section was an article on Ginevra and Kirsten's eyes moved hungrily over the text. She hoped to discover something new about the proposed nuclear site but was disappointed. The article was filled with the same old controversy, without any new facts or even a new editorial slant. However, the name of the journalist who had covered the story wasn't familiar to her so she tore the page from the paper and set it aside. Maybe when the lawsuit was behind her, she would be able to write an in-depth story on Ginevra without the fear of repercussions in court.

When the lawsuit was behind her. Would there ever be a time when she wouldn't be caught in a legal battle with KPSC? She shook her head and reached for the glass of wine. Right now it seemed as if the lawsuit would never end. She wondered how the as yet unselected jury would vote when they heard her side of the story.

Would Dane Ferguson make her appear nothing more than an irrational woman harboring a secret vendetta against KPSC? Was he capable and cruel enough to make her look like an incompetent two-bit reporter looking for a quick, easy buck? She closed her eyes against the vivid image of Dane, dressed in a conservative suit, smiling charmingly to the jury and pointing a condemning finger at Kirsten.

"Oh, dear Lord," she whispered aloud. "Why did I start

this?" After mentally reviewing her conversation with Dane earlier in the day, she decided that she hadn't said anything that was damaging to her case. However, if Dane decided to twist her words around, anything she might have casually mentioned might hurt her. And she had foolishly thought she could extract information from him!

To dislodge the disturbing thoughts, Kirsten pulled herself to a standing position, stretched and listened to the sounds of the coming night. The storm had continued to rage throughout the afternoon and evening and the rush of the wind had at times been strong enough to rattle the panes of the windows facing west. Kirsten walked across the small room and sat on the smooth wide sill of the bay window to peer into the darkness. Floodlights secured to the cliff cast eerie light onto the angry Pacific Ocean. Spray from the sea as it crashed against the rocks protecting the beach splashed upward into the blackened sky before running in frothy rivulets back to the turbulent ocean.

A movement of unfamiliar light caught in Kirsten's peripheral vision and she turned her head away from the view of the wild ocean. Pale headlights in two thin streams of illumination were advancing down the twisted lane toward the cabin. Kirsten squinted into the night and tried to determine the make of the approaching car.

Her elegant eyebrows lifted as she recognized the rental. Dane Ferguson was back!

Trying to ignore the sudden dryness that had settled in the back of her throat and the fact that her stomach had constricted into uncomfortable, tight knots, Kirsten waited until she saw Dane pull himself out of the car and hurry head-bent against the torrent of rain, toward the front porch.

Kirsten reached the door just as she heard his loud, impatient knock. Standing aside to allow him to enter the room, she opened the door and managed to hide the confusion gripping her.

"What happened?" she asked, staring at his wet clothes and dirt streaked across his face. He met the questions in her gaze directly and she noticed something in his disturbing gaze that she hadn't seen before. It was pain. Deep and raw. The kind of agony that was seldom unhidden.

"An accident—three cars piled up near a bridge that had washed out." His voice was low and strained with emotion. When he wiped the rain off his forehead with his palm, Kirsten noticed that his fingers were unsteady. It was something she hadn't expected to find—a crack in the firm resolve of Dane Ferguson.

"Wait a minute," she stated, and hurried into the hallway to search the linen closet. Within a few seconds she was back and handed him a dry bath towel. "Why don't you go into the bathroom and… Clean up." She eyed his mud-covered jeans suspiciously. "Do you have a change of clothes with you?"

"In the car."

"Go out and get them and then you can shower. I'll make some coffee and—have you eaten?" Her eyes rose to his, but he didn't answer immediately. "Doesn't matter. I'll throw something together—"

"You don't have to go to all this trouble."

"Of course I do," she asserted. "You're here, aren't you?"

"I could go to a motel…"

"The nearest one is miles away," she replied. "Just go get your clothes and clean up." Kirsten turned toward the kitchen as if she expected her commands to be obeyed. Her heart was beating unnaturally in her chest. The last thing she had expected was to have Dane return, but now that he was here, she found it inconceivably painful to think that he might once again disappear into the darkness.

She heard the door close as he went outside. Desperately she counted the seconds under her breath until he reentered the house. Just as she put the coffeepot on the stove, she heard the sound of running water from the bathroom. It was a warm and comforting thought to know that he was with her—one man and one woman caught together in the wild fury of the storm.

By the time she had poured the coffee and the chowder was simmering on the stove, the water in the bathroom was no longer running. She carried the hot food into the living room and set the tray on the coffee table before taking a chair near the fire and waiting.

Dane emerged from the short hallway leading to the bathroom a few moments later. His hair was still damp but neatly combed, and all of the traces of dirt were gone. He had put on clean corduroy pants and a sweater. When he looked at Kirsten he managed a tight smile, but she noticed that the haunted look in his eyes hadn't disappeared. There was something about that small glimmer of vulnerability that touched the deepest part of her.

He accepted a cup of coffee and took a long swallow of the hot liquid. "Thanks," he whispered, and his eyes never left hers as he drank from the steamy cup.

"I didn't mean to come racing back here," he said as if in apology.

"I know." Her words were sincere and encouraging. She sat across the room from him and the small coffee table separated them. She had crossed her legs and one slim calf parted the folds of the downy white robe.

He had to force his gaze from the enticing leg, back to the soft contours of her face. "I spent a little time driving up the coast before I started inland. I wasn't very far out of Cannon Beach when I came to the accident…."

"Where the bridge had washed away?"

Dane nodded thoughtfully. He frowned into the coffee cup and a muscle in the back of his jaw tightened. "I don't think there was a car on the bridge at the time, but no one knows. Apparently, the driver of the first car saw that the bridge had buckled and slammed on her brakes. The pick-up following her reacted a little too slowly. When the truck slammed into the car, the car slid down the embankment into a ravine." He paused for a sip of coffee to quiet the rage of wretched indignation boiling within him.

"A woman and her child were trapped in the car," Dane said, suddenly pursing his lips. "We were able to get them out...."

"But they were badly hurt," Kirsten guessed.

Dane shrugged. "The boy will be okay. At least the paramedics seemed to think so when they got to the bridge. But they weren't as optimistic about the mother." He finished the cup of coffee before continuing. "The state police asked that everyone at the scene give his name and phone number, in case there were any questions about the accident. When I told them I was from out of town, they asked me to give a local number where I could be reached—"

"And you gave them mine?"

"Yes." After setting his empty cup on the table, he pushed his hands against his knees and rose to a standing position. "Probably a mistake," he thought aloud, "but it's only for a little while—just until they have all the facts of the accident. They might not even call. I gave them your number because I didn't know where I would be staying tonight."

Kirsten attempted to hide her unease. "I thought you were staying in Portland."

"That was my original plan."

She lifted a dubious brow. "Then you still intend to drive inland?"

"I'll go down to Newport—see if the road is passable to Salem or Corvallis."

"And if it's not?"

"I'll stay in Newport." He leaned against the warm bricks of the fireplace and his thumb rubbed pensively along the hard line of his jaw. He seemed to be tossing a weighty decision over in his mind. "There's another reason I came here," he admitted reluctantly.

"Which is?"

"First of all, because I owed you an apology. I really had no right coming here and trying to get information from you." He shook his head and ran his tense fingers through the thick strands of his coffee-colored hair. "It's just that this case has me beating my head against a brick wall. No one seems to be leveling with me!"

Kirsten didn't respond; content to let him vent his frustration. She realized that she was witnessing a very personal side of Dane which he usually kept restrained.

He slammed his fist against the warm bricks before regaining his composure. "Another reason I came back," he conceded, "was that I wanted to see you again. I needed to know that you were still here—"

"I don't understand."

He smiled bitterly. "I don't blame you. I'm not sure I understand it myself." He drew in a long, ragged breath. "Something happened to me once. I lost someone very close to me. And while I was there at the site of the accident tonight, I had this feeling..." He shrugged as if suddenly embarrassed. "I just wanted to make sure that you were okay."

Kirsten shifted in the chair, unconsciously letting her robe gape open to expose the provocative curve of her knee protruding seductively against the plush fabric. Dane's intense gaze dropped to the slim leg before returning to her curious green eyes.

"I appreciate your concern," she said, disregarding the fact that her breathing had become uneven under his seductive stare. "But I've spent enough time at the coast to know how to weather an occasional storm." She smiled nervously and turned to gaze at the fire. The intimacy of the situation was unnerving her and she had trouble finding her voice. "I don't think you should spend any time worrying about me."

"If it were only that easy," he muttered before rolling his eyes to the exposed beams of the pine ceiling.

Her heart went out to him. The accident had brought back all of his dead wife and child. And now he was insinuating that he cared for her. She shook her head and caught her lower lip between her teeth. "Dane," she whispered, "you and I… we can't let this happen. It's no good for either of us."

"I've been telling myself that for several weeks," he said, "but I just haven't been able to convince myself." He witnessed the hesitance in her gaze and knew that she was wavering. Her green eyes had become unsure and inviting. Firelight caught in her hair, streaking the honey-brown strands with gold.

"I made some chowder," she offered, hoping to dissipate the seductive atmosphere in the suddenly intimate room.

"I'm not hungry." His intense eyes bored into hers and she felt her heart miss a beat. She was going to lose everything to this man. She knew it in one breathless instant.

The telephone rang sharply to break the sensual spell. Kirsten was relieved for an excuse to look away from the questions in Dane's eyes. She rose from the chair gracefully and hurried to answer the call. A rough male voice on the other end of the line identified himself as Officer Cooney of the state police and asked to speak to Dane.

Before Kirsten could call to him, Dane was at her side and took the receiver from her hand. The conversation was extremely one-sided, and only on a few occasions did Dane interrupt the officer. Kirsten returned to her position on the couch and slowly sipped the remainder of her wine. The Chablis had become warm but holding the glass in her trembling fingers and sipping the clear liquid helped hide her unease. Being alone with Dane in the middle of the night was

disturbing. Though she wanted nothing more than to spend the rest of the night with him, she couldn't allow herself to forget that he was a lawyer for the defense.

Just the realization that she had feelings for Dane made her uncomfortable. She hadn't been intimate with a man since her divorce. Nor had she wanted to. She had considered the fact that she might not ever meet a man whom she would desire, and she hadn't been concerned at the thought. The last thing she wanted in her life was a man. And yet, here she was, thinking about spending the night with the one man who could crucify her.

Slowly Dane replaced the receiver. His jaw had hardened and his thick black brows had pulled together. Wearily, he rubbed the tension from the back of his neck before sinking into the soft cushions of the couch. "She didn't make it," he murmured.

Kirsten swallowed with difficulty. "What about the boy?"

"He's all right. His dad is with him."

Seeing the angry pain on his face pierced Kirsten's heart. "Dane," she whispered. "I'm sorry."

"It's not your fault, Kirsten." He let out a deep breath. "I don't know why I'm taking it so hard."

"Because it reminds you of losing your wife and son," Kirsten said softly.

The skin over Dane's features tightened and his lips drew into a thin line against the injustice of life. "I suppose you're right," he conceded regretfully. "Doesn't matter anyway."

"Of course it does."

"Look, Kirsten, nothing's going to bring them back!" Dane snapped, the anger of six agonizing years resurfacing. He noticed her wince under the assault of his words. "I'm sorry," he apologized.

"It's okay—"

"No, it's not. I had no right to take it out on you. The last

few days have been rough, but that's not your problem." He gazed into her eyes and wondered at the bewitching mystery of Kirsten McQueen. The way she looked at him made his blood begin to boil with a passion he had once thought dead. The ache he felt for her made him push his hands deeply into the pockets of his cords. "I think I'd better go," he said huskily. His eyes wandered down the seductive column of her throat past her collarbones to the swell of her breasts hidden by the cream-colored robe.

"Then you still think you can make it to Portland tonight?" Her heart was pounding erratically in her rib cage. His gaze roved restlessly over her and she found it difficult to smile. Running nervous fingers through her light brown hair, she was conscious only of his compelling scrutiny.

"I think I should try." He took a step closer to her and Kirsten was held by the promises in his eyes.

"But the storm—"

"Kirsten, if I stay here any longer, I don't know if I'll be able to leave." He touched her shoulder. The soft fabric of the robe was familiar and evoked memories of a happier time in his life.

"It's just that…"

"What?" he asked, his voice low and commanding. Kirsten felt a shudder of anticipation skitter down her spine.

"It's already late—after midnight."

He stepped closer and his free hand traced the graceful angle of her jaw. She was forced to swallow and close her eyes as his finger moved slowly down her neck, along the collar of the robe, to rest between her breasts, just above her waist, where the downy garment was tied. "I want to stay with you," he admitted, his voice thick, "more than anything I've wanted in a very long time. But it has to be because you want me here."

Her head fell forward with the weight of her decision. She held her forehead in one hand and avoided looking into the

desire in his eyes. The warmth of his one finger lingered against her skin and argued with the logic in her mind.

"Look at me," he whispered. She raised her eyes to meet his probing gaze and couldn't hide the tears of frustration that had begun to form behind her eyelids.

"There's just so much more than the two of us," she murmured.

"That's why I think it would be best if I left—now—before we did anything we might regret."

"If it weren't for the lawsuit..."

"I never would have met you." The passion in his gaze had deepened. The intense hue was neither gold nor brown, but an erotic hazel. "Thank God for that damned lawsuit."

"This is very hard for me," she whispered.

"It's hard for both of us."

"Oh, Dane—"

"The hell with it," he muttered as the tension of the long night exploded. His free arm wrapped around her waist to pull her body fast against him. She felt the fever of his rapid breathing. His muscles tensed as his arms embraced her and his head lowered to allow his lips to capture hers. His kiss was bold, impatient, as if too many hours of frustration had ignited his smoldering passion.

Her breasts, where they crushed against him, ached for his touch. Ignoring the doubts lingering in her mind, she returned the ardor of his kiss and wound her arms around his neck. Her fingers twined in the thick, dark strands of his hair, and she ignored the fact that what she was surrendering to bordered on insanity.

One strong hand splayed against the small of her back, gently rubbing the soft fabric of her robe against her skin. His other hand caught in her golden brown curls and pulled her head backward, forcing her to stare into the seductive power of his hazel gaze.

"Tell me you want me to stay," he commanded.

"You know I do."

"Despite the circumstances?" he asked softly.

Kirsten knew that he was offering her one last chance to refuse him, giving her one final avenue of escape. "I'm thirty-five years old," she replied, "and I hope I understand myself well enough to know what I want."

"This is important to me," he murmured against her neck, holding her so tightly that she could scarcely breathe. "But you have to realize that it won't affect the way I defend KPSC. What happens tonight between us has nothing to do with what will take place in court."

"I wouldn't expect it to," she whispered.

"Then let me love you tonight," he pleaded as his lips brushed against hers. She responded by cradling his head in her hands and sighing against him. The invitation of her open lips sent a shudder of anticipation through his strained muscles.

His fingers found the knot of velour that held the creamy fabric together. Slowly it loosened. The robe parted to reveal an enticing glimpse of her body.

"You're beautiful," he whispered hoarsely as his eyes stole down the seductive slit in the garment. Her skin was flushed and the dusky hollow between her breasts invited his touch. His fingers probed beneath the soft fabric to inch up her rib cage before lightly touching one swollen breast.

Kirsten closed her eyes and let her head fall backward, exposing more of her throat to him. He pushed her hair aside and let his lips caress the soft shell of her ear while his hands accepted the weight of her breasts. Her heartbeat was lost in the wild fury of the night. It pounded as erratically as the angry waves against the sand.

She felt alternate currents of searing heat and arctic cold race through her veins. Thoughts of denial had long since escaped her, and she was conscious only of the seductive magic his hands inspired.

His finger moved slowly upward, past the swell of her breasts to her shoulders. Without hurry, as if he had all the time in the world, he gently pushed the robe off her shoulders and it fell to the floor in a puddle of plush ivory.

Kirsten stood before Dane, stripped naked except for her lace panties. He stared into her eyes before dropping to one knee and pressing moist lips to her skin. His hands pressed firmly against the small of her back while his lips caressed the soft skin near her breast.

Her knees started to give way, but he held her upright and slowly opened his mouth against one straining nipple. She moaned at the bittersweet agony his lips created against her soft flesh. "Dear God," she whispered, her fingers running through the wet strands of his hair.

All of his muscles flexed as he gently lowered her to the jade green carpet. Beats of sweat, evidence of the restraint he placed on himself, dotted his forehead. He moved away from her long enough to remove his clothes and toss them aside. Her eyes wandered down the solid length of his body. Lean muscles, looking as if they were oiled because of his sweat, gleamed in the firelight.

"Make love to me," he pleaded, pulling her against him. She felt his legs rubbing against hers. His fingers pressed against the naked length of her spine, pushing her against the hard desire straining in each of his corded muscles. "I've wanted you for so long…so long."

As if unable to restrain himself any longer, he removed the one small barrier of her underwear and slowly positioned himself over her. His hands trembled as they smoothed her hair away from her face and he kissed her quivering lips. His eyes had turned as dark as the night and he squeezed them tightly shut as he moved over her.

Her breathing was rapid and shallow with anticipation. Every nerve in her body wanted to be touched by this man with the powerful gaze. She felt the moment of their union, the power of his possession, and began to move in the sure rhythmic strokes he inspired.

Her fingers dug into the solid muscles of his shoulders as the tempo increased and the hot pressure within her swelled to burst in a rush of desperation and need.

"Dane…" she cried into the night just as his answering shudder announced his surrender. His body stiffened before falling against hers in satiation.

Tears of relief and fear pooled in her eyes before sliding down her face. His thumb caressed her cheek but stopped its gentle caress when he realized she was crying.

He reached for a blanket sitting on the edge of the couch and gently covered her body. "Shhh…" he whispered. "Everything will be all right. I promise."

"Just hold sme," she murmured.

"I will, sweet Kirsten." His arms wrapped securely and possessively over her body. "Forever."

CHAPTER SEVEN

Kirsten awakened to the inviting smell of freshly perked coffee. She raised a wary eyelid as unfamiliar noises disturbed her subconscious.

She was alone in the bed. The only evidence that Dane had spent the night with her was the impression still visible on the pillow near hers. She smiled and stretched. Vivid images of the night filled her mind and she realized that she was falling hopelessly in love with the seductive stranger from New York.

Why Dane? Of all the men in the world, why did it have to be Dane Ferguson who attracted her? For all she knew, she was just another in a long line of conquests. Worse yet, perhaps his seduction had been planned, a neatly staged scenario to break down her defenses.

"Stop it," she muttered angrily to herself. "What's done is done." She propped up on one elbow and surveyed the small bedroom. The dim light of dawn filtered into the room through the open weave of the airy draperies.

Her velour robe was lying on the foot of the bed. Kirsten smiled to herself when she saw it. Dane must have retrieved it from the living room and placed it on the bed this morning. That simple, thoughtful act touched her.

Approaching footsteps scraped against the hardwood floor and Kirsten smiled to herself. Holding the sheet over her breasts, she turned her eyes to the doorway.

He paused at the entrance to the room and his severe gaze yielded as he looked down at her slim form. Her hair framed her elegant face in tangled disarray. Green eyes, still seductive from recent slumber, peeked through thick dark lashes. She stretched and the sheet draped across her body molded to her slender figure.

Dane seemed more relaxed this morning, Kirsten decided as she met the invitation in his unguarded stare. The lines of strain around his mouth and eyes had gentled perceptibly. He was dressed in the same cords and sweater he had worn the night before and his chin was darkened by the morning shadow of his beard. His lean muscles moved fluidly beneath his clothes.

It could be dangerously easy to wake up each morning in Dane's arms, Kirsten thought to herself as an enigmatic smile curved her full lips.

Crossing his arms over his chest, Dane continued to stand in the open doorway. He propped one shoulder against the wooden frame of the door and leaned insolently against it as he regarded Kirsten with his penetrating, deepset eyes.

"I thought I heard sounds of life in here," he teased, reluctantly dragging his eyes from the seductive swell of her breast hidden beneath the crisp blue sheet up to her eyes.

Although she felt at an incredible disadvantage, lying naked between the sheets, she managed to return his engaging smile and ran her fingers through the tangles in her hair. She tried not to yawn and failed. "Have you been awake long?"

He shrugged his shoulders indifferently. "About an hour, I'd guess."

Kirsten's eyes swept to the digital display on her clock-radio. "But it's barely six—"

"Not in New York."

The statement settled like lead in the intimate room. Words caught in Kirsten's throat. "You're going back, aren't you?"

she asked quietly. The fingers clutching the sheet to her breast tensed, twisting the pale blue fabric.

His smile turned wistful and his shoulders slumped slightly. "I have to."

"Do you?" The look of disbelief in her cool green eyes challenged him.

"I've got a practice in New York."

"Of course you do. How could I forget?"

The minute the words were out, Kirsten regretted them. Every muscle in his body had stiffened in defense of her verbal assault.

"I hope you know that last night had nothing to do with your case against the station."

She took her eyes away from his uncompromising stare. "I'd like to believe that," she admitted in a rough whisper.

"Then just trust me."

She lifted a doubtful brow when she turned to face him again. "It's difficult for me."

"Why?"

"Maybe it's because all my life I've had to be wary of soft-spoken, smooth, manipulative men who would like to use me to get what they want."

"Like me?" he asked, the muscles in his arms flexing against his chest.

"Like you."

"Oh, lady." He sighed, looking up at the ceiling. "What have I done to you?" His eyes were shadowed in a self-reproachful pain.

Her heart twisted wretchedly. "Nothing I didn't want," she murmured. "Look, I'm sorry—I didn't mean to get so angry."

"It's just your nature?"

Her green eyes sparkled until she realized that he was teasing. "Call it a character flaw," she muttered with a self-mocking grin. "It seems to come to the surface every time I'm around a man who would like to crucify me on the witness stand."

"That's hitting below the belt, Kirsten," he cautioned.

She shook her golden-brown hair. "No that's telling it like it is, counselor." Before he could argue, she reached for her robe and slipped it over her shoulders.

He watched her precise movements and caught a provocative glimpse of her slim body as she put her arms through the sleeves, stood, knotted the belt and lifted her thick hair out of the collar of the robe. "Can I buy you breakfast?" she asked, hoping to hide the feeling of desperation growing within her. Dane was leaving! It was only a matter of time before he would disappear from her life only to resurface for a fleeting and heart-wrenching moment at the trial.

She attempted to walk past him, but strong fingers wrapped over the crook in her arm and held her fast. His chin had hardened and the rage in his eyes became deadly. "Are you trying to say that you regret what happened last night?"

The smile she tried to force trembled. "Regret is too harsh a word," she allowed. "I just think that I wasn't being very rational last night…and I hope that I never make that mistake again."

"Mistake?"

"Look, Dane, there's no point in arguing about what happened. I can't deny that what we shared was incredible. I'm just saying that it won't happen again… at least not until the court battle is resolved."

His dark eyes narrowed. "And when it is, what then? Do you honestly think that we'll be able to pick up where we left off—just as if the trial hadn't occurred?"

"No." She shook her head sadly and her slim shoulders sagged with an unfair burden. "No, I don't."

"Then what you're saying is that it's over," he deduced aloud.

"I'm saying it never began," she whispered.

The fingers around her arm slackened and Dane's hands clenched in frustration before making a disgusted sound in the back of his throat. "This is your choice, you know."

"Precisely my point. We don't have a choice, Dane."

He strode into the living room and picked up his suitcase before turning to face her. When he did, all trace of emotion had left his intense hazel eyes. "I think I'd better go," he stated as he picked up his windbreaker from the back of the couch. His eyes swept the top of a nearby table. Just as he reached for his keys, he noticed the newspaper article lying on the coffee table.

He paused as his eyes scanned the newsprint. Kirsten's breath caught in her throat. When Dane stood, he tossed the jacket casually over his arm, pocketed the keys and picked up the article. "Ginevra," he muttered softly, as if to himself. But he wanted a response. He expected one. She could read the unasked questions in his wary gaze.

Kirsten's spine stiffened and the smile she forced to her face was frail. "That's right."

"The proposed nuclear site?"

"Yes."

"You're still interested in it. Why?" He studied every movement on her face, looking for the slightest trace of emotion. Obviously Ginevra meant more to her than she had intoned during the deposition in Lloyd Grady's office.

"I free-lance. Anytime I read something that interests me, something I might do an article on later, I clip it from the paper and put it in my research file." She nervously ran her fingers along the belt of her robe. "I still have to make a living, you know."

Dane felt as if he had inadvertently stumbled onto something important. Kirsten was trying too hard to convince him that Ginevra meant nothing significant. From his years of practice reading people and attempting to make them say what he wanted to hear, Dane understood that Ginevra was somehow involved in the suit against KPSC. The first time the site had been mentioned, in Lloyd Grady's office, a look of caution had crossed the blond attorney's features. Kirsten had caught Lloyd's warning glance and had sidestepped the issue. Ginevra might be the key to the whole damned suit!

"And you're thinking about doing a story on Ginevra?" he prodded.

Dane assumed the same casual manner he had used in the depositions, and Kirsten realized that he was once again the attorney for the defense. Kirsten's heart bled when she knew that what she had feared was true: Dane had come to her seeking a hole in her story, a crack in the suit against KPSC.

Kirsten raised her palms indecisively to the ceiling. "Who knows? Maybe someday."

Dane dropped the subject. Pushing her any further wouldn't get him anywhere. He knew just how hard to press a person and when it was tactful to stop. He'd extracted all the information from her that she would give him. The satisfaction he should have felt in discovering her weakness was painfully absent. "I'll see you later," he stated, returning the clipping to the table and rotating once again toward the door.

"In court, counselor," she returned with a bitter smile.

"If that's the way you want it," he whispered.

"There's no other way. You know it as well as I do."

Without a smile or a regretful look over his shoulder Dane walked to the door, opened it, paused as if he thought better of his movements and then walked out of the house… and out of Kirsten's life.

"You're a damned fool," she told herself as she closed the door behind him and slumped against the wall.

A WALK ALONG THE beach didn't satisfy her, nor did it soothe her raw nerves. Evidence of last night's storm only served to remind her of Dane and the short romance they had shared together. The broken shells, tangled seaweed and discarded pieces of driftwood were scattered on the wet sand like pieces of her shattered life.

How could one man affect her so deeply? Kirsten huddled against the damp fog and pushed her hands deep into the pockets of her jacket as she stared out to sea. The gray waters of the Pacific lapped gently on the sand. Why had she let Dane into her heart? He would only destroy her.

Pursing her lips in determination, she forced herself to stand and abandon her post on the exposed rock near the tide pools. Whether she liked the thought or not, it was time to face the music and call Lloyd Grady. If she expected to win her fight against KPSC, her attorney would have to know everything about her conversations with Dane.

Bracing herself against the verbal attack she was sure to get from Lloyd, she mounted the stairs and walked back to the cabin. After discarding her shoes and jacket, she dialed Lloyd's office and after a brief wait was put through to her attorney.

"Kirsten!" He sounded relieved.

"I thought I should call and let you know that you were right," she said.

"About what?"

"Dane Ferguson showed up."

There was a pause in the conversation. "I knew it! That miserable bastard," Lloyd muttered. "I hope you sent him packing."

Kirsten hesitated. "He left, but we talked for quite a while."

"Dear God, Kirsten, what do you mean, quite a while? Ten minutes? An hour? What?"

"I think it ended up to be several hours," Kirsten admitted

with a frown. "I thought that maybe I could get some information out of him."

"And did you?" Lloyd asked, unable to hide his disgust.

"Not much..."

"Of course not! He's slick, Kirsten, and he's got the reputation to prove it. We're not talking about some two-bit penny-ante kid who's still wet behind the ears, for God's sake! He's one of the best Manhattan has to offer. His fee alone would choke a horse!"

"I know that."

"But you still talked to him." Lloyd let out a tired breath of air. "Damn it, Kirsten, what do you expect me to do? I can't win this suit for you unless you cooperate—with me, not with the defense! You have to remember that Dane Ferguson has only one objective in mind: to win this suit as fast as he can, by any means possible. You're not going to con him the way you conned Fletcher Ross."

Kirsten's anger snapped. "I didn't con Ross, Lloyd. I won the case because I was right! Remember?"

"And you didn't do it by handing over the defense any information I didn't know about."

"Okay, look, I'm sorry."

Lloyd's voice softened. "All right. There's no reason to panic about it. It's over. Just please, be careful, Kirsten. Don't make this kind of mistake again. What Ferguson's done is unethical, but there's not a whole lot we can do except make the best out of a bad situation. Why don't you tell me what you discussed?"

Kirsten repeated her conversations with Dane, excluding the personal aspect and tone. Lloyd listened intently, interrupting her only to clarify a point every now and then.

"It doesn't sound as if he learned anything that he didn't already know," Lloyd stated when Kirsten had finished her dissertation. The Portland attorney sounded relieved, and Kirsten hated to burst his bubble.

"Except for the fact that he found a clipping I'd taken from *The Herald*. It was an article on Ginevra."

"Great," Lloyd muttered, "I'd hate to see him open that can of worms…" He sighed audibly as he collected his thoughts. "Did he read the article?"

"Most of it."

"Did he ask about it?"

"Uh-huh. I told him that I was going to put it in my research file for an article I might write at a later date."

"Did he believe you?"

"I think so. After all, it's the truth."

"Okay, so we got lucky. Look, I don't want you to so much as look at Dane Ferguson when I'm not around. Anytime he wants to see you, tell him it's strictly by the book. Your attorney will have to be present." There was an edge to Lloyd's words, as if he were affronted that Dane had managed to see Kirsten alone. Kirsten sensed that it wasn't just because of the lawsuit.

"I don't think we'll have to worry about that," Kirsten replied. "He was planning to go back to New York."

"When?"

"I don't know…. I didn't ask."

"It doesn't matter. In the future, just use your head. You can't expect me to win this for you if you don't cooperate. And try to keep your perspective on this case. If you blow this, you'll lose that two hundred-thousand-dollar award."

"It's not the money, Lloyd. You know that, I just want to see that justice is served. KPSC had no right to treat me the way they did, and I hope that I can win this suit in order that other women like me won't have to put up with what I did."

"Then for Pete's sake, Kirsten, try to remember who's on your side and who's against you!"

"I will, Lloyd."

"Good."

"Talk to you later."

"And tell me if Ferguson tries to see you again."

Kirsten hung up the phone and went into the kitchen to pour herself a cup of coffee. The morning newspaper was still on the kitchen table, opened to the page Dane had been reading. Kirsten took a sip of the coffee and read the column about the previous night's accident.

An image of Dane with mud streaked across his cheek and rain glistening in his hair filled Kirsten's mind. Witnessing that accident had been hard on him. She had read it in the pain in his eyes and the tension of his jaw.

"If only things were different," she whispered, remembering the ecstasy of their lovemaking. "Maybe I could ease your pain… make you forget, just for a little while." Then, realizing that she had been daydreaming, she refolded the newspaper and poured her cold coffee down the sink.

The less she thought about Dane the better. Perhaps this morning was a good time to tackle the article about the timber sales slump. She walked back to the living room and sat down at the antique sewing machine on which her typewriter rested.

She tugged off the plastic cover and stared at the blank page rolled over the carriage. "This isn't going to be easy," she told herself as she placed her hands over the keys. "But somehow you've got to get Dane Ferguson out of your mind."

With new resolve she tackled the job ahead of her, and it wasn't until she paused in her work and rubbed the tension out of her shoulders that she saw the blanket folded on the corner of the couch.

Kirsten's throat went suddenly dry. She stared at the faded quilt and her lower lip trembled. The memory of Dane placing that blanket tenderly over her body last night while murmuring words of love into her ear wouldn't leave her, and she had to fight the tears beginning to sting her eyes.

CHAPTER EIGHT

Dane was impatient. He stared out the small window of Fletcher Ross's office and studied the gray skies shadowing the city.

Since leaving Kirsten, Dane had been uneasy. Listening to Fletcher Ross hadn't helped matters. Dane tapped his pencil angrily on the corner of Ross's oversized desk and tried to look pleased while being introduced to Aaron Becker, station manager for KPSC.

"Good to meet you," Becker stated as Dane rose from his chair to accept the station manager's handshake. The short man pumped Dane's hand several times before releasing it. As Becker dropped into the leather couch, he smiled at Dane. The grin was practiced and friendly: Dane didn't trust it for a minute.

"What can I do for you?" Aaron Becker asked pleasantly before he cocked he wrist and pointedly checked the time. He was a busy man. The seconds of his life weren't idly given.

"I just want to ask you a few questions about Kirsten McQueen's employment at KPSC," Dane suggested in an even, professional tone.

Becker responded. If there was anything he respected in a man, it was professionalism. "What do you want to know?" He leaned forward on the expensive couch, hiked his pants up and placed his clasped hands over his knees.

Dane studied the man. Becker was nervous, either by

nature or because of added stress. Maybe a combination of the two. "This isn't a deposition, you understand. I'm just trying to clarify a few points in the McQueen case."

"Good."

"How would you describe Ms. McQueen's attitude?" Dane asked the station manager.

"Toward me?"

Dane's dark brows rose slightly. "I was talking in generalities, but, since you brought it up, let's start with her relationship with you. How did Ms. McQueen react to you?"

Becker pulled an exaggerated frown. "Hard to say," he responded, tugging at the knot in his tie. "In the beginning we got along—you are talking about how she handled her work load, right?"

"What do you mean?" Dane's hazel eyes darkened.

"You're not asking about how she reacted to me ask a man, are you?"

Dane smiled tightly and his finger clenched around the pencil before he put it on the desk. "Did she? React to you as a man, I mean."

Becker grinned collusively at Fletcher Ross. The round attorney squirmed and wiped the sweat from his brow with his handkerchief. "Well, she didn't actually come on to me, if that's what you mean."

"But," Dane prodded, concealing his rage by leaning back in the chair and crossing his arms over his chest.

"But… you know how it is. A guy can feel when a woman's hot for him."

"You got that feeling with Kirsten McQueen?" Savage eyes drilled into Aaron Becker, but the anger in Dane's gaze was lost on him.

Becker shrugged uncomfortably. "Yeah, a couple of times. She went through a bad divorce and, well, I could tell she was interested."

"But you didn't pursue a relationship?"

Becker shook his head. The neatly styled hair didn't move. "Naw." He stuck out his lips as if in deep thought. "Probably was a mistake."

"Why do you say that?" Dane's jaw hardened, but he hung onto his façade of civility. The anger flowing through his veins was irrational and would only hinder his quest for the truth.

"Maybe if I would have given her what she wanted, we wouldn't be in this mess today." He laughed aloud. Neither Fletcher Ross nor Dane Ferguson cracked a smile. Dane's face remained impassive. Only the tightening of skin over his cheekbones gave any indication of his restrained emotions.

"So you think that Ms. McQueen's lawsuit was a vendetta aimed at you?"

Becker sobered. "I wouldn't go so far as to say that."

"Then what will you say when you're called to give testimony? Would you swear, under oath, that Kirsten McQueen was, let's see, how did you phrase it—" Dane eyed his notes. "Here it is. Would you swear that Ms. McQueen was 'hot for you'?"

"Of course not." Becker looked angrily at Fletcher Ross. "Hey, what is this? Isn't this guy on our side?"

Fletcher Ross raised his broad shoulders and with a shake of his head indicated to Aaron that he understood nothing about the New Yorker's tactics.

"I'm trying to defend KPSC," Dane pointed out, leaning over the desk. "And in order to do that I would like to understand Kirsten McQueen's motives for the lawsuit."

"You think I could understand that woman? No way!"

"But didn't you say that you could feel that she was interested in you as a man?"

"That's different than reading her mind, for crying out loud!"

"Is it?"

Becker's face had flushed scarlet and his fingers drummed

nervously on his knee. His full lips pulled into an introspective pout. "Just what is it you want to know?"

Dane forced a congenial smile onto his face. "I just want to know why Kirsten McQueen initiated the suit, an age-discrimination suit, against KPSC."

"I don't know." Aaron Becker looked from Fletcher Ross to Dane Ferguson. "I suppose she doesn't think she got a fair shake. She probably feels that she didn't deserve to get canned."

"Did she?"

Becker rose from his chair and began pacing restlessly in front of the desk. "She was getting pushy. She started demanding things I couldn't give her. She wanted to cover national stories and I was happy with the man I had covering national news. Then, she"—he paused as if carefully considering his words—"she wanted to do more investigative stories in and about Oregon. The whole idea would have thrown off our format. I told her no."

"How did she react?" Dane pressed his elbows on the desk and cradled his chin in his hands as he studied Aaron Becker. The grandstanding was over and the station manager was finally cooperating, or so it appeared.

Becker snorted in disgust. "Like any emotional woman. She flew off the handle."

"In your office."

"Right."

"Were there any other witnesses to her emotional outburst?"

"I can't remember—didn't I answer these questions during the last trial?"

"Some of them," Dane conceded. "So you fired Ms. McQueen and you think she filed a lawsuit in retaliation."

"Yeah, I guess so. Something like that."

"Did you?" Dane demanded, his voice stone cold.

"What do you take me for, an idiot? If Kirsten McQueen

had kept her nose clean, she'd still have a job at the station. She was getting to be more trouble than she was worth."

"So you used her argument with you as the excuse to fire her."

"I didn't need an excuse. She gave me reasons. Good reasons. It's all in her personnel file. Don't you have it?"

Dane's gaze remained cool when he leveled it on the hostile station manager. "I've got it. I'd just like to hear your impressions of the situation."

"Well, as far as I'm concerned, Kirsten McQueen is a real pain the backside. She was trouble all along."

"Not according to the employee records," Dane observed.

Becker waved off Dane's remark with a flip of his wrist. "Yeah, well I tried to give her the benefit of the doubt. Seems like that might have been a mistake." Once again the short man glanced at his watch.

"Back to the argument," Dane said, pressing the eraser of the pencil he had picked up to his lips and ignoring Becker's obvious ploy to end the discussion.

"The last argument with Kirsten?"

Dane winced at Becker's familiar use of her name. It soured Dane's stomach to think that anyone as slippery as Aaron Becker would know Kirsten personally. "Right. You stated that she was interested in doing more in-depth stories." Becker nodded. "Like what? Can you give me an example?"

Aaron tossed up his hand as if the question were irrelevant. "It didn't matter—anything slightly controversial."

Dane's hazel eyes fixed on Becker's smug face. "Such as Ginevra?" he asked.

The station manager blanched and shot Fletcher Ross a glance of fear before recovering himself. "That was something she was interested in," Becker conceded. "She also had her eye on an alleged drug ring and asked to do a report on one of the state senators who got himself into a little trouble in Salem…. There were a lot of stories she wanted to check into. Unfortunately for her, we didn't have the time or the money to finance some of her half-baked ideas."

Fletcher Ross hoisted his large frame out of his chair as if to end the discussion.

Dane wouldn't let go. "Wait a minute. You run a news program. Don't you cover all the news?" Becker's story wasn't adding up.

Aaron impatiently transferred his weight from one foot to the other. "The type of story Kirsten McQueen wanted to report was the flashiest, trashiest scandal to hit the streets. In my opinion, Kirsten was more interested in gossip than news. And that kind of reporting isn't compatible with the way I run my station. KPSC has a responsibility to its viewers and a reputation in the community.

"Now, unless you have any other questions, I've really got to get back to the station."

Dane nodded curtly and Aaron Becker strode hastily out of the tension-filled office.

"Need a ride to the airport?" Fletcher Ross asked, and Dane was forced to smile at the Portland attorney's tactless way of getting rid of him.

"No thanks. I asked your secretary to call me a cab the minute she saw Aaron Becker leave. It should be here soon." Dane snapped his briefcase closed and noticed the relief in Ross's dark eyes. Having Dane Ferguson set up camp in his office made the Portland attorney nervous.

"Is there anything I can do for you while you're in Manhattan?" Ross asked, hoping to look sincere.

"Pray," Dane suggested unkindly. "Unless I start getting some straight answers, we're going to need all the help we can get."

The portly man seemed surprised. "You think Aaron Becker lied to you?"

"Let's just say that I think he may have exaggerated a

little," Dane replied as he looked out the window and saw a cab pull up to the curb near Ross's office. Tossing his raincoat over his arm, Dane grabbed his briefcase and started toward the door.

"You'll keep me posted, let me know how you're progressing?" Ross asked uncomfortably. "And if I can be of any assistance—"

Dane flashed the Portland attorney his most disarming grin. "You'll be the first to know." With his final words he walked through the small maze of interlocking offices, pushed open the door and stepped into the cold Portland rain.

KIRSTEN DROPPED THE manila envelope into the appropriate slot at the post office. She knew it wasn't her most eloquent piece of journalism, but the article on the timber sales slump was precise and to the point—exactly what the editor of *Update* magazine had requested. With any luck, the magazine would buy the article and show some interest in the other ideas she had submitted with the article.

The post office was located in the business section of Newport and the offices of *The Herald* were only a few blocks east. Kirsten decided to talk to the reporter who had written the story on Ginevra. It took only a short time to walk to the brightly painted cabin that had been converted into the official headquarters of the newspaper.

"May I help you?" a pert redhead with an upturned nose and easy smile asked as Kirsten entered the building.

"I'm looking for Laura Snyder," Kirsten said, returning the young woman's friendly grin and wiping away the drops of rain that still clung to her flushed cheeks. The weather had turned cool again. "I don't have an appointment."

The redhead beamed. "I doubt if you'll need one. You're Kirsten McQueen, aren't you?"

"That's right…."

The receptionist extended her hand. "I'm Peggy Monteith. You're something of a legend around here, you know."

"A legend?" Kirsten took the young woman's hand, but the twinkle in her eye indicated that she thought the idea amusing and unjustified. "I don't think—"

Peggy waved off Kirsten's modesty with a flip of her wrist. "Don't give me that. It took a lot of guts for you to stand up to that television station the way you did. Around here, and probably throughout the entire state, you've become a local hero…or heroine."

"Were you looking for me?" another female voice asked. Kirsten turned to face a petite woman whose only indication of her age was the slight smattering of gray in her short black hair. "I'm Laura Snyder. I heard most of the conversation from my desk." Laura cocked her head in the direction of a thin partition. "There's not a whole lot of privacy in this office."

Kirsten offered her hand and Laura shook it. "I'd like to talk to you for a minute about an article you wrote. It was in the paper a couple of days ago," she explained.

"And I thought you were going to offer me an exclusive interview with the woman who stood up to KPSC and won."

Kirsten smiled wistfully. "Not yet," she admitted. "The station appealed. It looks as if my victory might be short-lived."

"So I heard." Laura crossed her arms over her chest and studied Kirsten carefully as she leaned against the corner of Peggy's desk. "But that's certainly no reason to think that you won't win the appeal. The way I understand it, you did a pretty good job of proving that the station discriminated against you."

"I'll have to give that credit to my attorney," Kirsten ventured. "He's the reason I won."

"He's still on your side, isn't he?"

"So far." Kirsten considered her conversation with Lloyd earlier in the day. He'd come close to withdrawing from the case—or at least he'd wanted her to think so.

"Why don't you come into my office, such as it is?" Laura suggested.

After leading Kirsten to the small area behind the partition and offering her a cup of coffee, Laura took a seat behind her cluttered desk and smiled at the slim woman with the intelligent green eyes. Folding plump hands over an unruly stack of papers, Laura asked, "What can I do for you?"

"I saw your article on Ginevra," Kirsten stated, noting that Laura didn't seem surprised in the slightest when she mentioned the article. It was almost as if Laura had anticipated what Kirsten was about to say. "I thought you might give me some information on what's happening over there."

"That article seems to have caught everyone's attention," Laura replied, shaking her head. "You're not the first person who's asked me about it. There was a man in here this morning. Tall fella. Good-looking man with an eastern accent. Seems he was interested in my article too." Laura's sharp brown eyes were mildly curious.

Kirsten's heart missed a beat and a sinking sensation swept over her. "Don't tell me. The man who was here this morning—his name was Dane Ferguson, wasn't it?"

"None other." Laura pursed her lips and nodded thoughtfully. "He's the hotshot KPSC hired to defend the station, isn't he?"

Kirsten met the friendly reporter's serious gaze. "The same. He'd already seen me earlier this morning—about the case. I didn't know he'd show up here."

"Strange, isn't it?" Laura conjectured with a thoughtful pout. "Why do you think he's interested in Ginevra?"

Kirsten lifted her shoulders. "I don't know, but I suspect it has something to do with my case."

"That's what I thought," Laura agreed.

"Did you ask him?"

"No. I thought I'd learn more from him by just listening to what he had to say."

"Which was?"

"Nothing." Laura's full lips pursed. "But I got the feeling that he wasn't happy about something. He seemed restless, as if he were trying to figure out something he didn't really understand." Her dark eyes warmed. "If you ask me, Kirsten, you've got him running scared."

"I doubt it," Kirsten admitted. "I don't think Mr. Ferguson is the kind to scare easily."

"Maybe you're right. He seemed like the type that would like a challenge." Laura rubbed her temple. "But just think what he's got at stake here. If you win your case against KPSC, he'll never live it down, just like before during the Stone Motor trial. You're just one woman with a grievance in Oregon and he's the best money can buy. He's got a lot to lose."

Noticing Kirsten's whitened pallor and realizing that she was straying from the reason for Kirsten's visit, Laura dismissed the subject with a wave of her plump fingers. "So what do you want to know about Ginevra?"

"Everything, I suppose."

"Don't we all. If we had the answers to that one, there wouldn't be much of a controversy over it, would there?"

"I guess not," Kirsten admitted, glad that the topic of conversation had shifted from Dane Ferguson. "How did you get interested in Ginevra?"

"That's pretty simple," Laura replied. "It's a pretty hot subject around here… probably because the location is so close. Anyway, I've got a couple of friends who are in an antinuclear power group, and they asked me to write an article against the site."

"But your article wasn't against it."

"No—I decided to point out both sides of the issue. Needless to say, my friends weren't too happy about it."

"It's not easy to be objective."

"Not on something as controversial as Ginevra," Laura agreed.

"Everything I know about the site was in my article, but if you want some more information, why don't you call June Dellany? She's a friend of mine—or at least she was until my article on Ginevra was published." Laura scribbled a name and telephone number on a small sheet of paper and handed it to Kirsten, who accepted the scrap of paper, stuffed it into her purse and finished her coffee.

"Thanks a lot," Kirsten stated as she rose to leave.

"No trouble at all," Laura replied with a slow-spreading grin. "And just let me know when I can get that interview."

"As soon as my case is decided," Kirsten promised as she left the small building.

Rain poured from the dark sky and the wind caught in her hair, but she didn't notice. Her thoughts had turned inward and her heart twisted in agony. So Dane had been checking on Ginevra. He'd noticed the clipping in her apartment and he'd looked up the source.

Her small fist clenched in anger. Whatever she had shared with Dane had meant nothing to him. He'd seduced her into thinking that he cared for her—if just a little. But when the chips were down, the truth of the matter was that Dane had used her solely to gain information about the trial. The seduction was just part of the plan to discredit her, and she'd been a fool to think otherwise.

At least now I understand, she thought grimly to herself. *The battle lines have been drawn.*

CHAPTER NINE

Jet lag. Or maybe it was general fatigue. Whatever the reason, Dane was irritable. The unscheduled two-hour layover in Denver hadn't helped matters and probably had contributed to the headache beginning to pound behind his eyes. The trip to Oregon had been a strain, and the worst part of it was that he was little better off now than when he had left New York City three days earlier.

Even the few hours he'd shared with Kirsten had turned against him. He had hoped to get information from her, but instead he had left her with the unlikely feeling that he had just given up the only thing of real value in his life. Discussing the case with her had only added to his misgivings, as had his meeting with Fletcher Ross and Aaron Becker. Dane had left Portland with the taste of disgust in his mouth.

It was evident that both Ross and Becker shared Harmon Smith's opinion that Kirsten McQueen was trouble. Dane didn't understand it. Though Aaron Becker had worked with Kirsten for several years, he had claimed that she had been a pain in the rear all along—a direct contradiction to the employee records in the files of KPSC.

Dane walked through the concourse at JFK and threaded his way past other, slower travelers who were making early morning connections in New York. He didn't have any baggage to collect, as he had carried his garment bag onto the plane himself and it was now draped over his shoulder as he pushed his way out of the crowded terminal.

Taxicabs, all a dingy yellow, were idling in wait as he walked out of the building and into the first gray streaks of dawn. After catching the next available cab, he sighed wearily and he braced himself for the ride back to Manhattan.

Relaxation was impossible in the battered Chevy as, without warning, it alternately lurched forward only to slow abruptly, according to the whims of the brooding driver.

Gratefully, the burly man wasn't inclined to make idle conversation at six in the morning, and Dane stared into the half light of dawn toward the winking lights of the heart of New York City. As the sun rose in the sky the lights of Manhattan disappeared and the dark skyline of the city took shape against the backdrop of what promised to be a brilliant summer day.

Dane closed his eyes and leaned his head against the worn cushion of the backseat before pinching the bridge of his nose with his forefinger and thumb. He couldn't shake the feeling that Fletcher Ross and Aaron Becker were covering their tracks in an attempt to pawn Kirsten off as a scapegoat. But for the life of him, Dane couldn't understand their motives. Kirsten had proved herself to be an intelligent and thoughtful woman. The image Ross and Becker had painted was decidedly less kind. Why?

Dane had suspected that the answer might lie in that proposed nuclear site, but when he'd questioned the reporter who had written the article on Ginevra, he'd come up empty. Again. The whole damned lawsuit was beginning to take on a new and sinister dimension. It was as if people were purposely trying to thwart him in his quest for the truth. But he should have expected it, Dane thought jadedly, his cynicism surfacing.

The cab screeched to a halt in front of Dane's apartment building. It was a modest but comfortable red brick structure on East 72nd Street. Though not luxurious, it served his needs. He had rented the apartment when he had first moved to Manhattan, and now that he could afford a much more expensive place to live, he found himself reluctant to move. He was comfortable where he was and he didn't want to disturb that comfort. A larger place might remind him of a time in his life that he would rather forget. Those happy memories of San and Julie had a way of making him incredibly despondent, twisting his brief joy into a melancholy pain that made his life alone seem empty and hollow.

Kirsten McQueen could change all that, he contemplated, and then abruptly changed the course of his thoughts. Until the lawsuit was decided, he had nothing to offer her.

His apartment was on the third floor. He unlocked the door, walked inside and threw his bag over the back of the modern rust-colored couch. Tugging uncomfortably at his tie, he strode over to the bar, splashed three fingers of bourbon into a glass and drank the warm liquor in one swallow.

It was the first time he'd taken a drink in the morning since Julie's death. The liquid hit his stomach and he felt no satisfaction in the sensation—nor in his life, for that matter. Maybe the bustling city wasn't for him. Maybe he belonged on the other side of the continent, where he could make love to a beautiful woman and watch the sun set in a burst of golden flame as it settled into the horizon of the calm Pacific. He considered another drink, and pushed the wayward thought aside.

Raking his fingers through his hair, he walked over to the desk he had pushed into a corner of the living room and reached for the phone. After calling the office and explaining that he wouldn't make it in until early afternoon, he showered, shaved and changed into a clean business suit. He was dog tired, and all he wanted to do was sleep for a solid twenty-four hours.

But he couldn't. The image of Kirsten lingered in his mind

and he knew that he wouldn't be able to rest until he'd found a way to defend KPSC. As he snapped his watch onto his wrist, he felt a twinge of guilt. He was torn between his feelings for Kirsten and the obligation of his promise to Harmon Smith. There was no room for any argument; regardless of what had happened between himself and Kirsten McQueen, Dane still owed Harmon Smith a very large debt, one that money couldn't begin to repay.

"Doesn't matter anyway," he reminded himself, remembering the cool manner in which Kirsten had dismissed him yesterday morning.

But why wouldn't anyone give him a straight answer? He tried to tell himself that it really wasn't his concern, that it wasn't so much the truth he wanted, but a perspective on the case. But his most convincing logic couldn't ignore the one obvious fact that everyone involved in this case seemed to be lying through his teeth. Including Kirsten. She hadn't been straight with him about Ginevra—he sensed it.

A cold feeling in the pit of Dane's stomach suggested to him that once before he hadn't been as concerned for the truth as much as he had been in proving his client's innocence. In the end it had cost him much more than his reputation, and he wouldn't let it happen again.

Without any further soul-searching, Dane called Harmon Smith's secretary and made an appointment to see the president of Stateside Broadcasting Corporation later in the day.

"DANE!" HARMON SMITH marched across the room and pumped Dane's arm furiously. His smile was genuine, if a little nervous. "Can I get you a drink?" Ignoring the negative sweep of Dane's head, Smith turned to the petite receptionist who had escorted Dane into the room. "Sylvie, pour him a drink, would you?" His watery blue eyes looked upward into

Dane's and his forehead wrinkled thoughtfully. "Bourbon, isn't it?"

Rather than risk a useless argument, Dane nodded. "Bourbon's fine," he replied with a slight grimace before accepting the hastily prepared drink.

Harmon Smith's office was as understated and elaborate as his residence. Brass lamps, expensive carpet, solid wood furniture, original oil paintings—the elegant trappings of wealth created an atmosphere of sedate affluence and comfort. The only thing seemingly out of place was Smith himself. The nervous man didn't blend into the complacent luxury.

He took a long sip of his Scotch and water, lit a cigarette and settled into his overstuffed leather chair. The receptionist left the room and he waved Dane into one of the side chairs near the desk.

"So you're back from Oregon, are you? Tell me, how's it going out there?" Smith asked with a worried frown.

"It's coming along," Dane said, taking a sip of his drink and regarding Smith intently. "Not as well as I'd hoped, but the defense is shaping up."

Harmon Smith appeared relieved. "Good," he uttered, taking a drag from his cigarette and letting the smoke filter out through his nose.

"It could be better, though, if I'd get a little more cooperation."

"Cooperation? From whom? What are you talking about? Isn't that bitch talking to you?" Faded blue eyes filled with concern settled on Dane.

A muscle in the back of Dane's jaw began to tighten at the abrasive words, and his back stiffened as if in defense, but he managed to hide his anger. Dane wanted information, and he wouldn't get it by letting the president of Stateside Broadcasting Corporation anger him. The best strategy was to give

Harmon Smith enough rope to hang himself—then maybe Dane could get to the bottom of this mess.

"The point is—no one is leveling with me."

Smith's face flushed and his palm slapped the desk. "Why that self-righteous little—"

Dane's hazel eyes blazed. "I'm not talking about Kirsten," Dane interjected. "And I think you'd better get used to calling her Ms. McQueen."

"Why?"

Dane shifted in his chair and regarded Harmon Smith with unforgiving hazel eyes. "It's unlikely you'll be called to testify, but if you are, the last thing we can afford is to have you, or anyone else remotely associated with running KPSC, come on like a vindictive male chauvinist out to get a woman." Smith looked as if he were about to interrupt, but Dane wouldn't allow it. The skin over his features had stretched taught; the corners of his mouth pulled grimly downward. "You'd better face it, Harmon, this is a tough case—one you can't afford to lose. And it's going to be tried on Oregon soil. We're the outsiders. We can't let anything we say rile the jury or prejudice even one member against us."

Harmon settled back in his chair, properly chastised, but still eyeing Dane speculatively. "Since when did you get so scrupulous?"

"Since I had my back pushed into a corner, Harmon. Now, you asked me to take on this case and I have, but we're going to play by my rules—or it'll be a sure bet that we'll lose. Lloyd Grady will see to that personally." He paused for a moment, letting his wrath slowly expire. "Don't forget that this case was already tried once."

"So what's your point?" Harmon grumbled, crushing his cigarette and reaching for another.

"No one is giving me straight answers. And I'm not just talking about the plaintiff."

"What do you mean?" Instantly, Harmon Smith was wary. His lighter clicked open and he paused to light the cigarette clamped between his teeth.

"Don't get me wrong. She hasn't exactly been helpful, and that attorney of hers, Lloyd Grady, isn't letting her say anything that might help our defense."

"You must have expected that, for God's sake." Harmon Smith finished his drink and pushed the empty glass aside.

"What I didn't expect was to find that my associate, Fletcher Ross, and one of my star witnesses, a guy by the name of Aaron Becker, don't want to level with me."

"You think they're lying?" Smith was mildly surprised but definitely not angry.

"I mean that Becker's testimony is inconsistent. And Ross doesn't seem to give a damn. I checked. KPSC's employee records, supposedly created and reviewed by Becker, state one thing; he says another. The discrepancy won't hold water in court."

"I thought you said things were progressing," Smith growled.

"As well as can be expected under the circumstances. But if I want to win this suit, I'm going to have to get a lot more cooperation from everyone out there."

"Including Aaron Becker?"

"And Fletcher Ross."

Harmon Smith stubbed out his cigarette and frowned. His sandy-colored brows rose, wrinkling his forehead. "Don't you think you misread the situation in Portland? What would Fletcher Ross have to gain by lying to you?"

"Beats me."

"He's supposed to be on our side, for Christ's sake—Becker, too, for that matter."

"Then why the secrecy?"

Harmon Smith shook his balding head. "Becker must have

been confused. As to Ross, he's probably a little resentful of you. It looks like a slap in the face to have you call the shots on the appeal, since he lost the first battle."

"I think it's more than that." Dane's hazel eyes knifed through Harmon Smith.

"Such as?"

"I think they're covering up for something. Nothing else makes much sense. And I think they're hoping that Kirsten McQueen will take the fall."

"That's ridiculous," Harmon protested.

"Is it?" Dane rubbed his thumb along his chin. "I don't think so."

"I told you why we're so eager to make an example of Ms. McQueen. We just can't let her get away with the lawsuit." Sweat was beginning to collect over Smith's anxious, watery eyes.

"I know, I know—a dangerous precedent, right?"

"Exactly!" Harmon Smith's fingers began drumming distractedly on his desk.

"Then you better tell your boys in Oregon to come clean, Harmon. The only way we'll win this case is to have all the facts and submit them to the jury in a manner beneficial to our defense. The minute we start lying, it's all over." Dane rose, as if to end the interview.

"But you do think we will win, don't you?" Harmon asked, attempting to hide his nervous concern.

"That depends, Harmon. But you can't expect me to work with my hands tied." Dane swung out of the office gritting his teeth. He'd suspected that Smith was aware of Ross's sleazy tactics, and now Dane was certain that Harmon Smith was stonewalling him along with Ross, Becker and everyone else associated with this damned case. An uneasy feeling tightened his stomach into knots, and for a desperate moment he felt trapped, caught in a web of deception he didn't understand.

Dane took the elevator downstairs and was in the lobby of the Stateside Building when he noticed Frank Boswick, Harmon Smith's assistant, hurrying out of the building. He was the one man who had been honest with Dane the first night that Harmon Smith had presented his case. In three swift strides Dane was beside the younger man, and Frank smiled in recognition.

"How are you—Ferguson, isn't it?"

"That's right, and I'm fine," Dane replied. "If you've got a minute, I'd like to talk to you about the McQueen case."

Boswick checked his watch. His smile was lopsided but genuine. "I've got a little time," he admitted.

"Good. How about a cup of coffee?"

Frank Boswick agreed and the two men settled on a busy café a few blocks west of Stateside Building. The small restaurant was doing a brisk noon business, but Dane was able to spot a table near the back that would afford a modicum of privacy.

The coffee was served by an efficient waitress whose plain face held no sign of expression as she placed the two steaming cups of black liquid on the Formica tabletop.

"What can I do for you?" Frank Boswick asked, taking a sip of the hot coffee and observing Dane over the rim of his cup.

"I hoped you could clear up a few problems I'm having with the McQueen case."

"Problems?" Frank's thick eyebrows shot over the rims of his thick glasses.

"I'm having trouble getting the truth from Fletcher Ross and Aaron Becker for starters—"

"Not to mention Harmon Smith," Frank guessed with a grimace.

Dane nodded patiently. "He hasn't been the most helpful. Yet, he expects me to win when the case comes to trial."

Frank chuckled, but the sound was hollow. "The whole thing's crazy, if you ask me."

"I'm asking. What do you mean? Why can't I get any straight answers? Why is Harmon so insistent that Kirsten McQueen is nothing but a money-grubbing ex-employee with a grudge? He seems to think that she initiated the suit out of spite."

"And you don't think she did?"

"I'm not sure—not until I get all the facts, and so far that hasn't been easy. I can't even count on my associate for any help."

"He's probably not too fond of you. If you win this case, it will only prove what everyone's thinking: that he did a lousy job during the first trial."

"But that's no reason to try to make it harder for me. We're supposed to be working for the same cause." Dane shook his head in frustration and disgust.

Frank stared into his coffee, absorbing all of Dane's words. He checked his watch before finally rubbing his fingers along his cheek and gazing out of the window at the front of the building. "You're right," he agreed. "I don't know why they haven't told you the whole story from the beginning." He shifted uncomfortably in his chair and drained his cup.

"As I understand it," Frank proclaimed, "the controversy over firing Kirsten McQueen started several months before she was actually let go." His dark eyes rose to meet Dane's curious gaze.

Nodding, Dane silently encouraged Harmon Smith's assistant to continue. "Kirsten had shown more than just a passing interest in a place called Ginevra. It's a site planned for the second nuclear power plant in Oregon."

"I've heard of it."

"Then you know that the construction of another nuclear power facility in the Northwest was subject to a lot of controversy and public interest due to the failed WPPSS or Whoops as it's called in that part of the country."

"I read something about it."

"To make a long story short, the Washington Public Power Supply System declared that it couldn't repay several billion dollars in bonds sold to the public to construct the project. On top of that, construction was never finished. It was a real fiasco, not only in the Northwest, but across the country. Thousands of investors lost their savings in confidence, and the municipal bond market dropped. Some financial advisers expect that the confidence level will never be the same. The people in the Northwest feel abused and an incredible amount of lawsuits are still unsettled."

Dane knew all about WPPSS, but he listened to Frank and was relieved to find out that someone seemed to be telling him the truth. "So what does this have to do with Kirsten McQueen?" Dane asked, finishing his coffee.

"For some reason that I sure as hell don't understand, Aaron Becker, the station manager for KPSC, didn't want Kirsten on the story. But she was persistent. She wanted more than the usual fluff stories assigned to women reporters at KPSC, and continued to press Becker about Ginevra."

Dane was forced to smile at Frank Boswick's description of the events. He could well imagine the green fire that would spark in her intelligent eyes if Kirsten were told certain stories were out of her league. Tethering her to mild human interest stories would only add fuel to the fire of challenge that burned within her.

"So you think the key to the entire lawsuit is Ginevra?" Dane surmised when he picked up the bill.

Frank shrugged as if he'd given away too many company secrets. "It looks that way to me."

The two men made their way out of the crowded café, shook hands and parted ways.

With renewed conviction Dane decided to return to Oregon. Unfortunately, the trip would have to wait until he'd cleared up a few things at the office. He had several cases that he had to review and couldn't be ignored. He found that thought discouraging.

He turned toward the street and hailed a passing cab. It had been less than forty-eight hours since he'd last seen Kirsten and it already seemed like a lifetime.

CHAPTER TEN

Two weeks had passed since she had seen or heard from Dane. Each day Kirsten felt a little less pain and a little more anger. Her wrath was aimed for the most part at herself—for letting Dane abuse her, and if she called herself a fool, she decided Dane was worse: a deceptive bastard who had intentionally seduced her in hopes of defaming her.

"You played into his hands," she reminded herself as she straightened and neatly typed pages of her résumé. She chided herself for being so naive. Once before a man had used her and she had sworn it would never happen again. The painful divorce from Kent should have been all the warning she needed about powerful men. Apparently it wasn't.

The telephone rang and the noise made her jump. Each time the damn instrument had rung in the past ten days, she had futilely hoped that it would be Dane. Of course, she had been wrong. Ignoring her racing pulse, she answered the phone on the desk and stared through the window at the blue-gray waters of the ocean.

"Kirsten!" Lloyd's voice rang enthusiastically over the wires when she answered the telephone.

"How are you, Lloyd?"

"Great, just great. Hey, listen, we've got a court date, and barring some unforeseen schedule changes, we'll be facing KPSC on September tenth." Lloyd sounded ready to do battle with the formidable foe.

Kirsten's heart pounded in her chest. The reality of the trial stared her in the face. The expressionless jurors, the judgmental looks of disdain from Fletcher Ross, the interest of hungry reporters—and Dane. With his unforgiving hazel eyes, his smooth Eastern manners, his ingratiating smile and his needle-sharp intent to destroy her character, Dane would crucify her during the trial.

"Is the tenth okay?" Lloyd asked. She could hear the worry in his voice. "Kirsten?"

She closed her eyes to compose herself. If she had any brains at all, she would tell Lloyd what happened between herself and the famous New York attorney. Maybe Lloyd would find a way to force Dane off the case. "The tenth is fine," she managed to say, her words faint.

"You're sure?"

"Of course."

There was a weighty pause in the conversation. "You're not having second thoughts, are you?"

"A little late for that, wouldn't you say?"

"Maybe not. I could suggest an out-of-court settlement," Lloyd proposed.

"No!" Kirsten drew in a steadying breath. "This suit isn't about dollars and cents, Lloyd, you know that. It's not the money—"

"I know. It's the principle of the thing, right?"

"Right"

"Tell it to the jury."

"I intend to. And I'm sure Ferguson will see to it that they don't believe me." She sighed.

"He's back in Portland, you know."

Kirsten's heart stopped and she had to lean against the wall for support. Dane was back! "No… No, I didn't."

"I thought he might have called you."

If only he had! Kirsten couldn't prevent the tears from forming in her eyes. "Why?"

"Because I ran into him—at the courthouse. I think he was waiting for Fletcher Ross. Anyway, I gave him a piece of my mind about talking to you without my presence, told him I might move for a mistrial."

"What did he say?" Kirsten asked breathlessly.

"He called my bluff, told me to go ahead."

"And are you?"

"Of course not. We've waited long enough as it is. Putting off the trial would only weaken our position. Right now, public sentiment is with you, but in six months, who knows? The public isn't known for its loyalty or memory."

"I see."

She heard Lloyd draw in a long breath. "What I hope you see, Kirsten, is that you can't talk to Ferguson, Ross, Becker or any of the lot unless I'm with you. This case is as important to me as it is to you, and I'm warning you not to do anything that might blow it."

"I understand," she whispered, knowing exactly what Lloyd meant. If Lloyd Grady should win against Dane Ferguson, it would be an important feather in his cap. With the national news coverage, Lloyd's fame in legal circles would be guaranteed and his new prestige would in turn bring him wealthier clients and more interesting cases. This was Lloyd's shot at the big time.

"We both have a lot at stake," Kirsten agreed.

"I'm glad you realize that. For a while I thought that you'd forgotten." His voice was filled with relief. "Then, let's go for it. I'll give you a call if anything comes up. Oh, have you heard any more about the job in San Francisco?"

"Not yet, but I've got my fingers crossed," she replied, her eyes drifting to the résumé stacked on the desktop.

"Good-bye."

Kirsten hung up the receiver with trembling fingers. The tears that had pooled in her eyes began to run down her face. "What am I doing?" she asked herself as she wiped her eyes with her fingertips, but vivid images of Dane assaulted her mind and continued to haunt her. "Why can't I hate him?"

Because I love him, she thought with a wry grimace. *I love him more than any woman should love a man.* Acknowledging this was more of a burden than she could bear and she had to find a way to rid herself of the torturous thoughts of Dane.

Without much enthusiasm she changed into her running shorts, a cotton T-shirt and her Nikes before dashing out of the house. As soon as she descended the weathered steps and her feet hit the beach, she took off, forcing herself to run northward. A cool breeze greeted her, but she bent her head against the wind and established her pace.

The run took nearly an hour and her muscles screamed against the abuse of seven miles when she finally returned to her starting point near the steps and stretched out her aching calves. Her hair was damp, as much from her sweat as the light mist that had begun to settle in the air. The dense gray clouds made it impossible to view the sun, which was probably settling behind the horizon.

Wearily, Kirsten trudged up the stairs, thinking of a hot shower and light dinner. She was exhausted, but at least the cobwebs that had gathered in her mind had disappeared and she could think clearly again.

She stopped her ascent before reaching the top step. Dane was waiting for her on the small landing from which the stairs angled down the cliff face. He stood on the weathered planks and leaned over the rail as he squinted against the wind.

Kirsten's heart twisted with inner agony when she recognized him. His dark hair caught in the wind and his brooding hazel eyes never left hers. Slowly, she finished the climb and silently braced herself against the magnetism in his eyes. Against the most feminine urges within her she told herself she had to avoid him—being with him was far too dangerous.

"What are you doing here?" she asked as she wiped her hands on her shorts and held his steady gaze.

"I came to see you."

"I thought I made myself clear the last time you were here."

"You weren't being honest with me or yourself."

"Look who's talking!" she blurted out.

"Kirsten, let's start over—"

"Forget it. I talked to my attorney. He's threatened to walk off the case if I make the mistake of talking to you without him." She managed to mask the turbulent emotions racing through her with the cool self-assurance she had assumed as an objective reporter in front of the news camera.

"He told me the same thing."

"Did he? Is that why you're here?" Her large green eyes narrowed as she stared up at him. "You'd like that, wouldn't you? If Lloyd dropped my case, it would certainly make it easier for you."

"The case has nothing to do with the reasons I came to see you," he stated, ignoring her taunts and the vibrant green anger sparking in her eyes.

"Save that for someone who'll believe it!"

"You believe it, Kirsten," he argued calmly as his dark eyes held her wrathful glare.

"I can't afford to believe anything you say." She attempted to walk past him, down the short path leading to the cabin but his fingers took hold of the crook in her arm.

"I just want to be with you for a while."

"Of course you do—so that you can pump me for information or snoop around my cabin and then go chase after clues. Look, Dane, I know that you went to *The Herald* and I know that you were trying to dig up some more information against me because of that article on Ginevra."

He seemed unperturbed as she challenged him. His square jaw remained rigid, but his eyes had softened as he gazed down at her. "I'm just trying to understand you."

She swallowed against the bitter taste of deception. "You're just trying to gather as much information against me as you can in order to prove that I'm a paranoid woman hell-bent to squeeze every last dime out of KPSC."

"I don't think that at all." His hazel eyes had clouded and his thick, dark brows drew together in an uncompromising scowl. She raised a doubtful eyebrow in disdain. "You're the most infuriating woman I've ever met," he muttered as he let go of her arm and pushed his hands into the pockets of his jeans.

"Maybe it's just the company I keep," she retorted. "If you'll excuse me—"

"I'd like to," he admitted. "Oh, lady, I wish I could just excuse you and leave you alone."

Her voice stumbled over the anger in her words. "Well, now's your big chance," she whispered.

"You're asking me to leave?" He stared at her intently, watching every trace of emotion evidenced in her confused green eyes.

Kirsten nodded mutely, the words never passing her lips. More than anything in the world she wanted Dane to stay with her and hold her in the security of his protective arms. But she couldn't.

"Why?" he asked.

"Because you scare me, damn it." Her voice quavered as she met his relentless gaze. "You scare the hell out of me, and I don't know how to deal with it."

"Because of who I am?"

She shook her head, fighting to keep the unwanted tears from pooling in her eyes. "Maybe," she murmured in a voice barely audible over the sound of the surf crashing against the sand. "I can't seem to forget that your mission is life is to try to prove that I'm nothing more than a chiseling employee bearing a grudge."

"Don't think of me as the attorney for the defense," he suggested.

"Oh, Dane." The pain in her eyes overshadowed her anger and managed to disguise her love. "Don't patronize me. I'm an intelligent woman and I know why you're here, why you're interested."

"You don't know a damned thing," he replied as he extracted his hands from the safety of his pockets to reach up and capture her shoulders. Warm fingertips caressed her skin and drew her body close to his. Lips, cooled by the cold sea air, touched hers tentatively.

She closed her eyes to reality. The response within her was immediate. A warm, uncoiling desire flooded her senses. The muscles that had previously ached were soothed as his lips pressed against hers. The scent of the sea mingled with the earthy male odor uniquely his. She sighed in despair when his lips drew away from hers.

"I've thought of nothing but you for the past two weeks," he admitted raggedly when he lifted his head from hers.

"I'll bet," she said.

"Shhh. It's not like that." His hazel eyes, filled with questions and pain, searched her face. "I wanted to be with you, not as opponents in the courtroom, but as a man to a woman."

"It's not that easy—"

"It's as easy as you make it," he whispered against her hair, and he held her gently to him. "I've wanted you, Kirsten, ached for you these past couple of weeks."

"But I haven't heard a word from you—you didn't call."

"Because that's the way I thought you wanted it." His arms tightened possessively against her back. "I knew that I couldn't… touch you over the phone… that I wouldn't be able to see into your eyes." His lips pressed soft kisses into her damp hair. "And I promised myself that I would look into those eyes again, not from across the courtroom, but here, alone, by the sea."

She felt her reservations melting, knew that her determination was crumbling with the power of his words. "It's not that I don't want to trust you," she admitted. "It's that I can't!"

He held her flushed face between his hands and forced her eyes to reach into the depths of his. "Let yourself go for just a little while."

"I did before… you used me."

The wind swirled restlessly around them, cooling the air as night began its imminent descent. Dane closed his eyes and held her as if he were afraid she might disappear. "I've done a lot of things I'm not proud of in my life, but you've got to believe that I've never abused you."

"Strong words—"

"The truth."

"What do you want from me?" she asked, giving into the raw female urges of her body.

He chuckled deep in his throat. "Nothing sinister, I assure you. I'd just like to take you to dinner."

She shook her head. "I don't think so. What if someone saw us? Not only would Lloyd quit the case, he'd probably skin me alive."

"He'll never know."

She smiled in spite of herself. "Already you're suggesting that I lie to my attorney."

"This has nothing to do with the lawsuit, remember?"

"Hmph." She eyed him suspiciously. "What if someone

from the press saw us together… maybe even managed to get a couple of pictures?"

"Who'd recognize us?"

"Let's start with Laura Snyder of *The Herald*." Kirsten pulled out of his embrace and started walking toward the house. "You're not exactly unknown," she pointed out when Dane caught up with her. "And for several years I was a reporter for local television. I'd say we should consider ourselves a highly visible twosome. Neither one of us can afford to be seen with the other." She kicked off her running shoes and unlocked the door before holding it open and silently inviting him inside.

"What are you suggesting—a clandestine rendezvous?" he asked with an inquisitive arch of one dark brow and a lazy half-smile.

"Isn't that what this is?"

He shrugged. "I offered to buy you dinner—"

"How about a raincheck—" she suggested, and then, realizing it would never happen, Kirsten sobered. "Let's not think about that." She closed the door behind him. "Just give me a minute to change and I'll scrounge something up in the kitchen."

She left him to his own devices and took a quick, scalding shower before stepping into a clean pair of jeans and an emerald green blouse. Her hair was still damp and she was rolling one of the sleeves of the blouse up when she stepped into the living room.

Dane was crouched before the fireplace and poking at the smoldering logs with a piece of kindling. His jeans pulled tightly across his buttocks ands strained against the muscles in his thighs. He had taken off his sweater, and through the thin fabric of a cotton shirt the muscles of his shoulders rippled as he worked.

He slid an appreciative eye in her direction. "You certainly don't dawdle," he said approvingly.

"Can't—not in my profession…or at least what used to be my profession."

The fire ignited, casting golden shadows into the room, and Dane stood, his eyes still appraising her as he dusted his hands on his jeans. "Are you giving up reporting?"

"Not exactly." The conversation was becoming too personal, wandering on forbidden territory, and Kirsten attempted to sidestep the issue.

Dane frowned thoughtfully. "You're a good reporter, Kirsten, you shouldn't give it up."

"That's a strange compliment considering the source."

Dane's scowl gave way to a slow-spreading smile that displayed the flash of nearly perfect white teeth. "I've seen several news clips—you knew your stuff." He cocked his head pensively. "A lady with a lot of class, savvy, intelligence and sexy enough to keep the audience interested." He chuckled at her stunned expression.

"That's what you think? Honestly? Or are you just trying to seduce me?"

"Perhaps a little of both," he admitted before turning his gaze from her face to look out the window at the dark sea. "By the way, it's not an opinion that I've spread around the office."

"I'll bet not." She warned herself that he might be disguising his true feelings; he was a master at ingratiating himself to a witness. But the honesty in his clear eyes made it difficult to doubt him. "I'd better start dinner," she said in an effort to change the course of the conversation.

He followed her into the kitchen, pulled out a chair, turned it around and straddled the seat while propping his arms and chin on the back. "Can I help?" he asked lazily.

She shook her head. "I think I'll do better on my own," she laughed, her eyes sparkling.

Content to watch her sprinkle lemon pepper on the steaks,

he didn't argue. Kirsten was efficient. After lighting the propane grill outside, she set the steaks over the coals and finished slicing red onions for the salad.

In a few minutes the meal was prepared and they were seated at the small table in the kitchen.

"Let me do the honors," Dane suggested as Kirsten reached into a seldom used cupboard and extracted an unopened bottle of Bordeaux she had been saving. He took the bottle, opened it and poured the wine while she lit the candles.

"Nice touch," he said, holding a chair for her.

"What? Oh, the candles? I thought they were appropriate for a…'clandestine rendezvous.'"

They managed to make small talk during the course of the meal, and the subject of the trial was carefully avoided. Kirsten learned a lot about Dane and found herself laughing at some of his more bizarre court cases.

"Do you like living in the city?" she asked, cutting a slice of French bread and offering it to him.

"There are advantages," he replied evasively. "At one time in my life I thought owning a practice in Manhattan would be all I could ever want." His eyes grew dark.

"But you changed your mind?"

"Some things in life are more important than money or fame," he observed, pushing his chair away from the table and cradling his wineglass in both hands. "I made the mistake of not realizing what was valuable in life a few years ago, and I'll never do it again." He smiled sadly before looking into her eyes. "Come on, let's go check on my fire…."

Once in the living room, she took a seat on the couch and curled her legs beneath her. He sat on the floor, content to stare into the glowing embers and drink his wine.

"Are you unhappy in New York?" she asked, wanting to know everything about him.

He shrugged and his shoulder brushed against her knee. "Not really."

"But not content?"

"Restless, I guess," he said. Setting down his glass, he turned to face her. "There are things I want in life—things I haven't found in the city." His eyes reached for hers and her breath caught in her throat as she gently touched his hair with her fingertips.

Dane closed his eyes as if in unbearable pain. His hand moved and slowly slid up the outside of her thigh, rubbing against the tight fabric of her jeans and creating a warm friction on her legs. He forced himself to swallow and open his eyes. "Being with you is very special," he whispered hoarsely.

"Because it's risky?" she challenged.

"Because you're the first woman I've met in a long while who's attracted me."

"Maybe it's because I'm the opponent," she ventured, her heart leaping wildly in her chest as his hands continued their upward assault on her body.

"Maybe it's because you're the most elegant woman I've ever met." It was a simple statement and it sounded honest. Kirsten had to look away from the intensity of his angled features. She set her wineglass on the table.

When his hands reached her arms he gently pulled her off the couch and caught her as she tumbled against him. Kirsten laughed and her thick brown hair cascaded around her face, framing her flushed cheeks and sparkling green eyes with softly tangled curls. Dan brushed a wayward honey-colored lock off her cheek before touching his lips to hers. The kiss as gentle and persuasive, catching Kirsten off guard.

"Let me love you," he insisted, his voice rough with the emotions tearing at him and the strain of his desire.

"If only you could," she replied, desperately hoping that she could believe, just for this onc magical night, that he loved her.

He let out a disgusted sigh and his jaw became rigid. "Oh, lady, if only you knew." His fingers twined in the thick strands of her hair. The fire's glow softened the dark corners of the room and the shadows in his eyes. When his lips found hers the kiss was demanding, and she sighed against the insistence of his supple tongue. Delicious warm feelings washed over her as he shifted and his tongue probed more deeply into the moist recess of her mouth.

Her heart pounded mercilessly in her chest, resounding in her eardrums. Tracing the lithe muscles beneath his shirt, Kirsten's fingers slowly caressed his back. She felt the tension in his spine and knew that he was suffering form the same primal urges that were taking charge of her body and mind.

Her skin became heated, her cheeks flushed and she returned the ardor of Dane's kiss with all the intensity of the fires of desire slowly consuming her.

"I've missed you," she whispered into the shell of his ear. "Oh, God, Dane, I've missed you."

His fingers toyed with the button on her jeans. When it slid through the hole, he tugged at the hem of her blouse, gently extricating the soft green fabric. She shivered when his hands touched the warm skin covering her abdomen and the tips of his fingers dipped seductively beneath the waistband of her jeans. Involuntarily her abdomen tightened, allowing room for him to touch her, inviting him to explore all of her.

His lips moved downward leaving a moist path in their wake. They caressed her cheeks, brushed against her neck and rested at the exposed hollow of her throat. His tongue rimmed the delicate bones at the base of her throat, gently probing the soft hollow and making the blood in Kirsten's veins pulse heatedly through her body. Her fingers tensed over his back and stroked him savagely, displaying the frustrated longing raging within her.

The lowest button of her blouse slipped through the hole.

Dane lowered his head and kissed the pliable skin covering her abdomen as he unbuttoned the next pearl in his path. The cool air touched her skin and his tongue moistened her flesh. His hands traveled upward and slowly, torturously, the blouse was removed to display the fullness of her breasts, straining upward, the taut dark nipples distended and waiting.

He shifted to look at her and his eyes traveled hungrily over her naked torso, which gleamed from the reflection of firelight on the thin sheen of perspiration covering her body. "Dear Lord, but you're incredible," he rasped and Kirsten could feel his despair cutting through the night.

When his fingers touched her breast she trembled in anticipation and moaned in contentment as his lips tugged gently on the nipple. His teeth teased her, tormenting her with a bittersweet pleasure akin to pain, and his hands slid down the smooth muscles of her back to settle beneath her jeans and ignite the womanly fires of desire smoldering within her.

"Let me stay with you tonight," he whispered, pulling her atop him and gently easing her jeans over her hips. "Let me stay and make love to you till dawn."

"It's more than I could hope for," she murmured, her passion blinding her to rational thought.

"Then promise me that there will be no regrets," he insisted, one gentle hand pressing against her back, forcing her to lay on him so that her breast filled his mouth.

"No regrets," she said, her throat dry, her heartbeat erratic. She felt the sweet pressure of his tongue and lips on her and she clung to him, reveling in the heat he inspired. While still wrapped in his embrace she helped him remove his clothes and slowly traced the swirling hairs around each of his nipples.

His hands forced her legs apart and he stroked her thighs, smoothing the lean muscles and preparing her for the rapturous moment he would claim her as his own.

"I love you, Kirsten," he promised as he slowly rotated her and forced her onto the faded carpet before the blood-red embers of the fire. The words spoken brought tears to her eyes, and when he pressed her legs apart with his knees, he felt her welcoming shudder of anticipation. "No regrets," he whispered, kissing a salty tear off her cheek and slowly entering her, bringing the union of her flesh to his in slow, powerful strokes of love that took her breath away and made her heart race.

The tempo increased and his breathing became as ragged as her own. The night became a sensual swirl of firelight and heat as their bodies melded to become one in a rush of liquid fire and shuddering surrender.

"Don't ever leave me," Kirsten cried in her moment of weakness.

"Never, dear one," he vowed as his body stiffened and the sweet pain of his weight crushed against her. "I'll always take care of you."

CHAPTER ELEVEN

Kirsten awoke early, just as the first golden rays of a beautiful July morning were streaming through the open window. A soft breeze gently rustled draperies and scented the bedroom with the tangy odor of the sea. Kirsten smiled to herself and stretched while remembering the passion-filled hours of the night before.

Dane was still asleep. One dark arm was stretched possessively over Kirsten's abdomen while the other dangled over the edge of the bed. His sharp features had tempered and the lines near the corners of his eyes had softened. The night's growth of his beard shadowed his chin, but his face was unworried in slumber. Tenderly, Kirsten brushed a wayward lock of sable-brown hair out of his eyes.

He groaned and turned his head into the pillow before shifting his weight and opening one wary eye against the bright sunlight invading the room. As Dane's eyes focused and he recognized Kirsten's intriguing green gaze, a drowsy half smile tugged at the corners of his mouth. "Good morning," he mumbled as he pushed his fingers through his hair. The arm over her abdomen tightened and he propped himself with his free hand. His smile broadened seductively as he gazed into the vibrant depths of her green eyes. "This could become a habit," he growled affectionately.

She laughed lightly and shook her head. "Unlikely, I'm afraid."

"You wouldn't want every morning to be like this one?" His thick brows rose dubiously as his eyes slid downward over the lavender sheet draped seductively over the curves of her body. His gaze lingered for a moment at the swell of her breasts, and one strong finger toyed with the smooth fabric stretched provocatively over her nipples.

"Logistics wouldn't allow it, counselor."

"You could move to New York—"

"Sure I could." She laughed. "And do what?"

"Newscasting—"

"Me and every other reporter in the country." She shook her head, but her eyes sparkled frivolously. "I'll take my chances here, thank you." The teasing smile with its wayward dimple sobered slightly as she stared into the incredible depths of his knowing eyes. Her voice became a whisper. "That is, if you leave me any chances."

The strong arm around her tightened and he softly kissed the thoughtful pout on her lips before brushing her hair away from her worried face. "I thought we weren't going to talk about the lawsuit—wasn't that part of the bargain? Your ground rules," he reminded her.

"I remember," she said, and avoided the contemplative look in his eyes by staring out the window to the sea. "You're so right, counselor," she agreed, forcing her infectious smile once again to her lips. Kirsten was determined to forget the lawsuit—if only for a little while. When she brought her attention back to his face, she smiled wickedly and threw back the covers, exposing his nude form. "What do you say about a run on the beach?"

He didn't seem to notice that he was lying uncovered. "Didn't you already do that?"

"That was yesterday."

He laughed at her spirit. "How about a walk? Humor me, I'm older than you."

Her eyes slid seductively down his body. "And not exactly

out of shape." She touched the lean muscles of his thighs and calves with her fingernail and watched him stiffen. "It's my guess that you jog every day in Central Park."

"That's the trouble with you reporters, always taking the facts and twisting them into a story."

"And lawyers are different, I suppose."

His eyebrows rose and his grin broadened. "You don't give up, do you?"

"Part of my on-the-job training."

His eyes narrowed to gleam devilishly as he rubbed his chin with his thumb. "Someone should teach you a lesson, you know."

"And let me just take a guess who'll volunteer for the job," she responded throatily, gazing at him through the thick sweep of gentle brown lashes.

"No job, Kirsten. A pleasure." In a lithe movement he hoisted his body upward and pinned her to the bed before she had the chance to argue or escape. His naked muscles moved suggestively over hers and the warm invitation in her eyes heated his blood. "A pleasure I could spend the rest of my life extracting from you."

"Promises, promises..." she teased.

The weight of his body combined with the feel of his supple muscles rippling sensually against hers, made her [illegible] the erotic depths of his hazel eyes [illegible] When his lips moist and aching for more of his sensual touch. His hand massaged each pliant mound as his tongue traveled from one delicious nipple to the next. Her back arched off the bed in readiness and he gently kissed her abdomen; her heart thundered in her chest with the agony of her need. Her fingers twined in the thick strands of his coarse hair when his tongue lapped leisurely upward, past her navel, between her breasts, against her collarbones to lick the sensitive skin of her ear.

"You're delightful," he murmured against her ear, "but addictive." Her skin tingled. "I don't think I can ever get enough of you."

"I hope not," she said raggedly.

When his lips returned to hers his fingers caught in her hair and he kissed her with a consuming passion that made her blood flow in molten rivulets throughout her body. She felt his knees move to position himself between her legs and she gasped when he entered her, savoring the sweet pleasure that his swift, sure strokes inspired.

She closed her eyes and emitted a sigh of pleasure as the heat pulsed through her body. His breathing was erratic and rapid when she felt the first bursting spasm of love overtake her. Reality blurred as the consuming tides of surrender rushed through her. Her throat was dry and hoarse when she called his name before letting her teeth sink into
muscles of his shoulder. The
on her lips,

"This is insane, you know," Kirsten ventured. The walk beside the sea had been sobering and the laughter and gaiety of her morning with Dane had already faded into a quiet, secret memory. They had breakfasted on sweet melon, muffins and hot coffee laced with brandy. Now, as she thought about the fated trial separating them, the morning happiness they had shared seemed a lifetime ago.

Kirsten slid a sidelong glance at Dane. A soft breeze blew his dark hair away from his face, displaying all too vividly the lines of concern creasing his forehead. His thoughts must have taken him unhappily back to reality, as had hers.

"We can't very well continue an affair without someone finding out about it," she thought aloud, her soft green gaze searching the horizon as if for an answer to her unwanted love for this man.

"Does that worry you?" he asked.

"Yes."

"Are you ashamed?" His voice as low, his hazel eyes troubled.

"Of course not—it's just the trial." She shook her head. "That damned trial."

"You could drop the case," he suggested with a shrug of his broad shoulders.

Her head snapped upward and her angry eyes drilled into his. "Is that what you want?"

"What I want isn't the question."

"This case is important to me, Dane, and I'm not about to give up on it now." Her voice was soft, but filled with resolve. "And if you think that you can come down here, jump into my bed and then talk me out of suing KPSC, you've got another think coming!"

"I wouldn't even want to try," he said. "It's just that the lawsuit isn't making much sense—at least not to me."

"Why not?" Her bright green eyes met his defensively.

"I can't buy the age-discrimination thing. I told you that before."

Her temper got the better of her and she stopped dead in her tracks to face him bitterly. "Then why don't you go work for KPSC? I'm sure you'd catch on very quickly."

"I talked to Aaron Becker."

"And you didn't get any straight answers," she surmised.

"I can't say for certain—"

"Of course you can't, you're an attorney—defending him and that station of his."

Dane smiled grimly. "I'll admit that he did seem to avoid some of the more sensitive issues."

"More sensitive issues? What's that supposed to mean? You're hedging, Dane, just like Aaron Becker," she charged, placing her hands resolutely on her hips.

"Maybe I am," he admitted. "It seems I've got myself caught in the middle—"

"Then let's not talk about it. I wouldn't want you to jeopardize the case, counselor," she bit out angrily. Pulling free from the protection of his arm, Kirsten started walking back to the cabin. Her small fists clenched at her sides and she was muttering under her breath. What did she expect from Dane? That he would believe anything she would say and take it as gospel? Attorneys didn't work that way, she reminded herself bitterly.

She was on the weathered stairs before she turned to see if Dane was following her. He wasn't. Standing where she had left him, Dane stared out to sea. There was something about his lone form staunchly watching the restless tide that disturbed Kirsten and twisted her heart. "Why you?" she whispered as she cast one final searching look at him. "Why not Lloyd Grady or anyone else? Why did I have to fall in love with you?" Finding no answers to her question, Kirsten started up the stairs.

DANE HAD CONSIDERED the fact that he might be defending the wrong side of the issue as far as the McQueen case was concerned. His determination was based on sound judgment and had little to do with the plaintiff. Or so he told himself as he watched the dark silhouette of a sip sliding silently across the distant horizon.

Harmon Smith's attitude along with the opinions voiced by Fletcher Ross and Aaron Becker reinforced Dane's fears that Kirsten was being abused and sacrificed for the sake of KPSC's reputation. The idea that Kirsten was being set up as a scapegoat sickened Dane and made his blood boil in anger and frustration. Despite his earlier promise to Harmon Smith, Dane knew he couldn't be a part of the character assassination of Kirsten McQueen.

The distant ship became a small speck on the blue expanse of sky and sea. Staring at the calm waters of the Pacific, Dane told himself that he shouldn't care what happened to Kirsten, that he shouldn't pursue the issue and that his entire career was on the line. Pushing his palms into the back pockets of his jeans, he kicked at a broken sand dollar and realized that he really didn't give a damn about his career or any hastily made promises to a man the likes of Smith.

If Smith were lying, as Dane suspected, Dane's career would suffer anyway and Dane had promised himself that he would never make the same naive error he had about the Stone Motor Company. He had come to Kirsten's cabin near Cape Lookout searching for the truth, and come hell or high water, he was determined to find it.

But he needed Kirsten's help. He had to get information from Kirsten, not trap her as he had originally planned, but discover the truth. He started to walk up the beach back to the cabin and smiled as he followed Kirsten's deeply etched footprints.

Lloyd Grady would refuse to help him—that much was

certain. The Portland attorney had insisted that Dane stay away from his client until the case had been tried. Dane didn't blame Lloyd—it was the same advice he would give his client, should the situation be reversed.

However, he had ignored Lloyd's warning and come to this lonely stretch of sand and sea to look for Kirsten. He had paid little attention to the fact that he might well be risking the entire suit by seeing Kirsten again, and had decided to let the cards fall where they may. He had been determined to see Kirsten and find out for himself what it was about Ginevra, Oregon, that bothered Harmon Smith and made him sweat.

Casting a final, rueful look at the sea, Dane strode across the final stretch of powdery sand. He climbed the staircase angling upward along the cliff and remembered the first time he had seen Kirsten on the news clip in Harmon Smith's office. From the minute he had stared at her incredible green eyes he had known that she wasn't the liar Harmon Smith had insisted she was.

KIRSTEN WAS SIPPING coffee and studying several neatly typed pages on her lap. Her reading glasses were perched on the end of her nose and she didn't look up when she heard Dane enter the cabin.

"Research?" he asked cautiously, still standing near the door. Kirsten wondered if he intended to escape.

"Um-hum. An article I plan to do on Ecola State Park—it's just a few miles north of here. Interesting place; good view of the ocean and lots of wildlife. Sea-lion and bird rookeries are located on off-shore rocks, and deer are supposed to roam through the park. Since this is for a nature magazine, it should be an inspiring article."

"Kirsten—"

She lifted her eyes to meet his disarming gaze. "What is it, Dane?" she asked, removing her glasses and her hostile manner.

"I think we should talk." He leaned against the door and observed her. Wearing little makeup and faded jeans, her hair unruly from the wind and her smile patiently frail, he decided she was the most beautiful woman he had ever known.

"There's nothing left to say." She sighed. "We've been over this all before, Dane." Her hands were trembling and she forced herself to take a long sip of coffee before she could trust herself to speak again. "Maybe you should leave now," she suggested.

"If that's what you really want." His voice was hoarse.

"It's a problem, isn't it? What I want, I mean. I'm not really sure myself anymore." She shook her head at the unfathomable thought and tears ran down her cheeks. "Me, the woman who knew just what she wanted in life and how to get it."

"But now you don't?"

Her smile was wistful and her eyes burned with unwanted tears. "Now I don't," she agreed. "And do you know why? It's because of you, damn it. You turn my head around, change my perspective, alter my objectivity. I know I shouldn't trust you, and I want to more desperately than I've wanted anything in my life." She sighed and her gaze became self-mocking. "The worst part of it is that I'm acting like a teenager."

She shook her head as if disgusted with herself. "I'm a thirty-five-year-old woman. In a few more months I'll be thirty-six. I always thought I had it together. Even through the pain of the divorce I knew I would find a way to survive. And I did. Somehow I managed to pull through." Her green eyes held his concerned gaze. "But with you it's different," she whispered, her voice catching. "I can't see any way of resolving this relationship, and sometimes I just want to sit down and cry my eyes out."

"But you don't let yourself," he guessed.

"I try not to. I'm not a child, Dane, and I don't want to act or feel like one."

"Is that what I do to you?"

"That and a whole lot more," she conceded wearily. "Would you like some coffee?"

He shook his head. "I can get it later." He noticed the tears in her eyes and her trembling fingers as she balanced the earthenware mug. "I've never meant to hurt you," he said, damning himself for the pain she was bearing.

"I know."

"I think I'm falling in love with you—"

"Don't!" She fought against the tears and held her hand out to forestall any vain promises. "Let's not complicate this with love," she whispered.

"I'm not a man to say things I don't mean." He leaned forward on his knees and clasped his hands in front of him. His features, angled and hard, were strained with the intent of his words. "I love you, Kirsten. You'll have to live with that whether you like it or not."

She shook her head, her honey-brown hair shimmering in the soft light with her denial. "I can't afford to love you, Dane, and I'd think you'd have the good sense to realize that the same is true for you." Tears glistened in her eyes and she apologetically brushed them away.

"Look at me," she demanded. "I'm a mess." His eyes, shadowed with an angry pain, held her gaze. "I'm a professional woman; I've seen things in my line of work that would make most men ill. And I could handle it! But here I am, crying like a baby, all because of my feelings for you."

"Because of the lawsuit."

"Because you're the attorney for the defense."

"Would it change things between us if I dropped the case?"

She was instantly wary and her eyes narrowed suspiciously. "Just like that?" she asked, snapping her fingers. "Why, Dane?"

"Because I'm not sure I believe the men I'm working for."

"Harmon Smith?"

"For starters. I think I'll throw in Fletcher Ross and Aaron Becker for good measure. As a matter of fact, the only person who seems to be telling me anything worthwhile is Frank Boswick, an assistant to Smith. Ever heard of him?"

Kirsten shook her head thoughtfully as Dane continued. "I don't even think you've leveled with me, Kirsten."

"I've answered all your questions."

"But you've evaded some as well—especially about this Ginevra thing. Frank Boswick seems to think Ginevra's the reason you were fired from KPSC. Is that so?"

Kirsten hesitated. "I—I don't know if we should be talking about this."

"You can trust me."

"I don't know—"

Abruptly he stood up, walked over to her, took the cup from her hands and placed his hands on her shoulders. "Lady, you're stuck with me. One way or another I'm going to find out about all of this, not just because of that damned lawsuit, but because I want to help you!"

"By defending Harmon Smith and Aaron Becker!"

His fingers tightened over her shoulders and the gleam in his eye became perilous. He started to shake some sense into her and stopped. "You haven't heard a word I've said." Her green eyes studied the honesty in his gaze. "I love you," he vowed, his voice thick.

Kirsten's hard exterior cracked and the tears threatening all morning began to spill. "But you're working for Smith—"

"Blast it, woman! Let me help you. Just answer my questions honestly. We can deal with Smith later."

"I don't know," she whispered, her voice faltering, her heart twisting in agony.

His fingers gentled and he pulled her to him. Strong arms surrounded her and he kissed the top of her head tenderly.

Kirsten softened against him and let her knees grow weak. She could feel Dane's strength surrounding her; hear the rhythmic beating of his heart.

"What do you want to know?" she whispered quietly.

"Everything."

CHAPTER TWELVE

"LET'S START WITH Ginevra," Dane suggested, sitting on the corner of the couch and taking a long swallow of his coffee. Kirsten was huddled on the opposite end of the sofa and her chin was resting on her knees. "Why do you think everyone's so touchy about it?"

Kirsten shook her head and her lips compressed into a thoughtful pout. "Good question, counselor. I don't really know much about Ginevra other than it's the proposed site for the next nuclear power plant in Oregon. There's lots of controversy, largely because of the failure of the Washington Public Power Supply System and all the national attention given to the pros and cons of nuclear power."

"Has the site been approved?"

"All the preliminary paperwork has been done, but there hasn't been an official announcement. At least not yet."

In the ensuing silence Dane finished his coffee, set the cup aside and tossed Kirsten's story over in his mind. "Aaron Becker didn't want you to cover the story?"

"He didn't want me near it."

"Surely the station had to give it some attention."

"Oh, they did. KPSC did a series of two minute reports on Ginevra one week." Dane's jaw tensed as if he had discovered an inconsistency in her story. Kirsten felt a moment of remorse. Maybe, after all, he was just looking for a way to trap her in the courtroom. "Anyway, all the reports ended up to be very shallow interviews of local people. You know, 'How do you, Mrs. Ginevra Homemaker, feel about construction of the site? Couldn't this be the economic boom the town needs? Wouldn't it give all of the unemployed citizens a chance to get back to work?'"

"You think that the reports were slanted, to give the public a positive view of Ginevra as the potential site."

"I don't know. It just seemed strange to me that with all the controversy over nuclear power, nothing negative was ever cast from KPSC, at least as far as I know."

"So you wanted to do an in-depth study on Ginevra, report the negative aspects as well as the positive."

"Right." Kirsten smiled bitterly and her green eyes widened with indignation as she remembered the tense moment when she had asked for the assignment and Aaron Becker had at first paled and then had laughed outright. "Forget it, sweetheart," Becker had commanded, still chuckling in nervous amusement. "You're better off covering that bake-off in St. Johns. Stick to things you understand." Kirsten's blood had boiled and she had left Aaron Becker's office determined to report on something more pressing than a local cooking contest.

"And Becker refused to let you report on it."

"That's putting it mildly." Kirsten's legs were crossed and her left foot bounced in agitation.

"But there were other stories you wanted to cover and were denied—other than Ginevra, that is?"

"Yes." Kirsten sighed wearily. "After I started asking about Ginevra, everything else I wanted to do was given to someone else."

"Someone younger?"

"Most of the time."

"But usually male," Dane guessed, and he noticed the spark of anger lighting Kirsten's eyes.

"This is not a sex-discrimination suit," she reminded him. "The reason that most of the stories were given to men is that most of the reporters for KPSC are men."

"So that brings us to the age-discrimination suit," Dane remarked, watching Kirsten's reaction. She held her head high, her chin tilted regally.

"I guess it does."

He settled back in the corner of the couch and studied her with undisguised interest. "Tell me about it."

Kirsten hesitated only slightly. "Nothing so out of the ordinary I guess. I'd been getting in some hot water with Aaron about the other stories I wanted to cover. I wanted to do something a little meatier than covering the selection of the Rose Festival court or the remodeling of the Grand theatre."

"Or the bake-off in St. Johns?"

Kirsten was forced to laugh, "Uh-huh. Until I started making noise about different stories, Aaron seemed satisfied with my work, but once I started asking for more interesting assignments, Aaron became sullen and started nitpicking everything I did."

"So what does this have to do with age discrimination?" Dane inquired.

Kirsten took in a long, steadying breath. Until this point everything she had told Dane was fact. Now she was going into nebulous territory: part fact, part conjecture on her part. "I was sure that Aaron was trying to phase me out of my job."

"How?" Dane's hazel eyes sharpened; he sensed her unease.

Kirsten stared into the bottom of her empty cup. "I'd seen it happen before, when a woman reporter became a little too old or outspoken to suit Aaron's tastes."

"So sexual discrimination was involved."

"To some extent, yes," Kirsten admitted. "Aaron preferred

younger women in front of the camera, women who looked as good on film as they did in his bed."

"Do you know what you're suggesting?" Dane asked, his voice low and his brooding eyes narrowing suspiciously.

"I know exactly what I'm saying," she assured him, her finely sculpted jaw elevating slightly.

Dane studied her dubiously and Kirsten knew that he was reassessing her. She knew she was beginning to sound like some of the gossiping women she detested, but she felt that Dane had to understand her position. If she were ever going to make him believe her, Kirsten had to tell him everything she knew. If he used it against her later—well, she would have to deal with his betrayal of confidence then.

"He expected you to sleep with him?" Dane's eyes darkened perilously.

The corners of Kirsten's mouth quirked. "It would have helped me with my job." The look of fire in Dane's hazel eyes made Kirsten's blood run cold. "Don't get me wrong. I didn't mean to imply that every woman who worked at KPSC slept with Aaron Becker. That's not the case."

"I wouldn't think so," he said, his temper barely restrained. Why did the thought of any man touching Kirsten make his jaw tighten and his fists clench? Dane wasn't a savage man by nature, but there was something about Kirsten that made him want to protect her from anything and anyone to the point of ruthlessness. "What about you?"

"I'd like to tell you that it's none of your business, counselor, and you can bet that if you ask me these questions on the witness stand, I will." The conversation was becoming more dangerous by the minute.

"But it is my business," he reminded her angrily.

Her clear green eyes didn't flinch under his wrathful stare. "I haven't slept with a man since my divorce—until you. I'm not comfortable with the idea of casual sex."

"I know that. I just find it hard to believe that you got away so unscathed—if Aaron Becker is the lech you say he is."

"Then you should know that I would never allow Aaron Becker, or any other man I work with, to touch me. Aaron was my boss. We had a professional relationship, nothing more."

"Not from any lack of want on his part, I'll wager," Dane decided as he rubbed his shoulders and tried to dissolve the tension from the muscles at the base of his neck.

"He made a couple of passes at me, if that's what you mean. During my separation and divorce from Kent."

Dane's hand stopped massaging his neck and his eyes grew deadly dark. "But you managed to deter him?" Dane sounded skeptical and his back teeth crushed together at the vivid scene in his mind.

"I've had a lot of practice," she admitted, taking her eyes away from him for a moment and setting her empty cup on the table. "Aaron got the message that I wasn't interested, and after a while he left me alone—that is until I turned thirty-five and started asking questions about Ginevra."

"Then he fired you." Dane's voice was flat, hiding the rage and indignation burning in his chest.

"That's about the size of it."

When Dane considered the ego of Aaron Becker, his jaw tightened and his back became rigid with tension. Dane remembered the interview with Becker where the man had insinuated that Kirsten had thrown herself at him wanting sexual favors.

"So what are you going to do now?" he asked, forcing his voice to remain even.

"Other than the lawsuit?" Kirsten asked. Dane nodded mutely, his eyes never leaving her face. "I'm looking for another job."

"In Portland?"

"Are you kidding? With all the publicity of the lawsuit, I don't have a prayer of getting hired in Portland. Or Seattle either." She looked at the ceiling. "I've sent résumés to several stations in San Francisco and L.A., but so far I haven't had any response. It's getting to be a problem though," she admitted thinking of her dwindling savings account. "Man does not live on free-lance alone, you know."

"But you won't consider New York."

She shook her head, but smiled fondly at him. "I think I'm better off here—away from you." She couldn't lie to him, as much as she would have liked to. What could be more pleasant than living near Dane, being with him?

"Are you serious?" he asked.

"Think about it, Dane. We've been kidding ourselves. How long can we continue to see each other?"

"As long as we like."

She closed her eyes and her heart twisted painfully. "We can't forget about the lawsuit. It's always there. We can't even be seen in public together."

"Look, Kirsten, there's no reason to keep rehashing this," he stated as he stood and stretched his weary muscles. "You're right. The lawsuit is a problem and it can't be resolved—not here, not today. But let's try to push it aside for just a little while, until we can sort everything out." He leaned over and gently pulled her to her feet. His eyes probed into hers as he drew her into the powerful circle of his arms. With a tenderness that warmed the deepest part of her, Dane kissed her forehead. "You worry too much," he whispered.

"Maybe because my entire future is on the line."

"Come on, let's go to dinner—"

"But we can't be seen together," Kirsten protested softly, her lips touching his shirt.

"We won't," he assured her with a devilish twinkle in his eye.

She tried to extricate herself from the comforting manacle

of his arms and eyed him with dubious interest. "Just what have you got in mind, counselor?"

"Something different. Hurry up." Without any further explanation the powerful arms released her and Dane reached for her jacket hanging on the hall coat-tree and tossed it to her.

"Where are we going?" she asked with undisguised interest. "Should I change?"

"You look great." To add emphasis to his words, his eyes slid seductively down her body. "And if we don't get going soon, I might be inclined to spend the rest of the afternoon here—in bed."

"Why the mystery, counselor?" she asked as she threw her jacket over her arm and walked through the door that he held open for her.

"Keeps you interested. Admit it."

She shook her head and laughed. "Life is anything but dull when you're around," she conceded. "I just hope you know what you're doing."

"Always." He opened the door of the rental car, and when she slid into the seat he shut it again. She watched him walk around the front of the car and take the driver's seat. With a roar the engine sparked to life and Dane put the car in gear. "There's something very macho about spiriting a beautiful woman to an unknown destination, don't you think?"

Her only response was a ripple of carefree laughter.

DEPOE BAY WAS crawling with tourists who had come to the unique coastal town. The business district of the small, bustling city was perched on the cliffs overlooking the rock-bound bay that slashed inland from the broad expanse of Pacific Ocean.

"You're out of your mind," Kirsten accused him when she understood what Dane was planning.

"And you're paranoid." He parked the car and opened the door. "Do you really think any of these people"—he motioned to the crowd of brightly dressed tourists leisurely walking on the sidewalk along Highway 101—"would recognize you?"

"I'm not about to take the chance!"

Just then the spray from the Spouting Horn, a gap in the rocks through which the tide raced upward in a geyserlike spray near the sidewalk, plumed into the air. Everyone on the street stopped to view the spectacle.

"I think you're safe," Dane commented dryly as he viewed the townspeople and tourists with interest.

He slammed the car door shut and disappeared into a local fresh seafood stand. He was back within minutes carrying a white sack filled with delicacies. After placing the bag in the backseat, he slid into the driver's seat once again and drove to a less public parking lot.

When the car stopped, Kirsten turned to face him. "You rented a boat, didn't you?"

His lazy smile gave him away.

"Do you know how to operate one?" she asked.

"Don't you?"

"Of course, but—"

"Then let's go."

He opened the car door, but she placed a staying hand on his arm. "Dane… why?"

His eyes sobered. "I wanted to be alone with you, Kirsten, but I don't like the idea of hiding. I thought we could spend a little time enjoying ourselves instead of always arguing and brooding about the lawsuit." His fingers touched the elegant line of her jaw. "Come on." Her pulse raced at the tender gesture and she slid out of the car.

The boat was moored in the bay. To get to the gleaming white vessel Kirsten and Dane had to walk down a bleached wooden staircase that led from the small town poised on the top of the cliff to the dark waters of the bay. The stairs were located near the bridge spanning Depoe Bay and as Kirsten walked toward the moorage she noticed barnacles clinging to the pilings supporting the bridge.

The boat was small but seaworthy, and Dane maneuvered the tiny craft through the fishing vessels and pleasure boats that clogged the small body of water. Once under the bridge and out of the crowded waters of the bay, Dane headed north.

"I thought you didn't know how to handle a boat," Kirsten accused him, her voice barely heard over the roar of the engine.

"I didn't say that. I just wanted to be sure you had your sea legs on you."

"But—I thought—I mean, you live in the city, for God's sake."

"We have an ocean on that side of the continent, too, you know," he stated with a mocking smile and wicked gleam in his eyes. After twenty minutes he cut the engine and let the boat drift on the sea. "There are a lot of things that you don't know about me."

"Such as?"

"Such as the fact that I grew up in a fishing village on Cape Cod."

Kirsten withdrew the food from the white sack and handed Dane a plastic carton filled with Dungeness crabmeat and tangy cocktail sauce. They ate without breaking the silence. The sea was calm and the small craft rocked gently on the water. The afternoon would have been hot except for the slight breeze moving gently over the water. To the west, dark clouds were drifting toward the shore and threatened to destroy the late afternoon sun. Kirsten stared at the rugged Oregon coastline in the distance. The jagged cliffs and sandy beaches appeared smoky-blue through the slight haze that had begun to settle on the sea.

"You're right," she said after a thoughtful silence.

"About what?" Dane's smile was engaging. It touched the darkest corners of her soul.

"I don't know much about you." Taking a drink of the cool white wine Dane had purchased, Kirsten leaned back and squinted against the ever-lowering sun. "On the other hand, you know everything about me, don't you?"

He finished his food and wiped his hands together. The wind caught in his hair and ruffled the coffee-colored strands. "I've been briefed, if that's what you mean."

"And you've read employee records, my original résumé and any other pertinent piece of information Aaron Becker and Fletcher Ross gave you. Besides which, I'll bet you did some digging on your own."

"A little," he conceded begrudgingly. And then, as if to change the difficult subject, his eyes scanned the darkening horizon. "We'd better head in; looks like we're in for a summer storm."

He had unbuttoned his shirt in an effort to stay cool, and Kirsten watched the supple movement of his muscles as he restarted the engine and headed the small boat inland. "You've got me at a disadvantage," she persisted, loud enough to be heard over the rapidly pulsing engine.

"I doubt that, Kirsten," he muttered, his eyes clouding. "I'd like to believe it, but I don't. Not for a minute."

She eyed him lazily and smiled to herself as she watched him guide the gently rocking craft back to its moorage in Depoe Bay. He's a handsome man, she decided, watching the jut of his square jaw and the narrowed eyes as he studied the water. His dark hair had only a few traces of gray and his lean physique was trim and well muscled. He looked at home behind the wheel of the boat, with the wind in his face and his shirttails fluttering behind him. It was hard to imagine that he was a famous New York attorney whose job it was to discredit her. Not only was he handsome, he was shrewd as well. Shrewd enough to know exactly how to read a woman.

Dane noticed the furrow of Kirsten's brow. "What are you thinking about?" he called over his shoulder.

"Nothing," she replied, lifting her shoulders.

"You're a lousy liar, Kirsten McQueen."

"Am I? Good."

He looked at her quizzically.

"Then you'll know that I'm telling the truth when we meet in the courtroom."

His lips thinned and he turned away from her to stare back at the prow of the boat knifing through the water and study the passage back to the bay.

THE DRIVE BACK to the cabin had been accomplished in silence. Dane hadn't responded to her barb about the courtroom and Kirsten didn't blame him. But how could he expect her to ignore the fact that the lawsuit existed? As each day drew to a close, the impending courtroom battle loomed nearer.

Dane had gone for a solitary soul-searching walk on the beach, leaving Kirsten to stay at the cabin. She told herself that it was time to analyze her relationship with Dane. She had to clear her mind and set her roiling emotions in some sort of order. How long could they continue to ignore the fact that they would meet in the courtroom and at that point be at each other's throat? Until September tenth?

She slammed her fist on the bureau top and gazed wearily into the mirror. How could she love a man so feverishly and still not be able to trust his motives? Her tired reflection had no answers.

The evening was hot and muggy. The dense air was filled with the promise of summer rain, which would be welcome relief to the sticky humidity.

Kirsten showered and changed into a sundress and sandals.

She waited for Dane to return, and after an hour she began to worry. What was taking him so long to return? Had he been that angry with her?

Anxiously her worried eyes scanned the beach, but the sun had set and it was rapidly growing dark. Though squinting at the silvery sand, she could see no sign of him. Desperately, her eyes searched the gathering darkness, hoping to see some trace of the man she loved so futilely.

"Damn it, counselor," she muttered as she hurried out the front door and down the path leading to the steps along the cliff face. When she got to the landing of the staircase her eyes again scanned the long stretch of white sand and noted the storm clouds rolling ominously off the sea.

With one hand on the rail to balance her she raced down the stairs and started running the minute her feet hit the sand. His footprints led south. She followed them and her concerned eyes scanned the darkness. "Where the devil are you?" she asked the rising wind.

She had run for nearly a mile when she saw Dane retracing his steps. Relief, like a welcome rain, showered her as she stopped to catch her breath and wait for him.

When he was close enough to hear her she ran to him and fell into his open arms, saying, "I was a worried sick. Where have you been?"

"Walking, thinking." His arms held her tightly against him. "I thought you were angry." Storm clouds rumbled threateningly and the wind gusted around them.

She shook her head and felt the first welcome drops of rain run down the back of her neck. "Just concerned, that's all," she whispered. As she looked up she could read the sorrow in his eyes. "I just don't know where all this will lead us," she admitted. "It worries me."

"You think I'm using you," he charged, defeat evidenced in his words and that tired slump of his shoulders.

"No, but I can't help but wonder what will happen once we're on opposite sides of the courtroom."

He pushed a weary hand through his hair. "Maybe it won't go that far—"

She stopped dead in her tracks. "I'm not giving up the lawsuit."

"Is it that important to you?"

"Yes." Couldn't he understand, feel her rage? Did he expect her to suffer those indignities in silence—alone?

"More important than—"

"Don't, Dane. Don't even compare what I feel for you to what I have to do. It's not fair." Her voice was trembling from the depth of her feelings and she shivered as if she were suddenly chilled. Tears threatened her eyes and her throat felt uncomfortably tight.

"It's just that I don't want to lose you," he whispered, clinging desperately to her. "I have this incredible fear that when the dust has settled and the lawsuit is over I won't see you again."

She smiled upward at him. "I thought you were the one who didn't want to worry about the future."

"Is that what I said?" She nodded and he kissed the top of her head. His warm breath caught in her hair. "I must be more of a fool than I thought."

She studied the lines of his face and noticed the agony shadowed in the depths of his eyes. Dread caught in her throat. "What's this all about, Dane?"

He shrugged but wasn't released from the weight of his burden. "A lot of things, I suppose. You, me, the lawsuit, Harmon Smith." His lips drew into a disgusted frown. "Especially Smith."

"Why would you let a man like Smith bother you?" Kirsten asked. "You act as if he owns you."

"Maybe he does," was the gruff reply.

"You can't be serious." Her comment was meant as a light attempt at humor, but the darkness in Dane's face and the tightness of his skin stretched over his cheekbones indicated that his relationship with Smith was more involved than the usual one between client and attorney.

Dane released her suddenly and began walking back toward the cabin. His strides were long and determined. "What do you mean?" Kirsten asked, nearly running to keep up with him.

"I owe Smith a favor—a big favor," Dane replied, stomping angrily toward the stairs. "And it's payoff time."

"Payoff? Dane? I don't get it—" But just as the words were out of her mouth, Kirsten began to understand. The lawsuit against her! That was the payoff. The cold-bloodedness of the situation hit her like a blast of arctic air. "Wait a minute," she called, but he was already to the stairs. She had to run to catch up to him. Her sandals caught on a buried piece of driftwood and she stumbled but she managed to catch herself.

Dane was already climbing the stairs. He heard her gasp and turned to face the noise.

Kirsten's throat was dry and tears began forming in her eyes. Rain from the heavens began to fall in earnest and she could feel the cool drops run down her bare back. She caught him and clutched his arm.

"What do you mean?" she choked out. "Don't tell me that you took this case to settle an old debt!"

He looked down at her with self-condemning eyes. "Would that surprise you, Kirsten?"

"I just hoped that you took the case because you wanted to and that once you found out the truth, you would drop it and—"

"Leave you alone?" he charged, his voice loud enough to be heard over the pounding surf and the rising wind. "Is that what you wanted?" His jaw was clamped rigidly, his mouth compressed into a thin, wrathful line.

He braced himself on the railing and pushed his face nearer to hers. "Then what about the seduction, Kirsten? Was that all for a quick thrill too? Or was it part of the plan? Did you intend to take me to your bed and then just let me go as soon as the case was resolved?"

"I didn't plan it at all. It just happened. Dear God, Dane, the last thing I wanted was to fall in love with you!" Her clear green eyes were filled with the honesty and pain of her confession.

He looked up to the dark sky as if asking for divine intervention. Warm rain slid down the collar of his shirt. "Dear God, woman," he whispered, reaching his hand down toward her. It was shaking but she took it and allowed him to help her up the stairs. Breathlessly he wrapped his arms around her and kissed the raindrops off the crook of her neck.

"I'm sorry, Kirsten," he whispered against her ear. He squeezed his eyes shut as if in physical agony. "The last thing I ever want to do is hurt you..." His lips claimed hers in a kiss filled with promise and pain. "I love you, Kirsten," he vowed. "More than you'll ever know."

"And I love you," she vowed, holding on to him as if for dear life. "I didn't mean to get angry..."

"Shhh... It's all right." He kissed her on the forehead and then wiped the tears from her eyes. "I think I should tell you about Julie."

"Your wife?" she asked weakly.

"That's right." His voice was raw with unnamed emotions. "Maybe then you'll understand why I have to repay Harmon Smith."

Her heart thundered erratically in her chest, and she had to swallow against the dread forming in her throat. Silently, she let Dane drape his arm over her shoulders before easing her to the ground. His lips whispered against the nape of her neck.

"Don't, Dane," she whispered, the blood within her beginning to warm. "You don't have to say anything. Just make love to me and never stop."

Ignoring the cool wind and the sultry rain, he untied the thin straps holding the lavender sundress in place. The body of the dress fell downward, exposing each of her rosy-tipped breasts.

"You're so lovely," he breathed, touching each nipple gently with his lips before burying his face in the folds of her skirt. "So lovely." Through the thin fabric his warm breath brushed against her legs and made her quake with the need of him.

"I didn't want to love you," he said, his hands sliding suggestively up her legs.

"Nor I you," she murmured huskily.

The raindrops began to filter from the sky in increased numbers. Her hair, dress and naked breasts were moist, and his hands slid easily against her skin.

Each breast was touched, kissed and sucked until the slowly spreading fire within her began to grow white hot. It was as if the more she had of this man, the more she wanted. Her need was all-consuming.

Her hands slowly removed his clothes and her eyes cradled every inch of his lean, rippling muscles. She cradled his head in her hands and offered him her breasts. He took first one and then the other into the warm moist recess of his mouth.

Kirsten sighed into the wind and felt as if she and Dane were the only two people in the universe. His hands traced her spinal column and splayed across the small of her back, gently encouraging her body more closely to his.

The warmth within her began to ache and she strained against him, hungry for him to fill that final, primal void within her.

Dane shifted and she felt the cool moist sand beneath her back. He straddled her and stared down at her, content for the moment to study every graceful line of her body. One shaking hand caressed a breast and she shuddered in anticipation before arching her body off the ground and crying out his name.

Slowly he came to her, gently parting her legs and finding the warm moist center of her womanhood. She moaned as he found her and reached up to hold him against her.

They moved as one, each offering pleasure and comfort to the other. Kirsten felt the fire and intensity build as the tempo increased, and when the final, shattering moment came, Dane whispered her name into the cool black night.

CHAPTER THIRTEEN

BY THE TIME THEY entered the cabin both Kirsten and Dane were soaked to the skin. The tension in the air had dissipated and Kirsten managed to laugh at the sorry sight they made in wet, bedraggled clothes.

While Dane heated the coffce and laced it with a touch of brandy, Kirsten changed into dry clothes. When she came back into the living room, a fire was crackling merrily in the fireplace. "It's too warm for a fire," she complained with a twinkle in her green eyes.

"Never." He had been kneeling on the hearth, but stood and dusted off his hands when she entered the room. His hair was still damp, and the firelight brightened the rich sable color to a sheen of gold. "When you've lived without the convenience of a fireplace for as long as I have, you learn to appreciate the smell of burning wood and the intense heat against the back of your legs."

"But it's the end of July—"

"And less than sixty degrees, unless I miss my guess."

She offered him a towel for his hair, which he refused; instead, he captured her wrist and pulled her against his wet body.

"Wait a minute," she protested with a merry laugh. "What do you think you're doing? I just changed."

"And you look great." He seemed to revel in her distress, and cared nothing about the fact that her crisp blouse and cords were becoming as wet as the clothes she had just thrown into the hamper.

"Dane—" she said weakly, but her words were lost in her throat when he kissed the exposed column of her neck, nibbling erotically below her ear. "You're wicked, you know," she moaned as her eyes closed.

"And you love it." His arms slowly released her and she felt oddly alone without his comforting touch. After bending to retrieve the towel, which had slipped to the floor into a fluffy blue mound, he dried his neck and hair.

"Anima," she muttered with a provocative grin.

"You wouldn't have it any other way, lady," he returned, snapping the towel against her backside.

"Oh, yes, I would," she whispered, suddenly uncomfortable. Her clear green eyes probed into the hazel depths of his seductive gaze.

"What would you change?" He handed her a mug of steaming coffee and took one for himself before bracing one shoulder against the mantle and eyeing her with undisguised interest.

"For starters…"

He held up his hand to cut off her response. "Oh yes, I know. The lawsuit." Shaking his head as if bewildered at the predicament of his life, he took in a long breath. "That's something we can't change—at least not now."

"So here we are, back where we started. Every time we start this conversation we end up at a stalemate." She tapped her fingers restlessly on the ceramic mug before frowning in frustration and dropping into the corner of the couch. Tucking her shoeless feet under her, she took a long sip of the warm liquid and felt it slide soothingly down her throat.

"Maybe we should try talking about something else." The smile on his face had grown tight, his voice low.

"Such as?" Her cloudy green eyes searched his.

"The reason I took on this case in the first place. It has to do with Harmon Smith and my wife."

Kirsten took in a shuddering breath. A mounting sense of dread crawled coldly up her spine. Talking about Harmon Smith made her uneasy and she wasn't sure that she wanted to hear about Dane's wife—a woman he had loved deeply. "Look, Dane, you don't have to tell me anything you don't want to. I don't expect any wild confessions from you… and it's not necessary to dredge up—"

"I think it is. There are things you should know."

He stared into the black depths of his cup as he collected his thoughts. Kirsten backed into the corner of the couch, bracing herself for what was to come.

"I met Julie in college," Dane announced, his voice soft and tortured. A wistful smile curved his lips, but his eyes remained dark and expressionless. "We went together for a couple of years, lived together and finally got married when I graduated from law school."

"You loved her very much," Kirsten surmised, witnessing the pain shadowing his sharp gaze.

Dane nodded. It was a slight movement, nearly imperceptible, but it acknowledged the depth of his feelings for his deceased wife. Kirsten felt as if a knife had been thrust into her heart and cruelly twisted.

"We were very happy. After a few years Sam came along." Dane took his gaze away from hers and looked out the window before quietly clearing his throat.

"I was foolish, young and thought I had the world in my pocket. My practice was flourishing upstate and I'd had a couple of offers to join an established firm in Manhattan. My biggest accomplishment was defining the Stone Motor Company and the Zircon. I suppose you read about that?"

Kirsten smiled wanly and nodded.

Dropping his head into his hand, Dane slowly massaged a throbbing temple.

Kirsten remained silent, knowing that Dane was offering her a glimpse of a part of his life he rarely exposed and preferred to keep buried.

"The Stone Motor decision was a real feather in my cap," he stated as his lips thinned menacingly. "There was lots of national attention to the case and several firms in the city wanted me to come work for them. The offers were very attractive. Full partnerships in some of the most prestigious firms in the country." When he raised his angry, self-mocking gaze to hers, Kirsten felt herself bleed for this man who had borne so much pain. Unwanted tears burned behind her eyelids.

Kirsten studied the lines of his face. It remained emotionless, other than those two glowing, angry eyes. She sensed that Dane had practiced hiding a past that was too ugly to remember.

"I thought I was on my way—" He shook his head as if to wipe away the distasteful thought. "That's the problem with youth, you feel that you're immortal, for God's sake."

He chewed thoughtfully on his lower lip and when he spoke his voice was hoarse. "And Julie… she was behind me every step of the way." Kirsten's stomach knotted painfully as she watched the agony in his eyes.

"Anyway, one day, when I was working at the office, Sam got sick. It was snowing and there was ice all over the roads. Julie called, and I told her to wait, that I'd be home in a couple of hours. She didn't—I don't know why, but I suppose that maybe Sam got worse." His voice faltered for a minute. "She was always worried about him because he wasn't very healthy.

"Since I had the Bronco she had to take the Zircon. She'd driven about five miles before she hit a patch of ice. The car slid sideways and rolled down an embankment." He hesitated, took a long swallow from his cup and closed his eyes, squeezing the eyelids. "Julie and Sam were killed instantly. At least that's what I was told."

"And you blame yourself," Kirsten guessed, surrendering to the hot tears pooling in her eyes.

"I had her car—because it was safer in the bad weather."

"You couldn't have known that Sam would get sick."

His dark eyes flashed angrily. "But I could have left her with the four-wheel drive, damn it! If I hadn't been so goddamn self-serving!" His fist crashed into the warm bricks of the fireplace in frustration.

"We all make mistakes," she offered lamely.

"But usually not ones that imperil the lives of the people we love. Oh, Kirsten," he moaned prayerfully. "I was still at the office when I heard about the accident. Still at the office, for God's sake! I raced like the devil over to the hospital, but it was too late."

"There's no need to talk about this," Kirsten volunteered, hoping to find a way to ease his pain. "It's all in the past and… and it's gone. Nothing will change that." She got to her feet and stood next to him, tentatively offering the support of her hand on his arm. "Don't carry this guilt—"

He refused the comfort of her gesture and tossed the remains of his coffee into the fire. The air sizzled as the liquid hit the flames. "But I was the one who defended the Stone Motor Company," he pointed out. "If I hadn't worked so damned hard to prove that the Zircon was safe, Julie and Sam might still be alive."

"You don't know that. It's just conjecture."

"But a chance, damn it." She turned away from the torture showing on his face. Tears had begun to stream down her face, and her stomach was knotted by futile sympathetic thoughts for him.

Dane straightened and his hands captured her shoulders,

forcing her to meet his defeated gaze. Firelight cast eerie shadows on his proud face. "There's a reason I'm telling you everything," he whispered. "I think you should know about the debt I owe Harmon Smith."

"It has something to do with the accident?" she asked, not sure that she wanted to hear any more of his confessions.

"I—I didn't handle the deaths very well and the guilt I felt was unbearable." Kirsten believed him. He still hadn't managed to let go of the responsibility. "I spend countless nights wondering if it would have made a difference. If I hadn't defended Stone Motors, or if I had lost the suit, would Julie and Sam have survived?" His broad shoulders slumped and the fingers gripping Kirsten's arms relaxed. "In the end I sold my practice and moved to Maine. I had a small cabin, no responsibilities and enough money to buy all the liquor I needed to drink myself into oblivion, should I feel the need."

Kirsten's heart bled for him, and all the words of consolation she wanted to say stuck in her throat. It was obvious that he had loved his family very dearly and that guilt was still gnawing painfully at him.

"I don't think I would have ever considered practicing law again if it hadn't been for Harmon Smith."

"What did Smith do?" Kirsten asked, pressing her ear to his chest and listening to the steady, rhythmic beating of his heart.

"He pulled me out of the bottle." Dane's arms tightened around Kirsten, but he avoided looking into her eyes, preferring to stare out the window at the stormy night. "Harmon Smith was an old family friend. He was close to my father and my uncle. He came to see me after my father died, probably at my uncle's behest, and made me an offer.

"Smith needed an attorney and he remembered me—probably because of the Stone Motor decision. My uncle gave him my address in Maine and one day he showed up on my doorstep. Fortunately it was one of my better days and he offered to finance an office for me in Manhattan at reasonable terms if I would agree to represent Stateside Broadcasting Corporation."

"So you accepted his proposal," Kirsten surmised, starting to understand the man she loved so hopelessly.

"I still had quite a bit of money left over from the sale of my practice in Buffalo, and that, along with the money I borrowed from Smith, was enough to start the practice. It was still a gamble, but one I couldn't afford to pass up." He let out a ragged sigh. "In other words, Harmon Smith saved my life. I know that I never would have accepted another case if Harmon hadn't helped me out."

"And that's the favor you owe him."

"Right." Dane released her and pushed his hands into the pockets of his jeans. After walking to the bay window he put a stocking foot on the sill, leaned on his knee and stared down at the turbulent black sea. "I still owe Harmon Smith over a hundred thousand dollars, and that doesn't begin to touch the fact that Harmon has handed me several important referrals and pushed a lot of business in my direction." He pushed impatient fingers through his hair. "I owe Harmon Smith, Kirsten."

"And he wants to be repaid?"

"Yes."

"I see," she whispered.

Dane turned from his position near the window and his eyes drilled into hers. "Then you have to know that Smith is determined to beat you—no matter what it takes."

Involuntarily, Kirsten's slender shoulders slumped, but she held her head upright. It was obvious that Dane was caught between a rock and a hard spot. There was no way he could bow out of the suit and let Harmon Smith down. And Kirsten would never voluntarily drop the suit.

Kirsten had too much pride in herself and love for Dane

to use their affair to her advantage. She realized that KPSC might back off if she let it be known that she had slept with the defending attorney, but she couldn't bring herself to stoop that low, not even against KPSC.

"I guess there's just no easy answer," she murmured.

"Maybe there never is." Dane didn't try to talk her out of the lawsuit again and she didn't offer. They were both trapped by their love and the hopeless circumstances that bound them.

She walked over to him and placed a comforting hand on his shoulder. "I'm tired," she whispered. "Come on, let's go to bed."

He smiled sadly and shook his head. "I'll be there in a minute," he murmured, gently kissing her forehead. She left him alone to stare out the window at the black night.

It was several hours later, after she had dropped into a fitful sleep, that she was awakened by the urgent persistence of his hands and lips on her body.

THE MORNING DAWNED foggy. Kirsten slipped quietly out of bed and watched Dane as he slept. The worries of the night before seemed to have melted with sleep and his face was relaxed and unlined. She smiled sadly at him before tenderly touching the tips of her fingers to his strong jaw. He groaned and shifted on the bed.

Without disturbing him she eased off the bed, changed into her shorts and T-shirt before collecting her running shoes on the porch. Though the fog still clung to the beach, Kirsten suspected it would burn off before afternoon and she would spend another glorious day with Dane.

She didn't think about the fact that he hadn't mentioned when he intended to leave, but Kirsten hoped that he would stay through the weekend. Life without him would be very lonely, very lonely indeed.

Shrugging off any lingering doubts, she started down the small trail leading to the stairs. She was smiling by the time she reached the weathered steps. After properly stretching her legs, Kirsten started northward on her early morning run, carefully avoiding the debris that had been kicked up on the sand by last night's turbulent tide. The sea air, fresh after the storm, cooled her lungs, and she felt the exhilaration of the exercise.

It was nearly an hour later when she returned to the cabin. She was winded and covered with perspiration, but managed to race up the stairs at the thought of surprising Dane.

As she kicked off her shoes and leaned against the railing surrounding the porch to stretch her muscles, she heard signs of life from within the cabin and realized that Dane had already awakened. The shower was running and the bed was empty.

After rinsing her face and hands she changed into her robe and knocked on the bathroom door to let him know that she had returned.

The thought of joining him in the shower entered her mind, but she rejected it when she touched the door to the bathroom and noticed that it was locked. With a shrug of her shoulders she turned her attention to breakfast.

The bacon was just beginning to sizzle when she heard the shower stop. By the time Kirsten heard him enter the room, breakfast was cooked.

She didn't look up, but felt the tingle of his cool lips against her neck. "I would have joined you," she said, smiling, "but the door was locked."

"A habit," he replied.

She turned and smiled at him. "Habit?"

Obviously you've never had children."

"Oh…" The sadness in his eyes when he looked at her told her he was leaving.

"They aren't particularly interested in giving you any privacy."

"I—I suppose not." She smiled despite the horrible pang

of sorrow knifing through her heart. "You're going back, aren't you?"

"I have to."

"I…thought you might stay through the weekend," she murmured, trying not to give in to the sadness overtaking her and failing miserably.

"Business."

Her voice was unsteady when he came over to her and tilted her head upward, forcing her to gaze into his eyes. "Will it always be this way?"

"I hope not. Look, I'll be back."

"Promise?"

His smile broadened. "What do you think?"

"I wish I knew," she whispered, motioning for him to take a seat.

"Trust me," he insisted, planting a warm kiss on her lips before sliding into a chair.

And she did. With all of her heart she trusted him.

Small talk prevailed during the light meal, and it wasn't until Dane had pushed his plate aside that his eyes became serious and intent while assessing her.

"Why didn't you have kids?" he asked.

Kirsten shifted her eyes away. "Kent didn't want them. And, well, I knew that our marriage wasn't very strong."

"So you divorced him?"

"It wasn't that easy," she said, sighing. "I wanted to make it work. Even when I found out about his girlfriend… well, I thought we could work it out. I made an appointment with a marriage counselor. He wouldn't go."

Dane was deep in thought. "I find it hard to believe that he wouldn't have fought for you tooth and nail." His dark brows drew over his eyes in puzzling agitation.

"He didn't want me—"

"What?"

"I was too threatening, I suppose. I was earning more money than he was and my career was more glamorous." She started stacking the plates nervously. "It was more than he could handle."

"Wasn't he proud of you?"

Kirsten sighed and shook her head. "I don't think so. Anyway, it didn't work out and he and I are both happier."

"And he's remarried."

"Yes, look, I'd rather not talk about it, okay?"

"Why not? Do you still care for him?"

She looked at the ceiling before letting her eyes settle on him. "I don't love him and I sometimes wonder if I ever did. But I don't feel comfortable talking about the divorce." She settled back in her chair. "I guess it all stems from the fact that I really don't believe in divorce. Once you're married, I think it's your responsibility to stick it out."

"But you couldn't—"

"Because he didn't want to. It seemed foolish to continue to live a lie and both be miserable." Her cheeks had colored and she was forced to look away from the honesty in his eyes.

"I didn't mean to pry," he said, setting his coffee on the table.

Her smile was frail. "You didn't. It's just not a subject that I'm particularly fond of."

"Then there's no reason to discuss it—unless that miserable son of a bitch comes near you again."

"I don't think you have to worry much about that. The last I heard, he and his wife were living in Alaska."

"Too bad it's not Australia."

Kirsten had to laugh. "I love you, counselor."

Dane's lips pulled into an amused smile and he rose from the table. "And I love you, Ms. McQueen. Now, if we could only find a way to deal with this petty little lawsuit you insist on holding over Harmon Smith's head, we'd be able to sort out our differences."

"I doubt it," she murmured playfully, her green eyes lighting with a seductive spark.

His brows rose in interest. "You're challenging me, and if you don't watch out, I'll be forced to..."

"What? Tar and feather me? Draw and quarter me?"

White teeth flashed against dark skin. "I've got a better idea," he suggested, pulling her out of her chair and pressing the length of his body against hers.

"I know—you'd rather bore me to death by reading to me from law journals."

His eyes grew dark. "You might be right. There was this case..." His hands pressed firmly against the small of her back, rubbing circles of desire against her flesh. "I think it was the notorious Ferguson versus McQueen decision, where the woman taunted the man into making love to her for a solid forty-eight hours..." His lips touched hers in a possessive kiss that warmed the womanly fires of desire smoldering within the most private part of her.

Her hands wound around his neck and her fingers twined in the dark strands of his hair. Her lips returned the ardor of his kiss and her tongue moved against the smooth polish of his teeth. "Guilty as charged, counselor," she said. Her body pressed urgently against his and he groaned in frustration.

"How am I ever going to leave you?" he whispered, holding her desperately.

"Don't, love. Stay with me," she murmured.

"Kirsten, I can't." But his hands reached upward to cup a straining breast. When he touched the taut nipple he surrendered to the desire burning in his veins. Slowly he eased her body to the floor. "I must be out of my mind..."

CHAPTER FOURTEEN

DANE HADN'T RETURNED to Oregon. Though he had called Kirsten several times, the telephone conversations had been cold and impersonal. Kirsten sensed that he sill cared for her, but as the court date approached, the unspoken tension over the wires made her uncomfortable. The lawsuit became an ever-widening abyss that separated them, and Kirsten chided herself for loving a man who would, no doubt, try his best to destroy her reputation.

She had tried to concentrate on anything other than the impending court date, but it had been impossible to get interested in the various articles she was researching and writing.

The first serious job opportunity since she was fired from KPSC had presented itself, and Kirsten had interviewed with the station manager of a small San Francisco television station. He had been a friendly sort, though reserved; and Kirsten hoped to land the job. The position wasn't available until October though, and Kirsten couldn't help but wonder if negative publicity over the lawsuit would kill her chances of getting it. What station manager in his right mind would hire a reporter with a track record of suing the station that employed her?

Time passed slowly. The weekend before the trial was scheduled Kirsten did anything to keep her mind off the forthcoming battle in the courtroom. She had already packed a suitcase, as she planned to stay in Portland during the trial, and she managed to find miscellaneous tasks to keep her busy.

She was now running five miles every morning and had managed to paint the cabin when she had too much nervous energy to work on her freelance assignments. Her appetite had fallen off sharply, but she realized that until the trial was over, she wouldn't have much interest in food, or anything else for that matter. The thought of seeing Dane from the opposite side of the courtroom tied her insides in uncomfortable knots and she shuddered to think what he could do if he really was a character assassin.

She was staring blankly down at the typewriter, her fingers poised hesitantly over the keys, when she heard a car door slam. Her painful daydreams were instantly shattered and her heart leaped to her throat as she thought for a wild, expectant moment that it might be Dane, She reasoned that sooner or later he'd have to come to Portland to try the case, though that didn't necessarily mean that he would jeopardize his position by risking a visit to her. But she couldn't help the hope from welling in her heart.

She had already gotten out of the chair and had reached the opposite side of the room when the visitor knocked. Kirsten opened the door with shaking hands.

Dane was standing on the porch. Kirsten found it difficult to swallow as the emotions of relief and quiet despair clogged her throat.

"Come in," she whispered, her small smile quaking.

"I shouldn't be here," he admitted, but accepted her quiet invitation and entered the familiar cabin with its lofty view of the sea.

Dane's tanned skin was stretched tightly over his cheekbones, and though he was dressed casually in gray cords and a lightweight cotton shirt, he seemed different from the last time she had seen him. He'd changed somehow, taken on a more aloof and sophisticated air. His eyes were more intense, his jaw line stronger and even his slight Eastern accent seemed more pronounced.

"Then why did you come?" she asked warily. *Dear God,* she thought, *he's going to tell me it's over and then he's going to go about his business of crucifying me in the courtroom.* She steadied herself against the door as she closed it.

When she had effectively shut out the rest of the world, his eyes, now flecked with gold, silently embraced hers and destroyed all her fears.

"Because I had to." He stared into her worried gaze and then let out a disgusted breath of air. Slowly he placed his arms around her waist and put his forehead against her hair. "I've missed you, Kirsten," he said. His voice was ragged with the emotions ripping him apart. "I had to see you again—it's been so long… so very long." His lips brushed her hair and Kirsten felt as if her knees would give way. The sting of wistful tears threatened her eyes.

"I know, love," she whispered hoarsely, feeling the warmth of his hands press against her back. She stood against him, matching each of his strong muscles with smaller counterparts. She could hear the irregular pounding of his heart and feel his ragged breath as it whispered through her hair. Possessively his arms held her and she thought she would cry with joy at his familiar touch. How long had she waited for this moment, wondered if he would ever again claim her body with his?

His lips touched hers and his hands moved upward, softly feeling the pulse jumping near her throat. She closed her eyes and gave in to the powerful feelings of love running through her veins like liquid fire.

When his hand slipped under the hem of her blouse to cup a breast, she gasped in anticipation. His tongue took advantage of the moment and slid past her teeth to flick against the deepest corners of her mouth. "I've wanted you so badly," he groaned when their lips parted and he lifted his head to look once again in the velvet-soft depths of her eyes.

Lovingly, he brushed a strand of honey-brown hair off her face and noticed the unbidden tears welling in the corners of her eyes.

"I've never intended to hurt you," he whispered before gently kissing a quiet tear as it ran down her cheek. Kirsten felt as if her heart would break with his earnest words of love.

"I love you, Dane—it doesn't matter."

"But it does, damn it," he thought aloud. "That's the whole point. If things were different..." His voice trailed off, the words lost in the still afternoon air.

"What?"

"If things were different, I'd ask you to marry me, Kirsten, and I wouldn't take no for an answer."

"If things were different," she repeated, her voice catching. But nothing had changed. They were still worlds apart, held together by a thin cord of physical attraction and the vague promise of love. "Look, Dane, I don't think we should be discussing hypothetical situations—" She tried to pull away from him and think rationally. She had to ignore the magic of his words, avoid contact with his sensual hands.

"I just want you to know how I feel."

"Let's not talk about it. Everything is just going to get more confusing and contradictory," she whispered, her heart wrenching painfully.

Shaking his dark head, he frowned. "I couldn't let you come into that courtroom without seeing you beforehand."

"I—I appreciate that. And I love you for it. But I think that us, being together, right before we go to court, will only confuse me and the issues...unless that's what you want."

His head snapped upward and he looked as if he'd been struck. His hazel eyes impaled her with needle-sharp honesty.

"I came only because I love you, Kirsten, and I want you to know that regardless of what happens on Wednesday, I care for you."

Closing her eyes and squeezing back the tears, she took her head and held up her palms as if in surrender. "We can't discuss this, Dane. It's too dangerous. It just won't work."

Suddenly his arms were around her and this time the embrace was fierce and demanding. He studied the doubt in her eyes. "I love you, Kirsten, and I want you to know it. Nothing. I repeat, nothing that happens in court will change that."

"Oh, God, Dane, I want to believe you."

"Then just try! For once don't try to reason everything out; trust your instincts!" When his lips found hers, the passion of six long weeks erupted. No longer was he careful or gentle. His hands were warm, possessive and demanding as they quickly removed her clothes and touched the most sensitive parts of her body in familiar caresses that made her breathing shallow.

His own desire was burning in his loins, aching to be relieved by the only woman he had let touch his mind as well as his body. Urgently, he pushed her to the floor, and she felt the weight of his torso crush against her breasts.

The warmth of his hands soothed her, quieted her fears and she was caught up in the furious storm of desire that only he could inspire. She felt his long legs through his trousers as they rubbed insistently against hers. His tongue touched her, tasted her and caused shivering sensations to filter through the whole of her being.

Her fingers deftly removed his clothes and then lingered to feel the rippling movements of his muscles. Desire, like a caged bird suddenly released, soared upward through her body, and her lips returned the fever of his kiss with each ragged breath she took.

"Make love to me," he urged, rolling on his back and placing her above him. The desire in his eyes coupled with the lines of worry on his face made it impossible for her to deny his bold request. His fingers touched each dark-tipped breast as she slowly molded herself to the strong contours of his body.

She felt his sweat mingling with hers, tasted the salt of it on her tongue when she kissed his neck. He groaned and propelled himself upward, his arms encircling her and his hands pressing firmly on her buttocks.

"Please," he cried, his eyes shutting as if in agony. "Kirsten…" Slowly she moved over him, positioning herself to accept the promise of his love. His neck strained as she lowered herself on him and began moving in the gentle rhythm of lovemaking.

Her warmth spread over him, heating his blood until it became white hot and pulsed violently in his eardrums. It rushed through him, increasing the pressure and the ache in his loins. He accepted her gentle rhythm and then began to move with her, increasing the heated tempo until Kirsten thought she would explode with the molten fires burning within her.

He stiffened and a shock wave passed from his body through hers, shattering her existence into fragments of sparkling light that touched her soul and blended with the universe.

"I love you," he whispered as the weight of her body rested against him and her breasts flattened over his chest. His fingers idly curled an errant lock of her hair. "I love you more than I thought it was possible to care for one woman."

"Then why, Dane?" she asked quietly. "Why must you defend the station?"

"I don't have any choice in the matter, Kirsten—not like you do."

"It's your job," the defeat in her voice made her sound weary.

"More than that. I explained it to you before." His hand

tenderly touched the gentle slope of her spine. "When this is all over, my lady, we have a few things to discuss," he promised.

"Such as?"

"Such as how I'm going to convince you to marry me."

She pulled away from him, just far enough to gaze into his eyes. "Are you serious?" she asked skeptically. But she couldn't contain the small smile that curved her lips.

"More serious than I've ever been in my life." He propped up on one elbow and stared into the mysterious depths of her eyes. "And if I can, I'm going to try to straighten out this mess of a lawsuit." He reached for his cords, jerked them over his legs and buckled his belt.

Kirsten had managed to get into her jeans and was buttoning her blouse. "And how do you propose to do that counselor?"

"I've been working on the Ginevra story."

"And?" she prodded him. Her heart was pounding frantically in her chest. Maybe there was still a glimmer of hope that they could find a way to be together, not as opponents in a court battle, but as one man and one woman.

He shrugged his tense shoulders. "And nothing, at least not yet. I feel that I'm close, but…"

"You're running out of time," she finished for him.

He nodded curtly, stood and paced between the window and the fireplace. "What about you?"

"Not much better, I'm afraid," she admitted. "I want to see that woman who heads up the fight against nuclear power, what was her name, the friend of the reporter at *The Herald*… June Dellany, that was it. She was very supportive, but she couldn't give me any information that would help."

Kirsten stood and ran her fingers through the tangles in her hair. "Even if I knew anything more, I don't know that it would help—especially not now. The trial starts Wednesday."

The conversation had become so intense that neither Dane nor Kirsten had heard the sound of a car as it ground to a halt in the gravel near the garage. It was only after the car door slammed and footsteps echoed on the front porch that Kirsten became aware of the visitor.

Dane's sharp eyes moved to the doorway and a small muscle in the back of his jaw tightened.

"Oh, dear God," Kirsten murmured as she stepped to answer the door. Dane's hand restrained her.

"I think I should leave."

"How? By the back door?" Kirsten's green eyes registered her indignation and she shook her head while attempting to straighten the tangled golden-brown curls with her fingers. "We have nothing to hide, Dane. It's probably just the paperboy coming to collect.

"You're sure about this?"

"Absolutely." She pulled free of his cautious grasp and jerked open the door.

On the porch, looking slightly perplexed and worried stood Lloyd Grady. He pondered Kirsten's face for a fleeting moment before looking into the cabin.

"I'm sorry I didn't call," he said half-apologetically, "but something's come up and I can't make our appointment on Monday. I though we'd better go over a few things today—and if you have any questions, we'll work them out this afternoon or on Tuesday, whichever is better for you..." His voice faded as he met the curious eyes of the man he was to oppose in the courtroom.

Lloyd's tanned face drained of all color. "What the hell?" After reconfirming what he had hoped was just a figment of his imagination, his furious gaze returned to his client. "What's going on here?" he asked in a clipped voice.

"Why don't you come in?" Kirsten suggested, her fluttering heart refusing to calm.

Lloyd placed his hands on his hips, pushing aside his suit jacket. "Wait a minute…"

"I think you'd better come in, Grady," Dane said, reinforcing Kirsten's offer. "Maybe we can talk this out."

"Look, Ferguson, I don't know what's going on here…." His pained eyes searched Kirsten's face. "I'm not sure I want to know, but I think we can forget about discussing it. The fact that you're here is not only unethical, it's—"

"It's my right," Dane finished for him. "Kirsten and I are friends."

"Friends!" Lloyd thundered, shaking his hands in the air. "If you're her friend, then you can't very well call yourself objective in this matter, can you? I think you owe it to Harmon Smith and Fletcher Ross to remove yourself from the case!"

"I can't do that."

"But you're the defending attorney, for God's sake!" Lloyd was shaking and red in the face, but something in the deadly glare in Dane's eyes made him pull himself together. The last thing he could afford was to let Dane Ferguson rattle him—in the courtroom or out of it. Nervously he tugged at one end of his blond moustache.

"Maybe we should be talking settlement," Dane ventured, moving out of the doorway and allowing Lloyd to pass.

"Not on your life, Ferguson. I've been working on this case day and night, and I'm not about to let it go."

"Don't you think you should consult your client?" Dane asked, cocking his head in Kirsten's direction.

Lloyd confronted Kirsten with a look that could kill. "I don't understand you, Kirsten," he said, his voice still shaking. "We've worked hard, won that first trial, and now you throw it all away on an affair with him? What the devil's gotten into you? Can't you tell your friends from your enemies?"

"I don't think you understand," Kirsten said.

"You bet I don't!" Despite his efforts to the contrary, Lloyd lost his cool. His fist crashed into the wall. "Kirsten, why didn't you tell me? If you wanted out of the suit, all you had to do was call!" He shook his head, his outrage evident in the scowl of frustration contorting his even features. "How could you have been so stupid?"

"I think that's enough," Dane interjected firmly.

"Excuse me, Ferguson," Lloyd lashed back. "I'm having a discussion with my client."

"Then quit yelling at me, Lloyd," Kirsten replied. "Treat me like your client instead of your wife."

Lloyd reacted as if Kirsten had struck him. After a moment's shock he began to speak, and his voice was considerably lower than it had been. He tossed an insolent thumb in Dane's direction, and his blond brows rose quizzically. "Didn't I tell you about him? Didn't I warn you that he would do anything to win this suit?"

"Wait a minute—" Dane cut in, striding over to Lloyd and staring at him with contempt.

Lloyd ignored him. "The trial is less than a week away, Kirsten. What the devil are you trying to do—sabotage the whole goddamn suit?"

"I think you should leave," Dane stated firmly. An angry muscle working in the corner of his jaw and his thumb was rubbing threateningly against his forefinger. The look in his eyes suggested that he would just as soon strangle Lloyd as confront him in the courtroom.

"I should leave? I was just going to suggest that you take a hike!"

"Stop it!" Kirsten's voice rose above the rage sparking between the two men. "Can't we talk this over like adults?"

"Sound advice," Dane agreed. "I still think a settlement is the best option for both parties."

"Not on your life."

"Lloyd, why not?" Kirsten asked. A settlement. It would solve all of her problems. No confrontation in the courtroom, and it would almost be like winning against Aaron Becker, Harmon Smith and the rest of the lot.

"Because we've got them running scared, that's why not!" Lloyd said, a sly smile pulling at the corners of his mouth. "Otherwise he would never have suggested it."

"I don't care, Lloyd. I'm tired, and I don't honestly know if I can go through another court battle. This way, the press will get wind of it, and it will seem as if I've won." Kirsten's eyes roved between the tense faces of the two men, one she loved as passionately as life itself, the other she had trusted most of her thirty-five years.

"I'll have to advise you against it." Lloyd's face was set in firm resolve. Kirsten knew he doubted that she would ever question his judgment.

A weary sigh escaped her. A settlement would represent an end to the fighting and a chance to be with Dane. It would also end any chance for the rumor of her affair with Dane to be made public. A scandal right now would be disastrous to her case and his reputation. "I want to settle," she said firmly.

Lloyd's lips compressed into a thin, tight line. "If it's what you want."

"It is, Lloyd. It's time for me to get back on my feet again and leave the lawsuit and KPSC behind me."

For the first time since setting eyes on Lloyd Grady, Dane smiled. "I'll call Aaron Becker and Harmon Smith."

Relief, like a cool wave, washed over Kirsten. "You can use the phone in the bedroom." Dane walked through the living room, down the short hallway and into the bedroom before closing the door softly behind him. Kirsten offered Lloyd a sincere smile and took Lloyd's arm. "Come on, let me buy you a cup of coffee."

When they were seated at the kitchen table, Lloyd took a long sip of his coffee and rotated the cup nervously in his hands. "You could have told me, you know," he said after an uncomfortable silence.

She shook her head and frowned. "No, I couldn't have. You threatened to walk off the case—"

"But I never imagined you were… involved with the man. Damn it, Kirsten, you should have told me."

"It's all working out for the best anyway," she said, avoiding the unnamed accusation in his eyes.

At the sound of Dane's approaching footsteps Kirsten turned to smile and face the man she loved. The look of defeat on his face when he entered the room shattered all her dreams as surely as if they were fine porcelain.

"Harmon Smith refuses to settle," Dane announced, leaning against the doorjamb.

"Maybe that's because his attorney advised him against it," Lloyd surmised with a triumphant gleam in his eye. He set his unfinished cup on the table. "So it looks like we'll meet in court after all."

Dane's dark brows rose. "That's about the size of it—unless your client wants to drop the case."

"No way," Kirsten replied, her lips tightening and her eyes cold. The thought of Smith forcing the issue made her blood boil. "If it's a fight Harmon Smith wants, it's a fight he'll get."

"Well, this sheds new light on everything, doesn't it?" Lloyd asked sarcastically. A grim smile spread slowly over his features as he turned his attention to Dane. "Mr. Ferguson, I suggest that the next time you want to see my client, you tell me about it first."

"Forget it, Grady. The lady makes her own decisions."

"Then use your head, Kirsten," Lloyd warned. "Think about whose side he's on." He cast a knowing look in Kirsten's direction before standing and straightening the cuff of his shirt. "I'll call you later, when we can discuss your side of the issue without the presence of the defense in the room."

Lloyd nodded a quick good-bye to Kirsten and brushed past Dane on his way to the door. When the front door slammed shut and the sound of Lloyd's car engine faded into the distance, Dane turned to Kirsten. "I'm sorry this didn't work out."

"Are you?"

"You know I am." He stared at her for a moment, as if memorizing the soft planes of her face. "Harmon wouldn't hear of a settlement. I really did try to convince him that it was in his own best interest, but he didn't buy it. He insisted that I help Fletcher Ross 'deal with you once and for all.'"

"And you owe him this incredible favor, right?"

"He did manage to bring that up."

"Nice guy," Kirsten murmured as she began picking up the dishes, and consciously avoided Dane's intuitive gaze. She had begun walking to the sink, but paused when he called her name.

"Kirsten, I—"

Turning to meet the questions in his eyes, she shook her head vigorously. The golden rays of the late afternoon sun poured through the window and highlighted the brown strands with streaks of gold. "I know," she whispered, reading his mind. "I think you should leave."

"When this is all over—"

"Shhh, don't even talk about it." Her smile was wistful. "You'd better go."

The frustration building within him was evident in the strained contours of his rugged face. His knowing eyes held hers for a silent moment, and then he left without saying good-bye.

When she saw Dane's car race down the long drive, Kirsten crumpled into a corner and let her quiet tears of despair run freely down her face.

THE COURTROOM WAS nearly filled by the time Kirsten took her seat. Newspaper reporters were hastily scribbling notes inside the room while camera crews from local stations were planted firmly outside the courtroom doors. Kirsten recognized several workers from KPSC, who would no doubt be called upon to testify on behalf of the station.

Lloyd was as reassuring as ever, though even he, in his impeccable brown suit, seemed nervous.

Kirsten hadn't slept more than two hours at a stretch from the time Dane had left the beach cabin. Every time the phone had rung, her heart had raced expectantly, and she had always been disappointed.

Dane hadn't called.

Nor had he come by to check on her.

The battle lines were drawn and the war was about to begin.

Lloyd was opening his briefcase when Dane strode into the courtroom. Even Kirsten was unnerved by his presence. She had warned herself that he would be formidable, but she hadn't expected that his self-assured stature and near arrogant pride in his eyes would be so noticeable. He looked as if he had already won the battle as he walked to his table on the opposite side of the room.

As she looked more closely, she noticed the lines of strain near the corners of his eyes. Though disguised by his East Coast sophistication and charm, the shadowed weariness was evident to her. Kirsten's heart went out to him.

Lloyd noticed the difference in her composure. "Don't forget why he's here, Kirsten," Lloyd warned her. "That smile isn't because he's seen you."

Maybe Lloyd was right. The triumphant smile on Dane's face might well be because he had found a way to completely discredit her, and she wondered fleetingly if he would use his affair with her to show how low she would stoop in her efforts to fight KPSC. In her heart she couldn't believe that he would use her, but he hadn't bothered to call since that last ugly scene with Lloyd at the cabin.

After setting his briefcase on the table, Dane advanced on Kirsten.

"Wait a minute, Ferguson. What's going on?" Lloyd asked, intervening on Kirsten's behalf when Dane was in earshot.

"I want to talk to Kirsten."

"You can't do that. Not here—not now," Lloyd argued, his feathers of protocol ruffled.

Dane's eyes drove into Kirsten's and she read the honesty in his gaze. "It's all right, Lloyd. I'll talk to him."

Begrudgingly Lloyd watched Dane take Kirsten's arm and maneuver her to a quiet corner of the courtroom.

"I've been busy," Dane whispered, letting his hand linger on the tailored sleeve of her linen jacket.

"I imagine—"

"As the lawyer for the defense, I had access to all the records at KPSC. Not just personnel records, but other documents as well."

"So?"

"It took a couple of days, but after poring over everything that the station had to do with Ginevra, I still felt that something was missing. I did some checking. The land for the proposed site is owned by a holding company."

Kirsten nodded. The company was obscure.

"Well, I dug a little deeper. The principal investors of that holding are none other than our own illustrious Aaron Becker and Harmon Smith. Fletcher Ross knew all about it. I wouldn't be surprised if he was in on the ground floor as well."

"What?"

Dane smiled, and a glimmer of hope entered Kirsten's

heart. "From what I can piece together, not only have Becker and Smith speculated and purchased the Ginevra land with the intent to sell it at an astronomical profit, they have also invested in the construction company that is most likely to bid and get the Ginevra job. When you became overly interested in the site, they got nervous and thought you might stumble onto their plans and expose them. The scandal would have ruined KPSC's reputation—or at the very least cost Aaron Becker and Harmon Smith their jobs once the board of directors got wind of it."

Kirsten shook her head at the deception. "So what does this mean?"

"I already talked to Smith. He's agreed to settle out of court with you. Though he hasn't really done anything illegal, he wants to avoid the embarrassment of any bad publicity and he feels that a quiet settlement would be in the interest of all parties concerned. He's agreed to pay all of the original award of two hundred thousand dollars."

Kirsten felt herself begin to stagger, but Dane's arm braced her until her knees became firm once again. "It's not the money, Dane, it never has been."

"You'd rather fight this thing?"

"What do you suggest—not as an attorney for the defense, but… as my friend."

His crooked smile broadened engagingly. "I'd say take the money and run."

"But what about the attempted fraud?" Kirsten asked in a tense whisper. "I can't let them get away with that!"

"I think fraud is too strong a term, but I wouldn't worry about it if I were you. When I was talking to Aaron Becker at KPSC, someone overheard part of the conversation. The way news travels in the land of television, you can bet that by the end of the day, it will be given national attention."

Kirsten smiled into Dane's intriguing eyes. "Counselor,"

she stated, "you've got yourself a deal. Just straighten out the facts and figures with my attorney."

Lloyd took the news in stride and seemed slightly relieved that he didn't have to battle the New York attorney. In his opinion the settlement was more of a win than a draw and a damn sight better than a loss. Any way you looked at it, it was a feather in his cap.

After the two attorneys advised the court that the case had been settled, Dane took Kirsten's hand and let her out of the courtroom. When Dane pushed the doors open and Kirsten stepped into the hallway, television cameras followed her and several microphones were thrust into her face.

"Ms. McQueen, can you give us any information on the settlement?" one reporter asked. Before Kirsten could respond, another question was put to her.

"Ms. McQueen, is it true that someone at KPSC was involved in the Ginevra scandal?"

"Ms. McQueen, do you consider the settlement a win and would you call it a victory for women workers?"

Kirsten had been walking away from the crowd, but turned gracefully on her heel and stared comfortably into the television cameras. "I'd just like to say that I'm very satisfied with the settlement and that I'd have to thank both the attorneys for the prosecution and the defense for helping to achieve it. Thank you."

"But Ms. McQueen? What about the defending attorney?"

"Mr. Ferguson? Wait a minute, he's the guy on the other side, isn't he? Mr. Ferguson! Could you give us a statement from KPSC?"

Dane shook his head and waved the cameramen away.

Kirsten hurried down the courthouse steps, not feeling the cool drops of rain pouring from the overcast Portland skies. It was over. She was with Dane and nothing else in the world mattered. Not the reporters, not the rain, not even Harmon Smith and Aaron Becker.

Dane helped her into his car and slid behind the wheel. In a matter of minutes they were driving west, leaving the city of Portland, the shimmering Willamette River, and the throng of reporters behind.

"That was rude, you know," Kirsten admonished Dane, snuggling against him.

"What?"

"Ignoring all those question."

"You think so because you're a reporter." He squinted at the road ahead and placed his hand on her knee. "Have I ever told you what I think of television people?"

"Spare me," she said with a laugh. "By the way, where are you taking me?"

"Home."

"Home?"

He lifted his hand from her knee and draped a possessive arm across her shoulder. "I've mentioned that I'd been busy?"

"Um-hum."

"Well, you see, one of the partners in the firm, he's been interested in buying me out for a long time… we finally agreed on a price."

Kirsten's heart missed a beat. "I don't understand."

"Only because you're not really trying. What's happening here, Ms. McQueen, is that I'm proposing to you. I knew that you wouldn't move to New York, and it's too far to commute, so I decided that I'd move to Portland and start a practice here. You don't think Fletcher Ross or Lloyd Grady would mind, do you?"

Kirsten smiled at the thought. "I doubt that they'll be pleased."

"How about you? I think you could use a new attorney as well as a husband. We could live in the city and keep the beach house for vacations—with the children. What do you say? Will you marry me, Kirsten?"

Tears of happiness welled in Kirsten's round eyes. Marriage to Dane and bearing his children were more than she could wish for. "I thought you'd never ask," she whispered throatily.

Dane laughed in contentment. "Let's go home."

Kirsten kissed his cheek and wrapped her arms around him. "Anything you want, counselor."

DOUBLE EXPOSURE

PROLOGUE

Taylor's Crossing, Oregon

THE WIPERS SLAPPED the snow away and the windshield fogged with the cold, but Melanie Walker barely noticed. She drove by rote, unseeing as the miles from the clinic downtown slipped beneath the old truck's tires.

One of her favorite songs was playing on the radio, fighting a losing war with static, but she didn't concentrate on the melody. She couldn't. Her mind wouldn't focus on anything but Gavin and the last time she'd seen him, three weeks before.

His naked body had been the only heat in the hayloft, and his legs and arms had been entwined with hers. The smell of musty hay and animals had filled the air.

"Wait for me, Melanie," he'd whispered against the curve of her neck. His breath had been as warm as a summer wind, his tawny eyes seductive in the half light of the barn. "Say you'll wait for me."

"You know I will," she had foolishly vowed, unaware that fate was against her. At the time she'd known only that she loved him with all of her young heart. And that was all that mattered.

Until today.

She swallowed a hard lump in her throat and shoved the gearshift into third. Her rendezvous with Gavin had taken place three weeks ago and she hadn't seen him since. And now, all their plans and her entire future had changed.

As she drove through the snow-packed roads, she forced her wobbling chin up and clamped hard on her teeth. She wasn't going to cry, no matter what.

Gavin was over a thousand miles away, chasing a dream, and she was alone in a small Oregon town—and two months pregnant.

Her hands clenched over the wheel as she struggled with the right words to explain to her father that she was carrying Gavin Doel's child.

Snowflakes drifted from a gray sky and melted against the windshield as the pickup rumbled along the slippery highway. To the west, the town of Taylor's Crossing nearly bordered Walker land. To the east, fields and pine forest covered the foothills of the Cascades.

Melanie snapped off the radio and glanced into the rearview mirror. Worried hazel eyes stared back at her.

Pregnant. And unmarried. And seventeen. Even in the cold, her hands began to sweat.

The fact that her father had let Melanie see Gavin had been a miracle. He despised Gavin's father, and heaven only knew why he'd allowed Melanie to go out with "that kid from the wrong side of town," the boy who had the misfortune of being Jim Doel's son.

"Help me," she whispered, feeling entirely alone and knowing she had no option but to tell her father the truth.

If only Gavin were still here, she thought selfishly, then whispered to herself, "You can handle this, Melanie. You have to!"

She shifted down and turned into the short lane near the house. The truck slid to a halt.

All Melanie's newfound convictions died on her tongue when she saw her father, axe propped over one shoulder, trudging through the snow toward the barn. The pup, Sassafras, bounded at his heels.

Hearing the rumble of the pickup's engine, Adam Walker turned and grinned. He yanked his baseball cap from his head and tipped it her way, exposing his receding hairline to the elements.

Melanie's mouth went dry. She cut the engine, pocketed the keys and sent up a silent prayer for strength. As she opened the truck's door, a blast of chill winter wind swirled inside. "It's now or never," she told herself, and wished she could choose never.

Stuffing her hands into the pockets of her fleece-lined jacket, she plowed through a blanket of snow. Four inches of powder covered the frozen ground of the small ranch—the ranch that had been her home for as long as she could remember. Though the town of Taylor's Crossing was steadily encroaching, her father had refused to sell—even after his wife's death.

Melanie shivered from the vague memory of losing her mother—and the sorry reasons behind Brenda Walker's death. Her father still held Jim Doel responsible.

Oh, Lord, why did it seem that her entire life had been tangled up with the Doels?

"I'd about given up on you." Her father squared his favorite old Dodgers' cap back onto his head, then brushed the snow from the shoulders of his jean jacket.

Melanie wanted to die.

"Go into the house and warm up some coffee. I'll be back as soon as I feed the stock and split a little kindling." Whistling, he turned and started for the barn.

"Dad?" Her voice sounded tiny.

"Yeah?"

"I'm going to have a baby."

Time seemed to stand still. The wind, raw with the breath of winter, soughed through the pines and cut through her suede jacket. Her father stopped dead in his tracks and turned to face her again. His jaw dropped, and denial crept over his strong features.

"You're pregnant?" he whispered.

Nodding, Melanie wrapped her arms around her middle.

"No!"

She shifted from one foot to the other and tried to ignore the sudden bow in her father's shoulders. All expression left his face, and he looked older than his forty-seven years. His throat worked and his brown gaze drilled into hers. "Doel?" he asked in a voice barely audible over the wind.

She nodded, listening to the painful drum of her heart.

His face turned white. "Oh—Mellie."

"Dad—"

"That black-hearted son of a bitch!" he suddenly growled, wincing as if physically wounded. The small lines around his mouth turned white.

Melanie didn't have to be reminded of the hatred that still simmered between the two families. And she hadn't meant to fall in love with Jim Doel's son; she really hadn't. But Gavin, with his warm eyes, enigmatic smile, lean, athletic body and razor-sharp wit, had been irresistible. She'd fallen head-over-heels in love with him. And she'd thought, foolishly perhaps, that the love they shared would bridge the painful gap between their families—the gap that had been created by that horrible accident.

"You're sure about this?" her father whispered, his gloved fingers opening and closing over the smooth wood of the axe handle.

"I saw the doctor this afternoon."

"Damn!" Adam's teeth clenched. He took up the axe and swung it hard into the gnarly bark of a huge ponderosa pine. "He's just like his old man!" An angry flush crept up his neck, and he muttered an oath under his breath. Kicking the toe of his boot into the base of the tree, he grappled with his rage.

"I should never have let you see him—never have listened to that stupid brother of mine!" he raged. "But your damned uncle convinced me that if I'd forbidden it, you'd have started sneaking behind my back!"

"Dad, I love Gavin—"

"Love? *Love!* You're only seventeen!" he bellowed, placing both hands on the fence. He breathed deeply, as he always did when he tried to regain his composure. His breath fogged in the air. "I don't have to tell you about the pain Jim Doel has caused this family." His face twisted in agony, and he leaned heavily against the tree.

"I—I know."

"He's a bastard, Mellie, a drunken, useless—" His voice cracked.

"Gavin's not like his father!"

"Cut from the same cloth."

"No—I mean, Dad, I *love* him. I—I want to marry him."

"Oh, God." Setting his jaw, he said more quietly, "And Gavin—how does he feel?"

"He loves me, too."

Snorting, Adam Walker ran a shaky hand over his lip. "He only loves one thing, Melanie, and that's skiing. Downhill racing was his ticket out of Taylor's Crossing and believe me, he's going to use it to stay away."

Melanie's heart wrenched. Some of what her father was saying was true—she'd told herself that the death-defying runs down the face of a rugged mountain were and always would be Gavin's first love, his mistress—but she didn't want to believe it.

Her father glanced through the trees to the snow-laden mountains in the distance. Absently he rubbed his chest. "I don't say as I can blame him."

"But, when he gets back from Colorado…" she protested as the wind tossed her hair in front of her face.

"He won't be coming back. He's gonna make the Olympic team." Her father's gaze returned to hers. The sadness in his eyes was so profound it cut to her soul. "Sweet Mary, you're just a child."

"I'm—"

"Seventeen, for God's sake!" His breath whistled through his teeth.

"It doesn't matter."

"Life hasn't begun at seventeen." He reached into the pocket of his work shirt for his cigarettes, then swore when he discovered the pack was missing. He'd quit smoking nearly three years before.

Walking on numb legs, Melanie crossed the yard and propped her elbows on the top rail of the fence. Through the pines she could see the spiny ridge of the Cascade Mountains. The highest peak, Mount Prosperity, loomed over the valley.

Her father's throat worked as he followed her. He touched her gently on the shoulder. "Doc Thompson at the clinic, he can—"

"No!" she cried, pounding her fist against the weathered top rail. "I'm having this baby!" She turned, appalled that he would suggest anything so vile. "This is *my* child," she said, tossing her black hair from her eyes. "My child and Gavin's, and I'm going to keep him and raise him and love him!"

"And where does Gavin figure into all this? Does he know?"

She shook her head. "Not yet. I just found out this afternoon."

Adam Walker looked suddenly tired. He said softly, "He may not want it, you know."

"He does!" Her fists clenched so hard that her hands ached.

"He might consider a wife and baby extra baggage."

She'd thought of that, of course. And it worried her. Gavin, if his dream were realized and he made the Olympic team, might not be back for months. Unless he felt duty bound to give up everything he'd worked for and return to support a teenage wife and child. Nervously, she chewed on the inside of her lip.

"What do you think he'll do when he finds out?"

"Come back here," she said weakly.

"And give up skiing?"

Though she felt like crying, she nodded.

He sighed loudly. "And that's what you want?"

"No. Yes! Oh, Dad, yes!" She threw up her hands. How could anything so wonderful as Gavin's child make life so complicated? She loved Gavin, he loved her, and they would have a baby. It was simple, wasn't it? Deep in her heart, she knew she was wrong, but she didn't want to face the truth.

She felt her father's hand on her shoulder. "I'll see you through this, Melanie. You just tell me what you want."

Melanie smiled, though her eyes burned with tears. "I want Gavin," she said.

Her father's hand stiffened, and when she glanced up at him, she saw that his face had turned ashen. He measured his words carefully. "You didn't plan this, did you?"

"Plan what?" she asked before she realized the turn of his thoughts. She felt the color drain from her face. "No!"

"Some women work out these things ahead of time—"

"No!" She shook her head. "The baby was an accident." *A glorious, wonderful accident!*

"Good." He pressed his lips together. "'Cause no man wants to feel trapped."

"I—I know," she whispered.

He touched her chin with a gloved finger, and his expression became tender. "You've got a lot going for you, girl. Finish high school and go to college. Become a photographer like you wanted—or anything else. You can do it. With or without Gavin."

"Can I?" she asked.

"'Course you can. And Gavin's not the only fish in the sea, you know. Neil Brooks is still interested."

Melanie was horrified. "Dad, I'm pregnant! This is for real!"

"Some men don't mind raising another man's child and some men don't even know they've done it."

"What's that supposed to mean?" she demanded, but a sick feeling grew inside her as she grasped his meaning.

"Only that you're not out of options."

She thought about Neil Brooks, a boy her father approved of. At twenty-two, he was already through college and working full-time in his father's lumber brokerage. Neil Brooks came from the right side of the tracks. Gavin Doel didn't.

"I'm not going to lie to Neil," she said.

"Of course you're not," her father agreed, but his eyes narrowed just a fraction. "Go on now, you go into the house and change. I'll take you into town and we'll celebrate."

"Celebrate what?" she asked.

He rolled his eyes to the cloud-covered heavens. "I suppose the fact that I'm going to be a grandfather, though I'll have you know I'm *much* too young." He was trying to cheer her up—she knew that—but she still saw pain flicker in his eyes. She'd wounded him more than he'd ever admit.

Gritting his teeth and flexing his muscles, he walked back to the ancient pine and wiggled the axe blade from the bole, leaving a fresh, ugly gash in the rough bark.

He headed for the barn with Sassafras on his heels again. But he was no longer whistling.

Melanie shoved her hands into her pockets and trudged into the old log house that had been in her family for three generations. Inside, the kitchen was warm and cheery, a fire burning in the wood stove. She rubbed her hands near the stove top, but deep inside she was cold—as cold as the winter wind that ripped through the valley.

She knew what she had to do, of course. Her father was right. And, in her heart, she'd come to the same agonizing conclusion. She couldn't burden Gavin with a wife and child—not now. *Not ever,* a voice inside her head nagged.

Climbing the stairs to her room, she decided that she would never stand between Gavin and his dream. He'd found a way to unshackle himself from a life of poverty and the ridicule of being the town drunk's son. And she wouldn't stop him. She couldn't. She loved him too much.

On his way to Olympic stardom as a downhill skier, Gavin couldn't be tied down to a wife and child. Though he might gladly give up skiing to support her and the baby, one day he would resent them both. Unconsciously, Melanie rubbed her flat abdomen with her free hand. She smiled sadly. If nothing else, she'd have a special part of Gavin forever.

Her pine-paneled room was filled with pictures of Gavin—wonderful snapshots she'd taken whenever they were together. Slowly, looking lovingly at each photograph of his laughing gold-colored eyes, strong jaw and wind-tossed blond hair, she removed every memento that reminded her of Gavin.

She closed her eyes and, once again, remembered the last time she'd seen him. His tanned skin had been smooth and supple beneath her fingers. His pervasive male scent had mingled with the fragrance of hay in the loft.

"Wait for me," he'd whispered. He had cupped her face in his hands, pressed warm kisses to her eyelids, touched a part of her no other man would ever find.

She remembered, too, how he had traced the slope of her jaw with one long finger, then pressed hard, urgent lips to hers. "Say you'll wait for me."

"You know I will," she'd vowed, her fingers tangling in his thick blond hair, her cheeks, wet from tears, pressed to his.

His smile had slashed white in the darkened hayloft. "I'll

always love you, Melanie," he'd sworn as he'd kissed her and settled his hard, sensual body over hers.

And I'll love you, she thought now, as she found a pen and paper and began the letter that would set him free.

CHAPTER ONE

Taylor's Crossing, Oregon
Eight Years Later

FLAGS SNAPPED IN the breeze. Barkers chanted from their booths. An old merry-go-round resplendent with glistening painted stallions pumped blue diesel smoke and music into the clear mountain air. Children laughed and scampered through the trampled dry grass of Broadacres Fairgrounds.

Long hair flying behind her, Melanie hurried between the hastily assembled tents to the rodeo grounds of the annual fair. She ducked between paddocks until she spied her uncle Bart, who was holding tight to a lead rope. On the other end was the apple of his eye and the pride of this year's fair—a feisty Appaloosa colt appropriately named Big Money.

Whip thin and pushing sixty, Bart strained to keep the lead rope taut. His skin had become leathery with age, his hair snow-white, but Melanie remembered him as a younger man, before her father's death, when Bart had been Adam Walker's best friend as well as his older brother.

"Thought you might have forgotten us," Bart muttered out of the corner of his mouth. His eyes were trained on the obstinate colt.

Melanie slid through the gate. "Me?" She looked up and offered him a smile. "Forget you? Nah!" Opening her camera bag, she pulled out her favorite .35-millimeter and removed the lens cap. "I just got caught up taking pictures of the fortune teller and weight lifter." Her eyes twinkling, she glanced up at Bart and wrinkled her nose. "If you ask me, Mr. Muscle hasn't got a thing on you."

"That's what all the ladies say," he teased back.

"I bet. So this is your star?" She motioned to the fidgeting Appaloosa.

"In the flesh."

Melanie concentrated as she gazed through the lens of her camera. *Okay,* she thought, focusing on the horse, *don't move.* But the prizewinning colt, a mean-spirited creature who knew he was the crowning glory of this fair, tossed his head and snorted menacingly.

Melanie smothered a grin. She snapped off three quick shots as the horse reared suddenly, tearing the lead rope from Bart's grip.

"You blasted hellion," Bart muttered.

Melanie clicked off several more pictures of the colt prancing, nostrils flared, gray coat catching the late afternoon sunlight.

"Come here, you devil," Bart muttered, advancing on the wild-eyed Big Money, who, snorting, wheeled and bolted to the far side of the paddock. "You know you're somethin', don't ya?"

The horse pawed the dry ground, and his white-speckled rump shifted as Bart advanced. "Now, calm down. Melanie here just wants to take a few pictures for the *Tribune*."

"It's all right," Melanie called. "I've got all I need."

"You sure?" He grabbed the lead rope and pulled hard. The colt, eyes blazing mischievously, followed reluctantly behind.

"Mmm-hmm. In next week's edition. This is the twenty-second annual fair. It's big news at the *Trib*," Melanie teased.

"And here I thought all the news was the reopening of Ridge Lodge," Bart observed. "And Gavin Doel's broken leg."

Melanie stiffened. “Not *all* the news,” she replied quickly. She didn’t want to think about Gavin, nor the fact that a skiing accident may have ended his career prematurely, bringing about his return to Taylor’s Crossing.

Uncle Bart wound the rope around the top rail of the fence and slipped through the gate after Melanie. “You been up to the lodge lately?”

Melanie slid him a glance and hid the fact that her lips tightened a little. “It’s still closed.”

“But not for long.” Bart reached into his breast pocket for his pack of cigarettes. “I figured since you were with the paper and all, you’d have some inside information.”

“Nothing official,” she said, somehow managing to keep her composure. “But the rumors are flying.”

“They always are,” Bart agreed, shaking out a cigarette. Big Money pulled on the rope. “And, from what I hear, Doel thinks he can pull it off—turn the ski resort into a profit-making operation.”

Melanie’s heart skipped a beat. “That’s the latest,” she agreed.

“Gavin tell you that himself?” he asked, lighting up and blowing out a thin stream of smoke.

“I haven’t seen Gavin in years.”

“Maybe it’s time you did.”

“I don’t think so,” Melanie replied, replacing the lens cap and fitting her camera back into its case.

Bart reached forward and touched her arm. “You know, Mellie, when your dad died, all the bad blood between Gavin’s family and ours dried up. Maybe it’s time you buried the past.”

Oh, I’ve done that, she thought sadly, but said, “Meaning?”

“Look up Gavin,” he suggested.

“Why?”

“You and he were close once. I remember seeing you up at the lodge together.” He slanted her a sly glance. “Some fires are tough to put out.”

Amen! "I'm a grown woman, Bart. I'm twenty-five and have a B.A., work for the *Trib* and even moonlight on the side. What would be the point?"

He studied her through the curling smoke of his cigarette. "You could square things up with Jim Doel. Whether your dad ever believed it or not, Jim paid his dues."

Melanie didn't want to think about Jim Doel or the fact that the man had suffered, just as she had, for that horrid night so long ago. Though she'd been only seven at the time, she remembered that night as vividly as any in her life—the night Jim Doel had lost control of his car, the night she'd lost her mother forever.

"As for Gavin," Uncle Bart went on, "he's back and unmarried. Seeing him again might do you a world of good."

Melanie shot him a suspicious glance. "A world of good?" she repeated. "I didn't know I was hurting so bad."

Bart chuckled.

"Believe it or not, I've got everything I want."

"Do you?"

"Yes."

"What about a husband and a house full of kids?"

She felt the color drain from her face. Somehow, she managed a thin smile. She still couldn't think about children without an incredible pain. "I had a husband."

"Not the right one."

"Could be that they're all the same."

"Don't tell your aunt Lila that."

"Okay, so you're different."

Bart scratched his head. "Everyone is, and you're too smart not to know it. Comparing Neil Brooks to Gavin Doel is like matching up a mule to a thoroughbred."

Despite the constriction in her throat Melanie had to laugh. "Don't tell Neil," she warned.

"I don't even talk to the man—not even when he shows

up here. Thank God, it's not too often. But it's a shame you didn't have a passel of kids."

Her insides were shaking by now. "It didn't work out," she said, refusing to admit that she and Neil could never have children, though they'd tried—at least at first. She and Neil had remained childless, and maybe, considering how things had turned out, it had been for the best. But still she grieved for the one child she'd conceived and lost.

Clearing her throat, she caught her uncle staring at her. "I—I guess it's a good thing we never had any children. Especially since the marriage didn't work." The lie still hurt. She would have loved children—especially Gavin's child.

Uncle Bart scowled. "Brooks is and always was an A-number-one bastard."

Melanie didn't want to dwell on her ex-husband, nor the reasons she'd married him. They came too close to touching Gavin again. With a sigh, she said, "Look, Bart, I really can make my own decisions."

"If you say so." He didn't seem the least bit convinced.

She said, "Not many people in town know or remember that Gavin and I had ever dated. I'd like to keep it that way."

"Don't see why—"

She touched his arm. "Please."

Deep furrows lined his brow as he dropped his cigarette and ground it out under the heel of his scruffy boot. "You know I can keep a secret when I have to."

"Good," she said, deciding to change the subject as quickly as possible. "Now, if you want to see Big Money's picture in the *Tribune* next week, I've got to run. Give Lila my love." With a wave she was off, trudging back through the dry grass, ignoring the noise and excitement of the carnival as she headed toward her battered old Volkswagen, determined not to think about Gavin Doel again for the rest of the day.

UNFORTUNATELY, GAVIN WAS the hottest gossip the town of Taylor's Crossing had experienced in years.

Back at the newspaper office, Melanie ran the prints in the darkroom and was just returning to her desk with a fresh cup of coffee when Jan Freemont, a reporter for the paper, slammed the receiver of her phone down and announced, "I got it, folks—the interview of the year!"

Melanie cocked a brow in her direction. "Of the year?"

"Maybe of the decade! Barbara Walters, move over!"

Constance Rava, the society page editor, whose desk was near Melanie's work area, looked up from her word processor. A small woman with short, curly black hair and brown eyes hidden by thick reading glasses, she studied Jan dubiously. "What've you got?"

"An interview with Gavin Doel!"

Melanie nearly choked on her coffee. She leaned her hips against her cluttered desk and hoped she didn't look as apoplectic as she felt.

"No!" Constance exclaimed.

"That's right!" Jan said, tossing her strawberry blond hair away from her face and grinning ear to ear. "He hasn't granted an interview in years—and it's going to happen tomorrow morning!"

Every face in the small room turned toward Jan's desk.

"So he's really here—in Oregon?" asked Guy Reardon, a curly-haired stringer and part-time movie critic for the paper.

"Yes, indeedy." Jan leaned back in her chair, basking in her yet-to-be-fulfilled glory.

"Why didn't we know about it until now?"

"You know Doel," Constance put in. She rolled her eyes expressively. "He's become one of those Hollywood types who demand their privacy."

Melanie had to bite her tongue to keep from saying something she'd probably regret. Her hands trembled as she set down her cup. Gavin had always created a sensation, probably always would. She'd have to get used to it. And she'd have to forget that there had ever been anything between them.

But the fact that he was back—*here*—caused her heart to thump crazily. Not that it mattered, she told herself. What Gavin did with his life was his business. Period. Except, of course, when it came to news. And though she was loath to admit it, Gavin Doel was news—big news—in Taylor's Crossing. The epitome of local boy does good.

Sidestepping the tightly packed desks in the newsroom, Jan threaded her way to Melanie's work area. "Can you believe it?"

"Hard to, isn't it?" she murmured, wishing the subject of Gavin Doel would just go away.

"Oh, come on. This is a coup, Mel. A real coup!"

"I know. But we've heard this all before. Someone's always going to reopen the resort."

"This is a done deal."

Melanie's heart sank. She'd hoped that, once again, the rumors surrounding Ridge Lodge were nothing more than idle speculation—at least as far as Gavin was concerned. Melanie welcomed the thought of the lodge opening, but why did Gavin have to be involved?

Jan wrinkled her nose thoughtfully. "I just got off the phone with Doel's partner, what's his name—" she glanced at her notes "—Rich Johanson. He said Doel would meet me tomorrow at nine at the main lodge!" Opening her hands in front of her, she added dramatically, "I can see it now, a full-page spread on the lodge, interviews with Gavin Doel and maybe a series of articles about the man, his personal and professional life—"

"Don't you think you're pushing things a bit?" Melanie cut in a little desperately. Few people had been with the paper long enough to know about her romance with Gavin, and she intended to keep it that way. "Constance just told us how private he is—"

"But he'll need the publicity if the ski lodge is to reopen for the season. And we all know how Brian feels about this story—he can't wait!"

Brian Michaels was the editor-in-chief of the paper.

"He'll want to run with this one. Now," Jan said, chewing on her lower lip, "we'll need background information and photos. Then, tomorrow, when we're at the lodge—"

"We're?" Melanie repeated, reaching for her Garfield coffee cup again. She took a sip of lukewarm coffee as her heart kicked into double time.

"Yes—us," Jan replied as if Melanie had developed some sort of hearing problem. "You and me. I need you for the shoot."

This was too much. Despite her professionalism, Melanie wasn't ready to come face-to-face with Gavin. Not after the way they'd parted. He'd asked her to wait for him and she'd vowed that she would. But she hadn't. In fact, within the month she'd married Neil Brooks. "Can't Geri do the shoot?" she asked.

"She starts vacation tomorrow, remember?" Jan shoved a stack of photographs out of the way and plopped onto the corner of Melanie's desk. Crossing her legs, she leaned over Melanie's In basket. "Don't you want a chance to photograph one of the most gorgeous men in skiing history?"

"No."

"Why not?"

Melanie dodged that one. There wasn't any reason to tell Jan all about her past—a past she'd rather forget. At least not yet. "I've heard he's not too friendly with photographers."

"Too many paparazzi," Jan surmised, waving off the statement as if it were a bothersome mosquito. "But that's what he gets for going out with all those famous models. It comes with the territory." She leaned closer. "Confidentially, this paper needs the kind of shot in the arm that Gavin Doel's fame and notoriety could give it. I don't have to tell you that the *Trib*'s in a world of hurt."

Guy, who had wandered over from the copy machine, glanced over his shoulder. "Do you think he brought any of his girlfriends back with him? I'd love to meet Gillian Sentra or Aimee LaRoux."

"You and the rest of the male population," Jan replied dryly.

Melanie's heart wrenched, but she ignored the familiar pain.

"I don't think there will be any women with him," Constance said from her desk. "He hasn't been seen with anyone since he broke his leg in that fall last spring. The way I understand it, he's become a recluse."

"But not a monk, I'll bet," Guy joked. "Doel's always surrounded by gorgeous women. Anyway, Melanie's right—the guy's just not all that friendly with the press. I can't believe he's going along with the interview."

"Well," Jan said, "I didn't actually talk to Doel himself. But Johanson says he'll be there." Jan checked her watch and glowered at the digital display. "Look, I've got to run. I want to tell Brian about the interview."

"He'll be ecstatic," Melanie predicted sarcastically. Since the rumors had sprung up that Ridge Lodge was reopening, the editor-in-chief had been busy coming up with articles about the lodge—its economic impact on the community, the environmental issues, the fact that one of the most famous skiers in America had returned to his small home town. Yes, Gavin was big news, and the *Tribune* needed all the big news it could get.

Jan's brown eyes slitted suspiciously. "You know, Melanie, everyone in Taylor's Crossing is thrilled about this—except for you, maybe."

"I'm all in favor of Ridge reopening," Melanie said, taking

another gulp of her coffee and frowning at the bitter taste. She shoved her cup aside, sloshing coffee on some negatives. Sopping the mess with a tissue, she muttered, "Idiot," under her breath and avoided Jan's curious gaze.

"So what's the problem?" Jan persisted.

"No problem," Melanie lied, tossing the soppy tissue into her wastebasket. "I just hope that it all works out. It would be a shame if Ridge Lodge reopened only to close again in a year or two."

"No way—not if Doel's behind it! I swear, that man has the Midas touch." Jan slung the strap of her bag over her shoulder just as Brian Michaels shoved open the door to his glassed-in editor's office and made a beeline for her desk. A short, lean man with prematurely gray hair and contacts that tinted his eyes a darker shade of blue, he dodged desks, glowing computer terminals and overflowing wastebaskets on his way toward the photography section.

"You got the Doel interview?" he asked Jan.

"Yep." Jan explained about her conversation with Gavin's partner, and Brian was so pleased he managed a nervous smile.

"Good. Good. We'll do a story in next week's issue, then follow up with articles between now and ski season." Tugging thoughtfully at his tie, he glanced at Melanie. "Dig out any old pictures we have of Doel. Go back ten years or so—when he was on the ski team for the high school, then the Olympic team. And find everything you can on his professional career and personal life. And I mean everything." He swung his gaze back to Jan. "And you talk to the sports page editor, see what he's got on file and double-check with Constance, see if he's up to anything interesting personally. It doesn't really matter if it's now or in the past. Don't forget to rehash the accident where he broke his leg—poor son of a bitch probably lost his career on that run."

For a split second, Melanie thought she saw a glimmer of

satisfaction in Brian's tinted eyes. But it quickly disappeared as he continued. "And check into his love life before he left town, that sort of thing."

Melanie's heart turned stone-cold.

"Will do," Jan said, then frowned at Melanie, who was standing stock-still. Jan pursed her lips as she glanced at her watch again. "I've really got to get moving—the park dedication's in less than an hour. I'll meet you up at the lodge tomorrow morning."

Unless I chicken out, Melanie thought grimly as Brian and Jan went their separate ways. So she had to face Gavin again. She felt a premonition of disaster but squared her shoulders. The past was ancient history. There wasn't any reason Gavin would drag it up.

Even so, her stomach tightened at the thought. How could she ever explain why she'd left him so suddenly? Why she'd married Neil? Even if she could say all the right words, it was better that he never knew.

She wasn't looking forward to tomorrow in the least, she thought grimly. The last person she wanted to see was Gavin Doel.

"I WANT IT OFF, and I want if off today!" Gavin thundered, glaring darkly at the cast surrounding the lower half of his left leg.

"Just another couple of days." Dr. Hodges, who looked barely out of his teens, tented his hands under his chin and shook his head. He sat behind a bleached oak desk in his Portland sports clinic, trying to look fatherly while gently rebuffing Gavin as if he were a recalcitrant child. "If you want to race professionally again—"

"I do."

"Then let's not push it, shall we?"

Gavin clamped his mouth shut. He wanted to scream—to

rant and rave—but knew there was no reason. The young sandy-haired doctor knew his business. "I've got work to do."

"The lodge?"

"The lodge," Gavin agreed.

"Even when you get the cast off, you'll have to be careful."

"I'm tired of being careful."

"I know."

Gavin rubbed an impatient hand around his neck. He hated being idle, hated worse the fact that he'd been sidelined from the sport he loved, but at least he had the resort to keep him busy. Though his feelings about returning to Taylor's Crossing were ambivalent, he was committed to making Ridge Resort the premier ski resort in the Pacific Northwest.

"Come back in on Friday. I'll check the X rays again and then, if the fracture has healed, you can go from a walking cast to only crutches. With physical therapy, you should be back on the slopes by December."

"This is September. It's already been over six months."

"That's because you rushed it before," Hodges said with measured patience. "That hairline fracture above your ankle happened during the spring season and you reinjured it early this summer when you wouldn't slow down. So now you have to pay the price."

Gavin didn't need to be reminded. He shoved his hands through his hair in frustration. "Okay, okay, you've made your point."

"Friday, then?"

"Right. Friday." Helping himself up with his crutches, he started for the door. He made his way through the white labyrinthine corridors to the reception area. He passed by posters of the skeletal system, the neurological system, the human eye and heart, but he barely noticed. He was too wrapped up with the fragility of the human ankle—his damned ankle.

And now he had to drive nearly three hundred miles back

to Taylor's Crossing, a town he despised. He would have picked any other location in the Cascades for his resort, but Taylor's Crossing, his partner had assured him, was perfect. The price was right, the location ideal. If only Gavin could get over his past and everything that the town represented.

Meaning Melanie.

Uttering an oath at himself, he shouldered open the door and hobbled across the parking lot to his truck. He shoved his crutches inside and climbed behind the wheel. As he flicked on the ignition, he told himself yet again to forget her. She was out of his life—had been for eight or nine years.

She was married to wealth and probably had a couple of kids by now. Scowling, he threw the truck into reverse, then peeled out of the lot. He didn't want to drive back to Taylor's Crossing tonight, would rather stay in Portland until Friday, when the cast had better come off.

Portland held no bittersweet memories for him. Taylor's Crossing was packed with them. Nonetheless, he headed east, back to Mount Prosperity, where so many memories of Melanie still lingered in the shadowy corners of Ridge Lodge.

AT FIVE-THIRTY, MELANIE ignored the headache pounding behind her eyes, stuffed her camera into her bag, snagged her jacket from the closet and headed out of the newsroom. The afternoon had flown by and she hadn't had a chance to dig through the files on back issues and dredge up pictures and information on Gavin. She was glad. She'd heard enough about him for one day, been reminded of him more times than she wanted to count. An invisible, bittersweet cloud of nostalgia had been her companion all afternoon. Seeing pictures of him would only intensify those feelings.

She would save the thrilling task of wading through Gavin's award-strewn past for tomorrow.

Tomorrow. She hardly dared think about it. What would

she say to Gavin again? What would she do? How could she possibly focus a camera on his handsome features and not feel a pang of regret for a past they hadn't shared, a future they would never face together, a baby who had never been born?

"Stop it," she chastised herself angrily, shoving open the door.

A wall of late summer heat met her as she walked out onto the dusty streets. A few dry leaves skittered between the parking meters lining the sidewalk. Melanie climbed into the sun-baked interior of her old Volkswagen, rolled down the window and headed east, through the heart of town, past a hodgepodge of shops toward the outskirts, where she lived in the log cabin her great-grandfather had built nearly a hundred years before, the home she'd left eight years ago.

She might not have returned except that her father's illness had coincided with her divorce. She'd come back then and hadn't bothered to move. There was no reason to—until now. If she could part with the home that was part of her heritage.

The log house had originally been the center of a ranch, but Taylor's Crossing, barely a fork in the road in her great-grandfather's time, had steadily encroached and now street lamps and concrete sidewalks covered what had once been acres of sagebrush and barbed wire. In the past few years there had been big changes in the place. Acre by acre the ranch had been sold, and now the property surrounding the house was little more than two fields and a weathered old barn. The log cabin itself, upgraded over the years, now boasted electricity, central heating, plumbing and a new addition that housed her small photography studio.

She parked her car near the garage, stopped off at the mailbox and winced at the stack of bills tucked inside. "Great," she muttered as Sassafras, her father's collie whom she'd inherited along with the house, barked excitedly. Wiggling, he bounded ahead to the door. "Miss me?" she asked, and the dog swept the back porch with his tail. She petted his head. "Yeah, me, too."

Inside, she tossed the mail and camera on the kitchen table, refilled Sassafras's water bowl and poured herself a tall glass of iced tea. Her headache subsided a little, and she glanced out the window to the Cascade Mountains. The craggy peak of Mount Prosperity, whereon Ridge Resort had been built years before, jutted jaggedly against the blue sky. She wondered if Gavin was there now. Did he live in the resort? Was he planning to stay after it was opened? Or would he, once his ankle had healed, resume his downhill racing career?

"What does it matter?" she asked herself, her headache returning to pound full force.

Tomorrow she'd have all her answers and more. Tomorrow she'd meet Gavin again. And then what—oh, God, what—could she possibly say to him?

THE NEXT MORNING, as shafts of early sunlight pierced through thick stands of pine, Melanie drove up the series of switchbacks to the ski resort.

A few clouds drifted around the craggy upper slopes of Mount Prosperity, but otherwise the sky was clear, the air crisp with the fading of summer.

Located just below the timberline, Ridge Lodge, a rambling cedar and stone resort that had been built a few years before the Great Depression, rose four stories in some places, with steep gables and dormers. The building had been remodeled several times but still held an early-twentieth-century charm that blended into the cathedrallike mountains of the central Oregon Cascades.

Melanie had always loved the lodge. Its sloped roofs, massive fireplaces and weathered exterior appealed to her as much today as it had when she was a child growing up in nearby Taylor's Crossing. She'd lived in the small town most of her life, except for the six years she'd been married to Neil and resided in Seattle. Ridge Lodge had been an important part of her youth—a special part that had included Gavin.

As she parked her battered old Volkswagen in the empty lot, her pulse fairly leaped, her skin covered in goose bumps. The thought of seeing Gavin again brought sweat to her palms.

"Don't be a fool," she berated herself, climbing out of the car and grabbing her heavy camera bag. *He's long forgotten you.* Shading her eyes, she looked over the pockmarked parking lot and noted that Jan's sports car wasn't in sight. "Terrific."

She started up the path, noticing the bulldozers and snowplows standing like silent sentinels near huge sheds. Behind the lodge, ski lifts—black poles strung together with cable—marched up the bare mountainside.

"It's now or never," she told herself. Keyed up inside, her senses all too aware, Melanie swallowed back any lingering fear of coming face-to-face with Gavin.

She pounded on the front doors, and they creaked open against her fist. "Hello?" she called into the darkened interior.

No one answered.

Hiking her bag higher, she squared her shoulders and strode inside. The main desk was empty, the lodge still, almost creepy. "Hello?" she yelled again, and her voice echoed to the rafters high overhead. Summoning all her courage, she said, "Gavin?"

The sound of his name, from her own voice, seemed strange. Her nerves, already strung tight, stretched to the breaking point. Where was Jan?

Maybe Gavin had changed his mind. Or, more likely, maybe Rich Johanson had spoken out of turn. Probably Gavin wasn't even here. Disgusted, she turned, thinking she'd wait for Jan outside, then stopped, her breath catching in her throat.

Blocking the doorway, crutches wedged under his arms, eyes hidden behind mirrored aviator glasses, Gavin Doel glared at her.

Melanie's heart nearly dropped through the floor. She tried to step forward but couldn't move.

He was more handsome than before, all boyishness long driven from the bladed angles and planes of his face. His expression was frozen, his thin lips tight. The nostrils of his twice-broken nose flared contemptuously at the sight of her.

In those few heart-stopping seconds Melanie felt the urge to run, get away from him as fast as she could. The once-dead atmosphere in the lodge came to life, charged and dangerous.

Gavin shifted on his crutches, his jaw sliding to the side. "Well, *Mrs.* Brooks," he drawled in a cold voice that disintegrated the remnants of her foolish dreams—dreams she hadn't even realized she'd kept until now. "Just what the hell are *you* doing here?"

CHAPTER TWO

GAVIN RIPPED OFF HIS sunglasses and impaled her with his icy gaze. "Well?" he demanded, his eyes slitting dangerously. His jaw thrust forward impatiently. Undercurrents of long-dead emotions charged the air.

"I was waiting for you."

"For me?" His mouth tightened. "Well, now, isn't that a switch?"

The words bit.

"You know, Melanie, you were the last person I expected to run into up here." He dug in his crutches and hobbled past her to the bar.

"I was waiting for you because—"

"I don't want to hear it. In fact," he said, glancing over his shoulder, "I don't think we have anything to say to each other."

Melanie was stunned. This cold, bitter man was Gavin—the boy she'd loved so passionately. Where was the tenderness, the kindness, the laughter she remembered so vividly? "Let's just get through this, okay?"

"What? Get through what? Oh, hell, it doesn't matter." He turned his attention to the dusty mirrored bar.

"Of course it matters! I've got a job to do—"

He frowned, his eyes narrowing on her camera case. "A job?"

"Yes—"

"Just get out."

"Pardon me?"

"I said 'Get out,' Melanie. Leave. I don't want to talk to you."

"But you agreed—"

"Agreed?" he roared, his fist banging the bar. "Unless memory fails me, the last time we agreed to anything, I was going to Colorado and you *agreed* to wait for me."

"Oh, God." This was worse than she imagined. "I couldn't—"

"And guess what? The minute I'm out of town, you left me high and dry."

"That's not exactly how it was," she snapped back.

"Oh, no? Then you tell me, how was it?"

"You were in Colorado—"

"Oh, right, I left you. Look, it doesn't matter. It's over. Period. I shouldn't have brought it up. So just go." Swearing under his breath, he propped himself up with his crutches and scrounged around behind the oak and brass bar, searching the lower cupboards.

From her vantage point, Melanie saw his reflection in the dusty full-length mirror. He was wearing cutoff jeans, and the muscles of his thighs, covered with downy gold hair, strained as he leaned over.

"You did leave me," she pointed out, refusing to back down.

"And you said you'd wait. Stupid me, I believed you."

"I meant it."

"Oh, I get it," he said, glaring at her again. "I just didn't put a time limit on the waiting, is that it? I assumed you meant you'd wait more than a few weeks before you eloped with someone else."

The hackles on the back of her neck rose as he turned his attention back to the cupboard. "You don't understand—"

"No, damn it, I don't. *I*—" he hooked a thumb at his chest "—wasn't there, was I? I didn't have the advantage of seeing you moving in on Brooks."

"I didn't move in on—"

"Okay, so he moved in on you. Doesn't matter."

"Then what're we arguing about?" she demanded, the heat rushing to her cheeks.

He let out his breath slowly, as if trying to control a temper that was rapidly climbing out of control. "What're you doing here, Melanie? I thought you lived in Seattle and probably owned a Mercedes and had a couple of kids by now."

"Sometimes things don't turn out the way you want them to," she said.

He glanced over the top of the bar, his brows pulled together. "Philosophy? Or real life?"

"Both," she replied, holding up her chin. "I'm here with the *Tribune*."

"The what?" he asked without much interest.

"The *Tribune*. You know, the local newspaper."

"Oh, right." He snorted, returning his attention to the contents of the bar. "So you're a reporter these days? What's that got to do with me?"

"I'm a photographer," she replied quickly. "Not a reporter, but I'm supposed to take pictures of you for the interview."

"I don't give interviews."

Melanie's temper began to simmer. "But yesterday your partner said you'd talk to us—"

His head snapped up, and the look he sent her over the bar was positively furious. "Rich said *what*?"

"That you'd grant an interview to the *Trib*—"

"No way!"

"But—"

"Hey, don't argue with me," he bit out. "You, of all people, should understand why I don't talk to the press. It has to do with privacy and the fact that there are some details of my life I'd rather keep to myself."

"Why me 'of all people?'" she flung back at him.

His lips thinned. "As I remember it, there's still some bad blood between our families and a whole closet full of skeletons that are better left locked away."

She couldn't argue with that, but she wanted to. Damn the man, he still had a way of getting under her skin—even if it was only to irritate her. But he did have a point, she thought grudgingly. She didn't want anyone dredging up their affair or the scandal concerning her mother and his father.

"I'll make sure this is strictly professional."

"You can guarantee that?"

"I can try."

"Not good enough. The *Tribune* doesn't have the greatest reputation around."

"I know, but—"

"Then no interview. Period," he growled, rattling glasses until he found a bottle, yanked it out and blew the dust from its label.

"Let's start over."

He didn't move, but his gaze drilled into hers. "Start over," he repeated. "I wish I could. I would've done a whole lotta things differently."

A lump jammed her throat. Her voice, when she found it, was soft. "I—uh, that's not what I meant. I think we should start the interview over."

"Like hell!" Wincing as he straightened his leg, he rained a drop-dead glance her direction.

Her temper flared. "Look, Gavin, I don't want to be here any more than you want me here!"

"Then leave." He cleaned the bottom of a short glass with the tail of his shirt, then uncapped the bottle.

"I have a job to do."

"Oh, yeah. Pictures for the *Trib*. I forgot." He poured three fingers of whiskey into the glass and tossed back the entire drink, grimacing as the liquor hit the back of his throat.

"Isn't it a little early—?"

"I don't need any advice," he cut in. "Especially from you!" A sardonic smile twisted his lips, and he leaned across the bar, holding the bottle in one hand. "Excuse my manners," he bit out, obviously intending to bait her. "Would you like to join me?"

Melanie narrowed her eyes, rising to the challenge. Why not? She'd taken all the flak she intended to, so she'd beat him at his own game! "Sure. And make it a double."

A spark of humor flashed in his tawny eyes. "The lady wants a double." He twisted off the cap. "You never did anything halfway, did you, Melanie? All or nothing."

"That's me," she mocked, but her pulse jumped as he looked her way again, and she remembered him as he had been—younger, more boyish, his hard edges not yet formed. He'd always been striking and arrogant and fiercely competitive, but there had been a gentle side to him, as well—a loving side that she'd never quite forgotten. Now it seemed that tenderness was well hidden under layers of cynicism.

She felt a stab of guilt. How could their wonderful love have turned so bitter?

Forcing a smile, she fought the urge to whisper that she was sorry. Instead she took the glass he offered and sipped the fiery liquor. "Ah…" she said, remembering the words her grandfather had used when tasting expensive Scotch, "smooth!"

"Right…smooth," he challenged, his eyes glinting again. "Good ol' rotgut whiskey. I'll give you a clue, Melanie, it's not smooth. In fact it burns like a son of a bitch."

He was right. The whiskey seared a trail down her throat. She pushed her glass aside and met his gaze squarely. "If you say so."

"I do."

"Then that must be the way it is," she replied smartly, wishing he wasn't so damned handsome. If only she didn't notice the way his dark lashes ringed his eyes, the cut of his cheekbones, the down hair of his forearms. "Now that we've gotten past going for each other's jugular—maybe we can quit sniping at each other long enough to get down to business."

"Which is?"

"The interview. And pictures for it."

His mouth tightened, and he shoved a wayward lock of blond hair from his eyes before taking another long, slow sip from his glass.

Several seconds ticked by, and he didn't move a muscle. The subject of the interview was obviously closed.

"Right. Well, I tried." With the tips of her fingers Melanie nudged her business card across the bar. "In case you change your mind. And when Jan gets here, would you tell her I went back to the office?"

"Who's Jan?"

"The reporter. The one from the *Tribune* who planned to write a stunning article about your lodge. As I pointed out earlier, I'm just the photographer and I don't care whether you want to be photographed or not. But Jan might see things differently. She's under the false impression that you agreed to an interview."

"She's wrong."

"You can tell her." She started for the door and said sarcastically over her shoulder, "Thanks for the drink."

Shoving his crutches forward, Gavin hobbled around the bar and placed himself squarely in her path to the door. "What is it you're really doing here, Melanie?" he asked.

A surge of anger swept through her. "You think I'm lying?"

"I don't know." His lips twisted cynically. "But then, you've had a lot of practice, haven't you?"

That did it! She slung her bag over her shoulder. "For your information, I don't want to be here. In fact, if I could, I'd be anywhere on God's green earth rather than here with you!" She spun, but quick as a striking snake his hand shot out, steely fingers curled over her wrist and he whirled her back to face him.

"Before you leave," he said so quietly she could barely hear him, "just answer one question."

Melanie's heart thumped, and her wrist, where his fingers wrapped possessively over her pulse, throbbed. Her throat was suddenly dry. "Shoot."

"Where is your husband?"

"I don't have a husband anymore."

His eyes narrowed as if he expected everything she said to be a lie. She turned back to the door, but he wouldn't release her. "So what happened to good ol' Neil?"

She swallowed hard. "We, uh, we're divorced."

Something flashed in his eyes. Regret? "I guess I should say I'm sorry."

"No need to lie."

His face softened slightly. "Believe it or not, Melanie, I only wanted the best for you," he said suddenly. "I just didn't think Neil Brooks could make you happy."

"I guess it's a moot point now."

"Is it?" Again the pressure on her arm, the spark in his eyes.

Nervously she licked her lips, and his attention was drawn for a second to her mouth.

His jaw worked, and he said softly, "You know, Melanie, I think it would be best if you didn't come back."

"I only came here because of my job."

"Oh?" he said, eyebrows lifting, the fingers on the inside

of her wrist pressing slightly against her bare skin. "So you weren't curious about me?"

"Not in the least."

"And you didn't think because you shed yourself of your husband that we could pick up where we left off?" His voice had grown husky, his pupils dilating in the darkened lodge.

"That would be crazy." But her heart was pumping madly, slamming against her ribs, and she could barely concentrate on the conversation as his fingers moved on her inner wrist.

"Probably—"

The huge double doors were flung open, and Jan, her briefcase swinging at her side, strode into the lobby. "So here you are! God, I've had a terrible time getting here—" She took one look at Gavin and Melanie, and her train of thought seemed to evaporate.

Self-consciously, Melanie yanked her arm away from Gavin.

"Well," Jan said, as if walking in on an intimate scene between one of her co-workers and an internationally famous skier were an everyday occurrence, "I see you've already started."

"Not quite," Melanie replied, but Jan plunged on, walking up to Gavin and flashing her businesslike smile.

"I'm Jan Freemont. With the Taylor's Crossing *Tribune*." She flicked a confused glance at Melanie. "But I suppose you already guessed."

"I assumed."

Jan dug into her heavy canvas bag. She withdrew a card and handed it to him. "So, you've already met Melanie."

Gavin's mouth quirked. "Years ago."

"Oh?" Jan's brows lifted in interest, and Melanie could have throttled Gavin right then and there.

Instead, she managed a cool smile. "Gavin and I both grew up around here," she explained, hoping that would end this turn in the conversation. She was probably wrong. Jan wasn't one to let the subject drop. Her reporter instincts were probably going crazy already.

"Sorry I'm late," Jan apologized. "I had trouble with my car again."

"I don't think it matters," Melanie said.

Jan was busy extracting her pocket recorder and steno pad.

Melanie threw Gavin a look that dared him to disagree as she said, "Mr. Doel and I were just discussing the interview."

"Mmm?" Jan asked, searching through her large black shoulder bag.

"There isn't going to be one," Gavin said.

Melanie lifted a shoulder. "Apparently he didn't know about it."

"I didn't," Gavin clarified.

Melanie charged on. "And he's not interested in going through with it."

"You're kidding, right?" Jan asked.

"'Fraid not," Gavin drawled.

"But I spoke with your partner, Mr.—" she flipped open a note pad "—Johanson. He said you'd be glad to talk to us."

"Oh, he did, did he?" Gavin seemed faintly amused. "Well, he was wrong."

Oh, this is just wonderful, Melanie thought, wishing she could disappear. She'd known this session would be a disaster, but neither Brian Michaels, the *Trib*'s editor-in-chief, nor Jan, the paper's crack reporter, had listened to her. Jan saw herself as a new Barbara Walters and Brian was hoping he could turn the *Tribune* into the *Washington Post*. Never mind that the *Tribune* was a small newspaper in central Oregon with a steadily declining readership.

Jan wasn't about to be thwarted. She explained about her phone call to Gavin's partner. She also went into an animated dissertation about how she wanted to write a "local boy does good then returns home" type of story.

Gavin wasn't buying it. He listened to all her arguments, but his hard expression didn't alter and his gaze drilled into her. "If you want information on the lodge, you'll have to get it from Rich," he finally said.

"But our readers will want to know all about you and your injury—"

"My personal life is off limits," Gavin muttered, and Melanie felt a tremor of relief.

"But you're a celebrity," Jan cooed, trying desperately to win him over. "You have fans who are interested—"

"Then they can read all about it in some cheap rag at the checkout counter of their local market. It might not be true, but it's guaranteed to be sensational."

"Now, wait a minute." Jan wasn't about to take this lying down. "Reopening Ridge Lodge is a big story around here! People will be interested and it's great publicity for you—"

"I don't want publicity," he said, glancing icily at Melanie. "I think I've had enough." He hobbled to the door. "If you want to do an article on the lodge reopening, that's fine with me. But I want my name kept out of it as much as possible."

Jan's smile was frozen. "But doesn't that defeat the point? It's your name that's going to bring people here, Mr. Doel. Your face in the paper that will make people interested. You're an international skier. You've endorsed everything from skis to lip balm. Your face will guarantee public interest, and that's what you need to reopen the lodge successfully." She gestured expansively to the inside of the resort. "I know I can convince my editor to do a series of articles about the lodge that will keep public interest up. I'll also free-lance stories to ski magazines that are distributed everywhere in the country, so by the time the snow hits and the season is here, you're guaranteed cars in the parking lot, skiers on the runs and people in the bar."

Melanie expected Gavin to say "Bully for you" or something along those lines, but he kept silent.

Jan pressed her point home. "My guess is you need all the publicity you can get."

"I've given you my answer. Rich'll be back here this afternoon. Since he's the one who agreed to this damned interview in the first place, you can talk to him."

He shoved his crutches in front of him and moved awkwardly through the front door.

"That man is something else!" Jan whispered, letting out her breath. "You know, he almost acts like he's got something to hide."

"Constance said he doesn't talk to the press," Melanie reminded her.

"Yeah, but she didn't say why." Jan's lips thinned as she turned to Melanie. "And what was going on between you two when I first got here? You looked like you were deciding whether to kill each other or make love."

Melanie's stomach tightened. "You're exaggerating."

"Nope. And you didn't tell me that you knew him."

Lifting a shoulder, Melanie replied, "It didn't seem important."

Jan's expression clouded with suspicion. "Oh, sure. That's like saying storm warnings aren't important when you're heading out to sea in a small boat."

Slinging the strap of her camera bag over her shoulder, Melanie said, "Look, I've got another shoot in twenty minutes, so I'm not going to waste my time here."

"But you'll fill me in later?"

"Sure," Melanie replied, wondering just how much she could tell Jan about Gavin as she shoved open the door and stepped into the warm mountain air.

Across the parking lot, near the equipment shed, she spied Gavin leaning hard on his crutches, talking to a man in an orange pickup. A sign on the pickup's door read Gamble Construction.

The two men were engrossed in conversation. Gavin's reflective aviator glasses were back in place, and the late morning sunlight glinted in his hair. His cast-covered leg looked awkward.

Melanie wondered if the rumors were true that his career was over.

He didn't glance her way as she unlocked her car, and she didn't bother trying to get his attention. The less she had to do with him, the better.

GAVIN WATCHED THE little car speed out of the lot and felt the tension between his shoulder blades relax. He hadn't counted on seeing Melanie again. What was she doing back in Taylor's Crossing, working at that rag of a paper? And why had she and Neil split? Maybe Brooks wasn't making enough money for her now.

But would she give up the good life of luxury to work on a small-time newspaper? Nope, it didn't make sense.

"…so the crew will be here at the beginning of the week, and I think we can make up for some of the time lost by the strike," Seth Gamble, owner of Gamble Construction, was saying as he leaned out the window of his pickup. Gavin forced his attention back to the conversation.

"Good. I'll see you then." Gavin thumped the dusty hood of the truck with his hand, and Seth, grinning, rammed the pickup into gear and took off.

Shoving the damned crutches under his arms, Gavin started back for the lodge and found Jan whatever-her-name-was, the blond reporter, sweeping toward him. Her expression had turned hard, and he was reminded why he didn't trust reporters. They didn't give a damn about the subject—just that they got the story.

"Mr. Doel!" she said, striding up to him and trying her best to appear hard-edged and tough. "My editor expects a story on the lodge—the story we were promised."

"As I said, you can talk to my partner."

"Is he here?"

"No," Gavin admitted.

"When do you expect him?"

"I don't know. He had business out of town."

"Then it looks like we're left with you if we want to make next week's edition. Right?" When Gavin didn't reply, she said, "I'm sorry if we inconvenienced you, Mr. Doel, but what's going on here—" she made a sweeping gesture to the lodge "—is news. Big news. And so, unfortunately, are you. You can't expect the *Tribune* to ignore it, nor, I would think, would you want it ignored."

She stood waiting, cool green eyes staring up at him, firm jaw set, and he couldn't fault her logic. Besides, he wanted to get rid of her. "All right," he finally agreed. "When Rich gets back. Tomorrow. He and I will tell you all about our plans for the resort, but I want my private life kept out of it."

"But not your professional life," Jan said quickly. "People will need to know why you're involved. Some people, believe it or not, might not be familiar with your name."

"My professional life is a matter of record."

"Good. Then we understand each other." She offered her hand, shook his and marched to a red sports car, which coughed and sputtered before sparking to life and tearing through the dusty lot.

"Now you've done it, Doel," he muttered. Inviting the reporter back was probably a mistake. No doubt Melanie would accompany her. His fingers tightened over the handholds on his crutches. Seeing Melanie again wasn't in his plans.

The sight of Melanie brought back memories he'd rather

forget forever, and touching her—good God, why had he done such a fool thing? Just the feel of her skin made his blood race.

Leveling an oath at himself, he plunged the tips of his crutches into the pavement and headed back for the lodge, intending to throttle Rich Johanson when he showed up. They'd had an agreement: Rich would handle all the publicity, the legal work and financial information; Gavin would supervise the reconstruction of the lodge and the runs. Gavin had made it clear from the onset that he wasn't going to have a passel of nosy reporters poking around, digging into his personal life.

He hadn't lied to Melanie when he'd mentioned skeletons in the closet. There were just too damned many. Unfortunately, Melanie knew about a lot of them. Her family and his could provide enough scandal to keep the gossip mill in Taylor's Crossing busy for years.

Gavin opened the door to the lodge. There on the bar was the bottle of whiskey. And two glasses—his and Melanie's.

Just what in the hell was she doing back in town?

BY THE TIME MELANIE shoved open the doors of the newspaper office, Jan had caught up with her. "Let me handle Brian," Jan insisted as she followed Melanie inside.

"He's not going to be thrilled about losing the interview," Melanie predicted.

Jan flashed her a grin and winked. "All is not yet lost."

Melanie stopped short. "What?"

"I think I've convinced the arrogant Mr. Doel to see things our way."

Melanie couldn't believe her ears. Gavin had been adamant. "How'd you do that?"

"Well, I did have to make a few concessions."

"I bet."

Constance, a worried expression crowding her features, was scanning the society and gossip columns of other papers. Looking up, she waved two fingers at Melanie, beckoning her over.

Jan made a beeline for the editor's office, but Melanie paused at Constance's desk.

"How'd it go?" Constance asked, once Melanie was in earshot.

"Not so good. You were right. Doel refused."

"Privacy is that man's middle name. So you got nothing?"

"Not so much as one shot," Melanie said, tapping her camera bag, "but Jan's convinced that he's changed his mind."

"I hope so." Constance's wide mouth pinched at the corners. "Brian's on a real tear. Geri called in and said she wanted to extend her vacation by a couple of days—and he told her not to bother coming back."

Geri was Melanie's backup—the only other photographer for the *Tribune*. Suddenly Melanie felt cold inside. "You mean—"

"I mean she's gone, kaput, outta here!" Constance sliced a finger theatrically across her throat.

"But why?"

"I don't know, but my guess is he's getting pressure from the owners of the paper." Her voice lowered. "We all know that sales haven't been so hot lately. In fact, Brian's counting on the interest in Ridge Resort to drum up business."

"Oh, great," Melanie said with a sigh. "In that case I'd better go help bail Jan out when she drops the bomb that we came up empty today."

She left her camera at her desk, then marched to Brian's office and knocked softly on the door.

"It's open!" Brian barked angrily.

Melanie slipped into the room as Jan coughed nervously. She was seated in a chair near the desk, notebook open, a pencil ready. "I was just explaining that getting an interview with Gavin Doel was tantamount to gaining an audience with God himself."

Melanie took a chair and nodded, swallowing a smile. "She's right."

"But somehow," Brian said, "she's managed to change his mind."

"Not somehow—I used my exceptional powers of persuasion," Jan remarked. "We're going back up there tomorrow. You know what they say about the mountain and Muhammad."

"He really agreed?" Melanie asked, dumfounded.

"Of course he did," Brian said with a sneer. He rubbed his chin with his hand. "No matter what else he is, Doel's no fool. And he can't snake his way out of this one. I've already devoted half the front page for the story."

Melanie couldn't believe it. What had made Gavin change his mind? And why was Brian so edgy?

"There is a catch," Jan explained.

Brian's lips turned down at the corners.

"Doel only wants his name used professionally. He doesn't want any part of his private life included."

Brian snorted. "That's impossible."

"But that's the deal," Jan insisted.

"Can't we hedge a little?"

Melanie shook her head. "I don't think that would be a good idea."

"Why not? As long as everything we print is true, he can't sue us," Brian argued. "And the way I see it, publicity will only help Ridge Lodge, of which he owns a large percentage."

Melanie squirmed. She wasn't afraid to speak her mind—she and Brian had locked horns more often than not, but when it came to Gavin, her emotions were still tangled in the past. "Gavin Doel won't take kindly to us digging through his private life. And I think we should keep good relations with him—at least as long as he owns and runs the resort."

Jan scribbled a note to herself. "Don't worry about it, Melanie, I'll handle the interview. Just get me some shots of the lodge, a few of the ski runs and the mountain and some closeups of Doel."

Brian tugged at his tie. "I'm counting on this article, men," he said, and Melanie laughed a little. Ever since she and the rest of the female staff had objected to being called girls, Brian had responded by referring to all reporters, photographers, secretaries and receptionists as men, female or male.

Melanie noticed the lines of worry etching Brian's forehead and the pinch of his lips. His complexion was pale, and she wondered, not for the first time, if he were ill. A bottle of antacids sat on the corner of his desk, next to his coffee cup and a half-full ashtray.

Brian's phone jangled, and he reached for it. "Okay, that's everything. Let's get on it," he said, lifting the receiver as he dismissed them.

"I want to talk to you," Jan whispered to Melanie as they walked back to the newsroom.

Here it comes, Melanie thought, but fortunately Constance waved Jan to her desk and Melanie escaped an inquisition on Gavin, at least for the time being.

She spent the rest of the afternoon sorting through the prints she'd taken of the fair the day before, picking out the shots of children riding the roller coaster and eating cotton candy. She worked on the shots of Uncle Bart's colt, as well, choosing a photograph of Big Money standing calmly by Bart for the next edition. She sorted through the shots again, found one she thought Bart would like and placed it in an envelope. She'd enlarge it later.

When she could no longer put off digging up pictures of Gavin, she set about looking through the files, sorting through old pictures and microfiche, rereading all about Gavin Doel. The photographs brought back memories of Gavin as a young man so full of life and expectation.

His skiing had been remarkable, gaining him a berth on the Olympic team and taking him on a road to fame and fortune. He'd been tough, fearless, and had attacked the most severe runs with a vengeance. His natural grace and balance had been God-given, but his fierce determination and pride had pushed him, driven him, to become the best.

Melanie stared wistfully at the photographs, noting the hard angle of his jaw and the blaze of competitive fire in his eyes before each race—and his smile of satisfaction after a win.

The most recent photographs were of Gavin losing that blissful God-given balance, tumbling on an icy mountainside and finally being carried off in a stretcher, his skin taut over nose and cheekbones, his mouth pulled in a grimace of pain.

"Oh, Gavin," she whispered, overcome by old feelings of love. "What happened to us?"

Hearing herself, she slammed the drawer shut and closed her mind to any of the long-dead emotions that had torn her apart ever since she'd heard he'd returned to Ridge Lodge. "Don't be a fool."

Stuffing the pictures she thought would be most useful into an envelope, she opened the drawer again. She slid Gavin's file into its proper slot and noticed the other slim file marked Doel, James.

Melanie's mouth went dry as she pulled Jim Doel's file from its slot and looked inside. She cringed at the first photograph of Gavin's father. Jim's eyes seemed vacant and haunted. His hands were shackled by handcuffs, and he was escorted by two policemen. In the background a frightened boy of twelve, his blond hair mussed, his pale eyes wide with fear, watched in horror. Restrained by a matronly social worker, Gavin was reaching around her, trying to get to his father as Jim was led to the waiting police car.

"Oh, God," she whispered. Her throat grew hot, and she pitied Gavin—an emotion he would abhor.

Chewing on her lower lip, she slipped the photograph from the file and tucked it quickly into her purse. No, that wasn't good enough. Jan or Brian would just dig deeper. Stomach knotted, she pulled the entire file from the drawer then took anything damaging from Gavin's file as well. There was no reason for Brian or anyone else from the *Tribune* to lay open Jim Doel's life and persecute him again. Nor, she thought, did she want to be reminded of her mother's death. She'd just take the file home and keep it locked away until all the interest in Gavin Doel faded.

She slammed the drawer quickly, and for the first time since returning to Taylor's Crossing two years before, Melanie wondered if coming home had been a mistake.

GAVIN RAMMED HIS crutches into a corner of his office and glared at his partner. "A reporter and photographer from the *Tribune* were here today," he said. "Seems you gave them the okay for an interview."

Rich shoved a beefy hand through his graying hair and sighed loudly. Tall and heavyset, he looked more like a retired guard for a professional football team than an attorney. "Don't tell me, you threw them out."

"You could have had the decency to let me know about it."

"You were gone," Rich pointed out. "Besides, I thought we agreed that we should start publicity as soon as possible."

"But not with personal interviews!"

Rich was irritated. "For God's sake, what've you got to hide?"

Gavin's jaw began to ache, and only then did he realize he'd clenched it. "I just don't want this to turn into a three-ring circus."

"Four rings would be better," Rich said, dropping into a chair. "The more interest and excitement we can generate, the better for everyone."

Gavin snorted. Ever since seeing Melanie again, he'd felt restless and caged and he'd been out of sorts. "Look, I'm all for publicity about the resort. But that's as far as it goes. I like my privacy."

"Then you chose the wrong profession." Rich stuffed his hands in his pockets and jangled his keys nervously. "I know you don't want to hear this, but I think public interest in you is healthy."

"Meaning?" Gavin asked suspiciously.

"Meaning that people aren't really all that interested in your professional life. Hell, the Olympics were eons ago. And only a few dyed-in-the-wool fans will care about ski clinics you developed." His pale blue eyes lighted, and he wagged a finger at Gavin. "But the fact that you jetted all over the continent, skiing with famous celebrities, dating gorgeous women, partying with glamorous Hollywood types—now *that* will get their attention!"

"The wrong kind."

"Any kind will help."

Gavin scowled. "The tabloids made more of it than there was," he said slowly.

"Doesn't matter. The public sees you as an athletic playboy—a guy who hobnobs with the rich and beds the beautiful."

Gavin grimaced. "Then the public would be disappointed if it knew the truth."

"Let's not allow that to happen," Rich suggested slyly. "What does it hurt to keep the myth alive?"

"Just my reputation."

Rich chuckled as he crossed the room and poured himself a cup of coffee. "Don't you know most men would kill for a reputation like yours?"

"Then they're fools," Gavin grumbled, hobbling over to the window and staring at the windswept slopes of the mountain rising high behind the lodge. Without snow, the ragged slopes of Mount Prosperity seemed empty and barren.

He thought of Melanie, and his frown deepened. No doubt she'd be back tomorrow, along with the pushy reporter. It didn't matter that he didn't want to see her again.

"Just one more session," he muttered to himself.

"What?" Rich asked.

"Nothing," Gavin replied. "I was just thinking about the interview tomorrow."

"What about it?" Rich blew across his coffee cup.

"I can't wait for it to be over!" he declared vehemently. Maybe then he could close his mind to Melanie. Even now, eight years later, her betrayal burned painfully in his gut.

Maybe he'd get lucky and they'd send someone else. But more likely he'd have to face her again and find some way of being civil. He doubted he was up to it.

CHAPTER THREE

THE MORNING SUN gilded the steep slopes of Mount Prosperity as Melanie again met Jan at Ridge Lodge Resort. She turned from the view of the mountain to the old rambling cedar and shake lodge. She wished she could be anywhere other than here.

"It'll be over soon," she muttered under her breath.

"What will?" Jan asked, approaching her car.

"This interview."

"You want it over? But why? This has to be the most interesting story we've done all year!"

"Is it?" Melanie asked, leaning inside her warm Volkswagen and snatching her camera case and tripod.

"What is it with you?"

"I don't like Doel's attitude," she replied, starting across the path leading to the front door of the lodge.

"Give him a chance. My bet is he'll grow on you."

"You'll lose your money," Melanie predicted.

They started to the building, but Jan suddenly stopped short. "Okay, Melanie, are you going to hold out on me forever or are you going to tell me what's going on between you and—" she cocked her head toward the lodge "—our infamous new neighbor?"

"There's nothing going on."

"Didn't look that way yesterday."

"We got into an argument, that's all."

"And it looked like a doozy," Jan exclaimed. "You know you're going to have to tell me the truth about all this. You grew up with the man."

"It wasn't all that interesting," Melanie lied, but Jan simply smiled as they headed up the path leading to the main doors.

Gavin was waiting for them.

Lounging at one of the tables near the bar, his leg and cast propped on the seat of another chair, he looked up as they entered but didn't bother trying to stand.

"So you didn't change your mind," he said, his tawny eyes moving from Jan to Melanie.

"Nope," Melanie replied.

"News in Taylor's Crossing must be slow." The weight of his gaze landed full force on Melanie, but she tossed her bag onto the table and unzipped the padded canvas, pretending she didn't care one way or the other that he was staring at her.

Jan slid into a chair opposite him. "Ready?" she asked.

"As I'll ever be." He glanced down at his stiff leg and the plaster cast surrounding his ankle. Grimacing, his jaw rock hard, he added irritably, "Rich isn't here right now."

"But he'll be back?" Jan asked.

"He'd better be," Gavin growled.

Jan looked smug. "We can manage without him."

Melanie set up her tripod near the bar and adjusted its height, then double-checked the film in her camera.

Frowning, Gavin muttered, "Let's get the damned thing over with."

"That's a healthy attitude," Melanie shot back, and Jan stared at her as if she'd lost her mind.

Scowling, Gavin reached behind him, grabbed his crutches, stood and made his way to the other side of the bar. Rock-solid muscles supported him, though he slouched to fit the tops of the crutches under his arms. "What do you want to know?"

"Everything," Jan replied brightly, reaching into her oversized bag for her pocket recorder, steno pad and pen. "The reopening of Ridge Lodge is big news. But then, everything you do is news."

"If that's true, then the world's in worse shape than I thought," Gavin remarked, setting out two glasses and his favorite bottle on the top of the bar. "Join Melanie and me for a drink?" he asked.

"A drink?" Jan's brows rose. "At eleven in the morning?"

"Right. Kind of a celebration, eh, Melanie?"

"Don't ask," Melanie advised Jan as she set her camera onto the tripod.

Gavin was already searching for another glass, but Jan held up her hand. "It's too early for me," she said, curiosity filling her gaze.

"Melanie?" he asked, motioning to the two glasses already placed on the bar. "Another *smooth* one?"

Jan shot her a look that said more clearly than words, *what's he talking about?*

Shrugging, Melanie found the lens she wanted and screwed it onto the camera. Then she checked the light with a meter. "Not today," she replied.

"Too early?" he mocked, pouring himself a hefty shot.

"I'm working." She moved to the windows with her light meter.

"All work and no play?"

"Oh, you know me, nose to the grindstone all the time," she flung back, unable to help herself. Why was he baiting her?

Jan eyed them both. "You two *do* know each other," she said speculatively while casting Melanie a look that could cut through steel.

"You could say that," Gavin answered evasively.

"How well?" Jan's eyes were full of questions when she turned them on Melanie.

"Gavin and I went to school together—grade school," Melanie replied quickly, silently cursing Gavin. What was he doing firing up Jan's reporter instincts? He was the one who wanted his damned privacy.

Gavin's jaw grew tight. "Small world, isn't it?"

Jan reached for her pen and paper. "Then you're family friends?"

Melanie's heart began to thud, and she felt sweat gather along her spine.

Gavin didn't answer, and the silence stretched long. "Not exactly," he finally said.

"Then 'exactly' what?"

"Acquaintances," he clipped. "Nothing more."

Melanie, wounded, nodded. "That's right. Acquaintances. Mr. Doel is—"

"Gavin, please," Gavin drawled. "No reason to be so formal."

Melanie bristled. "*Gavin*'s a few years older than I am." Jan lifted a brow as Melanie suggested, "Maybe we should just get started."

Gavin forced a cold smile. "I can't wait."

"So you went to school at Taylor High?" Jan began, but Gavin cut her off.

"Nothing personal, remember?"

You started it, Melanie thought.

"Okay, okay," Jan said amiably. "We can begin with the lodge. When is it going to reopen? Is it going to be changed in any way? And tell me why you think you and your partner can make it work when the last operation went bankrupt?"

Jan's questions were fair, Melanie decided. Her ear tuned to the conversation, she busied herself with her equipment. Now that Gavin had steered Jan to safe territory, she was sticking to questions Gavin could answer without much thought. Leaning on the bar for support, he ignored his drink and answered each question carefully. No more spontaneous remarks—just the facts.

Melanie lifted the camera and focused on Gavin. He didn't seem to notice, and the lens only magnified his innate sexuality, the hard slope of his jaw, the bladed features of his face, the glint of his straight white teeth and the depth of his eyes, cautious now and sober.

She clicked off a few shots, and he glanced her way. Her heartbeat accelerated as he smiled—that irreverent slash of white against his tanned skin that had always caused her heart to trip.

"You want a tour?" he asked, flicking his gaze back to Jan.

"That would be great!"

Melanie watched him maneuver to the main lobby. Beneath his shirt his shoulders flexed, straining the seams of the white cotton while his hips shifted beneath his shorts and his tanned thighs and one exposed calf strained.

Even though Gavin was on crutches, Jan had to hurry to keep pace with him. Melanie grabbed another camera, double-checked that she had film and switched on the flash as she followed.

Gavin moved quickly across the main lobby, gesturing to the three-storied rock fireplace, scuffed wooden floors and soaring ceiling. Around three sides of the cavernous room, two tiers of balconies opened to private guest rooms. The other wall was solid glass, with a breathtaking view of Mount Prosperity. Now the ski runs were bare, the lifts still, the pine trees towering out of sheer rock. Dry grass and wildflowers covered the slopes.

Showing off the office, kitchen, exercise room and pool room, Gavin explained how the lodge was set up, when it was built and how he planned to restore it. Eventually they returned to the main lobby, and Gavin stopped at a group of tables with chairs overturned on their polished oak surfaces.

Balancing on his good leg, he yanked three chairs down and shoved them around a battered table.

Jan plopped down immediately. Gavin kicked a chair Melanie's way, but rather than sit so close to him, she said, "I think I'll look around."

"Not interested in hearing about the lodge?" Gavin baited.

"I can read about it," she tossed back. "Fascinating as it is, I've got work to do."

Jan, sensing the changed atmosphere, said, "Melanie's the best photographer on the paper."

Melanie shot Jan a warning glance. "Right now I think I'm the *only* photographer." *Just let me get through this,* she prayed silently, wishing she could be aloof and uncaring when it came to Gavin Doel. She unzipped her bag and sorted through the lenses, cameras, light meters and rolls of film.

Jan leaned across the table to Gavin and turned the questions in a different direction. Writing swiftly in her own fashion of shorthand, she asked about his career as an international skier, his bronze medal from the Olympics nearly eight years before, his interest in the lodge itself. Gavin answered quickly and succinctly, never offering more than a simple, straightforward answer.

He's used to this, Melanie realized, wondering how many reporters had tried to pin him down, how many other newspapers had tried to dig into his personal life. Even though the *Tribune* had been known to downplay scandal in the past, especially about a local hero, there were other newspapers that wouldn't have been so kind.

Seeing this as her chance to escape, Melanie wandered through the old rooms, and memories washed over her. She'd been here often, of course, before the last owners had filed for bankruptcy and closed the runs and the lodge for good. She'd even skied here with Gavin, but that had been ages ago. She'd been seventeen, sure of her love of him, happy beyond her wildest dreams. And he'd been on his way to fame and fortune. She sighed. How foolish it all seemed now.

Measuring the light through the large glass windows, she caught sight of her own pale reflection and wondered what Gavin thought about her. Gone was her straight black hair, replaced by crumpled curls that fell past her shoulders. Her eyes were still hazel, her cheekbones more exposed and gaunt following her divorce from Neil. She'd lost weight since Gavin had known her. But it didn't matter. What had happened between Gavin and her was long over—dead. She'd killed whatever feelings he'd had for her, and she'd destroyed those emotions intentionally when she'd eloped with Neil Brooks.

She glanced back to the table. Gavin was leaning back in his chair, answering Jan's questions, but his eyes followed her as she moved from one bank of windows to the next.

She snapped off a few shots of the interior of the lodge, then, as much to get away from the weight of Gavin's gaze as anything else, wandered down the hallways to the spaces where the shops and restaurant had been housed in years past.

In the tiny shops the shelves and racks were empty. Dust collected on display windows, and the carpet was worn and faded where ski boots had once trod throughout the winter. Bleached-out Clearance signs were stacked haphazardly against the walls.

The interior seemed gloomy—too dark for the kind of pictures Brian wanted for the layout. Maybe exterior shots would be better. Even though there wasn't a flake of snow on the mountain, shots of the lodge, the craggy ridge looming behind its gabled roofline, would give the article the right atmosphere.

Outside, she snapped several quick shots of the lodge, a few more of the empty lifts and others of the grassy ski runs.

The mountain air was clear and warm, and a late September breeze cooled her skin and tangled her hair. The scents of pine and dust, fresh lumber and wildflowers mingled, lingering in the autumn afternoon.

"Get what you wanted?" Gavin's voice boomed, startling her.

"What?" Whipping around, she squinted up and found him seated on the rail of a deck, his cast propped on a chair, his eyes shaded by reflective glasses. The deck, because of the lack of snow, was some five feet in the air and he stared down at her.

"What I wanted?" she repeated, shading her eyes with one hand and attempting to hide the fact that at that height he was incredibly intimidating.

"The pictures."

"Oh." Of course that's what he'd meant. For a moment she thought he'd been asking about her life. *You're too sensitive, Melanie. He doesn't give a damn.* "Enough to start with." She noticed his mouth turn down at the edges. "But you never can tell. If these—" she patted her camera fondly "—aren't what Brian had in mind, then I'll be back."

Gavin's jaw clenched even tighter. "So when did you take up photography?"

"I've always been interested in it." *You know that.*

"But as a career?"

"It started out as a hobby. I just kept working at it," she replied, not wanting to go into the fact that after she'd married Neil, she'd taken photography courses. She'd had time on her hands and empty hours to fill without the baby.... Neil's money had provided her with the best equipment and classes with some of the Northwest's most highly regarded instructors, and she'd spent hour upon hour learning, focusing on her craft. When she'd landed her first job, Neil had been livid. It was ironic, she supposed, that her hours of idleness and Neil's money had provided her with her escape from a marriage that had been doomed from the start.

Clearing her throat, she looked up and found Gavin staring at her, looking intently, as if he could read her thoughts. "So you took your 'hobby' and started working for the *Tribune*."

"That's a shortened version of it, but yes." Why explain further? "Where's Jan?" she asked, changing the subject as she packed her camera back in its case.

"She took off."

Melanie was surprised. "Already?"

Gavin's lips twitched as she started to climb onto the deck. "She asked one too many personal questions, and when I objected, I guess she thought I was being rude."

Melanie skewered him with a knowing look as she crossed the deck. "Were you?"

"Undoubtedly. She asked for it." Wincing, Gavin swung his leg back to the decking and balanced on his good foot while he scrabbled for his crutches. "Damn things," he growled when one crutch clattered to the cedar planks. He twisted, and his face grew white.

"I'll get it."

Melanie started to pick up the offending crutch, but Gavin bent over and, swearing, yanked it out of her hands. "Leave it!"

Melanie's temper flared. "I was only trying to help."

"I don't need any *help*." He didn't say it, but from the flare of his nostrils she expected him to add, "Especially from you." A few beads of sweat collected on his upper lip, but his skin darkened to its normal shade.

"You know, Gavin, you could relax a little. It wouldn't kill you to let someone lend you a hand once in a while."

His lips thinned. "I learned a long time ago not to depend on anyone but myself. That way I'm never disappointed."

Her throat went dry and she felt as if he'd slapped her, but he wasn't finished.

"As for these," he said, shaking a crutch, "I can handle them myself. And I don't need your advice, or your help, or your damned pity!" By this time he was standing, leaning on his crutches and breathing hard as he glared at her through his mirrored glasses.

"Then I'm out of here," she said, forcing an icy smile. "If you don't want my help or my advice or my pity, then there's no reason for me to stay."

"No reason at all."

"And I'm sure the shots I've taken will be good enough for the paper. You won't have to worry about me intruding again."

"Good."

"Goodbye, Gavin," she said, swinging her camera case over her shoulder, "and good luck with the lodge."

"Luck has nothing to do with it."

"I'll remember that if we don't get any snow until next February," she said sweetly, turning on her heel and marching through the lodge to the main doors. Her footsteps rang loudly on the weathered flooring, and her fists were clenched so tightly her fingers began to ache. How could she have loved him? *How?* The man was rude, arrogant, and carried around a chip on his shoulder the size of a California sequoia! Muttering under her breath, she shoved open the doors and escaped into the hot parking lot. Heat rose from the dusty asphalt in shimmering waves, only adding to the fire burning in her cheeks.

How could he have changed so drastically? Gavin was positively insufferable! She unlocked her car door and climbed into the suffocatingly hot interior. Rolling down the windows, she wondered if somehow she were to blame for this new cynical, horrible beast named Gavin Doel. Had she wounded him so badly by marrying Neil—or had he, at last, shown his true colors?

Her father had always warned her that Gavin was cut from the same cloth as Jim Doel, but she'd never believed him. Now she wasn't so sure, and it worried her. Twice in two days Gavin had poured himself healthy doses of Scotch before noon.

But she hadn't seen him drink any this morning. It had just been a game. He'd been baiting her again.

"Well, he can drown in his liquor for all I care!" she grumbled as she rammed a pair of sunglasses onto the bridge of her nose and glanced in the side-view mirror. In the reflection she saw Gavin standing in the doorway of the lodge, leaning hard on his crutches and frowning darkly.

She ground the gears of her battered old car and sped out of the lot. Maybe, if she was lucky, she'd never have to deal with him again!

GAVIN SWORE ROUNDLY and stared after the car. "You're a fool, Doel," he growled, furious with himself for noting that Melanie was more beautiful than he remembered. Her black hair shimmered blue in the sunlight, and her eyes were round and wide, a fascinating shade hovering between gray and green.

So what? Her beauty meant nothing. He'd loved her more than any other woman and she'd betrayed him as callously as if his feelings hadn't existed. So why should he care?

"Damn it, why now?" he muttered. He didn't want to deal with any latent feelings he might still harbor for her. And he wouldn't. Just because she was in the same neck of the proverbial woods didn't mean he had to fall all over himself chasing after her.

No, he decided, his lips compressing thoughtfully as the dust from her car settled back onto the asphalt, this time he'd be in control. This time Melanie Walker Brooks wouldn't get close to him. No matter what.

"…HE MIGHT BE the rudest man I've ever met!" Jan charged. Her eyes were bright, her cheeks flushed at the memory of her interview with Gavin. "And, unfortunately, maybe the best looking."

Melanie couldn't agree more. She'd heard the tail end of the conversation between Jan and Guy as she returned to the office. "I take it you're talking about the new owner of Ridge Resort?"

"You got it," Jan said. "And I'm not kidding. I've met some jerks in my time—good God, I've dated more than my share—but this guy takes the cake!"

"What exactly did he say?"

Jan puffed up like a peacock. "I just mentioned that he'd been linked to several famous models and I brought up Aimee LaRoux's name."

"And?" Guy prodded.

"And he asked me who I'd been linked to. I, uh, said, it was none of his business and he said 'Precisely.'"

"That doesn't sound so bad to me."

"It gets worse," Jan assured them. "I kept bringing it up and he finally asked me why, if I was so interested in Aimee LaRoux's love life, I just didn't call her and ask her out! Then he had the audacity to scribble a phone number on a book of matches and toss it to me."

Despite her foul mood, Melanie laughed. "You're right," she said. "Doel's obnoxious."

Jan glared at her. "He's got one dismal sense of humor!"

"You think it's really Aimee's number?" Guy asked, his eyes bright.

"No, I don't!" Jan snapped. "And you can quit drooling."

Guy pulled a face. "Is it that obvious?"

"Very."

Melanie said, "Just be glad the interview's over. We won't have to deal with Doel again."

"Oh, I wouldn't be so sure of that," Guy disagreed. "Brian

seems to think that stories about Gavin Doel and Ridge Lodge can only increase circulation. I think he's planning a series of articles about Mount Prosperity and the lodge and guess who?"

"Gavin Doel," Jan said, grimacing.

"You got it."

Melanie sighed inwardly. She didn't think she could face Gavin again. And the thought of Gavin's personal life being ripped open put her on edge. "I think Brian's putting too much emphasis on Doel."

"Yeah, it's almost as if he has an axe to grind with him," Guy agreed.

"An axe? What're you talking about?"

Guy shook his head. "Just a feeling I have. I don't think there's any love lost between Brian and Doel."

"Do they know each other?" Melanie asked.

"Beats me."

Jan's purse landed on her desk with a thump. "Well, Brian had better get himself another reporter," she declared flatly. "I'm not going to put myself through that ringer again. Doel won't open up at all. Guards his privacy as if there's something dark and dangerous in his past."

"Maybe there is," Guy said, throwing a leg over Jan's desk and tapping the side of his face with the eraser end of his pencil. "After all, what do we know of the guy—really?"

Jan turned thoughtful eyes on Melanie. "We know more than most," she said, her mouth curving thoughtfully upward.

Melanie steeled herself. Obviously Jan thought she could get information on Gavin through her. Well, she could guess again. For now Melanie's lips were sealed.

"He grew up around here," Jan told Guy. "Melanie went to school with him."

"Did you?" Guy was impressed.

"Well, not really. He's five years older than I am," Melanie countered. "He was out of high school before I entered."

"But you said you knew him," Jan persisted, "and he concurred. In fact, I'd be willing to bet you two knew each other better than you're letting on."

"What's this?" Guy asked, interested.

Melanie decided it was time for evasive tactics, at least until she knew just how far Jan was willing to dig. "Jan's exaggerating. I knew *of* him," she corrected, her palms beginning to sweat. "Everyone in town did."

She should probably just tell Jan part of the truth right now and get it over with, but she couldn't. Where would she stop? How would she explain that she married Neil to protect Gavin from the burden of a wife and child? Gavin didn't even know that she'd been pregnant. She certainly wasn't going to tell Jan or Guy or anyone else.

And beyond that, she didn't want the scandal of her mother's death raked up all over again.

"What was Gavin like as a kid? Doesn't he have a no-good for a father?" Jan asked, the wheels turning in her mind.

"I thought you weren't interested in interviewing him again," Melanie said.

Jan shook her head. "You know me. I was just mad. I let the guy get to me. It was my problem, not his. But it won't happen again. Besides, Barbara Walters wouldn't have let Doel intimidate her, would she? Nope, I've just got to fight fire with fire. So, what was Gavin Doel like before he became famous?"

Melanie thought for a moment, remembering Gavin as he had been. "He was…determined and ambitious and dedicated to being the best skier in the world."

Jan sighed and blew her bangs out of her eyes. "I know all that. But what about the man behind the image? Did you know him?"

Better than anyone. Melanie lifted a shoulder. "Not well enough to be quoted. Besides, the way he is about his private life, I think the *Trib* would be better off if we asked him. That way there's a chance we won't get sued!"

"He won't sue us," Jan said.

"Why not?"

"Bad publicity. He can't afford it. But right now he won't tell me anything." She smiled slyly. "This is going to call for some research. What's in the files?"

"I checked yesterday," Melanie said, walking briskly to her desk and knowing there was nothing the least bit damaging in the envelope she snatched from her cluttered In basket. She tossed the packet on Jan's desk and waited while Jan quickly flipped through the stack of photos as if it were a deck of cards. "Nothing else?" she asked, looking disappointed.

"Nothing interesting."

"You checked the copy that went along with these?"

"Yep."

"Damn!" She pursed her lips and eyed the photographs again. "Well, these are good…." She picked up a glossy black and white of Gavin poised at the top of a ski run. His face was set, his body tight, his gloved hands wrapped around his poles, every muscle ready to spring forward at the drop of a flag. "But I think it would give some dimension to our story if we knew a little more about him." Tapping a long fingernail on the photograph, she said, "Privacy or no privacy, I think we should dig up *everything* we can find on one Mr. Gavin Doel. We can check with the high school, find out who he dated, if he was ever employed around town."

"I think most of his relatives moved away a long time ago. And as for his employment, he worked at the lodge before it closed down," Melanie offered, hoping to steer Jan away from Gavin's love life.

"Well that doesn't do us a lot of good. Unless he bought

the damned thing for sentimental reasons. But we'll find out. The next time I interview him, I'll be ready with a little personal ammunition to get him to talk."

"It's your funeral," Guy said, straightening from the desk.

And just possibly mine, Melanie thought inwardly. "I'll do the research," she offered, hoping that she could circumvent any old news story that might prove uncomfortable for Gavin or herself.

"Good." Jan checked her watch. "Look, I've got to run over to the school and talk to the principal about the new gym. Melanie—are you coming with me?"

"No, I've already got the pictures. They'll be on your desk tomorrow."

"Good. Thanks." Jan grabbed her bag and headed out of the office.

Melanie was left with the sinking sensation that Gavin's personal life—as well as her own—was about to be splashed all over the front page of the Taylor's Crossing *Tribune!*

CHAPTER FOUR

BRIAN MICHAELS DID indeed want to do a series of articles on Ridge Lodge and he wasn't the least bit concerned with Gavin's desire for privacy. In fact, he had his own reasons for wanting to see Gavin's life plastered all over the newspaper. But he kept those to himself.

"He's a public figure, for crying out loud," Brian said the next afternoon as he shook a cigarette from his pack. Jan and Melanie were seated on two worn plastic chairs near his desk. "And on top of that, he's rebuilding a lodge that will turn the economy of this town around. Doel can't expect to have a private life. If he does, he's a fool!"

"A man who's made several million dollars in five years isn't a fool," Jan argued.

Brian lit up and blew a cloud of smoke. "Look, I want to do several articles, one every other week until snow season. Front page stuff." He glanced at Mclanie. "I want to see the workers rebuilding the lodge, the furniture being moved in. I need photos of the lifts beginning to run, the first snowfall, that sort of thing. Then, find out about the ski school programs and add some schmaltzy stuff, you know, five-year-old kids on skis with their dads helping them, that sort of rot."

"Then you don't really need anything on Doel," she ventured.

"Oh, wrong!" Brian was just warming to his subject. "He's

going to open that lodge with a huge celebration of some kind. I want a copy of the guest list. Find out if any of the skiers he's competed against are invited and check to see who will be his personal date. If any of his old flames are going to show up, we have to know about it ahead of time." He stared straight at Melanie, waving his cigarette as he spoke. "And I'll want you at that grand opening with your camera. We'll want every bit of glitz on our front page!"

Melanie's throat went dry as Brian kept talking. "That's not all. I want to know everything about Doel—inside out. His old man is a drunk—why? And didn't he do some time years ago? What happened? And where is he now?"

Melanie said evenly, "I don't see that Jim Doel's tragedies have anything to do with the lodge reopening."

"Like hell. The man raised Gavin alone, didn't he? He shaped the kid. What happened to his mother? Is she still alive? Remarried? Does he have sisters or brothers or an aunt or uncle or cousin around here? You'd be surprised how easy it is to get people to talk about their famous kin. It makes them feel important, as if a little of that fame will rub off on them."

"This series is starting to sound like something you'd find at the checkout counter," Melanie said.

"Why?"

"Because you're more interested in finding out any dirt there is on Doel than reporting about the lodge."

Beside her, Jan drew her breath in sharply, but Brian didn't miss a beat. "I'm not interested in anything of the sort. I just want to sell papers. Period."

"No matter what the price or the standards?"

"I didn't say that, but listen, don't knock the tabloids. They make plenty!"

"And they're always getting sued!"

Brian flipped the ash from his cigarette into the already overflowing tray. "Hey—we won't print anything false. But we've got to generate interest in the lodge, interest in Doel, interest in the *Tribune*! You may as well know that the owners are putting pressure on us. Circulation's down, and we've got to do something about it."

"And that something is throwing Gavin Doel's life open for public inspection?" Melanie challenged.

"You bet it is." Brian took a final drag on his cigarette, then jabbed it out in his ashtray. "Look, he's the one who decided to come back to the small town where he was raised and reopen a resort that had gone bankrupt—a resort that represents a lot to the economy of this town. I can't help it that he's news—in fact, I'm thrilled that he jet-setted around the world and hung out with the rich and famous. All the better for the *Tribune*."

"How would you feel if it were you?"

"Listen, if I had Doel's money and his fame and I was interested in selling lift tickets, you can bet I'd grab all the press I could get my hands on!"

"No matter what?" Melanie asked.

"No matter what! Do you have a problem with that?"

Melanie could feel her color rising. "I'd just like to think that we were working with the man rather than against him."

"His choice. The way I see it, we're doing him a favor." Clasping his hands behind his head, Brian leaned back in his chair and squinted his aquamarine eyes. "So, let's not let Doel's sensitivity about his privacy bother us too much and get down to business. I'll call his partner, get the go-ahead for the articles and we'll take it from there."

Melanie left the meeting with a sense of impending doom. Brian Michaels could whitewash his intentions all he wanted, but Gavin, when he discovered that his life was going to be thrown open and displayed for every reader of the *Tribune*, would be livid. And Melanie didn't blame him. It occurred to her that she could tell him what was happening, but he'd probably lay the blame at her feet. Besides, nothing had been written yet. Maybe she could help edit the story. Crossing her fingers, she hoped that Brian would have a change of heart.

"LET ME GET THIS straight," Gavin said, eyeing his partner angrily. "You agreed to do a *series* of articles about the lodge."

"Sure. Why not?" Rich shrugged, opened the small refrigerator in the office and pulled out a bottle of beer. "I thought we agreed that we could use all the publicity we could get." He shoved the bottle across the coffee table and yanked out another.

"We did," Gavin said, trying to tamp down the restless feeling in his gut. "And I thought you were going to hang around and handle them. Instead you bailed out on me."

"I already apologized. Besides, I had to be at the courthouse—"

"Yeah, yeah, I know," Gavin said grumpily. "I guess I'm just suspicious of reporters."

"They're not all out for blood."

"No—just big stories." He twisted off the cap of the bottle and took a long swallow.

"So?"

"I've been burned before."

"The *Tribune* isn't exactly a national tabloid. It's just a little local paper with ties to the *Portland Daily*. And those ties—" he held up his beer to make his point "—are exactly what we need right now. We have to stir up public awareness and interest in Ridge Resort from Seattle all the way to L.A."

Gavin scowled. There was a chance that Rich was right, of course, but in Gavin's opinion, it was a slim chance at best. In the course of his career, he'd dealt with more than his share of reporters and photographers, but he'd never had to deal with Melanie before.

He took another long swallow and shoved all thoughts of Melanie aside. She'd shown her true colors long ago, and it was just too damned bad that he'd had the bad luck to run into her again.

"So when is the next session?" he asked Rich.

"Next week. They want some pictures of the crew working on the lodge."

He clenched his teeth. "So they're sending up a photographer."

"Mmm-hmm."

Chest tightening, he asked slowly, "Which one?"

"As far as I know they only have one."

"I think we should have our own photos taken."

Rich's brows shot up. "Why?"

"We'll get what we want. No surprises."

"You're the one who wants to stay within budget, remember?" Rich shook his head. "Relax a little and enjoy the free publicity, will ya? This is the best thing that's happened to us so far."

"I doubt it," Gavin growled, feeling suddenly as if he couldn't breathe. Swearing, he reached for his crutches and struggled to his feet. Only one more day of these wretched tools—then, at least, he wouldn't feel like an invalid. Shoving the padded supports under his arms, he moved with surprising agility to the door.

"You know," Rich's voice taunted from behind, "if I didn't know better, I'd say you were all worked up over some woman."

"Well, you don't know better, do you?" Gavin flung over his shoulder, and Rich laughed. Balancing on his good foot, Gavin unlocked the back door and hobbled onto the deck.

Rays of afternoon sunlight filtered through the trees, and the warm air touched the back of his neck where beads of sweat had collected. His hands were slippery on the grips of his crutches and his heart pumped at the thought of coming face-to-face with Melanie again. Melanie. He squeezed his eyes shut and willed her gorgeous, lying Jezebel face from his mind.

MELANIE SPENT THE rest of the afternoon in the darkroom developing the pictures she'd taken at Ridge Resort. Most of the shots were of the lodge itself, but a few of the photographs were of Gavin, his jaw hard and set, his mouth tight, his eyes intense as he studiously avoided looking at the camera.

"These are perfect," Jan said, pointing to the most provocative shot on the roll—a profile of Gavin, his hair falling over his face, his features taut, his mouth a thin, sexy line above a thrusting jaw. "Can you blow this one up?"

"Don't you think a shot of the lodge would be better?"

Jan tapped her finger to the side of her mouth and shook her head. "Nope—at least not for the female readers."

"And the male?"

Jan chewed on her lower lip, and her eyes narrowed thoughtfully. "I think even they would be interested in seeing what the enigmatic Mr. Doel looks like up close."

"Maybe we should use an overview of the lodge and a smaller inset of Gavin."

"Maybe," Jan said, but the pucker between her brows didn't go away, and Melanie realized she'd already made up her mind. "Or we could do it the other way around—a large profile of the man behind the lodge and a smaller shot of the resort itself."

"This isn't *People* magazine," Melanie pointed out. "The focus of the story is on the lodge, right?"

"Oh, right, but we'll have plenty of pictures of the construction. No, I think we'd better focus on Doel. He's the public interest."

"He'll have a fit," Melanie predicted.

Jan smiled. "And won't that be interesting?"

"Interesting? You mean like a hurricane or an earthquake is interesting?"

Jan eyed Melanie thoughtfully. "Just how well did you know Gavin Doel? The truth, now."

"I met him a few times."

"So why're you so defensive about him?"

Melanie toyed with the idea of confiding in Jan, but the phone shrilled and Molly, the receptionist, flagged Jan down.

"It's that call you've been waiting for from the mayor's office," Molly whispered loudly.

"I've got it," she said, before turning back to Melanie. "Has anyone ever told you you worry too much?"

"Not for a while."

"Well, you do! Everything's going to work out. For us and for Gavin Doel and his resort."

I hope you're right, Melanie thought, but couldn't shake the feeling that the *Tribune* and everyone on its staff were asking for trouble.

Hours later, she drove home and was greeted at the back door by a thoroughly dusty and burr-covered Sassafras.

"Oh, no, you don't," she said, wedging herself through the door, effectively blocking Sassafras's dodge from the porch into the kitchen. She left her camera case and purse in the kitchen, changed into her faded jeans and an old T-shirt, then squeezed through the door to the porch.

Sassafras whined loudly, scratching at the door.

Melanie plopped onto a small stool. "So, tell me, where've you been?" She laughed, reaching for an old currycomb and ignoring his protests as she combed out his fur. He tried to wriggle free and even clamped his mouth around her wrist when she tugged at a particularly stubborn burr. "Okay, okay, I can take a hint," she said, tossing down the currycomb. She brushed the dog hair from her jeans and held open the door. "Now, Mr. Sassafras, you may enter," she teased.

The old collie dashed inside before she could change her mind, and she followed him. She changed clothes again, throwing on a clean skirt and a cotton sweater before returning to the kitchen. She barely had poured herself a glass of iced tea when the doorbell pealed and Sassafras began to bark loudly.

Glancing at her watch, Melanie groaned inwardly at the thought of the next hour and the Anderson children she was supposed to photograph—four of the most rambunctious kids she'd ever met.

Sassafras growled, then settled in his favorite spot under the kitchen table.

"Coming!" Melanie called, hurrying through the cool rooms of the old log house.

Cynthia Anderson and children were huddled on the wide front porch when Melanie opened the door. In matching red crew-neck sweaters and khaki slacks, the wheat-blond boys, ages two through eleven, dashed past Melanie, down the hall and through wide double doors to her studio.

"Boys! Wait!" Casting Melanie an apologetic look, Cynthia Anderson took off after her brood.

By the time Melanie reached the studio, the boys were already jockeying for position around the single wicker chair Melanie used for inside portraits.

"Maybe we should have this picture taken outdoors," Cynthia suggested as Melanie tried to arrange the siblings—oldest with the youngest on his lap, two middle children standing on either side.

Melanie straightened the two-year-old's sweater, then glanced over her shoulder. "If you want exterior shots, we'll have to schedule another appointment. Right now there's not enough light."

Cynthia rolled her eyes. "No way. They're finally back in the swing of school and soccer practice is just about every night. I barely got them together to come today. Believe me, it's now or never."

Melanie was relieved. Though she loved children, one

session with these four was all she could handle. "Okay. Sean, you hold Tim on your knee."

"And turn his face to the right," their mother insisted. "He fell yesterday and he's got a black eye...." She rattled on, talking nonstop about the boys as Melanie worked with them. For the next hour Melanie positioned and repositioned the children, adjusted the light, changed film and cameras and took as many pictures as she could before all four boys started squirming and pushing and shoving.

"Brian kicked me!" Randy cried, fist curled to retaliate.

"Did not!" Brian replied indignantly. "It was Sean!"

Sean was smothering a sly smile, and Melanie wished she could have caught the act on film.

"Boys, stop that!" Cynthia said. "Sean—you and Brian quit it right now! Ms. Walker is trying to take your picture. The least you could is behave!"

"I think that'll do it," Melanie said, snapping the final shot.

"Good!" Sean, the oldest, pushed Tim from his lap. "I'm outta here!" He took off down the hall with his brothers following close behind.

"Thanks a bunch," Cynthia said, hastily writing a check for the sitting fee and handing it to Melanie. She shoved her wallet back into her handbag. "You know, I just heard today that Gavin Doel's back in town."

Melanie managed a smile she didn't feel. "That's right."

"Well, I, for one, am glad someone's doing something with Ridge Resort. This town's been dead ever since it closed."

That much was true. But Melanie wasn't sure that Gavin could bring it back to life.

"Mom!" Outside a horn blared.

"Got to run," Cynthia said, starting for the door. "The natives are restless!"

Later, after developing film in the darkroom, which was adjacent to the studio, and eyeing the strips of the Anderson boys, Melanie soaked in a hot bath, poured herself a cup of tea and relaxed on the couch with a couple of cookies. Sassafras curled on the braided rug at her feet, his ears pricked forward, his eyes on her, hoping for a morsel.

Smiling, she offered the dog a corner of one cookie and he swallowed it without chewing. "Glutton," she teased, and he lifted a paw, scratching her knee for more. "These aren't exactly on your diet." But she let him snatch the remainder of the final cookie from her palm. "Let's not tell the vet—he wouldn't understand."

She picked up the paperback spy thriller she'd been reading for the past week but couldn't concentrate on the intricate plot. Her mind kept wandering. To Gavin.

"Forget him," she chastised herself. "He's obviously forgotten you." Frowning, she tossed down the book, grabbed the remote control and snapped on the television. A local newscaster, a young dark-haired woman with intelligent blue eyes, was smiling into the camera.

"...and good news for central Oregon," she said. "All those rumors proved true. Gavin Doel and his partner, Rich Johanson, made a public announcement that they plan to reopen Ridge Resort on Mount Prosperity in time for the winter ski season. Our reporter was at Ridge Resort this afternoon...."

The screen changed to footage of Gavin, reflective aviator sunglasses perched on his tanned face, crutches tucked under his arms, standing behind a hefty, steely-haired man whom Melanie assumed was Rich Johanson.

The camera focused on Gavin's features, and Melanie's throat constricted. His face was lean, nearly haggard, partially hidden by the oversized sunglasses. Thin, sensual lips, frozen in an expression of indifference, accentuated his strong, square jaw.

His light brown hair was nearly blond, streaked by days spent bareheaded in the sun. His angled face was as rugged as the slopes he tackled so effortlessly, and there was a reserve to him evident even on the television screen.

Whereas Richard Johanson was dressed in a business suit and couldn't quit answering questions posed by the media, Gavin seemed bored and remote, as if he wanted only for the whole damn thing to be over with.

The screen flickered again, and the image changed to a steep mountain slope in France. A brightly dressed crowd gathered at the bottom of a ski run, and one woman, red-haired and gorgeous international model Aimee LaRoux, glanced at the camera before training her gaze up the hill.

The camera angle changed. Melanie's lungs constricted as another camera singled out a downhill racer. She'd seen this footage over and over again. Her throat went dry as Gavin, tucked low, streaked down the mountain. Seconds passed before one ski caught, flipping him high into the air. Skis and poles exploded. Gavin, in a bone-shattering fall, spun end over end down the icy slope.

Melanie's heart went cold, and she snapped the television off. Her hands trembled so badly she stuffed them into the pockets of her terry robe. She didn't need to be reminded of the accident that may have cost Gavin his career—the accident that had fatefully thrown him back to Taylor's Crossing—the accident that had shoved him back into her life.

No, that wasn't right. He wasn't back in her life. She wouldn't let him! Not even if he wanted back in, which, of course, he didn't.

"And that's the way it's got to be!" she said aloud, as if by saying the words she could convince herself.

GAVIN ROTATED HIS foot, wincing as the muscles stretched. His leg was pale, thinner than the other and not much to look at.

Several scars around his knee and ankle gave evidence to the wonders of medical science, though, according to his doctor, he still had weeks of physical therapy before he could hope to step into a pair of skis.

"Give it time," he told himself as he struggled into his favorite jeans and stood tentatively, placing only part of his weight on the injured leg. "Easy does it." He saw the cane sitting near his bed and ignored it, taking a few tentative steps around the small suite he'd claimed as his.

Located near the office on the first floor of the lodge, the suite boasted worn furniture he'd found in the basement, a small refrigerator, an oven, a fireplace and two closets. He had private access outside to a small deck. He'd added a microwave and coffeemaker.

"All the comforts of home," he said with a sarcastic smile as he steadied himself by placing his hands on the bureau. He'd never been one for carrying around extra baggage, never stayed in one place long enough to collect furniture, paintings or memorabilia. Aside from a few special awards, medals and trophies, he didn't keep much, was always ready to move on. Until now, moving along had been easy. But that was before the accident.

And what now?

Settle down? He made a sound of disgust. He'd given up those dreams long ago, when Melanie had showed him the value of love. His finger curled around the edge of the bureau top, and when he glanced in the mirror, he scowled at his half-dressed reflection.

He remembered all too vividly falling in love with Melanie, as if the years of trying to forget her had only etched her more deeply into his mind. Their affair had been short and passionate and filled with dreams that had turned out to be one-sided. Oh, he'd been good enough to experiment with, make love to, whisper meaningless promises to, but as his old man had predicted, in the end she'd decided he wasn't good enough for her. She'd married a wealthy boy from a socially prominent family rather than gamble on a ski bum.

"All for the best," he grumbled, reaching for a T-shirt he'd tossed over the back of a nearby chair and sliding his arms through the cotton sleeves. Just below the knee his leg began to throb, and he sucked in a breath between his teeth. Tucking the shirt into the waistband of his jeans, his wayward mind wandered back to Melanie.

She'd given him some very valuable lessons, though he doubted she realized that she was the single reason he'd become so self-reliant. Her betrayal had taught him and taught him well. Never would he depend upon anyone but himself, and as for women—well, he'd had a few affairs. They hadn't lasted and he didn't care, though it bothered him a little that he'd gained a reputation as a womanizer in some of the tabloids. The rumors of his sizzling one-night-stand dates stemmed more from the overly active imaginations of the press than anything else.

He slid into beat-up Nikes and, with the aid of the cane, walked carefully to the office, where he expected to find Rich.

Instead, rounding the corner and shouldering open the door, he ran smack-dab into the one person he wanted out of his life.

But there she was, in beautiful 3-D. Melanie Walker Brooks.

CHAPTER FIVE

MELANIE, WHO HAD been waiting impatiently in the office of Ridge Resort, reached for the doorknob, only to have the door thrown open in her face. Startled, she drew back just as Gavin, walking with the aid of a cane, pulled up short. A flicker of surprise lighted his eyes, and he drew in a quick breath.

Muttering ungraciously, he glanced rapidly around the room. "You're here—again?" he demanded.

She smiled. "Didn't you miss me?"

His mouth pinched at the corners, and a vein throbbed at his temple. She expected an insult, but he only asked, "Where's Rich?"

"I don't know."

"Are you waiting for him?" His eyes narrowed suspiciously.

"He told me to meet him here."

"When?"

"Today at eleven."

Gavin cast an irritated glance down at his watch, and Melanie had to smother another smile at his obvious frustration. He plowed rigid fingers through his hair, though the rebellious golden strands fell forward again, covering the creases marring his forehead. "What do you want?"

"*I* don't want anything. But, according to my editor, Brian Michaels, the article on Ridge Lodge has been expanded to a series."

"So I heard."

"Brian talked to Rich and sent me up here for more pictures. I was supposed to meet with your partner, that's all. It's no big mystery."

"So now you're my problem."

"I'm no one's problem, Gavin," she replied, surprised at how easily his name rolled off her tongue and how quickly she could be drawn into an argument with him. "And I suspect whatever problems you do have are all of your own making!"

"Not all." Gavin shifted, and his face, beneath his tan, blanched. Instinctively she glanced down at his leg, and he leaned against the door frame for support, effectively blocking all chance of escape. Not that she wanted to, she reminded herself. She could deal with Gavin one-on-one if need be.

"Didn't you get enough pictures the other day?"

"Not quite. But don't worry, I'll try not to get in the way."

He pressed his lips together.

"So why are you so camera shy?" she asked bluntly. "You've been photographed all over the world. Why now, when you can use the publicity, are you backpedaling?"

"Maybe I don't like yellow journalism."

"But the *Tribune*—"

"Peddles sleaze."

"No way!" she sputtered. "It's a small local paper—"

"With big ambitions. Oh, yeah, the *Trib* isn't that what you call it—" at her nod he continued "—is subtle and wraps all its smut in a cozy, folksy format."

"That's ridiculous!" she said, but she was still nervous with the memory of her last meeting with Brian and Jan.

"Is it?" Gavin asked, shaking his head. "I don't think so. I've dealt with Brian Michaels before."

Melanie caught her breath. "You have?"

"That's right."

This was news. Brian had never mentioned knowing Gavin. "When?" she asked suspiciously.

"Years ago. In Colorado."

She started through the door, but Gavin thrust out an arm, stopping her before she crossed the threshold. "What were you doing in here?"

"Rich said to meet him in the office. He wants to discuss some other work, I think. Anyway, that's what Brian said."

"What other work?"

"Your guess is as good as mine."

He frowned, the lines around his mouth tightening. "So when he wasn't here, what did you do?"

Melanie's heart began to pound. What did he think? "I waited."

"And while you were waiting?" he prodded.

Suddenly she understood. He thought she'd been snooping! She could see it in his eyes.

"While I was waiting, which has been all of eight or nine minutes, I sat in that chair—" she hooked a thumb at an overstuffed chair near the window "—and thought about the shots I'll need." Lifting her chin an inch, she said, "Oh, and I did snoop around a little—dug through your things, hoping to come up with some trashy dirt I can use in the paper and maybe sell to the tabloids for a few bucks—"

"I didn't accuse you of—"

"You implied, Gavin, and that's bad enough!" she cut in, unable to stop herself. "For your information, I didn't poke around your desk. I came here to take pictures and talk with your partner! I'm sorry to disappoint you but I don't have any devious plans of skulduggery!"

Gavin, using a cane for support, made his way past her and eyed the top of his desk. He frowned. "I bet your friend would have searched the room, if given the opportunity."

"My friend?"

"The reporter—what's her name? Jane?"

"Jan."

"Didn't like her."

"You don't like much, do you?"

He looked up sharply, and a golden flame leapt in his eyes. "Oh, I like some things," he admitted, his voice low.

"What? Just what is it you like these days?"

"I like expensive Scotch, steep mountains and women who don't ask a lot of questions."

"Dumb and beautiful, right?"

"Right," he said with a sarcastic smile. "It just keeps everything so much simpler."

"And that way you don't have to deal with a real woman, a person with a mind of her own, someone who might not deify you because you're some macho athletic jock!"

Stiffly, he dropped into the desk chair. "Seems to me you didn't mind too much."

"That was a long time ago," she shot back, closing her mind to the fact that she'd loved him. Now he was a stranger, a stranger with a biting cynicism that had the ability to slice deep. "And you've changed."

He leaned back in his chair, and his lips twisted. "I wonder why? It couldn't be because I trusted the wrong person, could it?"

Stunned, she swallowed hard. Pain welled up as if he'd struck her. "It doesn't matter," she replied, refusing to let him know he'd wounded her. "I'm here to do a job. That's all. What you think happened in the past really doesn't matter, does it?"

"It matters a hell of a lot!"

"Not anymore."

One of his golden brows lifted, challenging her, but she ignored it. Instead she picked up her camera case and said, "If you'll excuse me, I'll get to work. When Mr. Johanson shows up, point him in my direction. I'll be outside." Opening the door to the back deck, she flung over her shoulder, "I'll be at the blue chair."

Slamming the door shut, she marched across the deck, rested her palms on the thick weathered plank of the rail and took in three deep breaths.

Damn him, damn him, damn him, she thought, shaking inside.

She brushed her hair from her face and tried to calm down. The mountain air was clear and crisp with the promise of winter. Sunlight dazzled over the rocky cliffs and pine trees while dry grass and wildflowers added the fresh scent of a summer that hadn't quite disappeared. High overhead, against a backdrop of diaphanous clouds, a lonely hawk circled.

Melanie heard the door open behind her and braced herself.

"We don't have a blue chair anymore," he said, his voice soft and caressing. She dug her fingers into the weather-beaten railing but didn't turn to face him.

"Well, then, whatever you call it. You know the one I mean!"

"The Barbary Coast."

"The what?" Slowly she looked over her shoulder and caught him smiling, his eyes dancing with amusement at her bewilderment. But as quickly as it appeared, that fleeting hint of humor fled. "The runs have been named by the colors of their chairs for as long as there have been lifts."

"Then it's time for a change." He walked up to her and propped his injured leg on the lower rail.

What did she care? She wasn't about to argue with him. He could rename the whole damn mountain for all it mattered to her. She turned again, heading for the Barbary Coast chair.

"So where is that partner of yours?" he asked.

"I don't have one."

"The reporter who was here the other day."

Melanie shrugged. "I'm not Jan's keeper. I told her I'd get the shots we needed and she could arrange for another session with you. I didn't see that I needed to be involved."

His lips twisted. "How long is this going to take?"

She'd had enough of his foul mood. "I guess that depends on you," she said sarcastically. "If you're a good boy and answer all Jan's questions, it'll be over quickly, but if you start baiting her like you're doing with me right now, I guarantee you it'll be long and drawn-out."

"And what about you? How long do you plan to be here?"

"Believe me, I want it over as soon as possible. I plan to take some pictures now, a few more when the reconstruction really gets into swing and then, of course, more when the first snow hits and there are actually skiers up here. We'll probably end with a big spread when the lodge opens. That is," she added, "if you don't disapprove."

"Would it matter?"

"I don't know."

Suddenly she was staring at him as she had years ago—full of honesty and integrity. And she felt a very vital, private need to explain. "You're big-time, Gavin. Whether you want to admit it or not. Of course the press is interested. And it's not just your career, you know. It's your lifestyle."

His eyes darkened a fraction.

"You've been seen all over the world, in the glitziest resorts with the most gorgeous women, with a very fast, exciting crowd—actors, actresses, models, artists. You know, the beautiful crowd, the people middle-class America has an affair with."

His jaw clamped tight, and for a few long seconds he stared at her.

"Your name will become synonymous with Ridge Lodge Resort. It's only natural that the public will be curious. And face it, you and that partner of yours are counting on it. So why don't you quit fighting me every step of the way and enjoy it?"

"Enjoy it," he repeated on a short laugh.

"Most men would love your fame."

"I'm not most men."

"Lord, don't I know it," she said, hurrying across the deck, down the steps and through the tufts of dry grass. "I still need a few pictures of the interior of the lodge, you, your partner and...I don't know...something spectacular." She was thinking aloud, staring at the chair lift. "Something like a view from the top of the mountain." Her gaze landed at the hut at the base of the Barbary Coast lift. Twin cables, supported by huge black pillars, swept up the rocky terrain. Blue-backed chairs hung from the strong cable.

He followed her gaze. "You're not going up on that thing."

"Is it unsafe?"

"No, but—"

"It would be such a breathtaking view," she said, her mind already spinning ahead to the panorama that would be visible from the top of the lift. She'd been up there many times in winter, but never had she seen the mountains from that height before the snow season. "Oh, Gavin, it would be perfect."

Gavin shook his head. "No way."

"Why not?"

"Too risky."

She cocked a disbelieving brow. "I never thought I'd hear you say that." She started for the hut at the base of the lift and motioned to the cables. "Can't you turn this thing on?"

"Yes, but I don't think it would be a good idea."

"That's no surprise. You haven't thought anything about the *Tribune*'s interest in the resort has been a good idea." She was already climbing down the steps of the deck and heading for the chair.

Gavin, using his cane, was right on her heels. "What're you trying to prove?"

"Nothing. I just want to get my job done. Then I won't bother you for a while."

"Promise?"

Spinning, eyes narrowed, she said, "In blood, if I have to!"

He almost smiled. She could see it in his eyes. But quickly the shutters on his eyes lowered and no hint of emotion showed through.

"Then let's go."

"You don't have to come with me—"

"Like hell."

"Really—"

"Look, Mrs. Brooks, I don't know what kind of liability I have here, but I'm going with you to make sure you don't do something asinine and end up falling off the lift and killing yourself."

"Thanks for your concern," she mocked.

"It's not concern. It's simply covering my backside."

"And what can you do…?" She motioned to his injured leg and wished she hadn't.

His face tightened. "It's with me or without me," he muttered, turning away from her and mulishly crossing the remaining distance to the chair lift.

Telling herself she was about to make a grave error, she tucked the strap of her camera over one shoulder, pocketed a few rolls of film and followed him. "I must be out of my mind," she muttered under her breath but decided he was crazier than she as he struggled up the slight incline.

Gavin walked stiffly, jabbing his cane into the dry earth until he reached the hut, which was little more than a huge metal A frame, open at one end to allow the chairs of the lift to enter, revolve around a huge post, then, after picking up skiers, start back up the hillside. He went into a private glassed-in operator's booth that was positioned on one side of the hut. Inside, visible through the glass, he picked up the receiver of a telephone and punched out a number, then waited, his fingers drumming impatiently on the window.

She watched as he spoke tersely into the phone for a few seconds, then slammed the receiver back into its cradle.

"We're all set," he said, meeting Melanie in the shade of the hut.

"You don't have to—"

"Of course I do," he clipped. "All part of our policy up here at Ridge Lodge to keep the public and the press happy."

"Sure."

A wiry, red-haired man shouted from the lodge, then dashed across the rough ground to the hut.

"This is Erik Link. He's in charge of maintenance of all the equipment," Gavin said as the freckle-faced operator entered the hut. "Erik—Melanie Brooks—"

"Walker," Melanie corrected, extending her hand.

"Nice to meet you," Erik replied.

"Melanie's a photographer for the local paper and she wants some pictures from the summit of this lift." He turned back to Melanie. "Erik will make sure we get up and down in one piece."

"That's encouraging." Melanie said dryly.

Erik grinned. "Piece of cake." He withdrew a key ring from his pocket and went into the lodge.

Sighing, she glanced down at his cane. "Really, Gavin, I can handle this alone. You're still laid up—"

"Temporarily."

"Unless you do something stupid and injure yourself again," she pointed out. "I bet your doctor would have a fit."

He smiled then, that same blinding flash of white that had always trapped the breath in her lungs. "My doctor will never know."

"Then let's forget it."

He leaned forward on his cane and surveyed her through hooded eyes. "You've changed, Mel," he said quietly. "There was a time when you'd do anything on a dare. Including being alone with me."

"This has nothing to do with being alone with you."

"Doesn't it?" One eyebrow arched dubiously. "You're the one who wanted the best pictures for that damned paper of yours. I'm just giving you what you wanted."

She was tempted. Lord, it would be great knocking the wind from his sails! She eyed the lift with its tall black poles and hesitated.

"Come on, Melanie. I won't bite. I'll even try to keep a rein on my temper."

"Now you are promising the impossible!"

"We'll see." He motioned to Erik, who positioned himself at the station in the hut. A few seconds later, with a rumbling clang and a groan the chairs started moving slowly up the face of the mountain. Erik, smiling, stood at the attendant's box. "Any time," he yelled over the grind of machinery.

Melanie second-guessed herself. "What if we get stuck?"

"We won't."

"How will you get off?" she asked, eyeing his leg and cane. At the top of the lift, the platform had to be several feet below the chair to allow for snowfall. He couldn't possibly jump off the lift without reinjuring himself, and then there was the problem of climbing back on....

"I won't," he said, edging toward the moving chairs. "You'll have to take your pictures from the chair." Before she could argue, he shoved his cane into one hand, grabbed her fingers tightly, moved in front of the next chair and let the lift sweep them off their feet. Within seconds they were airborne.

"Nothing to it," he said, flicking her a satisfied glance.

"Right," she said, still steaming. "You always were bull-headed."

He frowned. "When I want to do something, I just do it."

"That could be dangerous."

"For me—or you?"

"Give me a break," she murmured, angry at being bullied into the chair but feeling a sense of exhilaration nonetheless. A rush of adrenaline swept through her veins as the chair began it ascent. The mountain air was clear, the sky a brilliant shade of autumn blue, broken only by high, thin clouds. A playful breeze was cool against her neck and cheeks and carried with it the fresh, earthy scent of pine.

Melanie slid a glance at Gavin and told herself firmly that the fact that her heart was beating as rapidly as a hummingbird's had nothing to do with the fact that his shoulder brushed hers or that his thigh was only inches from her leg.

Her throat grew tight, and she forced her gaze back to the view. Uncapping the lens from her camera, she stared through the viewfinder, adjusted the focus and clicked off several quick shots of the mountain looming straight ahead. The peak was dusted with snow, but the rest of the mountain above the timberline was sheer, craggy rock.

"Why'd you come back to Taylor's Crossing?" she asked as the chair climbed up the final steep grade of bare rock.

"Because the deal was right on the resort and because of this." He kicked up his injured foot and frowned at his leg.

"But that's only temporary."

"Maybe."

"Will you be able to race again?"

"It all depends," he admitted, "on how I've healed." His lips tightened. "Maybe it's time to retire."

"At thirty?"

He laughed, but the sound didn't carry any mirth as it bounced off the mountain face. "Looks that way."

The chair rounded the top of the lift and started downward. Melanie had to grit her teeth. Riding the chair up was one thing, but staring down the sheer mountain was quite another. Her hands began to sweat as she lifted the camera again.

Gavin's fingers clamped over her upper arm. "Be careful."

Melanie's concentration centered on those five strong fingers warm against her bare skin, heating her flesh.

She knew he could feel her pulse, hoped it wouldn't betray her as she forced the camera to her eyes and found breathtaking shots of the mountaintops. With her wide-angled lens, she caught the broken ridge of the Cascades. Thin, lazy clouds drifted between the blue peaks, and tall spires of snow pierced the wispy layer.

As the chair moved downward, past the timberline, she caught rays of morning sunlight. Golden beams sifted through the pine trees to dapple the needle-strewn forest floor.

Lower still, she focused the camera on the lodge, snapping off aerial shots of the weathered shake roof and sprawling wings.

"It is beautiful up here," she admitted, hazarding a glance at Gavin. Their gazes locked, and for a breathless instant Melanie was transported back to a place where things were simple and all that mattered was their love. He felt it, too; she could read it in his gold-colored eyes—a tenderness and love so special it still burned bright.

He swallowed and turned quickly to focus on the pines. His voice, when he spoke, was rough. "Look, Mel, I think we should get some things straight. I didn't know you'd be in Taylor's Crossing when I came back."

"Would it have changed your mind?"

"Probably—I don't know. Rich was hell-bent to reopen this lodge, but…" His voice drifted off, lost in the gentle rush of the breeze and the steady whir of the lift. "I—you—we made a lot of mistakes, didn't we?"

Her heart wrenched as she thought of their child—a child who hadn't even had a chance to be born. "More than you know."

"And I was wrong about a lot of things," he said, still avoiding her gaze. "And one of those things was you."

Bracing herself, she decided to try to bridge the horrible abyss that loomed between them, to tell him the truth. She placed her hand on his arm and said, "Look, Gavin, as long as we're talking about the past, there's something you should know—"

"All I know is it's over!" His face grew dark. "The past was just a means to an end. A way to get what I wanted." He stared straight at her. "And what happened didn't really matter. You and I—we were just a couple of kids playing around!"

"And that's why you're carrying this chip the size of Mount Everest on your shoulder," she mocked, "because it 'didn't matter'? Now who're you trying to kid?"

He smiled then, slowly and lazily. "If it makes you feel better to think you're the cause of my discontent, go right ahead. But that's making yourself pretty damned self-important, if you ask me."

"Why wouldn't I think it?" she challenged, angry again. "The minute you set eyes on me again, you went for my throat. There has to be a reason you hate me, Gavin."

A muscle worked in his jaw, and his voice, when he spoke, was barely a whisper. "I've never hated you, Melanie."

Her heart turned over. *Don't,* she thought desperately. *Whatever you do, Gavin, don't be kind!*

She opened her mouth, wanting to say something clever, but couldn't find the words. Besides, what good would it do, dredging it all up again? Instead, she fiddled with her camera, pretended interest in a few more shots and wished the ride would end. Being this close to Gavin, tangled up in old and new emotions, was just too difficult. "You're right," she agreed, forcing a cool, disinterested smile. "We were just a couple of kids. We didn't know what we wanted."

"Oh, I knew what I wanted," he said. "I wanted to be the best damn skier in the world."

"And nothing else?"

"Nothing else really mattered, did it?"

"No, I guess you're right," she replied tightly. "Skiing is all there is in life!"

His shoulders tensed, and the corners of his mouth tightened. At the bottom of the lift he motioned to Erik. The lift slowed, and Gavin helped her off, hopping nimbly on his good leg and swinging her to her feet as the lift stopped.

Leaning heavily on his cane, Gavin started hobbling back to the lodge, and she knew she couldn't leave things unsettled. Not if they were going to work together.

"Gavin..." Reaching forward, she touched his forearm again, and he spun around quickly, his expression stern, his eyes blazing.

"Go home, Melanie. You've got your pictures, though why you're taking them for that rag is beyond me."

" 'That rag' is the paper I work for."

He stopped dead in his tracks. "Couldn't you find a better one in Seattle?"

"I moved back here," she said, inching her chin up a fraction. "After the divorce."

He didn't respond as he propelled himself back to the lodge.

"Fool," she muttered, when he'd slammed into the building. "Why do you try?" *Because he has the right to know what really happened eight years ago.*

Drawing in a deep breath, she walked into the lodge and found Jan in the main lobby, chatting with Rich Johanson.

"...then we'll be back in a couple of days," Jan was saying.

Gavin was nowhere in sight. Slowly Melanie let out her breath, and Jan, spying her, waved her over and made hasty introductions.

"Sorry I was late," Rich apologized. "I got held up in court. I tried to call the paper, but you'd already taken off. I hope you weren't inconvenienced."

"No problem," Melanie said, hearing uneven footsteps approach. She stiffened.

"I took care of Ms. Brooks," Gavin said.

"Walker," Melanie corrected. "My name is Walker now."

"Again," he said.

"Yes, again." She forced a cool smile in Gavin's direction, though her fists were clenched so tight they ached.

Jan, delighted to find Gavin available, suggested they continue their interview.

He clenched his jaw but he didn't disagree, and they settled into a table in a corner of the main lobby.

"Looks like he's in a great mood," Rich observed.

"One of his best," Melanie remarked.

"With Gavin it's hard to tell." Rich shoved his hands through his hair. "Did you get everything you need?"

"I think so."

"Good. Good. Let's go outside." He motioned her into one of the chairs on the deck. "I've heard that you're the best photographer in town."

Melanie sat with her back to the sun. "You must've been talking to my uncle Bart," she said, laughing.

Rich waved off her modesty. "I've seen your pictures in the paper and looked over the work you did for the Conestoga Hotel. The manager couldn't say enough good things about you."

Melanie was pleased. She'd worked long and hard on the brochures for the Conestoga.

"And you did the photographs in the lobby of the hotel, right?"

Melanie nodded.

"Mmm. Look, I talked to several people in town because I need a photographer for the lodge, not only for pamphlets, brochures and posters but also to hang on the walls. We're reopening the resort with a Gold Rush theme and we'll need old pictures, blown up and colored brown—you know what I mean?"

"Sepia tones on old tintypes and daguerreotypes," she said.

"If you say so," he said a little sheepishly. "I don't know all the technical terms, but I do know what I want. We'll need between twenty and thirty for the lobby. Let me show you what I mean." He opened a side door to the main gathering room in the lodge and held it open while Melanie got to her feet and walked inside.

Jan and Gavin were still seated at the table, and from Gavin's body language Melanie guessed the interview wasn't going all that well.

Rich didn't seem to notice. He pointed to the walls where he wanted to hang the old photos. "Over here," he said with a sweeping gesture, "I'd like several mining shots and on the far wall, pictures of the mountain."

Rich rattled on and on. Though she listened to him, she was aware of Gavin talking reluctantly to Jan. She could feel the weight of his gaze on her back, knew he was glowering.

Eventually Rich guided her into the office where she was supposed to have met him two hours before and offered her a cup of coffee. Once they were seated, he said, "Besides the pictures for the lobby, we'll need photographs for brochures and posters. And we'll be selling artwork in one of the shops downstairs. We'd like some of your photographs on consignment." He opened up his palms. "So, if you're interested, I'd like you to become the photographer for Ridge Resort."

"Have you talked this over with Gavin?" she asked. Though a part of her would like to take the job and let Gavin rant and rave all he liked, the sensible side of her nature prevented her from jumping into a situation that was bound to spell trouble.

"I don't have to talk to him," Rich replied with a grin. "This is my decision."

"Maybe you should say something to him," she suggested, gathering her things.

"Look, Ms. Walker, I don't have much time. We plan to open in two months. I need brochures ASAP."

He offered her a generous flat fee and a percentage on all the posters sold, plus extra money for extra work. The job at Ridge Lodge, should she take it, would help establish her studio as well as pay off some of the debts she'd incurred since her divorce and give her a little cushion so that she wasn't quite so dependent on the *Tribune*. In short, Rich Johanson's offer was too good to pass up.

She cast a nervous glance in Gavin's direction, noted the hard, immovable line of his jaw and knew that he would hit the roof. But it didn't matter. She needed all the work she could get. "I'd be glad to work for you," she said, feeling a perverse sense of satisfaction.

Rich grinned and clasped her hand. "Good. I'll draw up a contract and we can get started as soon as it's convenient for you."

"I can work evenings and weekends."

"Will you have enough time?"

She shot another look in Gavin's direction. "Don't worry," she said, ignoring the tight corners of Gavin's mouth and the repressed fury that fairly radiated from him, "I'll make the time." She scrounged in her wallet, handed him her card and added, "You can reach me at my studio or at the office."

"Thanks." Rich stuffed the card in his wallet. "Then I'll see you in a few days." They shook hands again before Melanie, refusing to glance at Gavin one last time, gathered her things and headed for the front doors.

As she made her way down the asphalt path, she heard Jan's quick footsteps behind her. "Hey, Melanie, wait up!"

Melanie turned, watched Jan hurrying to catch her and noticed Gavin, hands braced on the porch rails of the lodge, glaring at her. She couldn't imagine what he'd think when he found out Rich had hired her. With a satisfied grin, she waved at him before turning her attention to a breathless Jan. "How'd it go?" Melanie asked.

"With Doel?" Jan sighed loudly and whispered, "I think it would be easier to interview a monk who's taken a vow of silence."

"Oh?"

Jan glanced over her shoulder,then said softly, "I want details, Melanie, *de*tails."

"About what?"

"You and Doel. I saw the looks he sent you. They were positively sizzling! And when we were up here before, I could've sworn there was something going on between you two. Now, what gives?"

"You're imagining things."

"And you're holding out on me. There's more to what happened to you than the fact that you went to school together." She reached her car and unlocked the door. "I mean it, Melanie. I want to know everything."

"It's not an interesting story," Melanie replied, though she knew sooner or later Jan would find out the truth—or part of it.

"Anything about Gavin Doel is interesting."

"Later," Melanie promised, needing time to sort out just how much she could confide. There was no getting around at least part of the truth. Jan would only discover the information somewhere else, and unfortunately, Taylor's Crossing was a small town. If Jan set her mind to finding out the truth, it wouldn't be too hard to dig up someone who would willingly remember. Only a handful of people had known that she and Gavin had been seeing each other—fewer still guessed they'd been lovers—but the townspeople in Taylor's Crossing had long memories when it came to gossip.

Frowning, Melanie slid into her sun-baked car. She glanced through the dusty windshield to the lodge. Gavin's eyes were narrowed against the sun, his jaw set in granite. How would she ever begin to explain the depth and complexity of her feelings for him? She'd been only seventeen at the time; no one, including Jan, would believe that her romance had been anything but puppy love.

But she knew better. As she slid a pair of sunglasses onto the bridge of her nose and drove out of the lot, she wished she could forget that she'd ever loved him.

CHAPTER SIX

"YOU DID *WHAT?*" Gavin roared, eyeing his partner as if he'd lost his mind.

"I hired Melanie Walker."

"Well, that's just great!" Gavin growled.

"What've you got against her?" Rich asked, his brows drawing together.

"I knew her years ago."

"So?" Sitting at his desk, pen in one hand, Rich stared up at Gavin as if he were the one who had gone mad.

"We dated."

Rich still wasn't getting the point. "I don't understand—"

"While I was gone, she married a guy by the name of Neil Brooks eight years ago."

"Neil Brooks—the lumber broker?"

"You know him?" Gavin growled, rolling his eyes and tossing his hands out as if in supplication to the heavens. "This just gets better and better."

"Of course I know him. Brooks Lumber is our major supplier for the renovation."

"No!" Gavin whispered harshly as he thought of Melanie's ex-husband—the man who had, in a few short weeks, stolen Melanie from him. He told himself he couldn't really blame Brooks. It had been Melanie who had betrayed him. Nonetheless, he loathed anything to do with Neil Brooks. "Find another lumber company."

"No can do," Rich said, assuming a totally innocent air. "Brooks Lumber is one of the few firms that service this area."

"There must be someone else! We're not exactly in Timbuktu, for crying out loud!"

"Brooks offers the best quality for the lowest price."

"I don't give a damn." This was turning into a nightmare! First Melanie and now Neil. Gavin's throat felt suddenly dry. He needed a drink. A double. But he didn't give in to the urge.

"Well, I do. I give a big damn. We don't have a lot of extra cash to throw around. Besides, we had a deal. I handle this end of the business—you help design the runs, bring in the investors and provide the skiing expertise."

"That's exactly what I'm doing. Providing expertise. Don't use Brooks. He's as slippery as a rattler and twice as deadly."

"Are you speaking from personal experience?"

"Yes! Damn it!" Gavin crashed his fist against the corner of Rich's desk, sloshing coffee on a few papers.

"Hey, watch it." Rich, perturbed, grabbed his handkerchief and mopped up the mess. "Look, even if I wanted to change lumber companies—which I don't—I can't. Not now. It's too late. We've already placed our order. Some of it has already been shipped and paid for. We don't have much time, Gavin, so whatever particular personal gripe you've got with Neil Brooks, you may as well shove it aside. And as for Neil's wife—or ex-wife or whatever she is—she's working for us. We both agreed that we'd employ as many local people as we could, remember? It's just good business sense to keep the locals happy!"

"I didn't know Melanie was back in town."

Rich grinned. "You've always had an eye for good-looking women, and that one—she's a knockout."

Gavin clenched his fist, but this time he did no more than shove it into his pocket. "I'm just not too crazy about some of your choices," Gavin muttered. He didn't want Melanie here, couldn't stand the thought of seeing her every day. He'd told himself he was long over her, but now he wasn't so sure. There was a moment up on the lift when he could've sworn that nothing had changed between them. But, of course, that was pure male ego. Everything had changed. "Was working for the lodge her idea?" he asked.

Rich shook his head. "Nope. In fact, I had to do some hard and fast talking to get her to take the job."

"You should have consulted with me first."

"That's what she said."

Gavin was surprised. "But you didn't listen, right?"

"No, I didn't listen. I wanted her. And as for consulting with you, that works both ways."

Gavin's jaw began to work, and he crossed to the window and stared out at the cool late summer day. A few workers dotted the hillside, and down the hall, in the lounge, the pounding of hammers jarred the old building.

"There's something else bothering you," Rich guessed, shoving back his chair and rounding the desk. Crossing his thick arms over his chest, fingers drumming impatiently, he stared at Gavin and waited.

"We don't need any adverse publicity," Gavin said flatly.

"And you think Melanie's going to give us some?"

Gavin hesitated, but only for a second. He trusted Rich, and they were partners. As his business partner, Rich had the right to know the whole story. He probably should have leveled with Rich before. But then, he had no idea he would run into Melanie again. If he had guessed she was back in Taylor's Crossing, he might have balked at the project.

"Well?" Rich was waiting.

"You know that I grew up here," Gavin said, seeing Rich's eyes narrow. "And you know that my father had his problems."

"So you said."

Gavin's muscles tightened as he remembered his youth. "Dad's an alcoholic," he said finally, the words still difficult.

"I know that."

"And he spent some time in prison."

"You said something about it—an accident that was his fault."

"An accident that killed the driver of the other car," he said quietly. "A woman, Brenda Walker. Melanie's mother."

Rich didn't move.

"Dad was legally drunk at the time."

Frowning, Rich said, "I'm sorry."

"So am I, and so was Dad—when he sobered up enough to understand what had happened. He came away with only a few scrapes and bruises, but Melanie's mother's car was forced off the road and down a steep embankment." Gavin relived the nightmare as if it had happened just yesterday. He'd been twelve at the time when the policemen had knocked on the door, the blue and red lights of their cars casting colored shadows on the sides of the trailer that he and his father had called home. He'd thought for certain his father was dead but had been relieved when he'd found out Jim Doel had survived.

However, that night had been just the tip of the iceberg, the start of a life of living with an aunt and uncle who hadn't given a damn about him.

Through it all, Gavin had escaped by testing himself. From the time he could handle a paper route, he'd spent every dime on the thrill of sliding downhill on skis. He'd landed odd jobs—eventually at Ridge Resort itself—and fed his unending appetite for the heart-pounding excitement of racing headlong down a steep mountain at breakneck speed.

In all the years since the night his father had been taken to jail, Gavin's only distraction from the sport he loved had been Melanie.

The only daughter of the woman his father had killed.

Rich asked, "And you think Melanie still holds a grudge?"

"I don't know," Gavin answered. "I thought I knew her, but I didn't. Ten years after the accident, against her father's better judgment, Melanie and I dated for a while." Gavin's gut wrenched at the vivid memories. "But then I had the opportunity to train for the Olympics."

"So you left her."

"I guess that's the way she saw it. I asked her to wait and she foolishly agreed." Gavin's lips twisted at his own naïveté.

"But she didn't."

Gavin felt again the glacial sting of her rejection. His nostrils flared slightly. "Adam Walker—Melanie's father—never approved of me or my old man. And while I was gone, Melanie married Neil Brooks. My guess is that her old man finally convinced her she'd be better off with the son of a wealthy lumber broker than a ski bum whose father was a drunk."

"And now?"

Gavin looked up sharply. "And now what?"

"Melanie and you?"

Gavin let out a short, ugly laugh. "There is no Melanie and me." His insides turned frigid. "There really never was."

Rich let out a sigh. "You should've told me this earlier, you know."

"Didn't see a reason. As far as I knew she was still living the good life up in Seattle."

"She's already agreed to the job, you know," Rich said, rubbing his temple. "I don't see how we can get out of this without causing a lot of hard feelings. Though I didn't sign a contract, if it gets out that we're not as good as our word—"

"Don't worry about it. Keep Melanie Walker," Gavin decided suddenly. He could find ways to avoid her. The lodge was large; the resort covered thousands of acres. Besides, he'd be too busy to run into her often. "Just as long as she does the job," he muttered, and added silently, *and doesn't get in my way.*

JAN WOULDN'T LET up. She'd camped out at Melanie's desk when they returned from the resort and wasn't taking no for an answer. "I saw the way he looked at you, Melanie! You can't convince me that there's nothing going on between you and Gavin Doel," she said, checking her reflection in her compact mirror and touching up her lipstick.

"I haven't seen him in years." Melanie walked into the darkroom and picked up the enlarged photograph of Uncle Bart and his prize colt, Big Money. She slipped the black-and-white photo into an envelope and, returning to her desk, pretended she wasn't really interested in Jan's observations about Gavin.

Sighing in exasperation, Jan tossed her hands into the air. "Okay, okay, I believe that you haven't seen him," she said, ignoring Melanie's efforts at nonchalance. "But what happened all those years ago? The looks he sent you today were hot—I mean, scorching, burning, torrid, you name it!"

Tucking the envelope into her purse, Melanie chuckled. "You're overdramatizing."

"I'm a reporter. I don't go in for melodrama. Just the facts. And the fact is he couldn't keep his eyes off you!"

"You're exaggerating, then." Melanie walked to the coffeepot and poured two cups.

"I'm not exaggerating! Now, what gives?"

Melanie handed Jan one of the cups, took a sip herself and grimaced at the bitter taste. She opened a small packet of sugar and poured it into her cup. "Well, I guess you're going to find out sooner or later, but this is just between you and me."

"Absolutely!" Jan took a sip of her coffee, but over the rim her eyes were bright, eager.

Haltingly, Melanie explained that she and Gavin had dated in high school, glossing over how deep her emotions had run.

"And so, when he went to train for the Olympics, we lost touch and I married Neil."

Jan shook her head. "You chose Neil Brooks over Gavin Doel?" she asked incredulously. "No offense, Mel, but there's just no comparison."

"Well, that's what happened."

"And nothing else?"

"Nothing," Melanie lied easily. "But what I told you is strictly off the record, right?"

"Oh, absolutely!" Jan looked positively stricken. "Besides, no one's going to care whom he dated in high school."

Jan slid a look at her watch and frowned. "I gotta run," she said, "but I'll see you tomorrow. When will the proofs of the lodge be ready?"

"I'll have them on your desk first thing in the morning."

"You're a love. Thanks." With a wave, Jan bustled out of the building.

Melanie spent the next few hours in and out of the darkroom, developing the photographs she'd taken at Ridge Lodge. The shots from the chair were spectacular, black-and-white vistas of the rugged Cascade Mountains. A few pictures of the workers, too, showed the manpower needed to give the lodge its new look. But the photographs that took her breath away were the close-ups of Gavin.

In startling black and white, his features seemed more chiseled and angular—as earthy and formidable as the mountains he challenged, his eyes more deeply set, his expression innately sexy and masculine. And though she'd seen little evidence of humor in the time she'd spent with him, the photographs belied his harshness by exposing the tiny beginnings of laugh lines near his mouth and tiny crinkles near the corners of his eyes. She wondered vaguely who had been lucky enough to make him laugh.

She circled the best shots, stuffed them in an envelope and

left the packet in Jan's In basket. By the time she was finished, most of the staff had left. Walking into the fading sunlight, she took the time to lock the door behind her, then noticed the cool evening breeze that chilled her bare arms.

The mountain nights had begun to grow cold.

She stopped at the grocery store on the way home and finally turned into her drive a little after seven. The sky was dusky with the coming twilight, shadows stretched across the dry grass of her yard, and a truck she didn't recognize was parked near the garage. Gavin sat behind the wheel.

She stood on the brakes. The Volkswagen screeched to a stop.

Surely he wasn't here.

But as she stared at the truck, her heart slammed into overdrive. Gavin stretched slowly from the cab. *Now what?* she wondered, her throat suddenly dry as she forced herself to appear calm and steeled herself for the upcoming confrontation. It had to be about Rich's offer.

Wearing faded jeans, a black T-shirt, a beat-up leather jacket and scruffy running shoes, he reminded her of the boy she'd once known, the kid from the wrong side of the tracks. No designer labels or fancy ski clothes stated the fact that he was a downhill legend.

Deciding that the best defense was a quick offense, she juggled purse, groceries and camera case as she climbed out of the Volkswagen. "Don't tell me," she said, shoving the car door closed with her hip and forcing a dazzling smile on slightly frozen lips. "You've come racing over here to congratulate me on my new job at the resort."

His jaw slid to the side, and he shoved his sunglasses onto his head. "Not exactly."

She lifted a disdainful eyebrow. "And I thought you'd be thrilled!"

"Rich handles that end of the business."

"Does he? So you didn't come over here to tell me that I'm relieved of my newfound duties?"

"I considered it," he admitted with maddening calm.

"Look, Gavin, let's get one thing straight," she said. "I'm not going to get into a power struggle with you. If you want me to do the job, fine. If not, believe me, I won't starve. So you don't have to feel guilty. If you want someone else to do the work, just say so."

"Rich seems set on you."

"And you?"

Brackets pinched the corners of his mouth. "I don't know. I haven't seen your work. At least, not for a few years."

She ignored that little jab and marched across the side yard to the back door. She kept her back rigid, pretended that she didn't care in the least that he'd shown up at her doorstep. Over her shoulder she called, "Well, if you're interested, come inside. But if you're just here to give me a bad time, then you may as well leave. I'm not in the mood."

Shifting the groceries and camera case, she unlocked the back door. Sassafras, barking and growling, snapping teeth bared, hurtled through. He didn't even pause for a pet but headed straight for Gavin.

"Don't worry," she called to Gavin over her shoulder, "he's all bark—no bite."

But Gavin didn't appear the least bit concerned about Sassafras's exposed fangs or throaty warnings. He flashed a quick glance at the dog and commanded, "Stop!"

Sassafras skidded on the dry grass but the hairs on the back of his neck rose threateningly.

"That's better," Gavin said, slowly following Melanie up the steps. "Damned leg," he grumbled, pausing in the doorway.

"Come on in," Melanie invited. "I don't bite, either—at least, not usually." She placed the bag on the counter. "Now, just give me a minute to get things organized." She kicked her shoes into a corner near the table and stuffed a few sacks of vegetables and a package of meat into the refrigerator.

She felt him watching her, but she didn't even glance in his direction. She pretended not to be aware that he was in the room, managing a fake calm expression that she hoped countered her jackhammering heart and suddenly sweating palms. Now that he was in the house, what was she going to do with him? The house seemed suddenly small, more intimate than ever before.

The fact that he was in her house, alone with her, brought back too many reminders of the past. The rooms felt hot and suffocating, though she expected the temperature couldn't be more than sixty-five degrees.

"Come on, my studio's down the hall," she said, opening the door for Sassafras. Cool mountain air streamed in with the old dog as he eyed Gavin warily, growling and dropping onto his favorite spot beneath the kitchen table. "See, he likes you already," Melanie quipped, suppressing a smile at Sassafras's low growl.

"I'd hate to think how he reacts to someone he doesn't trust."

"Just about the same." Melanie led Gavin to the front of the house and down a short corridor to her studio. He didn't remark on the changes in the house, but maybe he didn't remember. He'd been over only a few times while they'd dated and he hadn't stayed long because of her father's hostility.

As she opened the studio door, Gavin caught her wrist. "I didn't come here to see your work," he said, spinning her around so that she was only inches from him, her upturned face nearly colliding with his chest.

"But I thought—"

"That was just a ruse." He swallowed, his Adam's apple moving slowly up and down in his throat. Melanie forced her eyes to his. "I came here because I wanted to lay out the ground rules, talk some things out."

"What 'things'?" His hand was still wrapped around her wrist, his fingertips hot against the inside of her arm. No doubt he could feel her thundering pulse. The small, dark hallway felt close. It was all she could do to pull her arm from his grasp.

"I just want you to know that I don't want any trouble."

"And you think I'll give it to you?"

"I think that rag you work for might."

She bristled. "The *Tribune*—"

"We've been over this before," he said, cutting her off as she found the doorknob and backed into the studio. She needed some breathing room. With a flick of her wrist she snapped on the overhead light. "I have a feeling that reporter friend of yours would print anything if she thought it would get her a byline."

"Not true."

"If you say so." He didn't seem convinced. Glancing quickly around the studio, he slung his injured leg over a corner of her desk. "But she gets pretty personal."

"You don't have to worry about Jan," Melanie said, instantly defensive. "I told her a little of our history."

"You did *what*?" he thundered, gold eyes suddenly ice-cold.

"It's all off the record."

"You trust her?"

"Of course I trust her. We work together and she's my friend."

He snorted. "And I suppose you trust Michaels, too."

"Yes!" she replied indignantly.

Gavin muttered something unintelligible. "But he hasn't been your boss for long has he?"

"No," she conceded. "The paper changed hands about a year ago. Brian was hired to take charge."

"From where?"

"Chicago, I think. He's worked in publishing for years. Before Chicago, there was a paper in Atlanta."

"Right. Never planted his feet down for long, has he? And I wouldn't think Taylor's Crossing, Oregon is the next natural step up on the ladder of success. Atlanta, Chicago, Taylor's Crossing? Doesn't seem likely, does it?"

"What're you trying to say, Gavin?" she asked, bristling at the unspoken innuendos.

"I've met Michaels before. He was a reporter in Vail. I didn't like him then and I don't trust him now."

Folding her arms across her chest, she said, "You are the most suspicious person I know. You don't trust anyone, do you?"

"I wonder why," he said quietly, his features drawn.

Her heart stopped. "So you're blaming me?"

"No, Melanie, I'm blaming myself," he replied, his words cutting sharply. "I was young and foolish when I met you—naïve. But you taught me how stupid it is to have blind trust. It's a lesson I needed to learn. It's gotten me through some tough times."

"So you're here to thank me, is that it?" she tossed out, though she was dying inside.

"I'm here to make sure that you and I see eye to eye. I want our past to remain buried, and for that to happen, you'd better quit talking to Jan or anyone else at the *Tribune*."

"Is that so?"

"For both our sakes as well as my father's. No matter what happens, I want Dad's name kept out of the paper."

Melanie bit her lower lip. "I don't know if that's possible."

"Well, use your influence."

"I will, of course I will, but I'm only the photographer."

"And the bottom line is Brian Michaels doesn't give a

damn whose life he turns inside out!" He stood then, towering over her, his eyes blazing. "My father's paid for what happened over and over again. We all have. There is no reason to dredge it all up again."

"I agree. I just don't know what I can do."

Gavin sighed, raking his fingers through his hair. "Dad's moving back to Taylor's Crossing and I want to see to it that he can start fresh."

"I doubt that anyone will be interested."

"God, are you naïve! You just don't know what kind of an industry you work for, do you?"

"We report the news—"

"And the gossip and the speculation—anything as long as it sells papers!"

"I'm not going to stand here and argue about it with you," she retorted, wishing she felt a little more conviction. "If you're finished—"

"Not quite. Now that we understand each other—"

"I don't think we ever did."

"Doesn't matter. You stay out of my way and I'll stay out of yours. If you have any questions while you're working up at the lodge, you can ask Rich."

"And if he's not there?"

"Then I'll help you."

"But, don't go chasing after you, is that what you're telling me?" she mocked, simmering fury starting to boil deep inside her.

"I just think it's better if you and I keep our distance."

"Don't worry, Gavin," she remarked, her voice edged in cynicism. "Your virtue is safe with me."

He flushed from the back of his neck. "Don't push me, Melanie."

"Wouldn't dream of it," she threw back at him. "I'm not afraid of you, Gavin."

His gaze shifted to her mouth. "Well, maybe you should be," he whispered hoarsely.

"Why?"

He swallowed hard. His expression tightened in his attempt at self-control. "Because, damn it, even though I know it's crazy, even though I tell myself this will never work, I just can't help… Oh, to hell with it."

His arms surrounded her, and his lips slanted over hers.

Surprised, Melanie gasped, and his tongue slipped easily between her teeth, tasting and exploring.

She knew she should push him aside, shove with all her might, and she tried—dear Lord, she tried—but as her hands came up against his chest they seemed powerless, and all she could do was close her eyes and remember, in painful detail, the other kisses they'd shared. He still tasted the same, felt as strong and passionate as before.

Her lips softened, and she kissed him back. All the lies and the accusations died away. She was lost in the smell and feel of him, in the power of his embrace, the thundering beat of her heart.

Slowly, his tongue stopped its wonderful exploration, and a low groan escaped from him. "God, Melanie!" he whispered against her hair, his arms strong bands holding her close. "Why?"

She tried to find her voice, but words failed her.

Slowly he released her, stepping backward and shoving shaking fingers through his hair. She watched as he visibly strained for control.

"Gavin, I think we should talk."

"We've said everything that has to be said," he replied. "This isn't going to work, you know."

"We'll…we'll make it work."

His gaze slid to her lips again, and she swallowed with difficulty. "No."

"I need to explain about Neil," she said.

His features hardened. "You don't have to explain about anything, Melanie. Let's just forget this ever happened."

"I don't think I can."

"Well, try," he said, turning on his heel and striding out the door.

She didn't move for a full minute, and only after she heard his pickup spark to life, tires squeal and gravel spray, did she sag against the door.

The next few weeks promised to be hell.

"DAMN! DAMN! DAMN!" Gavin pounded on the steering wheel with his fist. What had gotten into him? He'd kissed her! *Kissed* her—and she'd responded. Suddenly, in those few moments, all time and space had disappeared, and Gavin was left with the naked truth that she wasn't out of his blood.

He cranked on the wheel and gunned the accelerator as he left the city lights behind and his truck started climbing the dark road leading to the mountain.

He couldn't hide from her. Not now. As a photographer for the resort, she'd be at the lodge more often than not. And then what? Would he kiss her again? Seduce her next time? Delicious possibilities filled his mind, and he remembered how the curve of her spine fit so neatly against the flat of his stomach, or the way her breasts, young and firm, had nestled so softly into his hands, or how her hips had brushed eagerly against his in the dim light of the hayloft.

"Stop it!" he commanded, as if he could will her image out of his mind. He flicked on the radio and tried to concentrate on the weather report. Temperatures were due to drop in the area, a weatherman reported, but Gavin's lips curved cynically. He decided that in the next month or two, his temperature would probably be soaring. All because of Melanie.

CHAPTER SEVEN

RIDGE LODGE AND Gavin were plastered over the front page of the *Tribune*. There were several pictures of the resort, including a panoramic shot Melanie had taken from the lift, showing the lodge sprawling at the base of the runs, and there was one photograph of Gavin—a thoughtful pose that showed off his hard-edged profile as he talked with the reporter.

He didn't like the picture. It showed too much of his personality and captured the fact that he felt uncomfortable and suspicious while being interviewed. Melanie obviously had a photographer's knack for making a flat black-and-white photograph show character and depth.

"Damn her," he muttered, forcing his eyes to the story. Bold headlines proclaimed: Doel to Reopen Ridge Resort. The byline credited Jan Freemont with the story.

Gavin's jaw clenched as he scanned the columns. But the article was straightforward, and aside from mentioning the fact that Gavin had grown up around Taylor's Crossing, his personal life wasn't included. His skiing awards and professional life were touched on, but the focus of the article was the resort.

So maybe Brian Michaels was playing by the rules this time. Perhaps the *Tribune* was a local newspaper that wasn't interested in trashing everyone's personal life.

Gavin didn't believe it for a minute. He'd met Michaels

before; the man's instincts usually centered on gossip and speculation. Unless Michaels had mellowed or developed some sense of conscience.

"No way," Gavin told himself as Rich, several newspapers tucked under his arm, a wide grin stretched across his jaw, strode into the office.

He dropped the papers onto Gavin's desk. "Looks like you were worried for nothing," he said, thumping a finger on the front page.

"We'll see."

"I told you, this is the best source of free publicity, and the story's been picked up by the *Portland Daily* as well as several papers in Washington, Idaho and northern California."

"If you say so," Gavin said, unable to concede the fact that he was wrong.

"And now the *Tribune* is doing a series on the resort with a final full-page article scheduled for the grand opening. What could be better?"

"Can't think of a thing," Gavin drawled, sarcasm heavy in his words.

"Well, neither can I." Rich stuffed his hands into his pockets and walked to the windows, looking out at a cloudy afternoon sky. "So, you be good to the reporters who start showing up."

"Wouldn't dream of anything else."

Rich sighed theatrically. "I know you gave Ms. Freemont a bad time."

"I was good as gold," Gavin mocked.

"It's your attitude, Doel. It's way beyond bad."

"I'll try to improve."

"Do that."

"Won't have to. You're the one going to handle the press from now on."

"I know, I know. But I'm not always here. In fact, I'm

taking off for Portland today, hopefully to settle a case. I need to check on my practice for a couple of days—make sure that legal assistant I hired is handling everything. I'll be back by the weekend."

"And in the meantime, you expect me to deal with—" he glanced at the byline again "—Jan Freemont."

"And anyone else who strolls in here looking for a story or pictures—and that includes Melanie Walker."

Gavin frowned. He'd already decided to try to work things out with Melanie. Bury the past. Forget it. Just treat her like anyone else. If that were possible. After kissing her, he wasn't convinced he could pull it off. One kiss and he'd been spinning—just like a horny high school kid. Disgusting. "I'll do my best," he told Rich, and flashed a cynical smile.

"Oh, God, Gavin, try harder than that," Rich said with a laugh as he stuffed some papers into his briefcase.

"Not funny, Johanson."

"Sure it was. That's your problem, you know. No sense of humor."

"As long as I've only got one problem, I guess I'm doing all right. Now, get outta here."

Rich snapped his briefcase closed. "Seriously, Gavin, try not to antagonize too many people—especially reporters—while I'm gone."

Gavin assumed his most innocent expression. "You've got my word. Unless the questions get too personal or way out of line, I'll be—"

"I know, 'good as gold.' God help us," Rich muttered, waving a quick goodbye as he left.

Gavin glanced again at the opened newspaper, his gaze landing on his profile. No doubt Melanie would return within the next couple of days. Well, he'd find a way to be nice to her. Even if it killed him.

MELANIE HAD EVERY intention of dealing with Rich Johanson and staying clear of Gavin. She'd already spent three sleepless nights thinking of Gavin and how easily she'd responded to him.

And he'd responded, too. Whether he admitted it or not. Her foolish heart soared at the thought, but she quickly brought it back to the ground. No matter how Gavin responded to her, that response was purely sexual. His emotions were far different from hers. He'd kissed her as he'd kissed a dozen women in the past year. She'd kissed him as she'd kissed only him. No other man, including Neil, had ever been able to cause her blood to thunder, her pulse to race out of control.

And that's why Gavin was off-limits, she told herself as she shoved open the door of Ridge Lodge three days after Gavin's visit.

Unfortunately, the first person she ran into was Gavin.

Thankfully, they weren't alone. A work crew was busy hammering and sawing, stripping old wood and refinishing. Men with sagging leather belts filled with hammers, chisels, nails, planers and files moved throughout the interior and scrambled up on scaffolding that reached to the joists and beams of the ceiling three stories overhead. Though it was late afternoon, the lodge wasn't dark or intimate because of the huge lights the construction workers had mounted to aid them in their restoration of the rustic old inn.

Blueprints, anchored by half-filled bottles, were spread upon the bar while power saws screamed and dust swirled in pale clouds. A radio blared country music, but Melanie was sure no one could hear it over the din.

"I'm, uh, looking for Rich," she shouted over the noise, aware that a blush had stained her neck. Gavin was standing near the bar, eyeing the ceiling. Wearing jeans and a loose

Notre Dame sweatshirt, he seemed to be supervising the restoration.

He frowned, dusted off his hands and moved closer so they wouldn't have to shout. "Rich isn't here. He left me in charge."

Great, Melanie thought, bracing herself for an inevitable confrontation.

"And I promised I'd be on my best behavior."

"I wasn't aware you had one."

His lips twitched. "It's buried deep. But you're in luck today. I'm going to try my level best to be charming and helpful."

"Bull," she replied, caught up in his teasing banter.

"Hey, look." He opened his palms. "Either you deal with me or you come back later."

"I thought you didn't want anything to do with me."

His eyes darkened. "Sometimes fate works against us."

Amen, she thought, but held her tongue. No reason to antagonize him. At least, not while he was trying to be affable.

"Rich left a contract for you on his desk," Gavin was saying, as if the other night hadn't existed—as if nothing had changed. "I'll get it for you. Come on."

Wondering how long his gracious manner would last, she followed him down a short hall and into the office.

Slamming the door behind him, he actually grinned. "Sorry about the mess."

"Doesn't bother me. In fact, I'd like to take a few pictures."

Nodding, he rummaged through the papers on the desk, found the typewritten contract and handed it to her.

Taking the document, she observed, "You're in a better mood today."

"Why not?" he tossed back, leaning over the desk. A few pale rays of afternoon sunlight streamed through the window to catch in the golden strands of his hair. Melanie's heart flipped over. "You and I got everything straight the other night, right?"

"Right," she agreed, not sure she was any more comfortable with this affable Gavin than she had been with the jaded, cynical man who had left her only three nights before—a man who had kissed her with a passion that had cut to her soul.

Gavin shoved his hands into the back pockets of his jeans. "And now that the construction's moving along, I feel that I'm not just spinning my wheels any longer."

"And so now everything is just wonderful?" she asked, unable to keep the disbelief from her voice.

He glanced up sharply, but a precision-practiced smile curved his lips. "Until something goes wrong."

She didn't believe him for a minute. This was all just an act, but she didn't argue with him. If he was going to be agreeable, it would make her job that much easier.

"Here's the contract. Take it home, look it over, have a lawyer look at it if you want to, but Rich wants it signed by the end of the week."

"No problem," she said as he handed her a stiff white envelope with the name and address of Rich's legal firm printed in the upper left-hand corner. She tucked the envelope into her purse, then settled down to business. "I've got some ideas for the brochure, but what I'd like are old pictures of the lodge and of you for background."

"I don't see why—" He stopped himself short. His sunny disposition clouded for a minute, and small lines etched his forehead. For the first time she understood how difficult it was for him to appear easygoing. "Sure. Why not?" he said. "Everything you'll need is in my suite." With a muttered oath, he grabbed his cane. "This way. Come on."

She followed him down a narrow hallway to a door near the back of the lodge.

Twisting the knob, he said with more than a trace of

cynicism, "Home sweet home." He held the door open for her, and she walked into his living quarters.

She'd expected a grand suite with lavish furnishings for a man as wealthy and famous as Gavin, a man who had desperately wanted to shed his poor roots.

Instead, she found the suite comfortable and sparse. A rock fireplace filled one wall. Nearby a bookcase was crammed with books, magazines, a stereo and a television. A faded rug covered the worn wood floor, and a few pieces of furniture were grouped haphazardly around the room.

Wincing, Gavin bent down to the bottom shelf of the bookcase, rummaged around and pulled out a couple of battered photograph albums and a box. He tossed everything onto a nearby table. "I think that should do it," he said, forcing a smile as he straightened. "If you need anything else, just whistle. I'll be supervising the renovation or working out in the weight room." He cast an impatient glance at his injured leg. "Physical therapy."

"It shouldn't take long," Melanie replied, trying to be polite, though her voice sounded strained.

"Good."

"I'll try not to bother you."

Oh, woman, if you only knew, Gavin thought, trying his damnedest to be civil. But every time he looked at her, gazed into her wide hazel eyes, he was reminded of how much he'd loved her, how deeply she'd touched his soul.

"Damn crazy fool," he muttered, leaving the room as quickly as he could. Just being around her made him restless. And though he knew rationally that he was through with her forever, there was a wayward side of his nature that wanted to flirt with danger, a wayward side that kept reminding him of their last kiss and the feel and smell of her yielding against him. What would it hurt to spend time with her—get a little back? Now that he was over her, he could handle any situation that arose—or could he? The other night hadn't gone exactly as planned. However, he was trying to keep the promise he'd made to Rich and himself, trying not to antagonize her. But it was hell.

In the lobby, he spent nearly an hour with the foreman and was relieved that the remodeling, though only a few days old, was still on schedule. Then, because he didn't want to run into Melanie again, he hobbled down the short flight of steps to the pool and the weight room.

Fortunately, this area needed very little work, and the long, rectangular pool was operational.

He stripped out of his work clothes, stepped into a pair of swim trunks and took a position at the weight machine. Slowly, he started working his leg, stretching the muscles with only a little resistance and weight and adding more pounds as he began to work up a sweat.

"Take it easy," Dr. Hodges had said. "Don't push yourself." Yet that was exactly what he felt compelled to do. Cooped up in this damned lodge with Melanie poking through old photographs upstairs while the upcoming ski season, which could make or break the resort, loomed ahead, Gavin had no choice but to push himself to release tension and nervous energy.

He pressed relentlessly on the foot bar of the thigh machine. Sweat trickled down his back.

The pain in his leg started to burn. He ignored it, pushing again on the weight, stretching out his knee and calf only to release the tension and hear the weights clang down. Gritting his teeth, he shoved again. Sweat dripped from his temples to his chin.

How the hell would he get through the next few weeks, unable to participate in the sport he loved, unable to trust a woman he'd treasured?

"Don't even think about it," he growled to himself, his

muscles bulging as he pressed relentlessly on the weights, his thigh muscles quivering. He slammed his eyes shut, but even in his concentration, Melanie appeared—a vision with a gorgeous body and seductive smile. She was older now, a little jaded in her own way. Yet he found her sarcastic remarks interesting, her sense of humor refreshing. The fact that she had the nerve to stand up to him was beguiling—or would have been if it wasn't so damned maddening. The nerve of her actually baiting him when she'd left him high and dry all those years before.

He wondered if she ever thought of him—of those nights they'd shared. God, with his eyes closed, he could still smell the scent of hay on her skin, see the seductive light in her hazel eyes, hear the sound of her pleasured cries as he…

He dropped the weights, and they slammed together, the noise ringing to the rafters. Climbing off the damned machine, he shoved his sweaty hair from his eyes and noticed he felt an uncomfortable swelling between his legs. "Damn it, Doel, you're a first-class idiot," he said, swearing beneath his breath.

Embarrassed at a reaction he would have expected from a teenager, he dived into the warm water of the pool and began swimming laps. Stroke after stroke, he knifed through the water, determined to push Melanie from his mind. With supreme concentration he counted his laps, losing track somewhere after thirty and not really caring. The water was refreshing, loosening his muscles, and he stopped only when he felt his ankle begin to throb. He glanced at the clock on the wall. Six-thirty. Nearly three hours had passed since she'd shown up. Surely she was long gone.

Dripping water across the aggregate floor, he snapped a clean towel from the closet and wiped his face. He was still breathing deeply, but at least his ridiculous state of sexual arousal had passed and he felt near exhaustion.

Towel drying his hair, he headed upstairs. The lodge was quiet and nearly dark. He'd go back to his room, change, then head into town for dinner.

With Melanie? a voice inside his head suggested.

"Not a chance." The only way he was safe from her was to keep his distance.

MELANIE LOST ALL track of time. Poring over the photographs of Ridge Lodge was fascinating. The old pictures created a visual and unique history of the lodge and Taylor's Crossing. She spent hours choosing those photographs she thought might enhance the brochure, and she'd had trouble deciding which shots she wanted to enlarge for the lobby and restaurant. She finally picked thirty pictures that had the right feel as well as clarity. She would let Rich and Gavin choose from these.

She should have quit then, but she picked up the second photograph album. The pages fell open to a picture of Gavin barely out of his teens, poised on the crest of a snow-covered hill. His face was tanned, his skin unlined, his hair blowing in the wind, his smile as brilliantly white as the snow surrounding him. She swallowed hard. She recognized the picture. She'd taken it herself on the upper slopes of Mount Prosperity.

Gavin had been an instructor at the time, paying for his skiing by earning his keep at the resort. And she'd spent every minute she could with him.

Her throat ached, and she pressed her lips together as she stared at the image. Memory after memory flashed in her mind, colliding in vital, soul-jarring images that she'd kept buried for eight years.

"Don't do this," she whispered, but she couldn't help herself and she slowly turned the pages, each slickly bound photograph a chronicle of Gavin's professional life. She saw pictures of breath-stoppingly steep runs, dazzling snow-covered canyons cut into narrow runs that sliced through the rugged slopes, and always Gavin, tucked tightly, skimming across the snow, throwing a wake of powder behind him.

And there were other photographs, as well: pictures of Gavin accepting awards or trophies or standing beside any number of gorgeous women, the most often photographed being Aimee LaRoux.

Melanie had composed herself and her heartbeat had nearly slowed to normal when she lifted the album and a single picture fluttered facedown to the table.

She flipped it over, and time seemed to stand still as she stared at a picture of herself with Gavin, laughing gaily into the camera. Seated at a booth near the huge fireplace in this very lodge, they snuggled together, their faces flushed from the last run of the day, their hair mussed, their eyes bright with love for each other. Gavin's arm was thrown carelessly across her shoulders, and he looked as if he had the world on a string. And he did. It was the night he'd learned that he was to train for the Olympic team.

Melanie took in a shuddering breath and released it slowly. "Oh, Lord," she whispered when she heard the creak of old floorboards and looked up to find Gavin standing woodenly in the doorway.

Wearing only swimming trunks and a towel looped casually around his neck, he didn't say a word. But his eyes were filled with a thousand questions.

She tried not to notice the corded muscles of his shoulders or the provocative way his golden hair swirled over his chest. Lowering her eyes, she noticed the thick, muscular thighs and a series of thin scars around his ankle.

"I thought you'd be gone," he finally said.

Oh, God, he'd caught her looking at the picture! Wishing she could slam the album shut, she forced her eyes upward again. He was already crossing the room, and his gaze was focused on the desk and the photograph still clutched in her fingers.

She searched for the right words, but they wouldn't form in her cotton-dry throat.

Stopping at the table, he stared at the photograph, and his lips curved down at the corners. "Reliving the past?" he growled.

"No, I—" She dropped the picture as if it were hot, then was instantly furious with herself for being so self-conscious. Inching her chin upward, she said, "It fell out of the album. I was just putting it back."

"Don't bother."

"Wh-what?"

"Just toss it."

To her horror, he snatched the picture from her fingers, crumpled it and dropped it into a wastebasket.

"No!" she cried, feeling as if a part of her past had just been wrenched from her soul.

"You want it?"

"No, but—"

"Then let's just leave it where it belongs, okay? It was just an oversight. I got rid of all those pictures a long time ago."

Inside, she was shaking. From rage? Or something else, a deeper, more primal emotion? She didn't know and she didn't care. But her voice was steady as she stood. "You can't just erase what happened between us, Gavin."

"*Nothing* happened."

"We loved each other."

"I thought you agreed we were just two kids fooling around."

"I lied."

His eyes narrowed. "Not the first time, is it?"

She sucked in her breath, feeling as if she'd been slapped. "I think I'd better go."

"Good idea."

She started gathering her things, picking out the photographs she needed and scooping them into a pocket of her case, but he grabbed her arm, forcing her to spin around and face him again.

She swallowed hard.

"Just explain one thing," he ground out.

"Name it."

"If you loved me," he said quietly, every feature on his face tense, "then why didn't you wait for me?"

"I didn't want to be a burden," she said quickly, thinking for a second that the truth was better than the lies they'd both been living with for years.

"A burden?"

"You had a future—a chance for a berth on an Olympic team. You didn't need a wife tying you down."

His eyes narrowed suspiciously and his nostrils flared, but his hard mouth relaxed slightly. "We could have waited until the Olympics were over and I had started my career."

She licked her lips. Could she tell him about the baby? Now, when honesty seemed so vital? Would he understand? Instinctively, she reached for his forearms, her fingers touching rock-hard muscles. "There's something else—"

But before she could finish, he lowered his head and his mouth slanted over hers in a kiss as familiar as a soft summer breeze. His arms surrounded her, crushing her against him. He tasted of chlorine and salt and whiskey, and she felt his thighs press intimately into the folds of her skirt.

She offered no resistance and kissed him back. Being held by him seemed so natural and right, and all the wasted years between then had now melted away. Once again she was seventeen, caught in the embrace of the man she loved.

Groaning, he shifted, his wet trunks dampening her dress, his fingers catching in the long strands of her hair. Her head lolled back, and her mouth opened to the insistent pressure of his tongue. Quick, moist touches of his tongue against the inside of her mouth caused her blood to boil, her knees to weaken.

He kissed her lips, her cheeks and her throat. Closing her eyes, she ignored the warning bells clanging wildly in her head. His touch was erotic, the hand against the small of her back moving deliciously.

"Melanie," he whispered hoarsely. With his weight, he lowered her to the floor and pinned her against the carpet. Still kissing her, he found the buttons of her blouse, and the thin fabric gave way to expose her breasts covered in lace.

Stop him! Stop him now! But when his palm glided over her breast, she could only moan and writhe as his fingers dipped beneath the lace, gently prodding, touching and withdrawing until her nipple strained tight against the bra and her breasts ached for more—so much more.

With agonizing slowness his tongue moved along her cheek and neck and rimmed the circle of bones at the base of her throat. Her own hands were busy touching and exploring the corded strength of his chest and the fine, furry mat of hair that covered suntanned skin. His shoulder muscles were hard as she reached around him, and her fingers dug into his back as he continued to kiss her, moving downward.

"Oh, Gavin," she cried as his mouth fit hot and wet over her nipple. His tongue touched her in supple, sure strokes that caused her blood to burn and wiped out any further thoughts she had of stopping him.

He suckled through the lace and moved one free hand to cup her buttocks, bringing her body so close to his that she could feel his thighs and hips straining against the fabric that separated him from her.

Lord, how she wanted him. Nothing else mattered but the smell, taste and feel of him.

Finally, he unhooked her bra; the lace gave way, and she

felt cool air against her bare skin before his mouth covered one breast and teased and laved the taut nipple.

She cradled his head against her, wanting more, knowing that only he could fill the ache that was beginning to yearn deep inside.

"Oh, God," he whispered, drawing up and away from her, staring down at her dishabille and groaning low in his throat. He squeezed his eyes shut for a few heart-stopping moments, and when he finally lifted his eyelids again, the passion burning so brightly in his gaze had died. "What're you doing to me?"

He rolled away from her and sat with his back to her, his rigid arms supporting him as he drew in deep, ragged breaths. "Damn it, woman, why can't you just leave me alone?" His voice was rough, the hand he plowed through his hair trembling.

"I didn't start this, Gavin."

"Well, you sure as hell didn't stop it!"

Humiliated, Melanie sat up and started working on her clothes. "This wasn't my fault," she said, still buttoning her blouse.

"Wasn't it?" he flung back at her, glancing over his shoulder before pushing himself upright. His features twisted in pain for just a second as he strained his ankle.

"Of course not!" she declared hotly. "And I'm tired of you always throwing the blame at my feet!"

"Maybe that's where it belongs."

She swept in a long breath. "You really can be a bastard when you want to be."

"Yeah, well, you don't seem to mind sometimes," he threw back at her.

"Maybe that's because sometimes, when you're not trying out for boor of the year, you're wonderful."

He stopped, his eyes locking with hers. Time stood still. His throat worked, and his face gentled for just a second.

Warring emotions strained his features. "You're dreaming! Living in a past that didn't exist!"

"Gavin—"

Swearing roundly under his breath, he hobbled toward the bookcase. He opened an upper cabinet, withdrew a bottle and glass, then poured himself a quick drink. "Why didn't you leave a couple of hours ago?" he asked suddenly. "What were you doing hanging around?"

"I wasn't finished sorting through the pictures."

He tossed back half his drink and stood rigidly near the windows. "Or you were waiting for me—because of that," he said, cocking his head toward the now ruined snapshot of the two of them.

"No, I just stumbled across it. But don't worry, I'm leaving now."

"Not quite yet," he said, slowly drawing the back of his hand across his mouth, as if he were wiping off excess whiskey—or the feel of her kiss.

Furious with him, she grabbed her camera bag and slung the strap over her shoulder.

Gavin set his unfinished drink on the window ledge and closed the distance between them. "There's something I have to know," he said quietly, though his anger was still evident in his uncompromising expression.

"It's too late for this discussion."

"Just one thing," he said again, his features set.

"What?"

"Why did you marry a bastard like Brooks?"

"It's none of your business," she lied.

"Like hell. Why, Melanie?" he thundered.

She slowly counted to ten. "There were reasons...." But they wouldn't come to mind. Melanie grappled with the truth, wishing she could just tell him about the baby they'd never shared.

"I'm waiting," he said, his voice low. "Was it because of his money, hmm? Is that what you found so attractive?"

"No!"

"God, I hope not," he muttered, shaking his head. "But I can't help wondering why you're hanging around here, lingering in my room, more than willing to seduce me."

"What?" she gasped. "I wasn't lingering and I had no intention of seducing anyone!"

"You could've left."

"I told you, I wasn't finished."

"Well, you are now."

"You got that right." She grabbed her purse and swung toward the door, but one of Gavin's arms snaked out and surrounded her waist.

"You haven't answered my question yet."

There was nothing she could say to change the past. With a sinking sensation, she realized that telling Gavin the truth about the baby would only increase the tension between them, making it impossible for her to work with him. "I don't think your question merits an answer."

"You walked out on me—"

"Correction, Gavin. You did the walking—or to be more precise, the skiing," she charged, unable to hide the bitterness in her tone. "You just skied your way out of my life and I fell in love with someone else."

The corners of his mouth twitched, as if he found her reason bordering on the ridiculous. "You loved Brooks? After me?"

"Yes!"

His eyes narrowed. "Save that for someone who'll believe it. You sold out, Melanie, to the almighty buck."

Without thinking, she slapped him with a smack that echoed through the room. Gavin's teeth set, and he clamped both hands over her arms. "Don't ever do that again."

“I’ll try never to get that close!” Her voice shook with anger.

“Then you’d better stay out of my bedroom.”

“You’re what? Oh, God, Gavin, don’t flatter yourself!”

His eyes blazed, and his fingers dug into her flesh. For a few seconds they glared at each other, breathing deeply, fury and other, more dangerous, emotions tangling between them.

Gavin sighed finally. “You make me crazy,” he admitted.

“Same here. It’s a bad combination.”

Something flickered in his gaze, and then his mouth crashed down on hers. She wanted to fight him, to stop this insanity, but when his lips molded over hers intimately, she couldn’t resist.

Closing her eyes, Melanie willed herself not to respond. Though her heart was thudding wildly, her blood on fire, she set her jaw and acted as if she could barely endure the kiss.

But Gavin didn’t give up. His lips coaxed, his hands moved magically across her back, and at last she gave into her weak knees and leaned against him.

“Oh, God, Melanie, why do we always have to hurt each other?” he whispered raggedly.

“I don’t know.” Her heart felt as if it might break all over again. Slowly Gavin released her.

“I don’t believe you ever loved Neil Brooks,” he said quietly.

“It doesn’t matter what you believe,” she lied. Reaching behind her, she found the door handle and yanked it open. As quickly as her legs would carry her, she walked through the dark lodge and outside, where she took in deep breaths of fresh air.

Her legs were unsteady as she walked to her car, but she held her chin up and decided that Gavin Doel, damn his black-hearted soul, was going to be harder to deal with than she’d ever imagined.

She tried to start her car, flooded it and swore. Slowly

counting to ten, she tried again. This time the old engine sputtered and caught. She didn't waste any time. Shoving the Volkswagen into first, she barely noticed the battered old pickup that pulled into the lot. She had other things on her mind.

"Oh, Melanie, don't be a fool," she told herself as she turned on her headlights, but she had the sinking sensation that she was falling in love with him all over again.

GAVIN GRABBED HIS drink, almost tossed it back but at the last second chucked the whiskey down the drain. He didn't usually drink—at least, not the way he had in the past few weeks. Having lived with an alcoholic father, he had always been careful with liquor.

Until he'd seen Melanie again. Just being with her, gazing into her intelligent eyes, seeing glimpses of her sense of humor, touching the slope of her jaw or burying his face into the clean scent of her hair, made him crazy.

"Get a grip on yourself," he said, knowing that alcohol didn't solve any problems. He twisted the cap on the bottle just as he heard footsteps in the outer lobby.

He froze. Melanie? Back? God, how was he ever going to keep his hands off her? He'd intended to kiss her to prove that he could kiss her without his emotions getting in the way, to prove that he really didn't care about her….

"Gavin?" a rough male voice called out.

"In here," he replied. So his old man had made it back to Taylor's Crossing. Ignoring his cane, Gavin crossed the room and held open the door, letting the light from his apartment spill into the hallway.

"Oh, there you are! This place is a goddamn maze!" Jim Doel, tall and gaunt, his hair snow-white, strode down the hallway to Gavin's apartment.

"It just takes awhile to get to know your way around."

Casting a critical eye on the rooms his son now called home, Jim took a seat on the raised hearth of the fireplace. "Quite a comedown from what you're used to, isn't it?"

"It's all right."

"And you're already fixin' it up. I saw the rigging." He rubbed his hands on the faded knees of his jeans.

"It should be finished by the time ski season opens."

"That's not so far away." Jim noticed the bottle of whiskey on the table and glanced meaningfully at Gavin. "I saw you had a visitor."

Gavin braced himself.

"That Walker girl still sniffin' around?"

"She's a photographer for the paper."

"So what was she doin' here so late?"

"Rich hired her to do some publicity for us. Brochures, maps, that sort of thing."

Jim raised an interested eyebrow. "And where is Rich?"

"In Portland."

"Convenient." Jim reached into his pocket for a pack of cigarettes.

"I think it'll work out."

"You thought that before," Jim observed. He lit up and clicked his lighter shut.

"What're you trying to say, Dad?"

"Nothin', nothin'." Jim drew hard on his cigarette. Gavin waited as his father blew smoke to the ceiling. "I'm just a little concerned, that's all. That girl hurt you once before."

"Water under the bridge," Gavin lied.

"Is it, now? I wonder. But then, I guess I don't have to point out to you that she didn't bother to wait for you when you took off for Colorado. No siree, she just up and married Neil Brooks within weeks after you left."

"What're you getting at?"

"That she's fickle, that one. Can't stick with one man.

First you, then the minute you're gone, she puts the richest boy in town in her sights, marries him, then when she gets bored, divorces him. Now she's back here, making herself available because you're back in town—and now you're probably the richest man in town."

"Not by a long shot."

Jim shrugged. "Well, she does seem to be developin' a pattern, doesn't she?"

"What do you know about her marriage?"

"Nothin' except it was short. Six years or so, I think, and then she comes back when her dad gets sick." Jim's face grew tense. "I never did like old Adam Walker, you know. He never forgave me for what happened to his wife."

"That was a long time ago," Gavin said, hoping to ease some of his father's pain.

Jim sighed. "But it's something that will stick with me until the day I die." He cleared his throat and tossed his cigarette into the grate. "You don't know how many times I prayed I could've changed things."

"Probably just about as many times as I did," Gavin admitted.

Scowling, Jim looked his son straight in the eye. "Don't get mixed up with Melanie, son. She'll only hurt you again."

Gavin bristled. "I survived."

"If that's what you call it."

"Look, I can make my own decisions. Now tell me, what else is on your mind?"

"I thought maybe you'd give your old man a job." Seeing that Gavin was about to protest, he held up one hand. "Hey, you've been good to me. If it hadn't been for you, I probably never would've dried out. And for that I owe you, son, I owe you big. But I'm tired of being a charity case. This time I want a job—a real, bona fide job. I'm not old enough to be sent out to pasture yet, and I'm handy with a hammer and nails. What d'ya say?"

CHAPTER EIGHT

THE NEXT THREE weeks went by in a blur. Indian summer waned, and the air turned brisk and chilly. Gray clouds lingered over the Cascades, promising early snow.

Melanie barely had time to notice the change in the weather, let alone eat or sleep. When she wasn't at the newspaper office, she was working in her studio or at the lodge, where she tried to keep her distance from Gavin. She wasn't always successful.

Fortunately, he, too, was working day and night. They spoke to each other only when absolutely necessary. She dealt primarily with Rich Johanson, unless he was out of town, and somehow managed to keep her relationship with Gavin strictly professional.

She was friendly, businesslike and cheerful, hiding her innermost feelings. Gavin was cordial but reserved, and glared at her suspiciously whenever she seemed in a particularly good mood.

The tension hovered between them, gnawing at her insides while all the time she plastered a smile on her face.

She was lucky on one count. Gavin and Rich had no trouble agreeing on pictures for the brochure. When she showed them her favorite shots, they weeded out the ones that didn't fit their image of the resort.

Rich slipped the good shots he needed into an envelope and said he'd take them, along with the copy he'd written for the brochure, to a printer in Portland.

Gavin handed Melanie a sealed envelope with a check inside and said, "Good job."

The words sounded hollow, and Melanie, despite her fake smile, was miserable. She couldn't wait to get through the charade and regretted taking the job.

As for the resort, the renovation of Ridge Lodge was on schedule, and the parking lot, lodge and lifts teemed with construction workers. A handful of employees had already been hired for the operation of the lodge and lifts, and a chef, a doctor, building supervisor and an equipment manager were already on staff.

Jim Doel, who had recently returned to Taylor's Crossing, had been hired as a handyman, and Melanie had kept her distance from him as well as from his son. Though Jim never was openly hostile, Melanie sensed his animosity whenever she dealt with him. And she, too, hadn't resolved all her feelings toward him. As much as she wanted to rise above it, the simple fact was that he'd killed her mother and robbed her of a normal childhood. Maybe that was Adam Walker's fault. Her father had spent years bad-mouthing the man.

"So, how're things going up at the lodge?" Jan asked late one Friday afternoon as Melanie handed her some pictures of people gathered at a city council meeting in city hall.

"I think everything's on schedule."

"Good. I've got another interview with our friend Mr. Doel next week and I wanted to be prepared. If there's any trouble at the lodge, I'd like to know about it. But everything's okay, right?" Jan asked, perching on the corner of Melanie's desk.

"No trouble," Melanie replied, carrying the pictures to the layout editor's desk. "In fact, when you go up to the lodge, I think you'll be surprised how smoothly everything's running."

"Is it?" Jan's eyebrows drew together, and she made a point of studying her nails.

"Uh-huh. Looks as if the resort will be a huge success,"

Melanie added, wondering why she felt compelled to defend Gavin.

Constance, who had overheard the tail end of the conversation, made her way to the coffeepot and asked, "So, do you know who'll be invited to the grand opening?"

Jan mumbled, "I wish."

Melanie shook her head. "I haven't the foggiest. It's not as if I'm on the inside, you know. I'm just doing some free-lance work for the resort."

Constance sighed. "I'd give my right arm for a look at that guest list."

"Why don't you just ask?"

"I have. I got Doel on the phone yesterday, but he told me very succinctly that it was none of my business. I just thought maybe you had some idea."

"Not a clue," Melanie replied.

"Well, I'm going up there Monday and I'll have a look around," Jan said, filled with confidence as usual. "Maybe I can convince Mr. Doel that a copy of the list would add public interest. He might just sell a few more lift tickets if people thought some celebrities were staying at the lodge."

"I wouldn't bet on getting anything more from him," Melanie said.

Constance agreed. Refilling her coffee cup, she said, "He's impossible. It's almost as if he resents the free publicity we're handing him."

"You were the one who pointed out that he was publicity shy," Melanie observed as Constance's phone jangled loudly from her desk.

With a dramatic sigh, Constance, said, "Jan, see what you can do." She hurried back to her desk. "Beg, borrow or steal that guest list."

"I doubt if I'll burglarize Gavin Doel's office all for the sake of a few names."

"Not just any names. We're talking names of the famous," Constance reminded her as the phone rang impatiently. "There's a difference. A big difference." Frowning, she picked up the receiver and plopped down at her desk, immediately absorbed in the conversation.

Jan turned her attention back to Melanie. "What do you think her chances are of getting the names of the invited?"

"From Gavin? Zero. From Rich Johanson?" Melanie lifted her hand and tilted it side to side. "About fifty-fifty."

Jan nodded. "Yeah, Johanson's always been more interested in publicity than Doel. And speaking of our local infamous professional skier, how're things going with you two?"

"Fine, I guess. We work together. That's it."

"That's it? Really?" Jan arched a skeptical brow. "Come on, Melanie, you can talk to me. I saw how he looked at you, and you said yourself that you'd been serious with him."

"I think I said I'd dated him."

"You said you were serious."

"Did I? Well, if I did, I meant I was serious for seventeen." Dear Lord, why had she ever brought it up?

"I know, but I read between the lines," Jan replied. "You two act as if you've never gotten over each other."

"That's ridiculous."

"Is it?"

"Of course it is," Melanie said, pretending to study an enlarged photograph of wheat fields to the south of town. "Gavin's not interested in me," she added tightly.

Jan laughed. "Yeah, right, and I'm the Queen of England! Don't try to convince me that you can't see the signs. That man is interested—whether he wants to be or not."

Melanie didn't comment and went back to work when Brian called Jan into his office.

The rest of the day she heard snatches of conversation in

the office and most of it centered around Gavin. As she drove home, she wondered if there was any way to escape from him.

Unfortunately, Taylor's Crossing was a small town and Gavin was highly visible and extremely gossip-worthy. She heard about him and the lodge everywhere she went. And it didn't end when she stopped by her uncle Bart's and aunt Lila's house that evening.

"The weather service predicts snow in the mountains by Friday," Bart said, squinting through his kitchen window to the night-blackened sky. Melanie dropped into a chair near the table, and Bart followed suit. "That should be good news for Doel."

Melanie, tired of all the talk about Gavin, took a swallow from the steaming mug of coffee Aunt Lila handed her.

"Now, Bart," her aunt said, "you quit fishing."

"Is that what I'm doing?" Bart asked, one side of his mouth lifting at the corner.

"Of course it is. She's barely been here ten minutes and you've brought up Gavin twice."

Bart lifted a stockinged foot and placed it on an empty chair. "I was just making an observation about the weather."

"Sure."

"And it wouldn't kill me to know how Melanie and Gavin are doing working so close together."

"You're worse than a gossiping old woman," Lila muttered, but smiled good-naturedly.

"Oh, for God's sake, I am not. I'm just interested in Melanie's welfare, that's all."

"She's old enough to make her own decisions without any help from you."

Melanie couldn't help but grin. Lila's and Bart's lighthearted banter had always been a source of amusement to her, and since she'd lost her mother at a young age, Aunt Lila had stepped in and filled a very deep void. "Well, if you must know," Melanie said, deciding to end the speculation about Gavin once and for all, "Gavin and I get along all right. We don't see a lot of each other, though. I deal primarily with Rich Johanson."

"That stuffed shirt!" Bart muttered.

"He's okay," Melanie said. "In fact, I like him. He keeps Gavin in line."

Bart smoothed his white hair with the flat of his hand. His faded eyes twinkled. "Does he need keeping in line?"

"All the time," Melanie said.

"And I heard he hired his old man, too."

This was dangerous ground. Melanie felt her equilibrium slipping a little. "That's right. Jim does fix-it jobs for the resort—things that the general contractor didn't bid on, I guess."

"How long is he staying on?"

"I don't know," Melanie said honestly. "We don't talk much."

"I'll bet," Bart said. "But Gavin can't be all bad if he takes care of his kin."

For once Aunt Lila agreed. "He's helped Jim more than any son should have to." Then, as if realizing she'd said too much, she added, "You're staying for dinner, aren't you?"

Melanie finished her coffee. "Another time. I've got an appointment later tonight. Cynthia Anderson is coming over to choose some pictures I took of her boys a few weeks ago, but I had something I wanted to give you." She reached into her purse and pulled out a small package wrapped in tissue paper.

"What's this?" Bart asked as she handed it to him.

"Open it and see," Lila prodded.

Bart didn't need any further encouragement. He unfolded the paper and exposed a framed picture of himself and Big Money taken on the day of the fair over a month before. Bart was grinning proudly, while the nervous colt tugged hard on his lead and tried to rear.

"Why, Melanie," Bart whispered, touched, "you didn't need to—"

"I know, but I wanted to. This was my favorite shot, but my editor preferred the one that ended up in the paper. I picked it out weeks ago, but it took a while to find the right frame."

"I have just the place for this," Lila said, eyeing the picture lovingly. "Oh, Melanie, thank you."

Melanie felt a lump in her throat as she finished her coffee and pushed back her chair. "You're welcome. Now I'd better run home before the Anderson boys show up and terrorize Sassafras."

Uncle Bart walked with her out the back door. Rain had started to fall, but the temperature had dropped. Goose bumps rose on Melanie's arms.

"Despite what your aunt said in there," Bart said, squaring an old Stetson on his head, "you know she thinks the world of Gavin. He used to do odd jobs around here, you know, and Lila's pretty soft where he's concerned."

Melanie eyed him in the darkness. "You already told me I should be chasing after him."

"I didn't say that." Bart's teeth flashed and his breath fogged. "But if he decides to do the chasing, I wouldn't run too fast if I were you."

"I'll remember that," she said dryly as she slid into the car.

Bart slammed the door shut for her, then paused on the step to light a cigarette. Melanie waved as she drove away. So now everyone thought she should try to start a new romance with Gavin. Jan, Uncle Bart and even Aunt Lila. It was enough to make a body sick.

And yet, falling in love with Gavin again held a distinct appeal. "You're hopeless," she told herself as she wheeled into her driveway and recognized Cynthia Anderson's gray van parked in front of the house. "And you're late."

As she climbed out of her own car, the side door of the van flew open and the boisterous Anderson brood, dressed in blue and white soccer outfits, scrambled out.

Cynthia herded them toward the front porch. "I know I didn't say anything when I made this appointment," she said quickly, "but do you have time to take a couple of shots of them in their soccer gear?"

Groaning inwardly, Melanie nodded. "I suppose."

"Good, good. Because Gerald would just love a picture of them like this—oh, but, boys, we mustn't tell Daddy, okay? It'll be a surprise. For Christmas."

Melanie wondered how the four boys could keep a secret for ten minutes let alone nearly two months. "Let's get started."

"Oh, thanks, Melanie," Cynthia said, whipping her comb from her purse and pouncing on the youngest one. "Okay, Tim, hold still while I fix your hair."

"No!" the boy howled. "No, no, no!"

"Aw, knock it off, Mom," Sean, the oldest, chided. "We look good enough. Besides, I'm freezin' my tail off out here. Let's go inside!"

Steeling herself, Melanie opened the front door, the boys thundered down the hall and Sassafras bolted outside, splashing through puddles as he headed around the corner of the house.

Melanie followed the Andersons through the door and hung her coat on the hall tree near the stairs. She didn't have time to think about Gavin for the rest of the evening.

THE FIRST SNOW arrived on Saturday in early November. Large powdery flakes, driven by gusty winds, fell from a leaden sky. Storm warnings had been posted, but Melanie decided to chance the storm, hoping that it would hold off for a few hours. She tossed her chains into her car and carefully placed five huge portfolios in her car.

The drive was tedious. Already tired from spending most of the previous night putting the finishing touches on the sepia-toned prints, she was anxious to take the pictures to the lodge and finish that part of her employment.

Because you want to see Gavin again, her mind tormented, but she pushed that unpleasant thought aside and ignored the fact that her heart was beating much too quickly as she drove through a fine layer of snow to Mount Prosperity.

Aside from half a dozen cars and a few trucks marked Gamble Construction and the snowplow, the freshly plowed parking lot was relatively empty.

Melanie drove straight to the lodge, and because she wanted to protect the prints as well as her car, she pulled into a parking shed that connected with the side entrance to the lodge. Grabbing her largest portfolio, she steeled herself for another cool meeting with Gavin. *You can handle this,* she told herself as she trudged up the stairs and opened the door.

Inside, the lodge was quiet. The screaming saws, pounding hammers and country music were gone. Only the few workers finishing the molding remained.

Most of the renovation was complete. The high wood ceilings had been polished, the oak floors refinished and new recessed lighting installed in the lobby and bar. Two snack bars boasted gleaming new equipment, and the restaurant had been recarpeted.

Fresh paint gleamed, and new blinds were fitted to the windows. An Oriental rug had been stretched in front of the fireplace, and several couches and lamps had been placed strategically around the room.

Melanie propped her portfolio against a post and eyed the renovations. Tugging off her gloves, she walked over to the bar to admire the polished, inlaid brass.

"Something I can do for you?"

She nearly jumped out of her skin at the sound of Jim

Doel's voice. She whipped around. Tall and lined, Jim settled a cap on his head and waited, his face tense, his eyes never wavering.

She and Gavin's father had never gotten along. Working at the lodge together hadn't made things any easier. She pointed to her portfolio. "I'm here to meet Rich. I have those old pictures he was interested in."

"He's busy."

"Then Gavin."

The older man's lips tightened. "He's busy, too."

"Are they here?"

Nodding, he motioned toward the back of the lodge. "Got some bigwigs with them. Don't know when they'll be through."

"It's okay," she said, forcing a smile. "I'll wait in the north wing."

"It may be awhile."

"I've got plenty of time," she replied, not letting him dissuade her. Jim Doel had never said why he didn't like her, but she assumed it was a combination of feelings—guilt for the death of her mother and anger that she, at least in Gavin's father's opinion, had betrayed his only son. He'd never know the truth, so she would have to get used to his glacial glances and furrowed frowns until she was finished with her job here.

Inching her chin up a fraction, she hauled her heavy portfolio off the floor and said, "Please let Rich know where he can find me."

Jim nodded grudgingly, and Melanie, rather than ask for his help, made two more trips to the car to pick up the bulky pictures. It took nearly half an hour to carry them into the north wing, and as she paused to catch her breath on her final trip, she heard the sound of voices coming from the banquet room.

The door was ajar, and her curiosity got the better of her. She looked into the crack and caught a glimpse of several men, all dressed in crisp business suits, clustered around the huge, round table. Smoke rose in a gentle cloud to the ceiling.

Gavin sat across from the door, and he looked bored to tears. His hair was combed neatly and he was wearing a blue suit, but his gaze lacked its usual life and he tugged at his tie and stuck his fingers under his collar.

Melanie couldn't help but grin. Where were the beat-up leather jacket and aviator glasses? she wondered, wishing she dared linger and watch him a little longer. She'd never thought of him as an entrepreneur, and she found it amusing to catch a glimpse of him in a starched white shirt and crisp tie, dealing with lawyers or accountants or investors or whoever the other men happened to be.

She made her way to the end of the hall and the north wing. As wide as the lodge itself, the huge room was vacant, aside from some chairs stacked in a corner and a few bifold tables shoved against the windows.

Melanie shrugged out of her coat, then began setting out the photographs that she'd selected for the sepia-colored pictures that were to decorate the main lobby. There were pictures of miners with pickaxes, wagon trains and mule teams, crusty old-timers panning for gold and younger men gathered around a mine shaft. There was a shot of a steaming locomotive and another of a nineteenth-century picnic by a river. She laid them out carefully, proud of her work.

She didn't hear Gavin walk into the room, nor did she notice when he stopped short and sucked in his breath.

GAVIN HADN'T EXPECTED to find her here, leaning over the table, her hips thrust in his direction and her black glossy hair braided into a rope that was pinned tightly to the back of her head.

Her lips were pursed, her eyebrows knitted in concentration, and her hips, beneath her denim skirt, shifted seductively as she arranged photograph after photograph on the table.

As if feeling the weight of his gaze, she glanced over her shoulder, and for a fleeting second her eyes warmed and her lips moved into a ghost of a smile.

Gavin's breath caught in his lungs for a heart-stopping moment, and he had trouble finding his voice. "Are you waiting for Rich?"

He noticed her shoulders tighten. Turning, she eyed him suspiciously. "Isn't he here?"

"Not now. He had business in Portland."

Her lips turned down. "But I just saw him—"

"I know. He got a call. There's some emergency with a case of his. He just took off."

"Well, that's great," Melanie said, motioning to the windows. "I hoped to get out of here before the storm really hit."

"What's keeping you?" he baited, and saw a spark flash in her eyes.

"My job. We have a contract, remember?"

"Rich's idea."

"Well, it doesn't matter whose idea it was, does it? Because, like it or not, you and I are stuck with it!"

"You could always leave," he suggested, and the look she shot him was positively murderous.

"I came here to do a job, Gavin, and I intend to finish it. The sooner it's done, the sooner I'm out of here." She placed her hands on her hips.

"Then let's get to it."

"Okay, first you need to figure out exactly where you want these hung. For what it's worth, I think you should hang them in chronological sequence…." Impatiently he listened as she explained about each of the pictures and how each shot had a particular meaning to the forty-niner theme of the lodge. Though she spoke with enthusiasm, he had trouble concentrating and was constantly distracted by the slope of her cheek, the way her teeth flashed as she spoke, or how her sweater stretched across her breasts.

"…and that picnic, it's my favorite," she was saying. "It took place at the base of Mount Prosperity sometime in the eighteen-eighties, I think, much later than forty-nine, but it still has a certain flavor…." Her voice drifted off, and her face angled up to his. "You haven't heard a word I've said, have you?" she charged, lips pursing angrily.

"Does it matter?"

Her eyes flashed. "No, I suppose it doesn't. I just thought since you were the owner of this place, you might be interested. I guess I was wrong."

"Go on," he suggested. His thoughts had taken him far from the photographs on the table. He knew that he and Melanie were virtually alone in the lodge. Rich had left with the accountant and investors, the workers had the day off, the carpenters who had come in were now gone, and even his father, after gruffly announcing that someone was waiting for Rich in the north wing, had left the premises.

Vexed, she placed her hands on her hips and tilted her head to the ceiling. "I don't know why I try," she muttered as if conversing with the rafters in the vault high overhead.

Gavin motioned impatiently at the table. "Look, they're all fine. You just tell me where to hang them and we'll do it."

"You and me?" she asked.

He felt one side of his lip curve up. "Face it, Melanie, we're stuck with each other."

She paled slightly. "But you're still laid up—"

"My ankle's fine."

"And you don't mind risking breaking it by falling off a ladder?" she said, sarcasm tainting her words.

"Won't happen," he replied, noticing how anger intensified the streaks of jade in her eyes. "Just give me a minute to change."

She didn't have time to protest. He dashed off, leaving her with the photographs. *Don't argue with him,* she told herself. *Take advantage of his good mood.* But she glanced through the windows to see the snow begin to drift around the lodge. Most of the mountain was now obscured from her view. They'd have to work fast. The railing of the deck showed three inches of new snow, and the wind had begun to pick up. Maybe she should just forget this and come back when the storm had passed.

Not yet, she decided. She had too much to do to let a little snow bother her. She'd grown up around here and she knew how to drive in the snow. She'd be fine. She hazarded another glance outside and decided she didn't have any time to lose.

By the time she'd hauled the photographs back to the main lobby, placing each matted print on the floor near the appropriate wall space, Gavin reappeared, tucking the tail of his blue cambric shirt into faded jeans. He strode quickly, without the use of a cane, to the huge fireplace on the far wall. Bending on one knee, he began stacking logs on the huge grate.

"Do we really need a fire?" she asked, glancing at her watch.

"Probably not."

"It'll go to waste."

Ignoring her, he struck a match. The dry kindling ignited quickly, sizzling and popping as yellow flames discovered moss-laden oak. His injury didn't seem to bother him, and when he straightened and surveyed his work, he nodded to himself.

"Now that we're all cozy," she mocked, hoping to sound put out, "let's get started."

"You're the boss," he quipped, gesturing to the stack of prints she had started positioning around the main lobby.

"Remember that," she teased back.

"Always." His eyelids dropped a little, and Melanie's breath caught in her throat as he stared at her.

Clearing her throat, she pointed to a picture of a grizzly old miner and two burros. “You can start with this one,” she said. “It should go near the door. And then, I think, the picture of the locomotive on the trestle. Next the mine shaft…” She walked around the large, cavernous room, shuffling and reshuffling the prints. Gavin was with her every step of the way, and her nerves were stretched tight. She felt the weight of his gaze, smelled the musky scent of his aftershave and saw the set angle of his jaw. *Dear God, let me get through this.*

When she finally decided on the placement of each picture, he took off in search of a ladder. Melanie sank against the windows and felt the cold panes against her back. *Just a few more hours.* She glanced anxiously through the window and noticed the storm had turned worse. The higher branches of the pines surrounding the lodge danced wildly in the wind, and the snow was blowing in sheets.

When Gavin returned with the ladder, his face was grim. “I just listened to the weather report,” he informed her. “The storm isn’t going to let up for hours.”

Melanie’s heart sank. Nervously, she shoved her bangs from her eyes. “Then I should leave now.”

“No way.”

“What?” She looked up sharply.

“It’s nearly a whiteout, Mel. Winds are being measured at over forty miles an hour. I’m not going to let you leave until it’s safe.”

“It’s safe now. Not that you have a whole lot of say in the matter.”

“Just wait. We’ve got a lot of work to do. Maybe by the time we’re done, the winds will have died down.”

“Is that what the weather service said?”

Tiny brackets surrounded his mouth, and he shook his head. “Afraid not. In fact, they predict it’ll last through the night.”

"Then I've got to leave now!"

"Hold on," he said firmly, one hand clamping over her arm. "If there's a lull, I'll drive you out of here in one of the trucks with four-wheel drive."

"I've got my car here. I'll—"

"You'll stay put!" he said, his eyes gleaming with determination. "Until it's safe."

"Oh, so now you're the one giving orders."

"While you're up here in my lodge, you're my responsibility," he said quietly.

"I'm my own person. I don't need you or anyone else telling me what to do!"

A muscle worked in his jaw. "Then use your head, Melanie. You know how dangerous a storm like this can be. Just wait it out. We can finish here."

"And then what?"

"I don't know," he admitted, "but at least you won't be in the ditch somewhere, freezing to death!"

"No, I'll just be suffocating in here while you keep ordering me around."

He couldn't help but smile. "Is that what I'm doing?"

"Damn right!"

He laughed then, and Melanie was taken aback at the richness of the sound. "So be it," he muttered. "Now, come on, quit complaining and let's get to work."

She hated to knuckle under to him, but the thought of driving out in a near blizzard wasn't all that inviting. "All right," she finally agreed, "but I'm leaving the minute the winds die down."

He didn't comment, just started up the ladder. She was afraid his ankle wouldn't support him, but he didn't once lose his balance, and slowly, as they hung picture after picture, the rust-tone prints began to add flavor to the lobby.

As she watched him adjust a picture of oxen pulling a

covered wagon, she noticed how quiet the lodge had become. The only sounds were the scrape of the ladder, their soft conversation and the whistle of the wind outside. "Where is everyone?" she asked.

"Gone," he replied, glancing down at her from the top of the ladder.

"Gone?"

"That's right. We're here all alone. Just you and me."

He was still staring down at her as she shifted uncomfortably from one foot to the other.

"Does that bother you?" he asked, one foot lower on the ladder than the other, his denim-clad legs at her eye level.

"No," she lied. "Why should it? As long as I've got one self-centered egotistical male bossing me around, I'm happy as a clam."

"Good." Gavin struggled to keep from smiling. He stepped up, and she tried not to watch the way his buttocks moved beneath the tight denim. "I figured the sooner this was done—"

"The sooner I'd be out of your hair."

He made a disgusted sound. "I was going to say, the sooner you'd be happy. If that's possible."

She didn't bother responding. And she tried to drag her gaze away from him to keep from noticing the way his shirt pulled across his broad shoulders and the lean lines of his waist as he reached upward. His hips, too, under tight jeans, moved easily as he shifted his weight from one rung to the next.

Without warning, the lights in the lodge flickered.

Gavin froze on the ladder. "What's going on..." But before he could say anything else, the only illumination in the entire building came from the fireplace. "Son of a bitch!" He shoved his hands through his hair, then climbed down the final rungs of the ladder. "Stay here," he ordered. "We've got an emergency generator, but I don't think it's operational yet." He started down the hall, his footsteps echoing through the huge old building.

Melanie watched him disappear into the darkness, then walked anxiously to a window. Snow, driven by a gusty wind, fell from the black sky to blanket the mountain. It peppered against the window in icy flakes.

Now what? she wondered, shivering. Rubbing her arms, she walked back to the fireplace and checked her watch in the firelight. Gavin had been gone nearly fifteen minutes.

The old empty lodge seemed larger in the darkness. The windows rose to cathedral spires and reflected gold in the firelight, and the ceilings were so high overhead they were lost in the darkness.

She heard the clip of Gavin's footsteps and saw the bob of a flashlight. "Well, so much for the generator," he said, his lips thin in frustration.

"What's wrong with it?"

"Nothing that some new parts won't fix, but that's not the bad news. We have a ham radio in the back, and I listened for a few minutes while I found these." He held up several kerosene lamps and a couple of flashlights. "The storm is worse than they expected. High winds have knocked down power poles and some of the roads are impassable."

With a mounting sense of dread, Melanie said, "Then I'd better leave now, before things get worse."

"Too late," he replied. "The road to the lodge is closed. I called the highway department. A falling tree took out several electricity poles and has the road blocked. This storm is more than the electric company can handle right now. The sheriff's department and state police are asking everyone to stay inside. The weather service now seems to think that this storm won't let up until sometime tomorrow at the earliest."

Her stomach dropped. "You mean—"

"I mean it looks like you and I are stuck here for the night, maybe longer."

"But I can't be. I've got work and my dog's locked in the house and…" Her voice drifted off as she saw the glint of determination in his eyes.

"You're staying here, Melanie," he said, his voice edged in steel. "You don't have any choice."

CHAPTER NINE

"I CAN'T SPEND the night here," Melanie stated, stunned. "That's a crazy idea."

"You have a better one?" Anger crept into his voice. So he didn't like the arrangements any better than she did. Good.

"No, but—"

"I don't have time to stand around and argue with you. Since we don't have any power, I've got to make sure that the pipes don't freeze, that the building is secure and that you and I find a way to keep warm tonight!"

"But—"

"Listen, Melanie, we just have to accept this," he said, his fingers gripping her shoulder.

"I can't."

He muttered an oath. "Can I count on you to help me, or are you going to spend the rest of the night complaining?"

She started to argue but clamped her mouth shut.

"That's better."

"I just want to go on record as being opposed to this."

"Fine. Consider it duly recorded. Now let's get on to business, okay?"

Ignoring the hackles rising on the back of her neck, she silently counted to ten. He did have a point, she grudgingly admitted to herself. There wasn't much she could do but make the best of the situation. Even if it killed her. "Okay," she finally agreed. "Let's start by being practical. Are the phone lines still working?"

"They were fifteen minutes ago."

"Good." She pushed her hair from her face and ignored the fact that he was staring at her. "I need to call someone to check on Sassafras and I'd better let Bart and Lila know where I am."

"You sure that's a good idea?" he asked, his face a hard mask.

She bristled. "Would you rather they send out a search party? No one knows I'm up here, and believe me, I'd like to keep it that way, but I can't."

Gavin crossed to the bar, yanked the phone from underneath and slammed it onto the polished mahogany. "Suit yourself."

Ignoring his black temper, Melanie picked up the receiver and dialed. "Come on, come on," she whispered as the phone rang and Gavin, blast him, stared at her in the mirror's reflection. Finally Aunt Lila picked up on the sixth ring.

"Mellie!" the older woman exclaimed, her voice crackly with the bad connection. "I was worried to death! Bart went over to check on you and brought Sassafras over here, but we didn't know where you were."

Melanie squirmed. She caught Gavin's tawny gaze in the mirror and turned her back on his image. "I brought the photographs for the lodge up to the resort," she said, trying to concentrate on anything other than the man glowering at her in the glass. Quickly, she explained how she'd lost track of time and the storm had turned so wild. "I just should have paid more attention and left before it got so bad outside."

"Well, thank goodness you're safe. Now, you just stay put until the roads are clear."

"That could be several days," Melanie said.

"I know, but at least you're safe."

Safe? Melanie doubted it. She cast a sidelong glance at

Gavin. His features were pulled into a thoughtful scowl, his lips thin.

She hung up and let out a long breath. "Okay, get a grip on yourself," she muttered.

"What?"

She shook her head. "Nothing."

He was standing at the end of the bar, lighting the wicks of several kerosene lanterns. He glanced up at her and nearly burned his fingers. "That's the first sign that you're losing it."

"I always talk to myself."

"I know," he said quietly. "I remember." He looked up at her again, his eyes warm in the firelight, the angles of his face highlighted by the flame of the lantern. Melanie's heart turned over, and she looked away quickly, before her gaze betrayed her.

He cleared his throat. "I'll go check on the pipes and you can see if there's anything for us to eat in the kitchen."

"Is that what I'm reduced to—cook?"

Gavin smiled. "Gee, and I figured that was a promotion."

"You're the most insufferable—"

"I've heard it all before," he said, striding down the hall.

"Cook, eh?" Indignantly, she grabbed a lantern and headed past the bar to the restaurant and the kitchen beyond.

Stainless steel gleamed in the light of the lantern. The refrigerators, freezers and pantry weren't completely stocked for the season, but there were enough staples to get through several meals. They might not dine on gourmet cuisine, but they wouldn't starve. And if she didn't decide to poison Gavin, he might be in for a rude awakening!

She found a Thermos and saved the rest of the coffee, then pulled a bottle of wine from the wine cellar. *This is dangerous,* she thought, eyeing the bottle of claret. Wine had been known to go to her head, and tonight, she knew instinctively, she should keep her wits about her. But what the hell? She intended to show Gavin up, and if a little claret could help, why not?

She couldn't resist the temptation and placed the wine and Thermos on a serving cart along with a huge copper-bottomed pot and some utensils.

Water presented another problem. Without electricity, the pumps wouldn't work. No problem, Melanie thought, refusing to come up with any excuses. She'd prove to Gavin that she could bloody well take care of herself—and him, if need be!

Melanie threw on her jacket and gloves and braved the elements long enough to scoop up snow in several huge soup kettles. She gritted her teeth against the wind that ripped through her clothes and pressed icy snowflakes against her cheeks. Even through her gloves, her fingers felt frozen as she lugged the filled kettles into the kitchen and placed them on the cart.

She pushed the cart to the lobby and placed the kettles in the huge fireplace, then headed back to the kitchen, where she grabbed spices, bouillon mix, tomato juice and all the vegetables she could find. Thinking ahead, she added bowls, utensils and a loaf of bread. She'd never considered herself a great cook—in fact, Neil had thought she was "hopeless," but she figured, as she shoved the cart back to the lobby, it really didn't matter. Haute cuisine wasn't the issue. Survival was—and, of course, showing Gavin up.

Once she was back in the lobby, she poured the juice into a huge pot, added bouillon and canned vegetables, then peeled and cut potatoes. She tossed the thick chunks into the simmering mixture and kept warm by staying close to the fire.

When Gavin returned half-frozen an hour later, he was greeted by the scent of hot soup heating on the grate. Candles and lanterns flickered on nearby tables.

He brushed the snow from the shoulders of his sheepskin

jacket, then warmed his hands by the fire. His eyes narrowed at the sight of the simmering pots. "What's this?"

"Oh, just a little something I whipped up," she tossed back.

"Sure."

He lifted a lid, and scented steam rose to greet the suspicious expression on his face. "You outdid yourself."

"I just aim to please, sir," she replied, smiling falsely.

"Okay, Melanie—what's up?"

"Oh, Mr. Doel, sir, I hope you're pleased," she said, her lips twitching at the way his eyebrows drew together. Served him right! "Here, take this." She handed him a cup of coffee, and he wrapped his chilled fingers around the warm ceramic and sipped. "What's your game, Melanie?"

"Game? No game."

"Oh, sure. Right."

She couldn't keep a straight face. "I just got tired of you barking commands at me and telling me what to do."

"As if you've ever listened." He frowned into his cup.

"I listen."

One of his brows lifted skeptically. "You do a lot of things, Melanie. And," he acknowledged, pointing to the kettles in the fire, "most of them very well. But listening isn't high on the list."

"And how would you know?"

"I remember more than the mere fact that you talk to yourself, Melanie." He paused, looking deep into her eyes. "In fact, I remember too much."

Her throat suddenly started to ache. She swallowed hard and whispered, "We'd better eat now."

Ladling the soup into bowls, she tried to ignore him. But she saw the snowflakes melting in his hair, the nervous way one fist clenched and opened, the manner in which he tugged thoughtfully on his full lower lip.

They ate in silence, both lost in their own thoughts as they sat on the floor in front of the fire. Melanie pretended interest in her soup and coffee, wishing she was anywhere but here, alone with the one man who could ignite her temper with a single word, the man who could turn her inside out with a mere look.

It's only for a few hours, she told herself, but the wind continued to moan and mock her.

It seemed to take her forever to finish her soup. She set her bowl aside, then, sipping her coffee, slid a glance at Gavin from the corner of her eye. She wondered what would have happened if, all those years ago, she'd told him the truth about the baby, if they had married, if their child had survived....

"What's this?" he asked, spying the bottle of claret for the first time.

"A mistake," she said.

"Oh?" He picked the bottle up by its neck, found the cork on the cart and slid her a knowing look. "Don't tell me, you were planning to get me tipsy, then, when I wasn't thinking properly, you were going to strip off all my clothes and have your way with me."

Blanching, she could barely speak. But when she found her tongue, she threw back at him, "Sure. That's exactly what I planned. Right after we both took a midnight swim in the pool, then ran naked through the blizzard."

His eyes darkened, and her throat closed. "There are worse fantasies."

"That's not my fantasy!"

"Isn't it?"

"Oh, Gavin, you're giving yourself way too much credit."

"Am I?"

"Yes!" she cried, the sound strangled. *Don't let him get to you,* she told herself, but couldn't stop the knocking of her heart.

"If you say so."

Good Lord, was there ever a more maddening man born?

He poured them each a glass of wine, then clicked the rim of his to hers. "To blizzards," he mocked.

She laughed. "Blizzards?"

"And running naked through the snow."

Melanie's pulse leaped, but she tried to appear calm. "Right. And running naked through the snow."

His mouth twisted wryly, but his eyes gleamed, and as he swallowed his wine, Melanie couldn't help but notice the way his throat worked.

The fire hissed and popped as a chunk of wood split. Outside, the storm raged, and Melanie, drinking slowly, caught alone in the lodge with Gavin, found that life outside the lodge seemed remote.

Don't let the night get to you.... But Gavin was so close, pouring more of the clear red claret, his hand touching hers as he steadied her glass, his gaze lingering on her mouth as she licked a drop on her lips. She remembered him as he used to be—so loving and kind. Their love had been simple and pure…and doomed.

"It's been a long time," he said quietly, his brows beetling, his thoughts apparently taking the same path as hers.

"We were children."

He shook his head. "I don't think so." His eyes held hers, and in that instant, she knew he intended to kiss her.

"Gavin, I don't—"

His mouth silenced the rest of her words, and her blood heated slowly. He tasted of wine, and the feelings he evoked were as violent as they had been years before. A thrill of excitement crept up her spine. Her heart began to pound, and she parted her lips willingly, moving close to him, feeling the contour of his body against hers.

"You don't what?" he asked, lifting his head and regarding her with slumberous golden eyes.

"I don't want to make love to you."

"Good. Because I don't want to make love to you." But his lips found hers again, and she yielded.

Gentle at first but more insistent as he felt her respond, his mouth moved over hers. Melanie's blood burned like wildfire as he clasped a hand around her neck, lacing his fingers in the loose knot pinned to the back of her head.

His heart thudded a rapid cadence, matched only by her own. She felt the pins slip from her hair, one by one, to fall on the floor as his kiss intensified and his tongue slipped familiarly through her teeth.

His weight carried them both to the carpet in front of the fire. Melanie's breasts pressed against the hard wall of his chest, and her arms circled his neck.

"Melanie," he whispered against the shell of her ear, and she shivered in anticipation. He pulled the final pin from her hair, and her thick braid fell over her shoulder.

Gavin touched the dark curls, his fingers grazing her breast. Beneath her sweater her nipples grew taut, and heat began to swirl deep inside.

Melanie knew the wine was going to her head, and even worse, the intoxication of being close to him was creating havoc with her self-control. She should stop him now, while she could still think, but the words couldn't fight their way past her tongue.

When he reached beneath her sweater and his hand touched her skin, the same old warning bells went off in her mind, but she didn't listen.

Instead she moaned and curved her spine, fitting herself perfectly against him. His breathing grew ragged as he lifted the sweater from over her head and gazed down at her.

"This is crazy," he muttered, as if his self-control, too, had been stripped from him.

He placed the flat of his hand between her breasts, his long, warm fingers feeling her heartbeat. His eyes closed for a second. "I want you, Melanie," he said, as if the words caused him pain. "I want you as much as I've ever wanted a woman."

Melanie's throat went dry. She didn't want to hear about his other women. This wasn't the moment for confession. "Shh…."

"But this could be dangerous."

More than dangerous, she thought, gazing up at his powerful features and focusing on the sensual line of his lips held tight with failing self-restraint. Making love to him was an emotional maelstrom. "I—I know."

"I wouldn't want to hurt you."

"Hurt me?"

"By getting you pregnant."

Tears threatened the corners of her eyes. "It's okay…."

"You're safe?"

"Neil and I couldn't have children."

He stared down at her for a long second.

Her throat ached, and she blinked as he lowered his head and kissed her with all the passion that had fired his blood years before.

Melanie lifted her hands, her fingers nimbly unbuttoning his shirt, her hands impatient as she shoved the fabric over his shoulders. In the glow from the fire, his skin took on a golden hue.

Her fingers swirled around his nipple, and he sucked in his breath, his abdomen concaving, his muscles a sexy washboard beneath his tight skin. Sweat dotted his brow, and she wondered vaguely if he was arguing with himself, listening to voices of denial screaming in his head.

She touched his waistband, and his eyes leaped with an inner fire. "Oh, God, you always could make me go out of my mind." Then his lips crashed down on hers, and gone was any trace of hesitation. His tongue pushed into her mouth, parrying and thrusting, exploring and claiming.

Melanie wrapped her arms around him, felt the fluid movement of his muscles as he shifted, lowering his lips down the slope of her cheeks, brushing across her skin. He kissed her eyes, her cheeks, her ears and lower, to her neck and the small circle of bones at her throat. His tongue tickled the pulse that was thundering in that hollow, and one hand moved in delicious circles on her abdomen.

Her breasts ached, and she moved impatiently.

"Slow down, Mel," he whispered hoarsely. "We've got all night."

His promise should have been a final signal for her to stop, before it was too late. But Melanie was well past turning back. And when he slid the strap of her bra over her shoulder, she moaned, her nipples strained upward, and he stared down at her. "God, I missed you," he admitted as he tugged on the ribbon and her breast spilled out of its lacy bonds, the dark nipple puckering under his perusal.

He touched a finger to his tongue, then to her breast. Melanie writhed at the sweet torture, wanting more, aching deep inside as he cupped her breast and kissed the hard nipple.

His tongue caressed her as his mouth closed over her. His arms wrapped around her torso, and his fingers splayed across the small of her back, pulling her urgently against him.

He kissed her again. Melanie exploded in her mind, memories of love and trust, passion and promises.

Quickly, he removed her bra and skirt, then kicked off his jeans and lay next to her, his naked body, bronze in the firelight, pressed intimately to hers. No words were spoken as he lay upon her, finding a path he'd forged long ago. Their bodies joined and fit, moving rhythmically, heating together, fusing into one.

Melanie gazed up at him, and her heart, pounding a thousand times a minute, swelled. His tempo increased, and she dug her fingers into the sleek muscles of his back, her body arching, her mind spinning out of control.

"Melanie, oh, Melanie," he cried hoarsely.

The earth shattered into a million fragments of light.

He collapsed against her, and she clung to him, holding on to this special moment, feeling his weight as a welcome burden as afterglow enveloped them.

I love you stuck in her throat, but she didn't say the words, nor did she hear them. The only sounds in the darkness were the gentle hiss of the fire and the moan of the wind outside.

When he finally rose on one elbow, looking down at her through warm tawny eyes, one side of his mouth lifted and white teeth flashed against his skin. "You know," he said, tracing the slope of her jaw with one finger, "I think we'd better go."

"Go? But I thought we had to stay here," she said dazedly. Shoving her hair from her eyes, she wondered what she was doing here, naked, still feeling the warmth of afterglow invade her.

"To my suite." He glanced to the shadowed rafters and sighed. "There's no way I can keep this room warm—not until the power comes back on. There's just too much space. But we'd be warm in my room."

And in your bed, Melanie thought. The thought of sleeping with Gavin, waking up in his arms, was inviting—but dangerous. Falling victim to him spontaneously was one thing; making love to him again was just plain foolish. "I don't think this is such a good idea."

"I know it isn't, but I'll be damned if I'm going to sleep alone tonight. We'd both freeze."

"Oh, so this is just a matter of convenience."

"No—pleasure."

"Stop this," she cried as he started to carry her. "Gavin, your leg!"

"My leg's fine."

"No, I mean it." She started to squirm out of his arms, then realized that she was probably doing more damage than good. "I'm perfectly capable of walking."

He chuckled deep in his throat. "Believe me, I'm not underestimating your capabilities."

"And I could carry things."

"We don't need anything."

"But the flashlight and the lanterns—"

"Unnecessary," he replied, carrying her down the dark hallway without once stumbling. He kicked open the door to his room. Red embers glowed from the fireplace, and a lantern, flickering quietly, had been placed on a bedside table.

"You planned this," she accused as he laid her onto the bed. The sheets were cold against her bare skin.

"No…well, yeah, maybe I did." He covered her with an antique quilt and crawled into bed with her.

"You're wicked!" she rasped, wishing she had the strength to climb off his bed and stomp back to the lobby.

"Absolutely."

"And beyond redemption."

"God, I hope so."

"And—"

His mouth found hers, and his hands wrapped around her waist, drawing her naked body to his. It was incredible, he thought, how perfectly she fit against him, how her curves molded to his muscles, how she seemed to melt into him. He'd stupidly thought that making love to her would purge her from his system, but he'd never been more wrong in his life.

It had been only minutes since they'd joined and he'd felt the wonder of her flesh wrapped around his, and yet he was ready again, his body fevered, his mouth hungry.

And she responded. Her breasts felt heavy in his hands,

her nipples willing buds that he brushed with his thumbs. And when he took her into his mouth, tracing those dark points with his tongue, she moaned, her body arching up to his, her moist heat enveloping him.

He rolled her onto him, suckling at her breasts, his hand firm on her buttocks. The windows rattled with the wind, and he thought vaguely that he hoped the storm would never end.

WITH THE MORNING came regret. What had she been thinking about? Making love to Gavin was asking for trouble. And yet, lying in his arms, she found it impossible to roll away from him and pretend that a one-night stand with him meant nothing to her.

Once a fool, always a fool, she thought, a willing prisoner in Gavin's arms. The storm had subsided, and the day promised to be clear and cold. Soon she would have to leave him.

She rested her cheek against his chest and fell back into a dreamless sleep.

Gavin, however, was very much awake. As he lay in the bed, gazing through the window, watching the sunrise blaze against the snow-covered mountain, the bedside phone rang loudly.

He groaned, unwilling to move. Melanie's cheek rested on his chest, and one of her arms was flung around his abdomen. Her skin was creamy white, her tousled black hair in sharp contrast to the white pillow case and sheets. His heart warmed at the sight of her tucked so close and lovingly beside him.

He wanted to protect her and cherish her and love her—

The phone rang again, and she stirred, lifting her head and shaking the hair from her slumberous eyes.

"Uh-oh," Gavin growled. "Looks like someone found us."

"Bound to happen sooner or later," she said, yawning through a smile.

"I suppose. Go back to sleep." He grabbed the jangling

receiver with his left hand while still holding Melanie with his right.

"Ridge Lodge."

"About time you answered! I've been trying to reach you all night," Rich grumbled.

"I've been here."

"Well, you didn't answer!"

"The phones must've been out," Gavin replied, not really interested.

"What's going on up there? No, don't tell me. You've probably got some beautiful woman waiting for you in bed."

"Get real, Rich," Gavin replied, smothering a smile. "The electricity has been out since last night."

"What about the backup generator?"

"Not yet fully operational."

"Oh, God," Rich groaned. "Any damage?"

"Nothing severe." Gavin stretched lazily. For the first time since he'd agreed to this project, he wasn't really interested in thc resort.

"Listen, we've got a million things to do. Now that there's snow, we're wasting big bucks every day we're not open. So I called all our suppliers and the trucks will deliver as soon as the roads are clear. Get ready. Make sure the lot is plowed and that Erik and some of the other boys are there when the shipment of rental gear arrives...." He rattled on and on, giving instructions, though he expected—and got—no answers. Gavin just grinned, and when Melanie tried to roll out of bed, he pinned her hard against him. He hadn't felt this good in years and he wasn't about to give it up.

He harbored no illusions that he and Melanie could ever get back together—not really. She hadn't wanted him when he was dirt poor and she probably didn't want him now. But while they were locked away from the rest of the world, he was going to spend every second with her. She was warm, willing and…and, damn it, she was the one woman who could make love to him as no other had ever…

"So I've called the ski patrol, and a group of would-be instructors will be at the lodge as soon as they can get through. Take their applications, talk to them, and for God's sake, make sure you see them on a pair of skis. Put them through their paces."

"I'll handle it," Gavin said, glancing down as Melanie looked up at him through the sweep of dark lashes.

"Right. And check on the—"

Gavin dropped the receiver back in its cradle and rolled over, giving her the full attention she deserved.

"Problems?" she asked.

"Nothing that won't wait." He fingered a strand of black hair that curled deliciously around her face, neck and breasts. Her eyes flashed silvery green in coy delight.

The phone began to ring again, and Gavin reached to the bottom of the bed and yanked on the cord. There was still a faint jangle from the phones in the lobby and bar, but Gavin didn't pay any attention. Instead, he wrapped his arms around her. "I think we have more important things to think about."

"More important than opening the lodge?"

"Mmm." He nuzzled her neck. "Definitely more important." And, kissing her, he proved it.

LATER, WHILE GAVIN was working elsewhere in the lodge, Melanie dialed the newspaper.

The receptionist answered on the second ring. "Taylor's Crossing *Tribune*."

"Hi, Molly, it's Melanie."

"Melanie! Where've you been?" Molly asked, her voice breathless. "Brian's been looking everywhere for you!"

"I got stuck up at Ridge Lodge when the storm hit last night," Melanie said, feeling more than a trifle guilty as she glanced at the still-rumpled bed. "The road's been closed. Is Brian there?"

"Yeah, I'll connect you."

Molly clicked off, and a few seconds later, Brian Michaels's voice boomed over the wires. "Where the hell are you?"

"Ridge Lodge," she said, repeating everything she'd just told Molly.

"And you were up there all night?" Brian asked.

"That's right."

"Hell, Melanie, I need you down here! We need pictures of the downed lines and the road crews and God only knows what else."

"I'll be there as soon as the roads are clear," she promised. "And I've got some great shots of the lodge."

"Good, good. According to the state police and the highway department, the road to the lodge will be open this afternoon."

A twinge of regret tugged at Melanie's heart. "I'll make a beeline to the office," she promised.

"Good. I'll be in all afternoon." His voice lowered. "And, since you're up on the hill anyway, there is something I'd like you to check into for me."

The hairs on the back of Melanie's neck rose. "What's that?"

"I want you to nose around. See if the resort is experiencing any financial trouble."

"Financial trouble," she repeated, her temper starting to rise.

"Right. There's a rumor circulating that an investor is backing out, that Doel's sunk all his personal fortune into this place and unless it opens and opens big, he's in trouble."

"I doubt it," Melanie replied tightly.

"Where there's smoke there's fire."

"I think that depends on who set up the smoke screen." She

kept her voice low, hoping Gavin wouldn't walk in on her. Clenching her fingers around the receiver, she felt trapped. To think she'd defended Brian to Gavin!

"Well, Rich Johanson spends a hell of a lot of time in Portland trying to keep that legal practice of his alive."

"So what?"

"Seems strange to me."

"You're fishing, Brian."

"Maybe, but you keep looking around. As long as you're there, you may as well keep your eyes and ears open."

"Listen, Brian, I'm the photographer for the *Tribune*. That's all. I'll take all the pictures you need, but that's as far as it goes! I'm not going to run around here trying to ferret out some dirt."

She hung up and slowly counted to ten. She'd gotten only as far as seven when the door to the apartment opened and Gavin strode in.

"Road crews are already working between here and Taylor's Crossing."

"So I heard," she admitted, motioning to the telephone. "I just called the office."

A lazy, self-deprecating grin stretched across Gavin's jaw. "And what did good old Brian have to say?"

"He misses me."

Gavin lifted a lofty brow. "Anything else?"

"Well, he did mention that I should poke around here and find out if you were financially stable."

"You're kidding." Gavin swore loudly.

"Nope."

"Then he was."

"I don't think so."

Gavin shoved his hands into his back pockets. "Michaels will stoop to anything," he said, disgusted. "The financial situation at the lodge is none of his business. You know, I wouldn't be surprised if he sent you up here just to find out what was going on."

Melanie hardly dared breathe. He wasn't serious, was he? Here, in this room, the bed still warm from lovemaking—how could he even say anything so cruel? "Brian didn't send me, Gavin."

"Of course he didn't," Gavin agreed. "But I wouldn't put it past him."

"And me?"

He snorted contemptuously. "I don't think you sleep with men to get the kind of story or pictures or whatever it is you want from them."

"I don't sleep with men, period. Except for you." She picked up a pen from the table and twisted it nervously.

His face lost all expression. "What about Neil?"

"Only while we were married."

He blanched.

"And there's something I should explain about that," she said quietly, her voice shaking as she struggled for the right words. "I married Neil because of the baby."

The room went still. Melanie heard her own heart thud painfully. She lifted her eyes to meet the questions in Gavin's gaze.

"I thought you said you didn't sleep with Neil until you were married."

"I didn't."

"And just last night—didn't you tell me you couldn't get pregnant?"

"I couldn't—I mean, I can't, not now, not with Neil—I mean… Oh, God." Her hands were shaking and her throat was cotton dry. She forced herself to stare straight into his eyes. "What I'm trying to say, Gavin, is that the reason I married Neil was because I was pregnant." She couldn't help the tears clogging her throat. It was all she could do to stand there, keeping her knees from buckling.

The air in the room was suddenly hot, the glare in Gavin's gaze positively murderous. "Pregnant?" he repeated slowly, quietly.

"Yes."

"But you said…"

She squeezed her eyes shut. "I know what I said. But I did get pregnant once, Gavin. And the baby was yours."

CHAPTER TEN

"MINE? THE BABY was mine?" he whispered hoarsely, his face devoid of color, his lips bloodless.

"Yes. I was pregnant when you left, but I didn't know it. When I found out you were already trying out for the ski team and—"

"Lies!"

"No! Oh, Gavin, why would I lie?" she cried.

"I don't know," he growled, stepping forward, his eyes gleaming menacingly. "But you must have a reason."

"I just thought you'd want to know."

"Now? After eight years?" His voice was so low and threatening that her skin crawled. "When it's so convenient? How stupid do you think I am?"

"I don't—"

He grabbed her upper arm, his fingers digging deep. "Just last night you told me you couldn't conceive. That's right, isn't it? Or has that story changed, too?"

She didn't blame him for being angry, but the explosion of emotion on his face scared her. She tried to jerk her arm away but he clamped down all the harder.

"I'm not lying, Gavin!"

"Oh, no? So where's the kid? Hmm? The son—or daughter, was it?—that I fathered?"

She crumbled inside. "Oh, God, Gavin, don't. Can't you see how hard this is for me?"

"I see that you lied eight years ago and you're doing it still."

"No—please, you've got to believe me."

"Why?"

"Because it's the truth!" she cried, desperation ringing in her voice. "The truth!"

"You don't know the meaning of the word!"

"How would you know? You never stuck around long enough to find out!"

He winced. "All right, Melanie. If you want to go on spinning your little tale, go right ahead." He released her suddenly, as if the mere touch of her made him ill. Crossing his arms over his chest, he muttered, "Go on. I'm all ears!"

Melanie lifted her chin and fought the tears that kept threatening to spill. "I was pregnant with your child, and my father talked me into not telling you."

"Wonderful guy."

"He was thinking of you."

"Sure."

"He said you weren't ready to be burdened with a wife and child, that you'd only grow to resent me because you'd have to give up your dream."

"Are you expecting me to buy any of this?"

"Only if you remember how much I loved you," she said, fighting fire with fire. His eyes betrayed him. Emotions, long hidden and tortured, showed for one instant, and he was again the vulnerable boy from the wrong side of the tracks. Her heart felt as if it were breaking into a thousand pieces. "I did love you, Gavin. All I thought about was loving you and living with you for the rest of my life. I—I didn't mean to get pregnant. It just happened."

"So you married another man. And Neil was more than happy to play daddy to my kid. Oh, come on, Melanie. This just doesn't wash."

"Why else would I marry a man I didn't love?"

"Money," he said cruelly, his voice filled with conviction.

"I didn't care about money. But I wanted a good life for the baby."

"The baby." He lifted his hands. "Where is he?"

She swallowed the hot, painful lump in her throat, "I miscarried. Six weeks after I married Neil."

"Now didn't that work out fine and dandy?" he mocked, his words cutting to the bone.

She shook her head at the memory. "No, it was awful—"

"It was a lie. Either you're lying to me now, or Neil Brooks is a bigger fool than I am for believing you."

"You think I made this up?"

"I don't know what to think, Melanie. But you just told me yourself that you couldn't get pregnant. How do you expect me to believe something as outrageous as this?"

"I didn't lie. Neil and I couldn't have children. I—we—after I lost the baby, we never used birth control. And, even though we hoped, there never was another baby."

"And how does medical science explain this incredible phenomenon?"

"It doesn't. Neil wouldn't go to the doctor and…well, I didn't bother. Things started falling apart, and we started sleeping in different rooms."

"So you're expecting me to believe that I got you pregnant and you, out of some convoluted sense of nobility, refused to tell me about it but you convinced Neil to marry you and raise another man's child as his own. Only, lo and behold, before the blessed event occurs, you lose the baby and never, ever conceive again?"

She fought the urge to snap back at him. Instead, curling her fists, she blinked against tears of frustration. "Yes."

"Well, Melanie, you missed your calling. You shouldn't have become a photographer. You should be an actress. You've just given one helluva performance!"

Melanie's temper exploded. How could he have become so cruel? So callous? So jaded?

She thought of their recent lovemaking; the scent still lingered in the air. He'd been tender and kind—and now, so heartless. Sick inside, she knew she had to leave. Now. Before whatever they'd shared turned ugly. Without a word, she started gathering her things.

"What're you doing?"

"Leaving."

"You can't leave."

"Watch me."

"But it's freezing, the roads are blocked and—"

"I don't give a damn about the roads or the weather!" she flung out as she found her camera and purse.

"You're angry."

"Try *furious*!"

"Just because I didn't believe your story."

"Forget it." She started for the door, but he grabbed her arm, spinning her around.

"You can't leave," he said again.

"Let go of me, Gavin."

"Your car won't make it."

"What do you care?" She peeled his fingers from her arm. "I'll walk if I have to."

"Melanie—"

She ran out the door and through the now familiar hallways.

The lodge was empty; her footsteps rang on the hardwood. She heard Gavin behind her, but she shoved open the front doors and was blasted with the rush of bitterly cold air.

Snow glistened and still fell in tiny flakes. She nearly slipped on the icy front steps and he caught up with her. "Melanie, listen, I'm sorry."

"No reason to be!" she snapped, plowing through the snow that nearly hit her at the knees. "You think I'm a liar or worse.

Fine. At least I know where I stand." She plunged on, determined to find a way to leave him.

"For crying out loud, Melanie…"

Her Volkswagen, even parked under cover, was under a pile of snow. Ignoring the wind, she brushed the icy flakes from the windshield, climbed into the car and turned the key. The engine ground slowly as she pumped on the gas. "Come on, come on," she whispered, sending up a silent prayer. She couldn't stay here a minute longer—she wouldn't!

Gavin opened the car door as the engine sputtered, coughed and died. "Now, just a minute—"

"Drop dead!"

"Look, I didn't mean to ridicule you."

"Well, you did!"

"It's just that your story is so unbelievable."

"So you said!" She stomped on the accelerator and twisted the key again. "Come on, come on," she muttered to the car. *Oh, please start! Please!*

His jaw worked. He was obviously struggling with his own temper. "Come back into the lodge. I'll make some coffee and we can talk this over civilly."

"Impossible! Just leave me alone! That's what you're good at—leaving!"

His lips tightened. "I'm trying, Melanie. Now the least you can do is meet me halfway."

"After what you said to me? After being accused of being a liar?" She turned furious hazel eyes up to him. "You know me, Gavin. You know I wouldn't lie about something like this. What would be the point?"

"I thought you needed an excuse for marrying Neil. Something I might understand."

The car gave a last sickening cough and died. When she turned the key again, all she heard was a series of clicks. Gavin's hand touched her shoulder. She shrank away.

"I'll buy you a cup of coffee and I'll listen to what you have to say. Besides, this car isn't going anywhere. Even if it did start, you'd never make it through the lot."

He was right about that. The lot was covered with nearly two feet of snow. The Volkswagen wouldn't get out of the shed before stopping dead—that was, if she ever could get it started.

"Come on, Mel," he insisted.

"Forget it! You won't believe me."

"I'll try." His voice turned gentle. "Melanie, you threw me for a helluva loop."

"Then you believe me?" she asked, her features tormented.

He glanced up at the sky, and snow collected in his hair and on his collar. Lines bracketed his mouth and eyes. "I don't know what to believe."

"Fine." She yanked hard on the door, but he wedged himself between the handle and the interior.

"As I said before, you're not going anywhere in this," he ordered tautly, taking hold of her and hauling her from the car.

She tried to climb back inside, but he pulled her out, bodily carrying her back to the lodge.

She wriggled and kicked, trying desperately to get back on her feet and find her rapidly escaping dignity. "Put me down! You'll slip and ruin your ankle and—"

"Oh, be quiet!" he growled, trudging through the snow, following the trail she'd broken only minutes before. "We're going back inside and you're going to start over, slowly, from the beginning."

"If you think I'm going through this again, you're out of your mind!"

"Probably," he said. "But I think you owe it to me to—"

"*I* owe *you*? Oh, give me a break. I owe you nothing! Nothing! I shouldn't have opened my mouth in the first place."

"But you did," he reminded her, slowly climbing the steps

and kicking open the front door. He didn't stop until he'd carried her all the way into his apartment. Plopping her onto the couch, he said, "Now let's start over."

"I've told you everything."

"A little late, isn't it?"

"I explained that I didn't want to burden you."

"Oh, yes, noble of you," he mocked, trying and failing to keep his temper under control. "So you, pregnant with my child, married Neil Brooks?"

"Yes."

"And he agreed to go along with your scheme?" he asked dubiously.

"It wasn't a scheme!"

He shoved shaking hands through his hair. "What I don't understand, Melanie, is, if this is true, why you didn't at least have the courage to tell me about it. Didn't you think I'd want to know?"

"I didn't want you to feel trapped," she said, her hands curling into fists of frustration.

"But if I was the father—"

"You know you were!"

"Then the child was my responsibility."

"A child you didn't want."

"You don't know that!" He crossed to the window, and anger fairly radiated from him. "If the baby had lived, would you have ever told me the truth?"

She opened her mouth, closed it again and struggled with the truth. When her words came, they sounded strangled. "I—I don't think so."

"And why the hell not?" He whirled, facing her again, his temper skyrocketing. His nostrils flared and his eyes blazed.

"Because I wouldn't want a scene like this one!"

Something flickered in his eyes, something dark and dangerous. "Or because I wasn't good enough for you?"

"What?"

"Is that why you ran to Neil instead of me? Because you wanted to raise your child—*our* child—by a rich man instead of the son of the town drunk?"

She couldn't believe it. Not now. Not after he'd sworn that he would listen to her. "I don't have to listen to this, Gavin. I loved you. I loved you so much I was out of my mind with wanting you. But I didn't want to make you hate me for the rest of your life!"

"So you married Brooks in order to pass off my child as his," he said, disgust heavy in his voice.

"No!"

"God, Melanie, this is one for the books—"

"You said you'd listen!"

The sound of footsteps rang through the hall. Someone had made it up to the lodge! The roads were clear! She could leave.

"Mr. Doel? Are you here? Mr. Doel?" Erik Link's voice echoed through the corridors, and Gavin's lips pursed.

He muttered an oath, then called over his shoulder, "In here."

The door flew open. "I just wanted to say that the roads are clear and—" Erik's voice fell away at the sight of Melanie, and she realized how she must look, her hair in tangles, her cheeks burning, her chin thrust forward like a recalcitrant child getting the lecture of her life. "I—uh, I didn't mean to interrupt."

"You didn't," Melanie informed him. She jumped to her feet and grabbed her things. "In fact, I'd really appreciate it if you'd give me a ride back to town. My car's given up the ghost."

"Sure." Erik's gaze moved from Melanie to Gavin.

"I'll drive you home," Gavin said. "If the roads are passable—"

Melanie tossed her hair over her shoulder. "Oh, I wouldn't want to bother you, Mr. Doel. You must have a thousand and one things to do before the resort opens."

"That's right, and the first one is to get you safely home."

He grabbed his keys from a hook near the door, gave Erik quick instructions about plowing the lot and keeping the lodge warm, then followed Melanie, who was walking briskly toward the back lot.

"You shouldn't have bothered," she shot at him when they were once again outside.

"I'd feel better about this if I made sure you were all right."

"I can handle myself. I don't need you bossing me around," she flung back, wishing she could hurt him as he'd hurt her. All his horrid accusations filled her head and she ached inside. Well, she'd done her duty, told him the truth. Now she couldn't wait to get away from him, from the lodge—from Taylor's Crossing if she had to!

They walked to the garage, and she climbed into a huge four-wheel-drive truck and waited while he turned the ignition. The engine caught immediately.

Gavin slid behind the wheel. Melanie didn't so much as glance in his direction. But he didn't shift out of park. Instead, he drummed his fingers impatiently on the steering wheel, jaw set, as if struggling for just the right words.

Well, she wasn't about to help him. He'd been wretched and he deserved to squirm.

He sighed, shifting uncomfortably, and the bench seat moved beneath her. If she could only get through this!

The cab of the truck was warm, the windows fogged, and Melanie, against her best judgment, sneaked a glance his way. He was staring at her, lips tight, eyes narrowed, as if he were trying to size her up. One wayward strand of honey-blond hair fell over his forehead.

The air between them fairly crackled.

Melanie broke the silence first. "I just wish you'd remember that you trusted me once," she said.

"That's the problem. I remember all too well."

"And you think I betrayed you."

"You did."

"Fine. Think what you want. Can't you start this thing?"

He shoved the truck into gear and let the wheels grab. The truck lurched, and he tromped on the accelerator, plowing through the unbroken snow until he was on the path that Erik's truck had broken through the parking lot.

The trip down the mountain took nearly an hour. Melanie turned an ostracizing shoulder to Gavin and stared out the window at the aftermath of the storm. Pine boughs drooped under a blanket of thick snow. The sky was gray, the clouds high, the air frosty and clean.

But inside the truck the atmosphere was thick. The miles rolled slowly by. At the sight of a road crew, Melanie yanked her camera out of its case and, asking Gavin to slow down, clicked off several shots of workers sawing through fallen trees and restringing electrical cable.

She didn't say another word until he reached her house. It took all of her willpower not to throw open the door and run up the front steps.

He ground the truck to a stop. "Melanie—"

She didn't want to hear it. Opening the door, she climbed out. "Thanks for the ride and all the hospitality," she said, her tone scathing. "Believe me, I won't forget this morning for the rest of my life."

And neither will I, Gavin thought as she slammed the door of the truck shut and stomped through the snow to the back door. He waited a few seconds, until he was sure she was inside, then he threw the truck in reverse.

He wanted to believe her. In his heart he desperately wished he could trust her again. But how could he? And this cock-and-bull story about the baby—his baby… Why the hell would she lie? Why now? It would have been easier for her to keep quiet.

There was obviously some truth to the tale. He knew her well enough to recognize her pain. And her private agony was matched by his when he thought about a child he would never know, a child he'd created with Melanie.

His hands gripped the wheel tightly, and an angry horn blared as the truck moved too close to the center line. Teeth clenched, he focused on his driving, but a thousand emotions tore at his soul.

He could have been a father—the father of a seven-year-old. For God's sake, he didn't even know what a seven-year-old was like!

And Melanie could have been his wife—not Neil's. If only she'd been honest with him way back when.

What kind of life could he have given her? Would he have given up his chances for glory on the Olympic team? Would he have forced Melanie and the kid to travel from one ski resort to the next while he tried to scratch out a living as a pro? Without the catapult to fame from the Olympics, would he have had the backing to race professionally, to get on his feet? Or would he have returned to Taylor's Crossing and become a ranch hand or a logger or given lessons to children during the weekends at Ridge Resort?

But there was no baby. An unfamiliar pain, raw and cutting, seared straight to his soul. If he'd stayed in Taylor's Crossing and married Melanie, would the child have survived? Hell, he didn't even know why a woman miscarried, but he felt tremendous guilt that he hadn't been around to offer support and comfort to Melanie for a child they would never share.

"Son of a bitch," he muttered, driving straight to the lodge. He parked near Erik's truck and noticed that several other vehicles had arrived. Two plows were working to clear the lot. Rich must have gotten through to the crew.

He walked into the lodge and made a beeline for the bar. Ignoring the looks cast his way by some of the workers, he grabbed a bottle of Scotch, twisted open the cap and took a long swig right from the bottle. It burned like hell.

"What's eatin' you?" his father asked. He glanced up, and in the mirror over the bar he saw Jim Doel's florid, lined face, an older version of his own.

"You wouldn't believe it."

"Try me."

Gavin shook his head and took another tug on the bottle.

His father approached and, laying an arm over Gavin's shoulders, said, "I don't know what you're fightin', son, but believe me, this—" he touched the bottle with his free hand "—isn't gonna help."

"Nothing will," Gavin agreed.

"It's that Walker woman again, isn't it?" his father guessed. "Don't you know it's time you got her out of your blood once and for all?"

"I wish I could," Gavin admitted. "But I don't think it's possible."

"Anything's possible."

"What I don't need right now is a lecture," Gavin grumbled.

"No. What you need is another woman."

Scenes of lovemaking filled Gavin's mind. He remembered Melanie snuggled tight against him, her hair brushing his bare skin. "I don't think another woman's the answer."

"'Course it is," his father countered. "I know that model has called you."

"I'm not interested."

"Well, maybe you should be." His father's eyes met his in the glass. "There's no reason for this girl to tear you apart."

Gavin clenched his teeth. What he felt for Melanie went way beyond the bonds of reason.

"SO THE LOST LAMB has found her way back to the fold," Guy remarked when Melanie shoved open the door and walked briskly past his desk.

Melanie, in no mood for humor, replied, "Since when was I a lamb?"

Guy held up his hands in surrender. "Only a figure of speech."

She unwrapped her scarf, shrugged out of her coat and hung them both in the employee closet near the darkroom. "Was I the only one who didn't make it in?"

"Are you kidding? The county was literally shut down. Constance and Molly were both out yesterday." He retrieved Melanie's Garfield mug from her desk, rinsed it out and poured her a cup of fresh coffee. "Even Brian's place lost power for a few hours. He came in late yesterday, and boy, was he fit to be tied."

"So things were just like usual," Melanie remarked.

Guy grinned. "I guess. Anyway, he's on a real kick to sell more papers."

"Isn't he always?"

"Yeah," Guy muttered, fidgeting with his watch and avoiding her eyes. "But this is different. I don't know what happened, but my guess is he got the word from the powers that be to increase circulation or—" Guy rotated his palms to the ceiling "—*sayonara!*"

At that moment Brian Michaels himself burst into the newsroom. His face was flushed from the cold, and he saw Melanie instantly. "So you're back," he said, yanking off his gloves and hanging his felt hat in the closet near the front door. "Good. We've got work to do. Come into my office."

"Be right there." Melanie grabbed a notebook from the top of her desk and, ignoring Guy's worried glance, followed Brian into his private office. "Now listen," Brian said before she'd even had a chance to sit down, "I'm serious about the rumors about the lodge being in financial trouble. I want to know all about it. You were up there—what's going on?"

"Nothing out of the ordinary. Because of the storm, they're hoping to open early."

"That's it?" he asked skeptically.

"That's it." She eased into one of the uncomfortable chairs near his desk.

Brian's brow furrowed, and he reached into his top drawer for a new pack of cigarettes. "No sign of any financial difficulty?"

"None. They were expecting delivery of the supplies and equipment as soon as the roads were clear."

Frowning, Brian tapped his cigarette pack on the edge of the desk. "You wouldn't keep anything from me, would you, Melanie?"

"No."

"But if you thought I was prying into someone's personal life, especially if that person happened to be someone you cared about, you wouldn't give up private information easily."

She felt heat climb up her back. "You're right. I wouldn't."

"Not even if it was news?"

"No."

He opened the pack and shook out a cigarette. "This job is important to me, Melanie. And it should be important to you. We owe it to our readers to report the truth, no matter how…uncomfortable…it might be."

"I didn't see anything at the lodge. As a matter of fact, I've been there when Rich Johanson has been paying bills." She leaned across his desk as he lit his cigarette and snapped his lighter closed. "I think you're barking up the wrong tree. The lodge looks solid as a rock. And if they can open earlier than planned, I would think there's a better chance than ever that they'll make it work."

Squinting through the smoke, he said, "How long were you at the lodge?"

"Less than twenty-four hours," she said uneasily. "I got there just before the storm hit."

"Who else was there?"

"Just Gavin Doel."

"Just Doel?" One sharp eyebrow arched. "How was that?"

"Cold," she lied. "The lodge lost power."

"And phone lines?"

"They were down—at least for a while in the middle of the night."

"So what did you and Doel do all that time?" he asked.

Was he suggesting something? She couldn't be sure. With effort she kept her voice steady. "We tried to keep the pipes from freezing, attempted to start the backup generator…that sort of thing."

"And in all that time Doel never once said anything that might indicate that things weren't running smoothly at the lodge?"

"Well, he wasn't too pleased about the lack of electricity."

"I mean financially."

"No." She leaned back in her chair. "What's this all about?"

"Just a rumor I heard."

"From whom?"

He grinned. "You know I won't reveal my sources."

"Well, I think your sources are all wet."

"But you won't mind checking into it when you're back up at the lodge doing whatever it is you do there."

Melanie's temper snapped. "Of course I'll mind!" she said, standing and glaring down at him as if he'd lost his mind. "I can't go creeping around spying on Gavin and Rich, and I wouldn't even if I could. I don't know why it is that all of a sudden you want to do some big smear campaign against Ridge Lodge, but I won't be a part of it!"

"This isn't a smear campaign. Think of it as investigative journalism."

Melanie's sound of disgust eloquently voiced her feelings.

"You don't have a choice," Brian added calmly.

"Of course I do…."

But his meaning was clear, and his face had hardened. "Not if you want to keep your job. Let's be straight with each other. Circulation hasn't picked up and I've got to make some cuts in expenses around here. I'm going to trim some people from the staff."

"Are you saying you're going to fire me?"

"Not yet, but I expect you to be a team player, Melanie. Now, why don't you develop the shots you've already taken up there, then go up with Jan and find out what's going on at the lodge?"

His intercom buzzed, and Melanie walked out of the office. She couldn't afford to lose this job, not yet. She still had debts to pay off from her father's illness and the addition to her house. But she'd be damned if she was going to help Brian ruin Ridge Lodge or Gavin Doel!

BRIAN MICHAELS STUBBED out his cigarette and watched as Melanie marched stiffly into the darkroom. Something had happened to her while she was up at the lodge, and his reporter's instincts told him she'd gotten herself mixed up with Doel.

Now *that* was interesting. Gavin Doel, internationally famous athlete, involved with a local woman?

For the first time all week, Brian smiled to himself. Maybe he was going for the wrong angle on Doel. Sure the man was newsworthy, but the readers just might be more interested in his love life than his lodge.

And Melanie Walker was beautiful as well as spirited. Exactly what was going on?

Jan had mentioned that Doel and Melanie had known each other way back when. Brian wondered just how well.

It wouldn't take much to find out. He had microfiche and old newspapers that went clear back to the fifties. There was also a town library filled with high school yearbooks and a lot of people who had lived here all their lives.

Surely someone would remember if Gavin and Melanie were involved before. Maybe it was nothing, just a passing friendship—or maybe not even that. But Brian wasn't convinced.

No, there was a spark that leaped to life in Melanie's eyes every time Doel's name was mentioned. He could see through her feigned nonchalance. And she'd been defensive as hell.

Oh, yes, it was time to do some checking on Gavin Doel. And this time, he'd put Jan on the story. Jan didn't have the same overrated sense of values that Melanie clung to.

In fact, he might even do some digging himself. He'd never liked Gavin Doel. Doel had once cost him his job, and from that point on, his career had gone downhill until he'd landed in this two-bit town. Well, maybe now Gavin Doel was his ticket out!

The guy had everything, Brian thought jealously. It was high time Doel was knocked down a few pegs, even if it cost Melanie Walker.

It was too bad about Melanie. Brian liked her. She worked hard, was nice to look at and was smart. Except when it came to Gavin Doel. Yep, it was too bad about Melanie. Brian felt an abnormal twinge of conscience and hoped she didn't get hurt—at least, not too badly.

But if she did, it was her fault. She was better off without an arrogant bastard like Gavin Doel. The sooner she knew it, the better for everyone.

CHAPTER ELEVEN

MELANIE RETURNED TO Ridge Lodge, determined that the next story in the *Tribune* would reflect the excitement of reopening the resort.

As she parked in the lot, she realized that the story would nearly write itself—if Jan would let it.

Ridge Lodge was frenetic.

Delivery trucks brought skis, boots, fashion skiwear, food, snacks, light fixtures, paper products, tourist information, utensils, medical supplies, souvenirs and on and on.

The ski patrol had already started checking the runs, and an area had been cleared near the Nugget Rope Tow for the ski school to meet. Chairs and gondolas moved up the hill as the newly named lifts became operational. Grooming machines chugged up the snow-covered slopes, while snowplows kept the parking lot clear.

A rainbow of triangular flags snapped in the wind, and the snow continued to fall, bringing with it hopes for a long and prosperous season.

Inside, the lodge was hectic. Employees manned the phones as the resort geared up for an early season. Others were briefed on the way the lodge worked, dishes were stacked, beds were made in the rooms, the bar was stocked and a new sound system was turned on.

Melanie smiled as she saw her sepia-toned pictures

hanging near mining equipment, adding to the Gold Rush atmosphere of the lobby.

In the huge stone fireplace a fire crackled and burned invitingly. Workers arranged furniture in the bar and lobby, and the Oriental rug where she and Gavin had made love was still stretched across the floor. A pang of regret tore through her.

Her smile disappeared. Hadn't she learned anything? Chiding herself for being a fool, she loaded a new roll of film into the camera and made her way past the bustling workers.

"Well, how do you like this?" Jan asked, breezing in the front door and stamping the snow from her boots.

"What—oh, the lodge?" Melanie glanced around. "Looks a little different, doesn't it?"

"*Very* different." Tucking her gloves in her purse, Jan eyed the walls. "Those your pictures?" she asked, moving closer to a print of miners panning for gold.

"Yes."

"They're not bad."

"Thanks."

Jan's mouth tightened. "You know I hate this, don't you?"

"Hate what?"

"Being the bad guy. I wouldn't be surprised if Doel and Johanson tried to kick me out of here."

Melanie was skeptical. "Would you blame them? You keep asking all sorts of personal questions."

She lifted a shoulder. "Brian wants a more personal story. I try to give him one." Jan's eyes clouded a minute. "Melanie, I think I should warn you…" She let the sentence trail off.

"Warn me about what?" Melanie demanded, then understood. "About Gavin?" When Jan didn't reply, she added, "Come on, Jan. Weren't you the one who thought I should chase after him?"

"Maybe that wasn't such a hot idea," Jan replied nervously. She looked as if she were about to say something else when she spotted Rich Johanson. "Look, just be careful," she said cryptically. "Don't do anything foolish."

Too late for that, Melanie thought as Jan, following Rich, took off in search of her story.

Melanie wandered down a long corridor to the shops. Mannequins were already dressed in neon and black jumpsuits. Sweatshirts, imprinted with the resort's logo or simply saying Ski the Ridge!, were displayed in a window case.

All around her, employees chatted and laughed, stocking the shelves or waxing skis or adjusting bindings on rental skis.

In the exercise room machines stood ready, and nearby, steam rose from the aquamarine water in the pool. Yes, Ridge Lodge was nearly ready for its guests. Despite Brian Michaels's arguments to the contrary, Ridge Lodge was destined to be a success. She could feel it. And the photographs she snapped off reflected that success—smiling employees, gleaming equipment, well-stocked shops....

She worked her way outside and changed film and lenses. Then she clicked off shot after shot of the moving lifts, a group of instructors in matching gold jackets as they practiced together, an operator in the cage at the bottom of Daredevil run, and above it all, Mount Prosperity stood proudly, a regal giant in a mantle of white.

She didn't notice Gavin for nearly two hours, then, as she trained her lens on a group of instructors making their way through the moguls at the bottom of Rocky Ridge run, she spied him in the lead, blond hair flying, skis so close together they nearly touched, his form perfect.

Her throat went dry as the camera zoomed in for a closer shot. She noticed the concentration in his face, the natural grace with which he planted his poles, the way he turned effortlessly, as if he'd never been injured.

"The man is awesome," Jan said as she stepped through

the snow to reach Melanie. Her eyes were trained on Gavin, as well. "Looks like he's good as new."

"I suppose." Melanie turned her camera on another instructor, a woman who was gamely trying to keep up with Gavin and losing ground with every turn.

"I wonder if he'll race again."

"I hope so," Melanie muttered, still adjusting the focus.

"You do?" Jan said. "Why?"

"Because he loves it. It's his life. He's not happy unless he's tearing down some mountain at breakneck speed."

Jan sighed wistfully as Gavin, flying over the last of the moguls, twisted in midair, tucked his skis together and cut into the hillside, stopping quickly and sending a spray of snow to one side.

"So you think once this lodge is up and running, he'll take off for the ski circuit?"

Melanie stiffened. "I don't know," she said honestly. "You'll have to ask him."

"Oh, I intend to." Jan's eyes darkened thoughtfully. "There's a lot more I'd like to know about Mr. Doel."

At that moment Gavin looked up. His gaze scanned the lodge before landing on Melanie. Through the lens, Melanie noticed his jaw tighten.

With a quick word to the instructors, he planted his poles and skied, using his arms and a skating motion with his legs, as he crossed the relatively flat terrain from the base of the run to the lodge.

Melanie's stomach knotted.

"Well, if it isn't the *Tribune*'s finest," he said, eyeing Melanie's camera and Jan's ever-present notebook.

Melanie ignored the jab and decided to try her damnedest to be professional. She would put what happened between Gavin and her behind her if it took all of her willpower. "You agreed to the series of articles, remember?"

"Yep," he said flatly, but his lips twisted. "What's the angle—isn't that what you call it?—for this week's edition?"

"Financial impact," Jan said as Gavin leaned over and shoved on his bindings with the heel of his hand. With a snap, he was free of his skis. "The *Trib*'s interested in the economic impact on the community, as well as how you keep a lodge resort this size out of the red."

"It takes some doing," he replied.

"Mmm. I'll bet."

"But we have backing."

"Investors?"

He straightened, his expression menacing. "Where're you heading with this?"

"Nowhere," Jan said guilelessly, but Melanie decided to step in.

"I thought I already mentioned that there've been rumors that the resort is failing financially," she said, warning Gavin.

Gavin's jaw set. His eyes turned as cool as the early winter day. "And I thought I explained that there are no problems, financial or otherwise."

"Then none of your investors is bowing out?" Jan asked.

Gavin whirled on her. "Not unless you know something I don't." His eyes narrowed threateningly. "Oh, I get it. Michaels is fishing again. Well, give him a reminder for me, will you? If he prints anything the least bit libelous about this lodge or me, I'll sue. Now, if you don't mind, I'd like to speak with Melanie. In private. And don't print that!" Lips compressed angrily, he took hold of Melanie's arm and, without a backward glance at the reporter, propelled Melanie up the few steps to the back deck.

"What the hell's going on?" he demanded once they were out of earshot.

"You know as much as I do," she replied, glancing over his shoulder. Fortunately, Jan, after casting them a questioning look, had turned back toward the main lobby.

"What's Brian Michaels's game?"

Melanie yanked her arm away from him. "All I know is he's looking for dirt. Any kind of dirt."

"On me?"

"Yes. Or the lodge."

"Then that brings him right back to you, doesn't it?" he countered, his expression hard. "Does he know about you and me?"

Melanie caught her breath. How could Gavin talk about their past without so much as a hint of emotion? "No," she replied levelly.

"You're sure?"

"Positive. A few weeks ago he asked me to look into your past—you know, dig through the files—and I told him I came up empty, that you walked the straight and narrow while you lived in Taylor's Crossing."

The lines near his mouth tightened, and he muttered a nearly inaudible oath. "And he doesn't know about Dad?"

Melanie shook her head, thinking about the pictures she'd lifted from the file cabinet. "There isn't a file on your father—at least, not at the *Trib*."

Gavin's brows shot up. "But—"

"Don't ask. Just don't worry about your father."

He studied her face for a second, and her breath seemed trapped in her lungs.

With all the effort she could muster, she inched her chin up a fraction. "Is that all you want? Because I've got work to do—"

He exploded, pounding a gloved fist on the top rail of the deck. "No, damn it." His voice lowered, and he grappled for control of his emotions. "No, Melanie, it's not all I want."

"I don't think I want to hear this—"

"Just listen. I've been thinking. A lot." His gaze touched hers, and she quivered inside. It took all her grit to hide the fact that he was getting to her. "Look, I know I came on a little strong the other day."

"A little strong? You mean your impersonation of Genghis Khan? Is that what you call a little strong?"

He shook his head and let out an exasperated sigh. "You shocked me, Melanie. And you threw me for one helluva loop!"

"I didn't mean to. I just thought you should know the truth."

"It came a little late."

Melanie had heard enough. She tried to storm away, but he grabbed her arms again and his face became tender. "Let me go, Gavin," she insisted, "before we cause a scene we'll both regret!"

He ignored her. "How did you expect me to act?"

As if you cared. As if you remembered how much we loved each other. "I didn't expect anything, Gavin. And I still don't!"

"I'm sorry," he said softly, his gloved hands still gripping her arms. "Really. But you dropped a bomb on me the other day, and it's all I've thought about ever since. I made some mistakes. We both did. I'm just sorry you thought I was too irresponsible to handle fatherhood."

"Not irresponsible," she said tightly. "But I just didn't want to be the one to destroy your dreams."

He dropped his hand and yanked off his gloves. "You don't understand, do you? Eight years ago you were part of that dream," he admitted, his eyes narrowing on her. "The skiing was great, don't get me wrong. But it wasn't the same after you married Neil."

Melanie froze. She could hardly believe him. Though the pain etched across his face seemed real enough, she didn't trust him. Couldn't. "Believe it or not, Gavin, I just tried to do the right thing."

"But it wasn't right, was it?" he said softly.

"I don't think there was a right or wrong."

His eyes searched her face. She thought he might kiss her. His gaze centered on her lips for a heartbeat, but, as if he had a sixth sense, he glanced over his shoulder and furrows lined his brow. "Oh, great," he grumbled.

Melanie looked past him and spied Jan heading for the deck.

Gavin touched her shoulder. "You and I need to talk somewhere quiet, somewhere without your friend." His mouth curved down as Jan climbed onto the deck.

"I don't mean to interrupt," she said, eyeing them with interest, "but I do have a few more questions and a deadline."

"Just a minute." He turned back to Melanie. "When things slow down here, I'll call."

Melanie shook her head. "You don't have to."

"I know. But I want to."

Their gazes held for just a second, and Melanie melted inside. Quickly, she squared her shoulders. "You do that," she quipped.

Gavin cleared his throat, took in a deep breath and, folding his arms over his chest, turned his full attention back to Jan. "All right, Ms. Freemont. What is it you want to know?"

Melanie didn't stick around for the rest of the interview. She took two rolls of film, then, trying to forget that Gavin wanted to see her again, returned to the office.

TWO DAYS LATER, all hell broke loose.

Melanie caught her first glance of page one of the *Tribune*. With a sinking heart, she read the headline that screamed: Financial Problems Plague Ridge Resort.

"This is outrageous!" she sputtered, skimming the article and feeling sick. How could Jan have reported anything so blatantly false? The article stated that Gavin himself was in serious financial trouble, that since his injury he'd become a recluse, not giving any ski clinics, not endorsing any skiwear, not making a dime.

He'd sunk his personal fortune, according to the story, into Ridge Lodge, and when he and his partner had run out of money, they'd sought private funds from investors, who were rumored to be upset with the way their money was handled.

By the time Melanie finished reading the article, her insides were in shreds.

The pictures she'd taken of the workers readying for the opening of the resort were sadly missing. The shots that were included were some she'd shoved aside—a worried profile of Gavin, a picture of an empty lift, another shot of chairs stacked on tables in the empty bar, a photograph of Rich and Gavin talking, their faces set and grim.

Anger burned her cheeks, and her fingers clenched the thin newsprint. "That bastard," she hissed.

Guy Reardon looked up from his desk. He seemed paler than usual. "I was afraid of something like this." He dropped his pencil and sighed. "I think it's only going to get worse."

"How can it get worse?"

Guy's eyes were troubled. "Believe me, it can."

"Do you know something I don't?" she asked.

He lifted a shoulder but avoided her gaze. "It's just a feeling I've got, Mel."

"Well, it's got to stop!" Brandishing the newspaper as if it were a sword, she walked swiftly between the desks to the editor's door. She didn't even bother knocking but shoved open the door and cornered Brian. He was just hanging up the phone.

"I can't believe you published this!" she said, tossing the paper onto his cluttered desk. The headline fairly leaped from the page.

"Why not?"

"Because it's not true! I've been up to the resort!" She thumped her fingers on the front page. "There's not a shred of truth in that story!"

"Maybe you're biased."

"What?"

"Close the door, Melanie," Brian said, lowering his voice. Her skin crawled, but she yanked the door shut and stood glowering down at him while he lit a cigarette. "Let's not pull any punches, okay?" he suggested.

"Fine with me. Why the smear job on the lodge?"

"Reader interest."

"And if readers are interested in gossip, in pure speculation, in anything no matter how damaging or incorrect, the *Trib* will print it, right?"

"This has never bothered you before."

"Because it hasn't happened before. I thought this newspaper had some pride, some integrity, some sound journalism behind it!" Melanie's blood was beginning to boil. "And what about libel? Aren't you afraid of being sued?"

He thought about that and shook his head. "I think you're too personally involved."

"I'm *what*?"

His eyes behind his glasses squinted. "I know about you and Doel, Melanie. I know you dated him in high school." He reached into the top drawer of his desk and withdrew an envelope.

Melanie's stomach turned over as Brian dumped the contents of the envelope onto the newspaper she'd dropped on his desk. She recognized her own face as well as Gavin's in the black-and-white shots. They were younger, obviously in love, and seated together at Ridge Lodge long before it closed. Eight years ago.

"Where did you get these?" she whispered.

"I had Jan dig through the files. When she came up empty,

I had her look through the high school records and check with people around town." He shook his head. "It seems that all the *Tribune*'s personal history on Gavin Doel is missing. As for Gavin's old man, Jim Doel, he doesn't even have a file here. Isn't that strange?"

"Not so strange. I took them, Brian."

"Big surprise. You know that's stealing, don't you?"

"I was just trying to protect my personal life."

He waved off her explanation and pointed to the prints on the desk. "It doesn't matter, does it?"

Her insides shredding, she said, "I just don't think any of our readers would be interested in this."

"And I think you're wrong. I think the readers will find everything about your…well, for lack of a better word, *affair* with Gavin Doel interesting reading."

"No!" she said vehemently.

"It'll be great. The angle will be The Girl He Left Behind But Never Forgot."

"It'll never sell, Brian. Too much schmaltz."

"I don't think so."

Desperate, she whispered, "You can't be serious."

Brian frowned. "Look, Melanie, I've got a problem. If I don't increase circulation, I'm out of a job. Now, from my experience, I can tell you what will sell papers."

"My life?"

"Not yours. Doel's."

"My private life is none of your business, none of the readers' business."

"Unless you're involved with a celebrity."

"Not even then!"

"Anyway, I know, for whatever reason, you broke off with Doel and married your ex."

Melanie's face drained of color. Sweat dotted her back. He couldn't know about the baby—or could he? Her knees were suddenly weak, but she forced herself to stand, her fists tightening, her fingernails pressing painfully into her palms. "My life is not open for inspection," she said quietly. "And neither is Gavin's!"

He studied the tip of his cigarette. "You know, this can work to our advantage. Mine, yours and the *Tribune*'s."

"How's that?" she asked suspiciously, not entirely sure she wanted to hear his rationale.

"I want you to get close to Doel again, see what you can find out."

"You're not serious," she whispered.

"Why not?"

Her eyes narrowed on the man she had once respected. "If you don't know, I'm not about to tell you."

"Hey, this is business—"

"Not to me, Brian. I quit!"

His eyes grew round. "You don't know what you're saying!"

"Oh, yes, I do," Melanie flung back with newfound conviction. "And you know what? It feels good. I should've done this the first time you suggested I dig up some dirt on Gavin!"

"I'm just doing my job, Melanie."

"Well, you can do it without my help!" With all the dignity she could muster, she turned on her heel and marched out of the office, letting the door bang closed behind her. More than one interested glance was cast in her direction, but she was too angry to meet anyone's eyes. She crossed the room to her desk. Grabbing her purse, briefcase, mug, camera case and coat, she took one final look at the newspaper office and started for the doors.

"What happened?" Constance asked, biting on her lower lip nervously.

"Ask Brian."

"You're leaving?"

"For good."

"But…" Constance glanced quickly to Brian's glassed-in office. "I'll call you."

"Do that."

As she headed through the front doors, Melanie ran into Jan and couldn't help saying, "I don't think Barbara Walters has too much to worry about."

"What?"

"Your story, Jan. It's garbage."

"You're the one who was holding out," Jan reminded her. "You knew a lot about Doel and then you took the damned files—"

"Wouldn't you, if you were in my shoes?" With that Melanie swung outside, not feeling the cold wind as it blew from the east.

"I TOLD YOU THAT girl was trouble!" Jim Doel flung a copy of the *Tribune* onto the empty bench in the weight room.

"What girl?" Gavin, working on strengthening his thigh muscles, let the weights drop with a clang.

"You know which one." Jim's face was florid, his mouth a firm, uncompromising line.

"You must be talking about Melanie."

"That's right."

Grabbing a towel, Gavin wiped the sweat from his face and ignored the churning in his gut. "What happened?"

"See for yourself!" Jim growled, motioning toward the newspaper.

The headline nearly jumped off the front page. "Son of a…" He bit off the oath as he saw that the article was written by Jan Freemont. "How do you know Melanie's involved?"

"She works for that rag, doesn't she?"

"Yeah, but she already told me that Brian Michaels was up to something. I doubt that she would tip me off, then be a part of it."

"Why not? That way she looks innocent."

"She *is* innocent," he retorted vehemently, wanting to believe his own words, instantly defending her.

"If you ask me, you've got it all wrong. If she works for the paper, she's part of the problem." Jim sank onto the empty bench, lifted his wool cap and scratched his head. "I know you've always been soft when it comes to Melanie," he said quietly, "but it seems to me she causes you nothin' but grief."

If you only knew, Gavin thought, reading the article and slowly seething. Though no concrete evidence was given, the story suggested that Ridge Lodge would close soon after it opened, leaving its investors, and anyone foolish enough to pay in advance for lift tickets and lodging, high and dry.

Gavin stripped the towel from his neck. "This is probably my fault," he admitted.

"Your fault?"

"For not playing the game."

"What game?"

"Years ago I met Brian Michaels. He was a reporter with the paper in Colorado. He wanted dirt on the ski team and then personal stuff on me and my teammates. I not only told him to get lost, I called the paper he worked for and complained. So did my coach. Michaels lost his job."

"And you think he'd hold a grudge?"

A corner of Gavin's lip lifted cynically. "I don't think he'd chase me down to get back at me, but since he's here and I'm here and I've got something to lose, I'd bet he can't resist a chance to get even."

"And so he's payin' you back?"

"Not for long," he muttered, his eyes narrowing. He wasn't about to take all the bad publicity lying down. Rich was a lawyer; he could deal with the legalities of libel. As for Michaels, he intended to talk to the owners of the paper.

But first he had to deal with Melanie.

Leaving his father sitting on the bench, Gavin walked through the shower, then threw on a pair of jeans, a sweater and a battered pair of running shoes. On his way out of the lodge, he spied the manager and left some quick instructions.

He couldn't wait to hear Melanie's side of the story.

Newspaper tucked under his arm, he shouldered open the door of the lodge. A blast of cold mountain air swirled in. Outside, dusk was settling around the mountain, shading the snow-covered landscape in shades of lavender and blue. He barely noticed.

As he climbed into his truck, Gavin told himself that Melanie wasn't involved in this—she wouldn't have used him for a story. But he couldn't ignore the seeds of doubt his father had planted.

After all, hadn't she lied to him, kept the secret of their child from him? If there really had been a pregnancy. His lips pursed in a grim line as he shoved the truck into gear and accelerated. The pickup lurched forward. She wouldn't have lied about the baby. There was no reason. No, he decided, his jaw clamped, her story was genuine—at least to a point. He still wasn't convinced that she'd kept the secret for altruistic purposes. No, she probably wanted to snag rich Neil Brooks all along.

Or had the baby been Neil's? Was there a chance she'd been sleeping with Neil at the same time she was having an affair with him? That made more sense. Neil would much rather claim his own child than a bastard of Gavin's.

"Stop it," he ground out, his fingers tight on the wheel.

His chest constricted, but he forced his thoughts back eight years to the hayloft where they had met, to the moonlight that had streamed through the window to cast her black hair in a silver sheen, to the look of sweet, vulnerable innocence that had lingered in her eyes.

No, he couldn't believe that she had lain with him one night and the next with Neil Brooks. No matter what had happened between them, he wouldn't believe that she was that emotionally cold and calculating. "Get over it," he growled at himself as he cranked the wheel. The truck skidded around the corner, then straightened.

In the distance, through the pines, the city lights of Taylor's Crossing winked in the darkness. It would take twenty minutes to get to Melanie's house. He only hoped that she was home—and alone.

CHAPTER TWELVE

MELANIE FINISHED MATTING some photographs in her studio, returned a couple of calls on her answering machine and tentatively planned two portrait shoots for the next couple of days. Since she was officially out of a job, she needed all the work she could get—and that included working at Ridge Lodge. With Gavin.

She dialed the resort's number and was told by a foreman that Gavin and Rich were out.

"Terrific!" she muttered, wondering about their reaction to the article as she fixed herself a meager dinner made from leftover chicken, vegetables and gravy. "Use your imagination, Mel," she told herself as she rolled premixed pie dough and laid it over the top of a casserole dish. Gavin would be furious—and hell-bent to avenge the article. "It's going to be trouble. Big trouble," she predicted, switching on the radio and adjusting the volume. The disk jockey reported that another storm was about to hit the central Oregon Cascades. More snow for the lodge, she thought. At least some news was positive!

Sassafras, hoping for a morsel of chicken, stood at attention near the stove. "Later," she promised, then eyed her creation. "We'll both have some—to celebrate."

Though not working for the *Tribune* created a score of financial problems, she felt a sense of relief.

Shoving the dish of chicken pot pie into the oven, she winked at the old dog. "Tonight, we dine like kings," she announced, then wrinkled her nose. "Well, not really kings, maybe more like dukes or squires or…well, peasants would probably be more appropriate. But we're celebrating nonetheless."

To prove her point, she pulled out the bottle of champagne she'd had in the refrigerator since her birthday and popped the cork. She found a glass high in the cupboard over the stove.

"Here's to freedom," she said, pouring the champagne. It frothed over the side of the glass, and she laughed. "I guess I won't get a job pouring drinks down at the Peg and Platter, hmm?"

Sassafras whined and lowered his head between his paws, still staring up at her with wide brown eyes as the doorbell pealed.

With a loud growl, the dog leaped to his feet and raced, toenails clicking on the old hardwood floor, to the front door. Melanie set her glass on the counter and followed.

Through the narrow window near the front door, she saw Gavin, collar turned against the wind, blond hair dark and wet, snow on the shoulders of his leather jacket, jaw set and stern.

A newspaper was folded neatly under his arm. Today's edition of the *Tribune*.

"Give me strength," she whispered prayerfully as she unlocked the door and swung it open.

"What the hell is this?" he demanded, shaking the paper in front of her nose.

"It's good to see you, too," she tossed back at him, the hackles on the back of her neck instantly rising.

He strode in without an invitation. "Whose smear job is this?"

Melanie closed the door behind him and braced herself. "Brian Michaels's."

"And what did you have to do with it?"

"Nothing."

His sensual lips compressed. "You're sure?"

"Absolutely. I didn't see the front page until this morning."

"Helluva way to bring tourists into town." He flung the newspaper onto a nearby table.

"Did you come over here to accuse me of something?" Melanie asked, unable to keep the irritation out of her voice. "Because if you did, let's get down to it."

"What would I accuse you of?"

"I don't know. It sounds like you think I was part of some conspiracy on the paper."

"No, I don't believe that," he said quietly, though he was still angry. White lines bracketed his mouth, and his jaw was clenched so hard a muscle worked beneath his cheek.

"Oh, so this is just a social call," she said, unable to resist baiting him.

"I just want to know what's going on. You work for the paper—"

"Worked. As in past tense."

His eyes narrowed. "What happened?"

She motioned to the newspaper. "That happened and… well, it's probably going to get worse."

"How?"

"Brian's not about to let up. Come on into the kitchen. I've got something in the oven and I've got to keep my eye on it." He followed her through the hallway by the stairs. The scent of stewing chicken and warm spices wafted through the air. "Join me?" she asked, holding on to the neck of the champagne bottle.

He lifted a shoulder.

"I'll take that as a yes." She poured his glass and handed it to him. "I'm celebrating."

Lifting an eyebrow, he took a sip from his glass. "Celebrating what?"

"My emancipation. I quit the *Tribune*."

He frowned. "You said things would get worse."

"They will. Brian found out that we dated in high school, Gavin. He plans to use it. He even asked me to get close to you again, get you to confide in me."

"Great guy, your boss."

"Ex-boss," she reminded him. "That's when I quit."

"How much does he know?"

She shook her head. "I don't know."

"About the baby?"

His words sliced through the air like a sharp knife. "I don't think so," she replied, shivering.

"Who does?"

Shaking her head, she frowned. "My dad did and Uncle Bart and Aunt Lila." She closed her eyes and rubbed her temple. "And of course Neil and the doctor."

"No one else?"

"I don't think so." Drawing in a shuddering breath she opened her eyes again and, grateful for something to do with her hands, lifted the glass to her lips. "I lost the baby before I'd started to show—before Neil or I had said anything to our friends."

Gavin's nostrils flared. "And you didn't mention it to your 'friend' Jan?"

"Of course not!" Melanie replied guiltily. She knew now that she should never have confided anything to Jan. "I told her we dated so she'd stop asking questions. I didn't think it would backfire." She finished her drink in one gulp.

"When reporters can't find news, they create it."

"Not usually," Melanie replied, noticing that Gavin's glass had been drained. She poured them each another glass and asked, "So why is it that Brian has it in for you?"

"You think he does?"

She nodded. "Don't you?"

"Probably. I met him a long time ago in Colorado. He

started sticking his nose in where it didn't belong, and I complained. He was fired shortly thereafter."

"He never mentioned it," Melanie said thoughtfully. "In fact, when your name was first linked with the lodge, Brian was interested, very interested. But I don't think it was because he wanted to dig up some scandal. At least, I hope not." She sipped from her glass again and stared over the rim at Gavin.

He was tense, his features hard, the muscles beneath his shirt bunched, but his gaze, when it touched hers, was warm and seductive. His tawny eyes were as they had always been, erotic and male, knowing.

Her mouth grew dry, and she quickly finished her second glass of champagne.

He stood near the windows of the nook, one shoulder resting on the door frame, large fingers wrapped around the slim stem of his fragile wineglass.

The soft noises in the house filled the room—the slow tick of the clock in the front hall, the steady rumble of the furnace, the muted strains of a love song from the radio, a creak of ancient timbers and the old collie's whispering breath as he slept under the table.

"So what're we going to do about this?" he finally said, his eyes searching her face.

"About what?"

"Us."

That single word caused her heart to start thumping. "I don't know if there is an 'us.' I'm not sure there ever was."

"Sure there was," he said easily, finishing his champagne and setting the empty glass on the counter.

"It was a long time ago."

"What about last week, when you were up at the lodge?"

Yes. What about those precious hours we spent together? "As I remember, it didn't end well."

"You shocked me." He let out a long, slow breath, but his gaze never wavered. "If I'd known about the baby..."

"What, Gavin? What would you have done?"

"Come home."

Her heart wrenched. "But that would have been no good," she whispered, her words difficult. "You didn't stay for me. You couldn't come back for a baby. You would've felt trapped." She saw the denial on his lips and held up a palm. "You would have, Gavin. Someday, sometime. You would have wondered, 'what if?'"

"And you weren't willing to gamble that I would decide it didn't matter?"

"No."

He crossed the room slowly, his gaze moving deliberately from her eyes to her lips. "You didn't give me enough credit, Melanie."

"I just wanted you to be happy—"

Wrapping strong arms around her waist, he drew her against him. "Happiness is elusive," he whispered before he kissed her, his lips molding over hers. He smelled of snowflakes and tasted of champagne.

Knowing she shouldn't give in, Melanie closed her eyes and leaned against him, content to feel his hands splayed possessively against her back. She welcomed the feel of his tongue as it slid easily between her teeth, his hard body pressed so intimately to hers. His thighs moved, pinning her legs to his. Her pulse leaped, and her heart thundered.

When at last he lifted his head, his eyes were glazed. He touched her wet lips with one finger, tracing her pout, his gaze searching hers. "I thought that if I ever saw you again, it wouldn't matter," he confessed. "I told myself that I was over you, that you'd been a boyhood fascination, nothing more." Disgust filtered through his words. "Obviously I was wrong."

The timer on the stove buzzed so loudly Melanie jumped.

"What's that?" Gavin asked.

"Dinner."

"It'll wait." In a quick motion, he turned off the stove and the buzzer. Noticing the coat rack near the back door, he tossed a long denim coat in her direction, grabbed her hand and tugged, pulling her outside.

"Hey, what're you doing?" she said, laughing as he led her down the back steps and through the snow. "I'm not dressed for this."

"Don't worry about your clothes," he said, sliding a hard look over his shoulder.

"Gavin…?"

He didn't answer but just tugged on her arm, leading her across the yard. The sky had turned black, in stark contrast to the white earth. Snow covered tree branches, roofs, eaves and ground, drifting against the fence and piling onto the stack of wood near the barn.

The barn.

The air was suddenly trapped in her lungs.

With a tingling sense of déjà vu, she knew where he was taking her. Her throat went dry, and time seemed to spin backward.

He tugged on the handle of the door, and it slid to the side on rusted rollers, creaking and groaning. Inside, the dark interior smelled of dust and old hay. There were no more cattle or horses, and the barn itself was in sad need of repair.

Melanie balked. Her breath fogged. "You're not seriously thinking of—"

"Let's go," he insisted, leaving the barn door open, letting in a pale stream of illumination from the security lamp near the garage and the silvery reflection of the snow.

He paused at the bottom of the ladder to the hayloft, and Melanie stopped, yanking her hand from his. "They say you can never go back, Gavin."

"I'm not going back."

"This might not be a good idea."

"Why not?"

"Eight years."

His arms surrounded her, and his mouth closed over hers. Memories rushed through her mind, yet they paled to the here and now, to the rough feel of his jacket against her cheek, the smell of his cologne mingling with the dust, the warmth of his hand pressing hard against the small of her back. She'd been kidding herself, she realized, when she'd made love to him before and thought she could remain emotionally detached.

Groaning, he half pushed her up toward the loft. Melanie's throat went dry, but a thrill of anticipation skittered up her spine and she stepped onto the ladder.

With each rung, she wondered if she were making a mistake she would never be able to undo, but she kept climbing, one step at a time, until she stood in the cold, darkened loft and Gavin was beside her, his breath stirring her hair as he slid the coat from her shoulders and tossed it onto the old straw. Then, holding her chin between both his palms, he ground a kiss against her lips that made her shiver from head to toe.

A tremor passed through Melanie, and she was sure he could feel it as his tongue pressed insistently against her teeth and into her mouth, searching, tasting, plundering.

His hands held her tight against him, his thighs pressing against hers, her breasts crushed to his chest.

"I never forgot you, Melanie," he admitted, his voice rough. "Never." His hands slid lower, cupping her buttocks, pulling full against him. Through their clothes, she felt the hardness between his legs, the urgency in his touch.

"I tried. God, I tried. And there were other women—women I hoped would make me forget."

"Shh," she whispered, the breath torn from her lungs. She touched his lips with the tip of one finger. "I don't want to hear about them."

He drew her finger into his mouth and sucked, his tongue playing havoc with her nerve endings as it tickled and toyed.

Melanie's abdomen tightened. Liquid heat scorched her veins, and she couldn't stop the moan that slipped through her lips.

Kissing her again, he pulled her closer, forcing one of her legs to move upward and rest against his hip. Her head lolled backward, and her arms wrapped around his neck as they fell to the hay. The old denim coat was a meager blanket against the cold air and the rough hay, but Melanie didn't notice. She was on fire inside, and the scratch of the straw only heightened her already tingling senses.

Gavin's mouth found hers again. Hot, anxious lips pressed hard against hers in a kiss that was as punishing as it was filled with promise.

"Gavin," she cried wantonly. She arched upward, closer, closer. He stripped away her sweater and took both lace-covered breasts in his hands. Burying his head between the mounds, he kissed the skin over her breasts as he pulled the bra away. The stubble on his chin was rough, his lips and tongue wet and wild and wonderful as his hot breath whispered across her nipples and caused a fire to burn deep within.

He teased her. His tongue grazed a nipple, parrying and thrusting, wetting the tight bud until Melanie was wild with desire.

An ache stole through her, and she cradled his head to her breast. He suckled long and hard, and Melanie grasped his hair in her hands, her fingers tangling in his thick blond locks.

He began to move against her, and she felt his rhythm, still holding him close as he struggled out of his clothes and kicked his jeans away. Lord, she wanted him. She could barely think for the desire rippling deep within.

His eyes were gold and glowing with a passion matched only by her own as he discarded her clothes quickly. And then they were naked. Again in the barn, but this time the love between them was a savage, forceful desire that stripped them bare. "You make me crazy," he muttered, as if trying to get a grip on his exploding passion.

Was he going to stop? Now? Oh, God, no! "Gavin… please…" Writhing, she lifted her hips, and he ran his hand along her inner thigh, touching her moistness at the apex of her legs, and groaning in satisfaction at the evidence of her desire.

"Melanie…" he whispered, his breath fanning her skin, his tongue wetting a trail against her leg. "Oh, Melanie…" And she shivered in anticipation.

His hands once again found her buttocks, and she moved closer to him, trembling with desire as he found her, pleasuring her until she could stand the sensual teasing no longer.

"Gavin, oh, please…" She reached for him, drawing him up along her body, her hands forcing his head to hers, and she kissed him with all the desire flooding through her veins. Touching the flat nipples in his mat of golden hair, she sucked on his lower lip and he lost control.

"What do you want from me?" he rasped, his voice echoing off the old beams.

"Everything!"

Shifting, he opened her legs wide with his knees. He mounted her then, his legs fitting inside her own, before he plunged deep and she arched upward, meeting the fervor of his thrusts anxiously, closing around him again and again, their bodies fusing in savage fury.

Her fingers dug into the supple flesh of his arms as he entered and withdrew, pushing her to the edge of rapture, until at the sound of his primal cry, she shuddered, convulsing against him, a thousand sparks igniting and sizzling.

With a dry gasp, he collapsed atop her, crushing her breasts and pressing her hard against the rough denim coat. Perspiration fused their bodies, and his curling chest hair tickled her sensitive bare skin.

"Melanie, oh, Melanie," he whispered, his voice raw and hoarse. "Oh, God, what am I going to do with you?"

And what am I going to do with you? Wrapping her arms around him, she closed her eyes and tried to slow the still-rapid beating of her heart. She wasn't going to fall apart now, to weep for what might have been. But she held on to him tightly, as if afraid he might disappear.

When he slowly rolled to his side, she reluctantly released him.

"This is insane," he said. "Just plain crazy." He plucked a piece of straw from her hair and sighed loudly.

"So what're we going to do about it?"

"I wish I knew," he muttered. "I wish to Holy God I knew."

CHAPTER THIRTEEN

"I THINK IT WOULD be best if we went low profile," Gavin stated, finishing his second helping of slightly burned chicken pot pie. As if the passion that had exploded between them less than an hour before had been forgotten.

"Low profile?" Melanie repeated, unable to touch her food.

"If Michaels is really serious about making us the lead story in his next issue, we should diffuse it."

"By not being together?" Why did it hurt so much?

As if noticing her pain, he reached across the table and wrapped warm fingers around her palm. His thumb slowly rubbed the back side of her hand. "I just don't want the focus of attention shifted from the lodge to us." He offered her a patient smile. "It's only for a little while, till the lodge gets on its feet. And believe me," he added with a devilish twinkle in his eyes, "it'll be as hard on me as it is on you."

"You think so?"

"I know it." With a sigh, he scraped his chair back and reached for his coat. "I've got to get back, but I'll see you at the resort, right. Rich says you've got some pictures on consignment in the ski shop?"

"That's right."

"And you'll be there for the grand opening?"

She nodded, though her throat was tight as she walked with him to the back door. "Of course."

"Bring your ski gear. Maybe we could take a few runs together."

"You'll be too busy."

"Then come up sometime before." He reached for the handle of the door.

"I thought we were going low profile," she teased, though she didn't feel much like joking.

"We will. I doubt if Michaels will catch us on Devil's Ridge or West Canyon." He smiled as he mentioned two of the toughest runs on the mountain.

"It's a date," she said as he drew her outside and swept her into his arms. His lips caressed hers in a kiss that was full of promise and pain.

When he lifted his head again, he groaned. "We've got to do something about this," he whispered, his voice rough as he rested his chin against her crown and held her close. Wrapped in the smell and feel of him, she hated to let go.

When at last he released her, she stood on the porch and watched as he ran across the yard and climbed into his truck. With a roar the engine caught, and as the pickup backed out of the drive, the beams of his headlights flashed against the old barn and the trunks of the trees in the backyard. As the light receded, she noticed the huge ponderosa with the gash in its bark, the ugly cut her father had made when he'd first learned she was pregnant all those years ago.

She closed her eyes for a second and wondered where she and Gavin would go from here. Would the future be bright and filled with happiness, or black with the loss of a love that was never meant to be?

"Don't even think about it," she told herself as she walked back into the house.

"I'VE GOT GOOD NEWS," Dr. Hodges said as he switched on the light and illuminated an X ray of Gavin's leg.

"I could use some." Gavin eyed the X ray but couldn't make head nor tail of it. He hadn't seen Melanie in days, and he was irritable. The lodge was opening the day after tomorrow, and he was up to his eyeballs in preparations. But he really didn't give a damn. He just wanted to be with her.

"The fracture's healed." Hodges studied the X ray again, narrowing his eyes, looking for some sign of the flaw that had sidelined Gavin.

Gavin felt a slow smile spread across his face as he thought about the season ahead. "I can race again."

"Well," Hodges said, his lips protruding thoughtfully, "there's no physical reason why you can't, at least not in your ankle. But if I were you, I'd give it a year before I raced competitively again."

"So you're releasing me?"

Hodges smiled a boyish grin. "For the time being. But if you have any pain—any at all—I want you back here, pronto."

"You got it." Gavin stood and shook Hodges's hand. He felt as if a ton of bricks had been lifted from his shoulders and he wanted to celebrate. With Melanie. This afternoon!

MELANIE WAS MISERABLE. The past few days without Gavin she'd been cranky and upset and her stomach had been queasy. "All because of one man," she chided herself as she snapped on the lights in the darkroom and walked into the kitchen.

"About time you finished in there."

Melanie nearly jumped out of her skin. Gavin was there, half-kneeling, scratching Sassafras behind his ears.

"How'd you get in?" she asked, drinking in the sight of him. Dressed in gray slacks and a pullover sweater, his skin tanned and his hair unruly, he was as handsome as ever. He glanced up at her and her heart turned over.

"Breach in security. The front door was unlocked. I heard you in the darkroom and I didn't want to bother you." He straightened and his eyes sparkled. "Come on, get your gear."

"My gear?" she repeated as his arms surrounded her.

"We're going skiing."

"Now? But I have work—"

"No time. We're celebrating." Wrapping strong arms around her waist, he spun her off the floor.

"Hey, wait. Stop! Your leg!" she cried, though it was her stomach that lurched.

"That's what we're celebrating," he said, dropping her back to her feet and planting a kiss against her forehead. "My health."

"Your health? Gavin, you're not making any sense."

He winked. "The doctor's released me. Given me the okay to race again!"

She felt her face drain of color. "This season?"

"As soon as I can pull it off. I'm rusty, of course, and older than most of the guys on the circuit. It'll take some intense training, but I can work out at the lodge. And once Ridge Lodge is up and running, Rich and the manager can handle the rest."

So he was leaving! Again! All her private hopes disintegrated. Her father was right. Gavin's first love was and would always be the thrill of downhill racing.

"Are you all right?" he asked, his eyes suddenly serious.

"I'm fine," she lied, forcing a smile that felt as fake as a three-dollar bill. "Just let me get my things." Wriggling out of his embrace, she ran out of the kitchen and upstairs. Her head was pounding, and when she looked in the mirror she noticed that her face had turned ashen. "Great, Melanie—you're a real trooper," she chided, changing into a black turtleneck and her new jumpsuit, a purple and sea-green one-piece that she'd found in a local shop before she'd quit working for the *Tribune*.

She found her skis, poles and boots and packed a small bag

for her goggles, gloves, sunglasses and an extra set of clothes. Then, before she went back downstairs, she splashed water on her face and fought a sudden attack of nausea.

"Hang in there," she said angrily, furious with herself for overreacting to the news that he was leaving. A little blush and lipstick helped, and when she hurried downstairs, she'd pushed all thoughts of life without Gavin from her mind. They still had a little time together, and she was determined to make the best of it.

They drove to the lodge, and while Gavin changed, Melanie waited for him outside. The sky was blue and clear, and other skiers tackled the runs, gliding gracefully down the slopes or, in the case of the less experienced skiers, grappled with their balance as they snow-plowed on the gradual hills.

Melanie smiled as she heard the crunch of boots behind her. Turning, she expected to find Gavin but was disappointed. Jim Doel was walking toward her, and his face was firm and set.

"I'm surprised to see you here," he said.

Nervously, she replied, "Gavin and I decided to ski together before the crowd hits this weekend."

Jim frowned. "Look, I don't see any reason to beat around the bush."

Melanie braced herself.

"A lot of things have happened between your family and mine, and Lord knows if I could change things I would. I'm the reason you grew up without a mother and I've lived with that for eighteen years. I've also lived with the fact that I wasn't much of a father to Gavin, but he made it on his own. Became one of the best skiers in the whole damned country."

"You should be proud," Melanie said icily.

"Of some things. All I'm saying is that I'm sorry for the accident. If I could've traded places with your ma, I would've. But I couldn't."

"If you're expecting me to forgive you—"

"Nope. What I expect is for you to leave Gavin alone. You've messed with his mind enough." He raised faded eyes to hers. "He's got a second chance, you know. Most people don't get another one. And he loves racing."

"I know."

"So let him go."

She inched her chin up a fraction. "I'll never stand in the way of Gavin's career."

He didn't look as if he believed her, but she didn't care. She had something else she had to get off her chest. And, though a part of her longed to blame him for the tragedy, she knew it was unfair. He'd paid for it with every day of his life. "As for my mother's death, it was a long time ago," she said, offering a slight smile. "I hope you can put it in the past where it belongs. I have."

His jaw worked.

"And, though I doubt you and I will ever be close, regardless of how we both feel about Gavin, I'd like for us to try to be fair with each other."

His lips compressed. "All I want from you is a promise that you won't interfere in his life."

"How Gavin lives his life is Gavin's business."

"Glad you see things my way."

"But I do care about him very much."

"Then do what's best for him." With that, he strode toward the machine shed, and Melanie let out her breath slowly. She watched as Jim disappeared inside the shed, then she headed toward the lift. She wondered if she and Jim Doel could ever be comfortable around each other. Probably not.

Frowning, she adjusted her bindings and practiced skiing on the flat area behind the lodge.

"Hey! Let's go!" Gavin, already on skis, was making his way to the Daredevil lift. Wearing a royal blue jacket and black ski pants, he planted his poles and she followed. Her heart soared at the sight of him, and she shoved his father from her thoughts. Today she was going to enjoy being with the man she loved.

The lift carried them over snow-covered runs, thick stands of pine and a frozen creek. Gavin rested one arm over the back of the chair, and they laughed and talked as they were swept up the mountainside.

Cool air brushed her cheeks and caught in her hair. Gavin touched her cheek and she smiled, happy to be alone with him. At the top of the lift, they slid down the ramp.

"Follow me," Gavin urged, his voice excited, and Melanie only hoped that she could keep up with him.

Melanie's ski legs were better than she remembered, and she flew down the mountainside, snow spraying, hair whipping in the wind. Gavin, far ahead of her now, skied effortlessly. His movements were sure and strong, and as he glided from one plateau to the next, he waited for her.

At one plateau, she didn't stop to catch her breath but flew past him, her laughter trailing in her wake. Gavin gave chase and breezed past her along a narrow trail that sliced through the trees.

Exhilaration pushed her onward, and the wind rushed against her face, stinging her eyes and tangling her hair. She rounded a bend and found Gavin stopped dead in his tracks, flagging her down.

"Giving up?" she quipped as she dug in her skis and stopped near him. She was breathing hard, her chest rising and falling rapidly.

"No, I just thought you could use a rest." To her amazement, he pressed hard on his bindings, releasing his skis from his boots.

"Me?" she mocked, still gulping breaths of fresh air. "Oh, no, I could do this for hours! You're just wimping out on me."

"Ha!" He glanced up, and his smile slashed his tanned skin. "Well," he drawled, "I did have an ulterior motive."

"And what's that?"

"I wanted to get you alone up here."

For the first time she realized that they had skied away from the major runs and that the lifts were far in the distance. The area was secluded, trees surrounding the trail and the frozen creek that peeked from beneath drifts of snow.

Gavin reached down and unfastened her bindings, as well.

A thrill raced up Melanie's spine. "And what did you plan to do with me?"

"Just this," he said, taking her into his arms and pressing ice-cold lips to hers. They tumbled together in the snow and laughed as the icy powder tickled their noses and caught in their hair.

"Someone could come along at any minute," she protested.

"Let them." He kissed her again, and his lips warmed hers, heating her blood, easing the chill from her body.

Melanie's heart knocked loudly, her pulse leaped and she wished she could stay here forever, locked in his arms, the pristine stillness of the snow-covered forest surrounding them.

When he reluctantly drew back, his gold-colored eyes gleamed and he smiled at her as if they'd been lovers for years, as if all the pain and twisted truths of the past had never existed. "I love you, Melanie," he said, and tears tickled the corners of her eyes. She could hardly believe her ears. Gavin loved her? If only she could believe it was true.

"Well?" he asked.

"You know I love you, Gavin. I hate to admit it, but I probably always have."

He laughed. "What're we going to do about that?"

"I don't know," she replied honestly.

"Well, I do." He kissed her again and, pulling her against him, lay with her in the snow. Warmth invaded her body, and she closed her eyes, remembering how much she'd loved him. That love seemed to pale compared to the emotions that tore at her now.

Shouts and hoots interrupted the stillness, and Gavin, with a groan, struggled to his feet. He pulled her upright just as two teenagers swished past them, spraying snow and hollering loudly.

"Come on," Gavin said, eyeing the retreating figures. "Let's get in a couple more runs before I lose control completely."

"Or I do," Melanie thought aloud, stepping into her skis.

They spent the rest of the afternoon on the mountain, laughing and talking.

Finally, after dark, Gavin drove her home. He lingered on the doorstep, holding her close and pressing urgent lips to hers.

"You could stay," she offered, surprised at her sudden boldness.

"I have to be at the lodge."

"Tonight?"

"I should be."

She grinned up at him. "What would it take to change your mind?" she asked coyly, her fingers crawling up his chest.

He grabbed her hands. "You're dangerous."

"Am I?"

He kissed her again, harder this time, his lips sealing over hers, trapping the breath in her lungs. When he finally lifted his head, his eyes had darkened. "Oh, the hell with it! Since when was I responsible?"

Lifting her off her feet, he carried her inside, slammed and locked the door with one hand and hauled her upstairs, where he dropped her unceremoniously onto the bed.

A second later he was beside her, kissing her and removing

their clothes, anxious to love her. And Melanie didn't stop him. Sighing, she wound her arms around his neck, tangled her fingers in his hair and pulled his head to hers.

Tonight, she thought. *I'll just think about tonight....*

SHE WOKE EARLY the next morning. It was still dark outside, but Gavin was staring down at her, his hand moving slowly against the smooth texture of her shoulder. She could see his face in the half light from the moon sifting through the window.

"I've got to go," he whispered.

"Already?" She clung to him, his body warm as it molded to hers.

"No choice. The grand opening is tomorrow."

"At least let me make you breakfast."

He brushed a wayward strand of hair from her eyes. "You don't have to."

"I know I don't," she said crankily, unhappy that he was leaving her, "but I want to."

"Sure you do." He laughed as she climbed out of bed and, slipping into her bathrobe, struggled with the belt.

Downstairs, she started the coffee, opened the back door for Sassafras, then decided to get the paper. Donning a ski jacket over her robe, she hurried to the mailbox, grabbed the paper with near-frozen fingers and returned to the warmth of the kitchen.

She tossed the paper onto the table and returned the coat to the rack, then set about making waffles and sausage, suppressing a yawn and listening to the sound of water running as Gavin showered.

How right this all felt, she thought dreamily, wondering what it would be like to be married to him.

Within minutes Gavin hurried downstairs, his hair combed and wet, his expression positively devilish. "Well, aren't you the domestic one?" he joked, wrapping strong arms around her waist and standing behind her.

"Watch it," she warned, lifting her spatula. "I'm armed."

He laughed, his breath stirring her hair. "And I'm worried."

"Sit," she ordered good-naturedly, pointing with the spatula to the table. "You're the one who had to get up at this ridiculous hour."

He did as he was told, and as Melanie plucked the first waffle from the iron, Gavin snapped open the paper. Melanie placed the waffle and a couple of sizzling sausage links onto a plate, turned and set the plate on the table. As she did, Gavin's hand grabbed her wrist.

She giggled, thinking he was still playing, but when she caught his glance, she realized that something was horribly wrong. His eyes were hard, his nostrils flared and his mouth a grim, hard line.

"What—what's wrong?"

"Everything!"

"I don't understand."

Confused, she looked down at the table, then stood frozen, reading the headlines of the front page of the *Tribune*:

Gavin Doel Returns To Taylor's Crossing For Long Lost Love.

"Oh, God," she whispered.

"It just gets better and better," he said, his lips tight.

Swallowing hard, she read the article, written by Jan, which detailed their romance and the feud between the two families. There was a picture of her and Gavin at the lodge, obviously young and in love, and a picture of Jim Doel, the man who went to jail for negligently killing Melanie's mother.

"This is too much," she whispered, reading on and feeling sick to her stomach. There was nothing written about the baby, just Melanie's quick change of heart and short marriage to Neil Brooks.

"It could be worse," he muttered, "and it probably will be."

"What do you mean?"

"Just that Michaels isn't about to let up. Each week he's going to find something to dredge up. Again and again."

"The baby?" she whispered.

"Eventually."

"Oh, no." She sank into the nearest chair and told herself to be strong, that there was nothing more to worry about. She reached for Gavin's hand, but he stood slowly and impaled her with angry eyes.

"I think I'd better leave."

"Why?"

"Because I've got things to do." His face darkened with determination. "And I can't be sure that some reporter or hotshot photographer isn't camped outside your back door." There wasn't the least spark of friendliness—or love—in his eyes. His expression was murderous.

"You—you think I was a part of this?" she whispered, disbelieving.

His jaw clamped together. "I don't know, Melanie. Were you?"

"That's absurd! You know I wouldn't do anything…" But she could see it in his eyes—all the past lies and accusations surfacing again. Her world tilted, and her fantasy shattered. "You're right, you'd better leave," she said, standing on legs that shook and threatened to buckle.

He hesitated just a moment as a glimmer of love glinted in his eyes, but he grabbed his jacket and stormed out of the house, letting the door bang behind him.

"And good riddance!" she said, tossing his uneaten breakfast into the trash before she collapsed and slid down the cabinets to the floor. Tears flooded her eyes, and she tried to fight them back.

Pounding an impotent fist against the cabinets, she hiccupped and sobbed, and then her stomach, already on edge, rumbled nauseously. She scrambled to her feet, dashed to the bathroom and promptly threw up.

When she was finished, she sluiced cold water on her face and looked at her white-faced reflection in the mirror. *You've really got it bad,* she thought sadly. She hadn't wretched in years. The last time had been—

Time stopped. The world spun crazily.

With numbing disbelief Melanie realized that the last time she'd been so ill had been eight years ago, when she'd been pregnant with Gavin's child.

CHAPTER FOURTEEN

MELANIE STARED IN disbelief at the blue stick from the home pregnancy test. But there it was—physical proof that her monthly calendar wasn't inaccurate. She was, in fact, pregnant. With Gavin's child. Again.

Ecstasy mingled with pain. What could she do? Sitting on a corner of the bed, she weighed her options and decided not to make the same mistake twice. She had to tell Gavin and she had to tell him soon.

Sighing, she shoved her hair from her eyes. She had to confide in him—there was no question of that. But she didn't have to marry him. In fact, she'd be more than willing to raise his child alone.

No longer a frightened girl of seventeen, she could handle the demands of a child and a career—if she ever got her career going again. Never again would she turn to another man. Marrying Neil had been a mistake she would never repeat. If and when she married, it would be for love.

And she couldn't imagine loving anyone but Gavin.

"You're hopeless, Melanie," she told herself, but couldn't ignore the elation that she was pregnant.

Suddenly she wondered how she'd be able to speak with Gavin alone tonight—opening night. She thought about avoiding the party but knew that both Gavin and Rich expected her to attend. As official photographer for the lodge, she could hardly beg out now.

She spent the day wondering how she would tell him. There was no easy way.

Finally, that evening, she took an hour getting ready for the formal party that would officially kick off the season and reopen Ridge Lodge. Tomorrow there would be races, sleigh rides, an outdoor barbecue and snowboarding and skiing demonstrations, but tonight the lodge would be ready for dancing and hobnobbing.

Not in a party mood, Melanie stepped into her one long dress, a royal blue silk sheath with high neckline and long sleeves, then added a slim silver necklace and matching bracelet. She brushed her hair and let it fall in curls that swept past her shoulders.

"Here goes nothing," she told Sassafras as she petted him on the head and slid her arms into the sleeves of her ankle-length coat.

She drove carefully to the lodge, joining a procession of cars up the steep grade and smiling to herself as snowflakes landed on the windshield. If Gavin's lodge failed, it wouldn't be for lack of snow.

The lodge was ablaze with lights. Torches were lit outside and every room cast golden rays from the windows and dormers. Melanie parked near a back entrance and, squaring her shoulders, walked through the main doors, where her pictures were now highlighted by concealed lamps.

Guests, employees, caterers and musicians already filled the lobby. In one corner a piano player and backup band were playing soft rock. In another a linen-covered table was arranged with silver platters of appetizers, and behind the bar two barkeeps were busy refilling glasses. Waiter and caterers hurried through a throng of bejeweled guests.

Smoke and laughter floated up the three stories to the ceiling, and Melanie wished she was just about anywhere else on earth. She spotted some local celebrities and a couple of famous skiers and their wives, as well as some of the more prominent townspeople.

She mingled with the crowd, searching for Gavin, wondering how she could break the news.

"Well, what do you think?" a male voice whispered in her ear. She turned to find a beaming Rich Johanson surveying the crowd.

"Looks like a success."

"I think so," he agreed anxiously. "And Gavin was worried!"

"That's what he does best."

"I—um, sorry about the article in the paper," Rich said. "I had no idea—"

"None of us did," she said. Then her heart thumped painfully. Behind Rich, through the crowd, stood Gavin, tall and lean, impeccably dressed in a black tuxedo. At his side, her arm threaded through his, was the most beautiful redhead Melanie had ever seen. With a sinking heart she realized the woman was Aimee LaRoux.

Rich, following her gaze, frowned. "Surprise guest," he said with a shrug.

"She wasn't invited?"

"Not by me."

But by Gavin. Melanie cast the unhappy thought aside. She trusted Gavin, and he had told Melanie he loved her, hadn't he?

"If you'll excuse me," she said, wending her way through the guests to Gavin. He hadn't seen her yet—his head was bent as he listened to Aimee—but when he raised his eyes and found her standing in front of him, he managed a tight smile.

Melanie returned with one of her own. "Congratulations, Gavin," she said. "The party looks like a big hit."

"Thanks."

"Oh, this resort is just fabulous!" Aimee said, bubbling. "But everything Gavin touches turns to gold."

"Not quite," Gavin said.

Melanie drew on her courage. "When you've got a minute—no, not now—I'd like to talk with you."

"Alone?"

She nodded. "That would be best."

Gavin glanced at his watch, whispered something to Aimee, then, taking Melanie's arm, propelled her quickly to the back hall. "Hey, wait, you've got guests," she protested.

"Doesn't matter." He strode quickly to his private suite and locked the door behind them.

"There's something you should know—"

"Mr. Doel?" A loud knock thudded against the door.

Gavin, swearing, opened it quickly. "What?"

The caterer, a tall man of thirty or so, stood fist in the air, poised to knock again. "I'm sorry to bother you, but the champagne is running low—"

"Open another case—there's more in the refrigerators near the back door," Gavin said, unable to keep the irritation from his voice. "And if you have any other questions, talk to Mr. Johanson."

"Yes, sir," the caterer replied.

Gavin closed and locked the door again. "Now—what's so all-fired important?" he demanded.

Her stomach, already knotted, twisted painfully. "You left the other morning in a hurry," she said, reaching for the back of a chair to brace herself. "And I didn't get a chance to say goodbye."

"Goodbye?" he repeated, frowning. He folded his arms over his chest and waited.

Her palms began to sweat. "Aren't you leaving soon…to rejoin the racing circuit?"

"I don't know. I haven't made definite plans. It all depends on what happens here." He crossed the room and stood only inches from her. "What's going on, Melanie?"

She cleared her throat. "I'm pregnant," she whispered, facing him and seeing the shock and disbelief cross his features.

"You're what?"

"Pregnant." When he paled, she added, "Of course, the baby's yours."

"But you said—I thought you couldn't have children."

"I couldn't—not with Neil."

"You're sure about this?" he said, still not making a move to touch her, his suspicious gaze drilling into hers.

"I took a home pregnancy test this morning, but no, I haven't seen a doctor. I'm late and I've been throwing up and I haven't felt this way since the last time." Her fingers were digging into the back of the chair, and she felt herself begin to shake.

"We'll get married," he said without a second thought.

"No."

His head snapped up, and he regarded her in disbelief. "What do you mean, 'no'?"

"I'm not going to trap you, Gavin. You have your life and it doesn't include me or a baby. You won't be happy unless you're racing headlong down a mountain as fast as you can."

"And so what do you plan to do? Marry another man?"

She sucked in a swift breath. "No. I'm going to raise this baby alone, the way I should have the first time. And I'm going to love it and—"

"You lost the first one."

The words crackled through the air, burning deep in her heart. "I won't lose this one," she vowed, "no matter what."

"You're right about that," he said, his disbelief giving way to a new emotion. His lips twisted, and his eyes turned thoughtful. "I won't let you," he said softly, kicking the chair from her hands and throwing his arms around her.

"Mr. Doel?" Pounding erupted on the door again.

"Let's get out of here," he whispered against her ear.

"But..." She cast a worried glance at the door.

"Come on!" Taking her hand, he opened the back door and hustled her down the steps of his private deck.

"Where are we going?" she asked, and his answer was a ripple of laughter.

When her high-heeled shoes sank into the deep drifts, Gavin lifted her easily into his arms and carried her toward the base of Rocky Ridge, where a gondola sat.

"You're not serious..." she whispered, but he was. He started the lift and ushered Melanie inside the gondola. The operator, recognizing Gavin, took instructions, and within seconds Melanie and Gavin were moving quickly uphill, the night dark around them.

"You're insane," she chided.

"Crazy. The word is crazy and I'm crazy about you." When the gondola was at the top of the lift, it stopped suddenly.

Melanie gasped. "What's going on?"

"Tony's giving us half an hour of privacy." Gavin drew her tightly into the circle of his arms. "And in those thirty minutes, I'm going to convince you to marry me."

"Gavin, you don't have to—"

His mouth closed over hers, and his tongue slipped intimately between her teeth.

Melanie's knees sagged, and he propped her up against the side of the car. "Marry me, Melanie."

"But I can't—"

He kissed her again, and this time she gave in, kissing him with all the fire that raced through her blood. She closed her eyes, unaware of the view of the lodge or the surrounding night-darkened hills.

Groaning, he lifted his head. "Well?"

"Yes!" she said. "Yes, yes, yes!"

His grin slanted white in the darkness, and he reached into

the pocket of his tuxedo. Taking her hand, he placed a soft velvet box in her palm.

Breathless, she opened it to discover a large solitary diamond ring nestled in a tuft of black velvet. He slipped the ring on her finger, and it fit perfectly.

"You had this planned," she whispered.

"That's why the operator was standing by at the base of the lift," he admitted. "I was going to wait until the party had wound down a little, but I had already decided that I wanted to marry you and I wasn't going to take no for an answer. I planned to take you up here and propose."

"You did?" she asked incredulously. "But what about the *Tribune*? You accused me of—"

"I know. But we don't have to worry about the *Tribune* anymore."

"Why not?"

"I bought it yesterday."

"You did what?" She stared up at him, sure that he was teasing her, but his face was dead serious.

"Remember, I told you I had things to do. When I left your place I called the owners of the paper, made them a more than generous offer and bought them out. As for Brian Michaels—he's already packing, along with Jan."

Melanie could hardly believe it.

"Yesterday I decided that it was time to set a few things straight. So—if you want it, you can have your old job back, with a raise."

"And what about you?"

"I've decided that I don't need to race in Europe, unless my family needs a vacation."

"Will you be happy living here?" she asked.

"Only with you."

"But what about your father?"

"Oh, I straightened him out. And it seems that you two had

a chat the other day. Dad's decided maybe he was wrong about you."

Melanie could hardly believe her ears. "So why did you put me through all this—this confession? Why didn't you propose *before* I told you about the baby?"

He took her into his arms again and pressed a kiss to her forehead. "Because I wanted to hear what you had to say—I had no idea you were pregnant. And then I wanted to make sure that you really wanted our child."

"Oh, Gavin, did you doubt that?"

"Not for a minute, love," he said, grinning ear to ear. "But I had to know that you were marrying me because you wanted to, not because you wanted the baby to have a father."

"That's convoluted thinking."

"No more than yours." He kissed her again, and she snuggled against him. "I can see it all now—the headlines in the next edition of the *Trib*: Doel Marries Girl of His Dreams."

Melanie laughed and glanced down at the diamond on her left hand. "It's my dream, you know. I've dreamed about this for so long."

"It's our dream," he replied, his voice tight with emotion. "And it's a dream that will last forever."

* * * * *

Don't miss the sizzling new Lone Star Sisters series by *New York Times* bestselling author

SUSAN MALLERY

Sibling rivalry takes on a whole new meaning as the high-society Titan sisters vie for their tyrant father's business and respect…and fall unexpectedly in love with three sexy men along the way!

Available wherever books are sold!

And don't miss the final Lone Star Sisters tale, HOT ON HER HEELS, coming this winter!

We *are* romance™

www.HQNBooks.com

PHSMT2009

HQN™
We are romance™
Some secrets are better left buried....
New York Times bestselling author
MERYL SAWYER
New York Times Bestselling Author
MERYL SAWYER
DEATH'S DOOR
"For romance, passion and thrills, read Meryl Sawyer."
—New York Times bestselling author Susan Elizabeth Phillips
Madison Connelly is tired of lies and betrayal. She wants answers…answers that will draw her deep into a complicated web of intrigue, deceit and murder. And she'll need more than detective Paul Tanner's growing attraction to keep her safe.
Death's Door
Available now wherever books are sold!
www.HQNBooks.com
PHMS374

From acclaimed author
RHYANNON BYRD
Dangerous passions
awaken an ancient hunger
impossible to deny....
RHYANNON BYRD
EDGE of HUNGER
RHYANNON BYRD
EDGE of DANGER
RHYANNON BYRD
EDGE of DESIRE
April 2009
May 2009
June 2009
Don't miss the debut of
the scintillating Primal Instinct
paranormal series
in April 2009!

HQN™
We are romance™